D0269876

Class No. ___F___   Acc No. _C/145268_

Author: _Butts, C_   Loc: ~~1 MAR 2004~~

LEABHARLANN
CHONDAE AN CHABHAIN

1 4 DEC 2014

1. This book may be kept three weeks. It is to be returned on / before the last date stamped below.
2. A fine of 25c will be charged for every week or part of week a book is overdue.

2 2 APR 2004		
2 6 JUL 2004		
1 1 APR 2005		
1 6 MAY 2005		
2 8 JUL 2005		
2 - SEP 2005		

a bus could
run you over

Also by Colin Butts

Is Harry on the Boat?
Is Harry Still on the Boat?

a bus could
run you over

COLIN BUTTS

ORION

First published in Great Britain in 2004 by Orion,
an imprint of the Orion Publishing Group Ltd.

A CIP catalogue record for this book is
available from the British Library.

ISBN 0 75285 588 3 (hardback)   0 75286 026 7 (trade paperback)

Typeset by Deltatype Ltd,
Birkenhead, Merseyside

Set in Stone Serif

Printed in Great Britain by
Clays Ltd, St Ives plc

All the characters in this book are fictitious,
and any resemblance to actual persons living or dead
is purely coincidental.

The Orion Publishing Group Ltd
Orion House
5 Upper Saint Martin's Lane
London, WC2H 9EA

part one
reasons to be fearful

chapter one

'Not too tight, is it?'

Gina wriggled, gave Connor a dirty smile and tried to bite him. The rope tightened around her gloved wrist, as he secured the other end to the post of his wrought-iron bed, the most recent addition to his Camberwell flat.

'C'mon, Gina. Let me take this make-up off. At least let me get rid of the skirt.'

'Think of it as a kilt.' Gina tried not to laugh. 'Of course, if you don't want to carry on making this video, then just untie me and—'

'All right, all right.'

He couldn't believe she had gone to so much trouble. Oversize women's clothes from a charity shop was bad enough, but when she insisted on applying mascara and lipstick to his face . . . home porno, loved up on pills and MDMA powder or not, he'd almost called it off.

It was due to the age-old problem: what happens after a home porno is made? Who gets to keep it? What happens if the relationship ends? Is there a handover ritual? How can each party be sure copies haven't been made, or vindictively placed on the internet?

Gina had therefore insisted that Connor appear in drag, the theory being that he would be too embarrassed ever to let anyone else see it.

Of course, this worked both ways.

'Gina, what if you show it to one of *your* friends?'

'Girls aren't interested in pornos.'

'Bullshit. *You* watch them.'

'Only ones with a decent storyline and good-looking actors.'

'Good-looking! What about Ron Jeremy?'

'He's got a huge willy.' At this Connor looking slightly concerned. 'It's OK, babe, you've got nothing to worry about. Don't you remember we measured it? You're well above average.'

'Only because I had the tape measure halfway up my sphincter.'

'Well, if I were you, I'd be more worried about looking like Dame Edna Everage's mutant sister.'

'Right, that's it!' Connor leapt up and playfully tightened the rope still further.

'Have we started?' she asked.

'Huh? Oh, why not? I'll just get a drink from the kitchen then come back in character, OK?'

Gina giggled. 'Hurry up. I can feel myself coming up on that last bit of MDMA powder.'

Role-play. He hadn't felt entirely comfortable with the idea when Gina first suggested it. Not that he was prudish, or had any kind of averseness to the rough sex she liked, it was just that sometimes he felt, well . . . slightly embarrassed, almost as though he could imagine one of his mates watching and thinking what a prat he looked. Also, it wasn't always easy to get in character, especially last time when she'd suggested he pretend to be a psychotic dentist who tied his patients up before having his wicked way. (The Ikea office chair Gina suggested as a prop simply did not cut it.)

But this time it was going to be much easier. Firstly, the MDMA had made him infinitely less self-conscious. Secondly, in the fantasy scenario they were about to play out, Connor was to interrogate Gina about a fictitious drugs stash hidden by her two brothers, Rik and Buster. They were bouncers at a local club and, it was commonly known, second division drug dealers. Connor had never been keen on them so he was almost looking forward to the opportunity of verbally abusing them – albeit from the safety of make-believe.

As he went to the kitchen he caught sight of himself in the hallway mirror and almost screamed. Gina was clearly more astute than he gave her credit for – he doubted if even *he* would ever watch the video dressed like that.

'Scary!' he said to his reflection.

He too could feel the effect of the last dab of MDMA powder. Fantastic. He *so* needed a night like tonight. An escape. A chance to switch off. The last few months felt as though he had jumped on a treadmill that somebody else was controlling. There was no option other than to keep on running, yet the more tired he became and the more he wanted to stop, the faster the bastard machine would go. His work as an IT recruitment consultant, an upcoming big deal, his relationship with Gina; all these seemed ever present in his mind, despite his attempts to ignore them.

4

Connor wandered back from the kitchen as the MDMA crept up on him.

Gina Searle. He knew that if ever they were to split up she would have to be the one who ended it. Connor always preferred to be the dumpee rather than the dumper, primarily because it meant that come Judgement Day he was absolved of responsibility, just in case he had inadvertently missed out on the love of his life, or as he called it, the 'Big Adventure'. Gina had not started out as the Big Adventure but with his thirtieth birthday recently under his belt, he was beginning to wonder if being reasonably compatible with someone was enough.

Of course, the fact that Gina had such fantastic tits and was up for making a home porno and necking loads of pills made her more compatible than most.

He entered the bedroom and slowly paced around the bed, trying to ignore his quickening stream of consciousness, attempting to forget how stupid he looked and to concentrate on matters carnal.

'Right then,' he said, getting into character, 'I've just spoken to the rest of the gang and they've told me to do whatever it takes to find out where those drugs are hidden.'

'Do what you want.'

'I intend to.'

He took her nipple between his thumb and index finger and gave it a sharp pull. Gina didn't make a sound. He nodded slowly then grabbed her hair.

'If you don't tell me where those wanker brothers of yours have stashed the gear, you're going to get this,' he pulled out a rubber dildo from under the pillow, 'and this,' he lifted the asinine skirt he was wearing and pointed to his own bursting member.

'Never! I don't care what you do, I'll never tell you.' Gina glared and grinned.

'Right then.'

He tied her legs together and pulled them up so that they too were fastened to the bedstead. Then, picking up a belt, he lightly whacked her backside.

'Do you know what your problem is?' he said, still in character. 'You respect your brothers too much. Repeat after me: "My brothers are a pair of muscle-bound wankers." Come on, say it.'

'No.'

He just managed not to laugh. 'Didn't you hear me? "My brothers are a pair of cardboard gangsters who watch too many films." ' *Whack.* ' "My brothers are a pair of fags who just act tough." ' *Whack.* 'Say it.'

'Fuck off.'

'Don't tell me to fuck off.' *Whack*. 'They shag each other up the arse.' *Whack*. 'They're full of steroids and they're pansies in the gym.' *Whack*. 'They're wankers.' *Whack*. 'Ugly wankers.' *Whack, whack*. 'Ugliness runs in your family, you fucking whore.' *Whack, whack, whack*.

'*Hey*!'

'Oh, sorry. Was that too rough?'

'Lay off the ugly family stuff, Connor.' She ignored the faint trace of a smile forming on his lips. 'I tell you what, I don't think I can wait any longer. Untie me.'

He contained his urge to laugh and undid the ropes. Once Gina's hands were free she grabbed his rock-hard manhood and guided him in. He felt a mini-rush as her warmth enveloped him. She let out a long satisfied groan as he slowly buried himself.

A little onward lend thy guiding hand . . .

Fuck off! It always happened when he was really buzzing. Poems he'd studied more than a decade earlier would suddenly burst into his consciousness. It wasn't normally even stuff from his English degree, but half-remembered lines learned for his 'A' level. And it always seemed to happen when he was having sex, or dancing with a girl in a club. He'd concluded this had to have something to do with Miss Cooke, his old English supply teacher, whose cleavage had sent adolescent boys into hormonal apoplexy and Kleenex shares soaring.

He who shall teach the child to doubt

The rotting—

'Connor, not quite so hard, honey.'

'What? Oh, sorry.'

Must concentrate. All those pills earlier. Now that MDMA powder is kicking in. That's it, nice and slow. Not too hard to start.

Gina's not a bad girl really. But there's something . . . can't put my finger on it. Shame about her brothers. Nasty pieces of work. Won't ever catch me anywhere near her flat. Haven't been near it since I found out she was related to them. But God. Sex with her is soooo good . . .

Yeah, Gina's all right. At least I don't have to go to weddings on my own any more to get fixed up with some mingin bridesmaid. And you know what? I actually quite like getting Christmas cards to Connor and Gina. And the sex . . .

Maybe it's time. Maybe that's what getting older is all about – compromise. Maybe the Big Adventure, the ten out of ten, doesn't exist. I've already compromised with work, after all. Positive Solutions. Positive bloody Solutions. The fastest growing IT recruitment company in the UK. So they say anyway, with their poxy pseudo-Californian ra-ra-ra attitude. Why is it the more I hate it there the better I do? Weekend trips away, prizes, flash restaurants. New company car next week. Mercedes no less. Assuming I get that big deal. Gina does go on about it a lot though. When are you getting the big deal, Connor? Don't forget you promised me that bracelet, Connor. She loves a bit of Tom. Loves going out, and the status. Oh yes, she fucking loves it.

Without realizing, Connor was thrusting more aggressively.

Living in the material world . . .

Where did that come from? Hardly fucking Blake or Wordsworth. Makes a nice change. Change. Maybe that's it. But what though? No, fuck it. Things are good. The sex is good. What have I got to be unhappy about? Earning decent money. So what if I don't enjoy it? Gina loves it. Gina loves it. Give it up, Connor. Why chase the dream? Look at Stuart King. Sorry, Mr King. Boss. Only a bit older than me. Wanker. But is he happy?

. . . In solitude

What happiness? who can enjoy alone

Or, all enjoying, what contentment find?

Fuck off, Milton. Where was I? Stuart King. Stuart 'it's what you've earned, not what you learned' King. What a tosser. His stupid Ovation guitar, never missing an opportunity to play it on sales conferences, always slipping in a couple of 'songs I've just written'. Wanker. Fucking wanker.

'Aahhhwoow.' Gina half moaned in pleasure, half in pain as Connor pounded away ever more forcibly.

And what are those stupid photos of him playing in a band on his office wall all about? And those faded press clippings from local papers? No way is he happy.

'Steady, Connor.' The comment barely grazed Connor's consciousness.

When I get that big deal this week, that'll show him. Maybe I'm not doing something I really like. But what do I like? What is the dream? Going back to Ibiza? Yeah, right! The boy most likely to become a recruitment consultant – what a joke.

'Connor!' The bed was banging against the wall like a kick drum at a Jungle rave. Connor was still lost on planet ecstasy.

Am I happy? But what is happiness? Doing what you want? Being a good person? I nearly always treat people with respect. I try not to hurt people . . .

'Ooooowww – my head!'

This time Gina's scream was shrill enough to drag Connor back. He stopped and looked down at her.

'What's up?'

'You were going too hard. My head was banging against the wall. Get off a minute.' As Connor rolled off, Gina went to sit up. 'Ouch. Shit, I can't move. My head's stuck.'

Sure enough, the top of Gina's head was squashed between two of the bedstead's bars.

'You're winding me up. Here we go . . .' Connor tickled her, which made her wriggle involuntarily, then yelp in pain, as her head remained where it was. 'Fuck. Let's try to ease it out slowly. I'll put some baby oil on it.'

He poured liberal amounts of oil around her temples then put one hand through the bars and rested it on the top of her head ready to push down. He put the other on her shoulder. Gina gripped hold of the bars.

'Right, are you ready? One, two, three . . .'

They pushed.

'Ow, ouch, fuck, stop, *stop*! You're going to turn me into a bloody conehead.'

They pondered different ideas for a few moments, had another couple of tries, then gave up.

'This could be a job for the fire brigade,' said Connor, only half-joking.

'Oh, great. Rik and Buster would be over the moon if they found out.'

'Yeah, well we don't want that.' Connor cogitated several impractical solutions before clicking his fingers. 'I've got it! A car jack. That'll ease the bars apart. I'll borrow one from the boys up at Bounty FM; they should be up and transmitting this time in the morning.'

He switched on the alarm clock radio next to the bed and was greeted by the familiar sound of UK Garage, courtesy of the new pirate radio station his two best friends, Dex and Luc, ran. 'Yep, they're on air. It should only take me half an hour. I'll be back by . . . no later than seven. Shall I leave the curtains drawn or do you want some daylight? Radio on or off?'

'Radio on, and don't even think about opening the curtains.'

Connor went into the kitchen and came back with a glass of fresh orange juice and a large saucepan.

'What's the saucepan for?'

'In case you need to . . . you know . . . call of nature.'

'Don't you *dare* take that long.'

chapter two

Rik and Buster Searle heard the message in their earpieces at the same time. It was the third dealer caught in Brazen that night. They left the door and sprinted down the stairs, barging through the crowd, hoping to impress a few females with their display of machismo.

The Searles were thugs, with gangster aspirations. They were huge men with non-existent necks, and pecs, lats and triceps that were so over-developed the brothers walked as though oranges were glued into their armpits. They were vicious, and lacked any compassion or conscience when dealing with their enemies; they also lacked the quickness of thought and the perception so vital to those who understand the psychology of violence, rather than just its mechanics. It was unlikely they would ever ascend the echelons of their chosen profession.

On Fridays they worked for Goliath Security, which held door contracts on four leading London clubs. Each week, they would be rotated to a different venue; Goliath wanted to keep a clean reputation and felt this reduced the risk of their doormen becoming too familiar with any one club and involved in controlling its supply of drugs.

This was wise, because every Saturday this was exactly what the Searle brothers did at Brazen, where they ran the security *and* controlled the drugs. It was therefore always a highlight of their night's work when a dealer was found operating in 'their' club.

The brothers ran into the back room where another bouncer called Blue was standing next to the young dealer.

Rik Searle's pace quickened as he approached them. 'You come into my fucking club and start selling gear without my permission . . .'

Rik went for the dealer, but Blue stepped between them.

'I'll sort him.' He had seen the result of bodies pumped full of steroids, cocaine and adrenalin too many times. He turned to the dealer. 'Turn your pockets out and drop your pants.'

The dealer began to protest but saw the look in Rik's eyes and thought better of it. He handed over a bag with just over twenty pills in it and about £500 in cash. Rik snatched it and Blue pushed the dealer towards the door.

'Go on, fuck off while you still can – and don't let me ever see you in here again.'

As the dealer left, Rik turned to a wiry lad with a wispy goatee beard and gave him the pills.

'There you go. More for the collection. Now get out there and sell 'em.'

The Searles swaggered back towards the main room and bar with Blue close behind. Rik winked at the barmaid, and leaned over, helping himself to three beers.

'Arse still playing you up, Buster?' he said to his younger brother with a grin as he handed him a bottle.

'Of course it fucking is. I only had the op four days ago. I've still got the poxy stitches up there.'

'What's all that about?' asked Blue.

'He had a dirty great spot up his arse that he had to get removed,' laughed Rik.

'It was an abscess on my rectum,' corrected Buster, with surprising anatomical accuracy.

'What caused that?' asked Blue.

'Haven't got a clue. All I know is it's fucking sore.'

Blue laughed then left to patrol the club; Rik and Buster went back to work on the door, where the queue had grown considerably in their absence. They nodded at the massive bouncer who spent all night at the entrance, and the expectant clubbers slowly began to trickle in once again. Rik lit two cigarettes, passing one to Buster.

'Cheers. What time's Jock due down?'

'Usual,' replied Rik. 'Between seven and eight this morning.'

'Is Gina still seeing that bloke – Connor?'

'Yeah, I think so. Why's that?'

'He won't be at the flat when we get back, will he?'

'Course not. He wouldn't come near the place after he found out it was ours.' Rik and Buster shared a small, self-satisfied smile. 'Besides, Gina knows to stay away until midday every Sunday.'

'Yeah, but she always moans about it.'

'Tough shit. Who owns the place? We spend hardly any time there and we don't charge her a penny rent. All she has to do is keep the place clean. She's got a good deal and she knows it.'

In return for the peppercorn rent on the waterfront Rotherhithe flat,

10

Gina turned a blind eye to the drugs transactions her brothers carried out there when she was at work during the day, and early on Sunday morning, after they'd finished at Brazen, when their courier made his weekly journey on the sleeper from Glasgow. For nine months the Searle brothers had been organizing cocaine and ecstasy deals with a Scot, whom they had never met in person. This was to be the last delivery until October; the mysterious Caledonian was apparently taking a summer break. With this in mind, the Searles had in fact already sourced some gear from elsewhere, but they had chosen not to share this information with the Scot or his deliveryman. They would be more than happy to buy an extra load, and if the courier had made the trip, they reasoned, he would happily reduce the price rather than take it all the way back to Scotland.

Part of the cause for their complacency was the courier himself. He was an insignificant looking man in his mid-forties, about five foot six with a maturing, middle-aged paunch, and always sported a cravat, irrespective of whether he was wearing a suit or T-shirt. Curiously, the top of his wedding ring finger was missing; the Searles assumed this to be the result of an industrial accident, or a bar room brawl that he had inevitably lost. They had little respect for anybody who couldn't bench-press at least 250 pounds, so had never even bothered to ask his name, referring to him only as 'Jock'. They were too puffed up with their own sense of importance to notice the veiled menace in the Glaswegian's hooded eyes. If they'd had any idea who it was they were dealing with, their attitude would have modified.

Dawn was breaking when the brothers turned up outside the door of Gina's flat. Their Scottish connection was waiting outside.

'Nice cravat,' remarked Buster, containing a snigger.

'How is it that I travel best part of six hundred miles and get here on time, yet you two locals are late? It doesn't look good me standing out here, especially with a kilo of Charlie and five thousand pills in my overnight bag.'

'Keep your hair on, Jock,' said Buster. 'We're here now, ain't we?'

Jock had long since abandoned the idea of telling these two retards his real name, which was Mac and, in any case, just as much of a cliché.

Of all his customers, Mac found the Searles the most annoying. He could see straight through them, the cogs painfully turning in their Perspex skulls. It was as if they believed their intellect grew with their muscles. The bigger they got, the less they thought things through. Maybe they laboured under the misconception that the brain was a muscle too, growing in size with every steroid injection. Mac laughed to himself. How could they possibly even consider that they could outsmart him? He was one step ahead of them. He always was.

They walked into the flat and Buster headed straight for the coffee table where a small mirror tile sat. He took a wrap of cocaine from his pocket and started to chop out some lines on it.

'Do you want one, Jock?'

'No. I want to give you this, take my money, then bid you farewell until October, miss you though I shall.'

Rik walked in from the kitchen, twisting open the top of an imported Belgian beer. 'We need to have a chat to you, Jock me old mate. We've got a bit of a problem.'

Quelle surprise, thought Mac. 'And what might that be, pray tell? I assume you are not referring to your brother's recent operation to have his piles removed?'

'It wasn't piles. That's what old gits like you get. It was an abscess.'

'Congratulations.'

'The thing is, Jock,' continued Rik, 'we don't really need the Charlie. We're fine with the pills though. Because it's your last delivery for a while, we needed to find a different supplier and the one we found for coke had some top gear about him. We had to show willing so we bought it.'

Mac just nodded.

'Yeah, so we don't really need yours now. Sorry to fuck you about and all that,' added Buster.

'Oh no, that's quite all right. I'm always happy to put my liberty on the line for nothing. If I get arrested on the way home, maybe you'll both be good enough to drop me the odd postcard?'

'Well, I tell you what we could do,' said Buster, too hurriedly. 'Like I said, we don't really need it but seeing as it's partly our fault, we'll take it off you if we can sort out a deal.'

'Oh, would you?' replied Mac. 'Are you sure you don't mind?'

The Searles looked at each other and grinned.

'Course not,' said Rik. 'I'm sure you'd do the same for us.'

'And what figure were you thinking of offering me for this kilo of finest Colombian produce, with a normal RRP of twenty-four grand?'

'We-ell,' stretched Buster.

'Fifteen,' interjected Rik abruptly. 'Take it or leave it.'

'Goodbye,' said Mac, and sighed. He picked a wad of notes from the table. 'Is this the money to cover the pills?' Rik nodded. 'I'd like to say it's been a pleasure doing business with you, but you can't have everything you like.'

Mac walked to the door, counting the money with practised dexterity. Buster nodded at Rik.

'Just a sec, Jock.' Rik guided him back into the room.

Mac didn't look up, whispering the count as the notes flicked swiftly between his fingers. Rik and Buster were silent while he finished, Rik staring at Mac's left hand with its truncated finger.

'Problem, big man?'

'Huh?' The suddenly calm aggression and icy stare took Rik by surprise. 'No,' he said, shaking his head. He felt uncomfortable in Mac's presence for the first time and, for a few moments, was unsure where to cast his gaze. He caught his brother's eye. Buster was mouthing, 'Go on.' Rik quickly re-composed himself and continued. 'All right, fifteen was a bit low. You are up for dropping the price though . . . aren't you?'

'Try me.'

'Sixteen and a half.'

'Try me again.'

'Seventeen.'

'And I thought the Marx brothers had the monopoly on sibling comedy. Now, if you don't mind, I've a train to catch and a country of sane people to return to.'

'OK, OK. What's your best price?'

'Twenty-two,' replied Mac, poker-faced.

'Eighteen,' tried Rik.

Mac stayed silent and Rik upped his offer within seconds. 'All right then, twenty. If you won't take that you can piss off back to sweaty sock land with it,' he quickly added, with an unconvincing air of bravado.

'Twenty it is. And may I say, that was the finest piece of bartering I've witnessed this side of Monty Python.'

The Searles nodded and smiled, missing the reference. Mac took a packet from his bag and put it on electronic scales, which Buster had placed on the table.

'Vacuum-sealed as always, gentleman. You can see it's in the same kind of packaging as the last lot. That's because it's from the same batch. I assume there were no problems with quality last time?' The Searles shook their heads. 'Good. Well, I'll be on my way.'

'No problem, Jock,' replied a beaming Rik.

Once outside, Mac took out his mobile phone and dialled a number.

'Kyle? It's Mac. All right to talk on this phone?'

'Aye. What happened?'

'Just as I predicted.'

'The wee bastards. Did they try it on with just the Charlie or the pills as well?'

'Just the Charlie.'

'And they went for it?'

'Hook, line, and sinker. The Searle dimwits are now in possession of the most expensive kilo of glucose in Britain.'

'Excellent, excellent. That'll set us up nicely for a bit of spending money on the Isla Blanca. Right then, Mac, I'll be into Gatwick just after three p.m. Our flight to Ibiza leaves at five fifty-five so I'll meet you by the check-in.'

'Where's the diving boat?'

'It's got its own mooring right outside the dive school.'

'And it's up to the job, yeah?'

'Well it's no' gonna be at the Earl's Court fuckin' boat show but for something that's been in the water for nearly twenty years it's in pretty good nick. It used to belong to a Kraut, until his diving school went bust the year before last. As part of the deal there's a Spanish guy who's going to captain the boat for us when we're doing diving lessons.'

'I'm still not convinced it's a good idea.'

'Are you joking? It's perfect. The Spaniard's OK – he doesn't ask any questions. And I tell you what, Mac auld son, I've got an English girl working as a diving instructor – fit as fuck.'

'Kyle, why do you have—'

'And we've even taken a few bookings already. *Tranquillo*, Mac. Just pack your suntan cream and leave that fucking cravat at home – everything's sorted.'

In the flat, the Searles toasted each other. Then the phone rang. Buster could tell by Rik's face it wasn't good news.

'What's up?'

'That was our Charlie man in Bermondsey. He thinks he's being watched.'

'He what?'

'I'm sure it's nothing to worry about. You know what he's like. He's probably been sampling too much of his own stock and got on a bit of a para one. He wants us to keep hold of the nosebag for a few days.'

'Oh, for fuck's sake . . . What are we going to do with it?'

Rik scanned the room. 'We'll just leave it here. One of the boys'll be round to pick up the pills so that's taken care of.' His eyes rested on the video. 'Let's put it in that old thing. It looks like it's been here a while.

We'll come back Thursday and take it out. No point in telling Gina –
she'll just get a strop on.'

Buster nodded, went to the kitchen and got a screwdriver and began
to take the cover off the video recorder.

The kilo of glucose fitted inside it perfectly.

chapter three

'*It's . . . a . . . Lon-don . . . thing.*'

'Yeah, this one goes way back to November ninety-seven. Hold tight, the Peckham massive. Going out to the one like the Everton, from Tanya. Hold tight, the one like the Mikey in Stratford. Hold tight, the B-line massive. This is DJ Dex and you're locked on to Bounty FM, pirate stylee. Quick time-check of a quarter to seven on a Sunday morning. Summer's on its way . . .'

Dex pulled back the fader and allowed himself a little self-congratulatory nod at another mix well executed. There was a small mirror next to the mixing desk and Dex had a quick look at his own reflection. He still hadn't quite got used to seeing the number one shave instead of the dreadlocks, which, until three days before, had been his crowning glory. When he noticed that the just-arrived, grinning Connor was watching him, he buried his face in his record box, slightly embarrassed his mild display of vanity had been noticed. He pulled a record out and turned back to Connor and Luc, his other best friend.

'So, let me get this right,' said Luc. 'You've been making a video with Gina Searle in your flat and now her head's stuck between two bars of your bed, and you need a pump car jack to force the bars apart?'

'That's right.'

Dex and Luc, who were semi-stoned, burst out laughing.

'Hurry up! I promised her I'd only be half an hour and it'll take me ten minutes to get back even if I run.'

'Chill, man, chill,' said Dex. 'Sit yourself down and have a toke on this. Look at you, you're still wired from last night.'

Connor swept a hand through his hair and took a long, slow toke on a spliff, then slumped into a battered armchair.

'I don't suppose another ten minutes will hurt, will it?'

Dex and Luc had commandeered the empty Camberwell flat three weeks earlier and had been broadcasting their pirate radio station from the living room ever since. The monitors were turned down low so as not to cause feedback. A shaft of early Sunday morning sunlight bisected the room through the balcony window, transfixing the stoned occupants as they realized that exhaling sharply changed the direction of the dust particles. With a combination of the previous night's narcotic intake and the spliff now in his system, Connor's brain locked on to the music rather than the clock. Conversation virtually ceased, apart from the odd shout of, 'Tune!' when Dex put on a track one of them liked. Every so often, the mobile phone would ring with another request or dedication. A map of Greater London was on the wall with little pins in it to show where the station was being received. Most were dotted around the east and south-east of the capital.

Luca Torres (his Spanish father and English mother moved to London from just outside Madrid when he was four and all his English friends called him Luc) was sitting on the floor skinning up. Connor noticed the first flecks of grey appearing in his goatee beard. He had started receding at just nineteen and although at twenty-six he was four years younger than Connor (though a year older than Dex), he was more than a little touchy when it came to his pate. To his credit, rather than opting for any kind of hirsute cover-up, he had shaved the whole lot, which suited his sullen Latin features.

The contented semi-silence was punctuated by the station's mobile phone exploding into life, playing a digitized version of an old classical tune. It caused the stoned Luc to jolt with a start, sending the contents of the nearly finished spliff flying everywhere. Dex kicked the phone to Connor, who answered. The voice was female and very distant.

'Connor. Is that you?'

'Hello . . . Gina? I can hardly hear you. It's a terrible line.'

'It's not a terrible line. I've managed to reach the phone by your bed and put it on to hands free. It's the only way I can use it because I can't quite get my fingers to the handset. What are you still doing there? Why haven't you come back? It's nearly seven-thirty.'

'Is it? Oh shit, I mean, yeah, I know. Luc's had to go home to, er, get the jack. He's only just got back. I'm leaving right now. See you in ten.'

'You'd better.'

Connor switched the phone off. It immediately rang again.

'Hello, Bounty FM,' he said.

'Get off our fucking frequency!'

Connor pulled the phone away from his ear as if it had nipped his earlobe.

'Who's this?'

'It's Skunk FM an' you're on our frequency. I've warned you before, man. Get off – right now.'

'I haven't got time for this.'

'Just get off our waves, you blood clat.'

'Who the fuck do you think you're talking to?'

There was a moment's silence. 'Ja, man, if you don't get off air I'm gonna come over there an' bus' up your bones, see?'

'You what?'

'I'm serious, man.'

'Do me a favour and just fuck off.' He ended the call and turned to Dex. 'Skunk FM?'

'Yeah,' replied Dex. 'What's up?'

'Reckons you're on their frequency and if you don't get off he's gonna come over and "bus' up me bones".'

'Oh, it's just one of their silly little DJs. He keeps ringing up. He's a pain in the arse.'

'So there won't be any trouble then?'

Dex shook his head. 'Doubt it.'

'Cool. In that case I'm going to make a move.'

'Hang on a minute.' Dex held out a spliff.

Feigning reluctance, Connor took it. 'Just this one and then I'll go.'

'So then, Connor,' said Luc, following him into the kitchen, 'big contract signed at work this week, new Merc next week. Can't be bad.'

'No, guess not.'

'You don't seem that excited.'

'Well, you know . . .' Connor trailed off.

'Who'd've thought it, eh? Connor Young a fully paid-up member of the rat race.'

Connor laughed. 'Maybe you should try it some time instead of running back to Ibiza again. What's this – your third summer?'

Luc nodded. 'If you hadn't raved about it so much after you worked there, I probably wouldn't have gone in the first place. You know what it's like – addictive.'

'Yeah, but you've got to come back to the real world one day, you know.'

'Who's to say what's the real world?' replied Luc. 'Why can't Ibiza be the real world?'

'Because it's not, and anyway, what would you do when you get old?'

'Die happy with a nice tan. You know, a few years ago, this conversation would've been the other way round. It was always me who wanted to settle down. I remember you saying to me once that if you got run over by a bus, then you'd be at the pearly gates saying, "Can't complain. I've crammed a lot in," and St Peter would've said to me, "You twat, fancy saving for a rainy day and working a nine to five." What happened?'

Connor stood up. 'I guess you can't go through life assuming you're about to get run over by a bus.'

Ten minutes later, Connor was using Dex's spare car key to get the car jack out of Luc's Mondeo. It was ten to eight, an hour and twenty minutes since he left Gina, so he popped into a nearby Costcutter to purchase some peace offerings.

As he came back past the main entrance to the estate, Luc came hurtling round the corner with a baseball bat. Dex was hot on his heels and they almost knocked Connor over as they sped around the corner.

'Quick, that DJ from Skunk FM has nicked the antennae,' screamed Dex, out of breath but not stopping. 'Three hundred quid's worth of fucking antennae.'

Luc went one way, Dex the other. By the time Connor put down the Costcutter bag, they were both out of sight. He trotted round the estate trying to find them. After a couple of minutes, he heard the crunch of gears and the furious revving of an engine coming from the adjacent lock-ups. As he turned the corner, a red, three-series, brand-new BMW with a Skunk FM sticker in its rear window was frantically trying to accomplish a three-point-turn within the confined canyon of the garages, the driver and passenger screaming at each other to hurry up. Luc was smashing the bodywork of the car for all he was worth with the baseball bat. Instinctively, his temper rising in support of his friends, Connor swung the car jack, which shattered the back windscreen, and grabbed the antennae that were poking out of the open rear window, hauling them out on to the tarmac. The car had almost completed its manoeuvre but Luc was ideally placed to smash the front windscreen too and was just about to bring the baseball bat down again when Dex came running into the garages.

'No, Luc, stop!' he yelled.

It was too late. Luc caught the edge of the windscreen on the passenger side and although it didn't shatter completely, the damage was significant. The car sped past Dex, who tried to see who the two occupants were, and out into the road before roaring away.

'Oh, man, what have you done?' wailed Dex.

'I managed to get the aerial back,' declared a triumphant Connor.

'And we trashed the car,' grinned Luc.

19

Dex put his head in his hands. 'Don't you know whose car that is? Don't you know who owns Skunk FM?' Luc and Connor looked at him blankly. 'Victor James!'

Luc's expression changed.

'Who?' said Connor.

'Victor James,' Luc repeated, the colour draining from his face. 'What's he got to do with Skunk FM?'

'He fucking owns it,' replied Dex.

'Why didn't you let me know that before?'

'I've only just found out myself. I rang my brother Steve to see if him and his little crew were up and about because I wasn't sure how many of the Skunk lot were going to be waiting for us here. He just told me. Anyway, surely you recognized Victor's car?'

'*That* was Victor's car?' groaned Luc.

'You must have seen it outside clubs. It's his pride and joy.'

'Not any more,' observed Connor.

'Great,' said Luc. 'Bang goes the station.'

'What's the big deal with Victor?' asked Connor.

'What's the big deal?' repeated Dex aghast. 'Man, Victor James was one of the main gang leaders in Moss Side until he came down here just under a couple of years ago. He's got a tattoo on his shoulder blade that's a list of all the gang members killed. The man is serious.'

'But if he's turned his back on it—'

'Listen,' Dex interrupted, 'he might not be involved in gangland shit no more but you can bet he's got his fingers in a few pies, like Skunk FM. One thing's for sure – we're in deep shit now you've trashed his car. I'm surprised he didn't get out of the car and shoot you both.'

'Do you know him well?' asked Connor.

'We're not bosom buddies but yeah, I chat to him when we're out. He was always asking me to DJ for him.' Dex shook his head, still unable to believe what had just happened. 'Why didn't I find out before he was behind Skunk FM?'

'So, can't you just give him a call, explain it was a misunderstanding and maybe tell him we'll go off air for a while,' offered Luc.

'Off air? With Victor after me I'd rather get off this planet! It's all right for you two, you're off to Ibiza, and Victor doesn't know Connor. I'm stuffed.' They were silent as they walked back off the estate. After a few moments, Dex stopped and his eyes lit up. 'Unless . . .'

'Unless what?' asked Luc.

'I might not be able to get off this planet but I can get out of this country for a while.'

'How?'

'By coming with you to Ibiza. I can work there for a while. I've got no ties here.'

'It's not that easy,' said Luc. 'You don't speak the language like I do. You haven't got a job—'

'I shouldn't have any trouble getting a job as a DJ.'

'Are you serious? There are hundreds of DJs over there,' insisted Luc. 'When the British flights land there're more record boxes than suitcases going round the baggage carousel.'

'I'll get a job, no sweat. Going out there could be the making of me.'

'Or the breaking of you,' noted Connor.

'You're the one who always used to tell me that I hadn't seen nut'ing. Man, I've only ever been to the Caribbean and a day trip to France. It'll be cool.'

Back at the car, Connor picked up the Costcutter bag, shaking his head. 'You can't run away from your problems, Dex. All they do is get worse.'

'The only problem I've got is a pair of boring mates. For once in my life I'm gonna do something because *I* want to. By the time I get back Victor will have cooled down. Sorry, guys, but I've made up my mind.' He turned to Luc. 'I'll get my stuff and stay round yours until we leave, just in case Victor comes knocking. You've got room in that Mondeo of yours for me, haven't you?'

Luc nodded. 'If you're sure, then yeah.'

'Cool.' He turned to Connor. 'What about you, Connor? Fancy it? We all know that you secretly hate that job of yours. How about returning to your old stomping ground?'

Connor felt a familiar hollow feeling in his stomach. The truth was that Connor considered going back to Ibiza every summer. May was the worst time of year, when friends were planning their trips, organizing their jobs and places to stay. Then there'd be the music press and the constant TV programmes and documentaries, inevitably with people he knew popping up in the background, all tans and smiles. What did they know? Ibiza was *his* island.

Unfortunately, as Connor realized only too well, nearly everyone who spent any length of time in Ibiza considered it their island, such was its magic. Connor loved the place, yet he always sensed it was unrequited. Ibiza fed off the vitality of youth, and callously moved on. Connor did not want to return to Ibiza as last year's model, nor feel relegated or replaced in its peculiar hierarchy.

Yet, just thinking about it . . . he could almost feel the excitement of

21

coming in to land, almost smell the plane fuel mixed with the warm, pine-scented air. Then once out of the airport, the sweet scent of honeysuckle battling with the stench from the salt flats, the taxis with their little green lights scurrying between clubs, hotels and the airport.

Working for Positive Solutions was certainly not what he ultimately wanted. It did however, seem the 'right' thing to do. Connor wasn't scared of going to Ibiza – he was scared of never coming back.

'No,' he said slowly. 'Not for me, Dex. I've done my time. I've got a good job, an all right girlfriend, a big deal coming off this week, and a new Merc arriving next week. Why on earth would I want to give all that up for a few months in the sun?'

'Because you know exactly what's round the corner,' replied Dex, animatedly. 'Who knows what might be waiting for you in Ibiza?'

'Might be a bus,' said Luc, with a glint in his eye.

Connor shook his head. 'I've had my time-out. You go over there and have yours. I've had the pause button on for long enough – time to hit play.'

'So what now?' asked Dex.

'Now?' Connor sighed. 'Now I'm going home to grovel.'

chapter four

Chocolates, champagne, flowers . . . nothing worked. Gina was angry, he was being dumped, and that was that.

During the two hours Connor had been at Dex's, Gina had had to pee in the saucepan. She accomplished this particular task with the pride of a two-year-old. However, when she tried to move the full saucepan from the bed on to terra firma, she managed to spill the contents all over herself. Unable to reach a towel and with the duvet just out of reach, she remained in this drenched and unpleasant state until Connor's tardy return at eight-thirty. If there had been a Generation Game challenge where contestants had to pass a saucepan full of pee from a bed to the floor, then Gina would have been lucky to score a consolation point.

The jack worked perfectly. Once free, she grabbed her mobile from her bag and stormed off to the bathroom, leaving a stoned and pissed Connor coming down and contemplating the news that they were no longer an item.

He could hear her muffled voice and guessed she was ringing friends to tell them about the demise of their relationship. The first person she would be calling would undoubtedly be the psycho-bitch from hell, Chrissy. This troubled him. A few weeks earlier, Connor, out with his mates, had bumped into Chrissy in a bar just off Regent Street. Although they normally had little time for each other, the extremely strong Mitsubishi pill he had taken persuaded him to rebuild bridges, and in an attempt to bond, he told her certain things about his relationship with Gina. Exactly what, he couldn't recall.

Gina eventually emerged from the bathroom, her resolve clearly stiffened by the support of her friends at the other end of her cellular. She grabbed her things, checked her watch, and barked her desire to be taken home.

They drove back to her flat in silence. He had only visited it once since the discovery that Gina's brothers were Rik and Buster Searle. Gina always made an excuse why she couldn't go home too early on a Sunday and Connor guessed the reason. Half of Connor's mates got their gear from the Searles, either directly or indirectly. A role-play about it was one thing, to mention it quite another.

Connor knew that he should be talking to Gina about their relationship, apologizing even more profusely, and coming up with some extravagant proposal, like a romantic weekend away together. Yet each time his mind wandered, the existence of *that* video would yank him back to reality. As Connor turned his car into Long Lane from Borough High Street he made a lame attempt to broach the subject.

'Do you want me to take the video? Obviously I'll wipe over it.'

'Oh, that's all right. I'm sure I can manage myself.' Gina looked positively evil.

Connor fidgeted uncomfortably. They'd had a few minor arguments before but this was different. She was calm and had taken all of her things from his place. She had allowed him to give her a lift home rather than get a taxi, but had made it clear that this was to pick up his few possessions from her flat.

'Are you sure you're going to wipe over it? I mean, we don't want anyone to see it.'

'By "anyone", you wouldn't happen to be referring to my brothers, by any chance, would you? I mean, you've not been sitting there for the whole of this journey, dying to ask me if I'm going to let them see it?'

'Of course not,' lied Connor. 'I just meant anyone.' Gina smiled smugly. Connor knew she wanted to see him squirm. 'Anyway, I can't for one moment imagine that you'd want your brothers to watch it.'

'Can't you?'

'Are you honestly telling me that you'd let your brothers see you tied to a bed, getting whipped with a belt and a dildo shoved—'

'While you're calling them wankers, pansies, and God knows what else.' She gave him a withering look of disdain.

Connor slunk back into his seat. Had he not been driving he would have probably curled up in a ball in the hope that he would disappear altogether. Eventually he spoke, as feebly as he could manage.

'So, are you going to tell them?'

'Might, might not.'

'How will I know?'

'Just listen out for your door being broken down.'

When they got to Gina's, Connor helped carry her things to her flat. It was on the first floor of a newly built block, designed to feel as though it was an old warehouse conversion. Inside, he noticed a small mirror tile

24

on the dining table, smeared by the remnants of cocaine. Gina went into her room to gather Connor's belongings, mainly sweatshirts she'd left his flat wearing, or CDs she'd borrowed. While she was doing this, Connor noticed a vinyl of India's 'Love and Happiness', which Gina always referred to as 'their tune'. He slipped it on to the record deck.

He walked into the kitchen and looked across the Thames towards the stepped building on the opposite bank, Cascades. It was a grey day, which wholly reflected his mood. He put the kettle on and made two of cups of tea, then walked back into the large living room.

'Gina, I've made you a cup of tea.'

Gina came out of her bedroom carrying a black bin liner containing most of his things. Connor noticed that she'd been crying. Good sign.

'Here,' she said, handing him the bag. 'Everything's in there apart from the old video recorder you lent me. I took the plug off, so I'll have to get you a new one.'

'Don't be silly.'

They looked into each other's eyes and, as India's voice soared over the speakers, Gina's face slowly began to crumple. She buried her head into Connor's shoulder and he stroked her hair, breathing a huge sigh of relief.

'I'm really sorry, Gina. I know I should have got back earlier but—'

Gina gulped some air and pulled away from him. He wiped a tear from her cheek with his thumb. She smiled. 'I'm OK. Things have been getting to me lately, that's all. I overreacted.'

They kissed then Connor went into the kitchen and brought back a packet of biscuits, a simple action but something he could not have possibly imagined ever doing again just a couple of minutes earlier. As he sat down on the cream leather sofa, Gina made her way to her answerphone, where the red light was flashing.

Connor happily dunked a biscuit into his tea. The first message was from a colleague, asking if she wanted to go to an exhibition at Olympia. When Connor heard the second voice though, he shifted uncomfortably. It was a very drunk psycho-bitch from hell.

'Gina. It's Chrissy. I got your message. Why aren't you there? What's that bastard Connor done this time? You said it was something outrageous. I never knew why you were with him. You could do so much better. Anyway, now you've split up, there's something I've been meaning to tell you . . .'

Connor was on the verge of leaping for the answerphone, but unsure what Chrissy was going to say, he sat still rather than immediately condemn himself.

'You remember that night I bumped into him? We had quite a long chat, old Connor and I. He told me he thought you weren't the – oh, what did he call it? – Big Adventure. I reckon he's just marking time with you. I wasn't going to say anything but now you've split up, well . . . He's a loser, Gina. You're well shot of him. Call me later.'

Connor had never seen Gina's face look so scary. For one horrible moment, he could see the family resemblance to her brothers.

'Gina, wait. I'd done a couple of pills, I was fucked—'

'Why were you discussing our business, in particular with *my* friend?'

'I wasn't . . . I didn't . . . I was buzzing . . .' Connor realized how pathetic this sounded.

Gina stamped her foot, 'I know why you're doing this. It's because you're going to be earning all that money next month and getting the Merc, isn't it? You want to be single again and give it large with all your mates. You don't care about me.'

'Don't be so silly. You should know all that means nothing to me.'

'*Liar*!'

'Gina, this is stupid.'

'You planned this.'

'Why would I plan it? You know I think a lot of you—'

'Ha!' Gina wiped her nose on the back of her sleeve. 'But do you love me, Connor?'

He went quiet. 'Gina, you know the "L" word is not something I do lightly.'

'You can't even *say it*!'

Connor paused, then took a deep breath. 'Yeah, I guess in a way I do love you.'

Gina's eyes welled up again. '*In a way*? What does that mean? You're not actually *in* love with me, are you?'

Connor started to pace up and down the room. 'Fucking hell, Gina. What is love? You're asking me to define a word that songwriters and poets have been struggling with for ever. How on earth do you expect me to be able to do it? I care about you and I think a lot of you. Who knows where it could lead?'

Gina wasn't listening. 'Just say you're in love with me.'

Connor looked at her, frustration in his eyes.

'Just tell me that you really, really love me.'

Connor held her gaze for a few moments more, then cast his eyes to the floor.

'I knew it.'

'But it doesn't mean—'

Gina picked up the bin liner with his stuff in it and threw it at him. 'Get out, Connor. Get out now.'

Connor could tell things had passed the reasoning stage.

'All right, I'm going. Just give me that tape. Please.'

Gina's lips mutated into a snarl and she pointed to the door. Defeated, Connor picked up the bin liner and left. As he turned the latch, she called after him.

'Haven't you forgotten something?'

For one beautiful moment, Connor expected to turn around and see her holding the videotape. Instead, she was standing with the video recorder he'd lent her.

'And you can get your own plug,' she snapped as she shoved it into his hands.

chapter five

In a luxurious villa in Ibiza's Benimussa hills, Kyle Goldwell pressed the release button on the flick knife, the Spanish sun glinting against the blade, to open the bag of creamy powder Mac was tossing from hand to hand. He allowed himself a smile. It wouldn't be long now. Purer gear, fewer people taking their cut . . . They were back. They were in control.

'Five years, Mac, that's all it's taken. Five years. I knew this place was wide open. No organization, see. All the wee scallies did was earn it and spunk it.' He tapped the side of his head. 'No brains. Just like the Searles. Mind you, I didn't think for one minute you'd get away with ripping them off like that. Are you sure you've never pulled that scam before?'

'Never. I just knew that they'd try it on. It was obvious they'd be so pleased with themselves for getting such a good price that they wouldn't check the gear. Also, they had me marked as a mug and thought I wouldn't dare stitch them up. The fools probably still haven't opened it.' Mac loosened his plum-coloured cravat. His torso was bare. 'We've got planning and brains; they haven't.'

'Exactly. Now that the Atlantis complex is built I'm a bona fide bar owner.' Kyle puffed his chest out a little. 'Respectable. We're getting in with the bizzies, Smacker is into its third year . . . Even without the masterplan we'd make a good living out of just those. It's all about getting the right people on our side.'

'True, though we both know where the real money is.'

'Aye, we're moving into the fucking big league, right enough, and these guys don't fuck about. They didn't bat an eyelid when that local lad copped it last week.'

'Did you find out what happened?'

Kyle nodded. 'It was an accident. They were about to drop the trunk, the one we're going to use for our pick-ups. The sea was quite rough and just as they were moving it to a smaller boat they got caught by a wave and the trunk slid off. The local guy got his sleeve snagged and was dragged down. The bloody trunk was lined with concrete so weighed a ton and it's fucking deep there by all accounts. They dived down for him as quick as they could but the trunk was on his arm – not the nicest way to go, eh? They didn't have any way of getting the trunk up so they just left him, even though the area's quite popular with divers. So he's still there now, as far as I know. They're sinking another trunk at our site within the next few days. We've gotta just keep checking it's there cos they wanna stay *incommunicado* until the first drop. So you see, Mac, this is serious shit. We know these guys are real players. That's why we've gotta be that little bit smarter.'

'I know, but I'm still not certain the diving school is the best cover. Why didn't we just get a boat of our own and do it like that?'

'First of all there was that other unit next to the bar – I didn't want anyone else renting it and it's perfect for a little dive school office. Also, you can't be too careful, Mac auld son. They've all sorts of technology these days. They track people right across the world, watching for patterns. Even if we're no' being watched that doesn't mean the boys we're getting it from aren't. Sure, they're safe and we've known them a while but we're no' talking a little eighth of puff. Trust me – the diving school is ideal. A few trips out, a few practice runs, one small drop, then the biggie. Plus of course, there's Marina . . .'

'Who?'

'The wee lassie I told you about who I've got working for me. Wait till you see her . . .'

Mac shook his head. 'Everyone's got one.'

'What?'

'An Achilles heel. You and your pursuit of the supposed fairer sex will be your downfall one day.'

'Away to fuck, you miserable wee sod. What's the point in being on this island, with all the trappings we've got, if we don't use them to enjoy ourselves? There's more to life than Stanley blades. Talking of which . . .'

Kyle nodded towards the drive where a tall, good-looking lad was talking to his pretty, dark-haired passenger in a navy-blue Ford Focus. Then he trotted up the path to the villa. There was a gentle knock on the door.

'It's OK, Terry,' said Kyle, 'it's open.'

A young lad peered around the door, squinting as his eyes adjusted from the bright sunlight.

'Who's that with you?' asked Kyle.

'Oh, me bird. Met her back home in Manchester. Fit but headstrong. Didn't want to stay indoors.'

29

'You shouldn't have brought her here. We don't like people knowing our business.'

'I ain't stupid. She doesn't know who you are. I even told her you were Spanish.'

'Oh, that's all right then,' said Kyle sarcastically. 'Right, let's get down to business, shall we? How does this wash up?'

'I don't know, I'm just the delivery boy.'

Terry nervously took the blue hairband from his wrist and swept his light brown hair back into a ponytail.

'What do you reckon, Mac?' said Kyle.

'What do I reckon?' replied Mac. 'I reckon our young friend here thinks we're a pair of daft old fools.'

'Hang on a sec,' said Terry, trying not to appear intimidated. 'Who's this old sod? It's you I deal with and you I answer too. What the fuck's it got to do with him?'

'Terry, Terry,' sighed Kyle. 'Have you never heard of showing respect for your elders? That's no way to be speaking to Mr McGrath. It's a good thing that he's got a calm disposition. Isn't that right, Mac?'

'Absolutely.'

'Actually, his friends call him Mac the Knife.' Kyle laughed. 'Corny, isn't it?'

Terry was over six foot and well built, but sensed he was out of his league.

'Look. I don't want any trouble. Why are you getting all stroppy? Like I said – I'm just the delivery boy.'

'Aye. But you're not though, are you, Terry?'

'What?'

'Mac . . . ' Kyle nodded at Mac.

Before Terry knew what was happening, Mac had his hand in Terry's pocket and pulled out a small bag containing about a quarter of an ounce of cocaine.

'Well, well, well,' said Mac. 'Now what have we here?'

'Cocaine – what does it fucking look like? And what the fuck do you think you're doing going through my pockets, you short-arsed—'

Mac was a good six inches shorter than Terry, so it was with some ease that he punched him in the groin, cutting him off in mid-sentence and causing him to tumble to the floor in agony.

'We can see it's cocaine, you long streak of pish.' Kyle grabbed him by the hair. 'It's our fucking cocaine you've been helping yourself to, eh?'

'No, it's not,' groaned Terry between grimaces. 'It's a delivery for someone else.'

'Oh, is that right? OK,' Kyle grabbed his mobile phone, 'let's make a call to your boss and find out. I'm sure he'd love to know that one of his boys has been dipping into his best customer's gear. I wonder what he'd do to you, huh? Probably be a lot worse than what we'd do, right enough. Well – shall I call him?'

Terry pulled himself from the floor on to a chair. 'No.'

'I didn't think you would. You daft wee fuck. Did you no' think we'd notice the bag had already been opened? So what have you put in it? Whizz? Glucose? What?'

'Crushed up homeopathic hay fever tablets.'

'Hay fever tablets. He's put fuckin' hay fever tablets in my Charlie, Mac. What do you make of that?'

'Most insulting, Kyle. Your nose isn't running and any tear in your eye is probably only because you're upset at being let down so badly by our young friend here.'

'Aye, fuckin' right.' Kyle stared at Terry, causing him to shift uncomfortably on his chair. After a long silence he nodded to Mac, who punched Terry on the jaw, knocking him to the floor again. Kyle quickly knelt on his chest, holding his head still between his hands.

'The thing is, Terry, I lied when I said that your boss would be worse than us. For sure you'd've been better off letting him deal with you, because Mac the Knife here didn't get his name singing Frank Sinatra songs.'

Mac picked a knife from the table, pulled Terry's right ear and cut through the top part, so he was left holding a bloodied half-inch of gristly skin between his thumb and forefinger. Terry didn't immediately realize what had been done. He saw the severed ear first then felt an intense stinging. He started screaming, but before any sound came out, Kyle had his hand over his mouth. Terry's eyes bulged with fear.

'Sshh, sshh. No noise. It's your own fault for bringing someone with you, otherwise you could have screamed the place down.'

Slowly, Kyle took his hand away from Terry's mouth. He started to whimper and clutched the side of his head.

'There, there. That's a brave boy.' He stood up and whistled. 'Fifi – where are you, girl?'

A pitbull terrier hurtled into the room.

'There you go, Fifi.' He nodded to Mac, who tossed the severed part of Terry's ear on the floor. As the dog tried to stop, it slid on the marble floor, before scampering back to gulp down the grisly offering. Kyle bent down to make a fuss of the dog.

'Enjoy that? Better than Chum, eh? Yes, good girl. Do you want some more?'

The dog barked.

'Looks like auld Fifi here loves your ear, Terry. Hey, we might be on to something here, Mac. Aye, maybe we could get some kind of sponsorship, you know like, get a Crufts winner to go on about how they were raised on Terry's ear. They can clone pigs' ears so maybe we could get both of Terry's and grow a load more. You wouldn't miss them, eh?'

'You're fucking mad,' cried Terry, his palm pressed firmly against his wound, trying to stop the flow of blood.

'Aye, that's true. Blame Quentin Tarantino though. Mac's a huge fan. Always copying him when he gets the chance.' Kyle clapped his hands together. 'Right, Mac, shall we get Zed and the gimp in?' Terry's eyes opened even wider. Kyle smiled. 'Another wee joke, Terry. This isn't the movies – this is real. I bet your fucking ear hurts, eh? If this was a film it wouldn't. It's not like we can say, "Cut." ' Kyle looked at Mac and they laughed. 'Shall we try it anyway? Got the knife, Mac? Right – ready . . . cut!'

Terry screamed and scurried across the floor.

'Terry, Terry, come back,' laughed Kyle. 'You don't think we're sadists, but? All we've done is taught you a lesson. We're no' mad or anything.' He nodded at Mac who went to the kitchen. 'Actually, we are mad because we're going to let you walk out.'

Terry's face registered genuine shock. 'You're what?'

'Go on, you waste of space – get to fuck before I change my mind.' Kyle gave a dismissive wave.

Terry picked himself up and dashed for the door. Kyle called after him, 'And if I were you, I'd get off the island, because when your boss finds out what a thieving little shite you are, you might well be losing a few other body parts.'

Mac walked back into the room with two opened bottles of San Miguel. They both flopped on to the massive L-shaped settee. Kyle reached across and they clinked bottles.

'Ah, Mac, me auld amigo. It's great to be back, eh? You don't get pads like this in Coatbridge either,' he said, sweeping his arm around the room.

'True, but we make more money in Glasgow.'

'*Did* make more money Mac, *did*. That's all going to change this year. If all goes according to plan—'

'And there's no reason why it shouldn't.'

'Exactly. More money and this lifestyle. Nobody fucks with us plus I've a nice wee bar, my own nightclub, a scuba-diving school, a speedboat, a lairy motor and more women than I can wave a shitty stick at. All we've got back home is rain, hassle and wankers.'

'True, but wankers have an extremely agreeable habit of paying twenty thousand big ones for a kilo of glucose.'

They clinked bottles again.

'To the Searle brothers,' said Kyle. 'I hope they've got a sweet tooth.'

chapter six

Connor enjoyed being best mates with Robbie Williams

Robbie got all the attention in the clubs, but, on balance, that wasn't important. Quite why the ex-Take That star was with Connor in a down-market student club in New Cross was, admittedly, puzzling. Even more confusing, was how the club, The Venue, had suddenly turned into an American football stadium and Connor and Robbie found themselves at either end of a cricket pitch, with Carol Vorderman as wicketkeeper in a pink bikini and cricket pads.

As the bowler came thundering in, the roar of the crowd building to a mighty crescendo, the handle of the cricket bat began to shrink until Connor could only hold it with one hand. Robbie Williams, his best friend, stood at the bowler's end, pointing at the bat and leading the other players and spectators in mocking laughter. Connor dropped the bat and turned to the wicketkeeper. Carol Vorderman may not have had the safest pair of hands in the game and her pink bikini didn't exactly match the pads, but at least she probably knew how many balls were left to bowl in the over . . .

It took Connor thirty seconds or so to tune back into reality and focus on his bedside clock. Fuck, the skunk was strong. It was the Wednesday after his Sunday split from Gina and he'd been living in fear that the Searles would be coming through his door at any moment. The only way he'd been able to stop worrying and get any sleep had been to get stoned, which resulted in him having increasingly weird dreams and missing work on Monday and Tuesday. He'd phoned Mr King to say he had a stomach bug and would be in that afternoon.

The dream was probably something to do with feeling powerless, impotent even, to do anything if the Searles chose to come after him, the sexual imagery pointing to the fact that his current predicament was a result of his carnal pursuits. He leaned across and sparked up the remainder of a spliff in the ashtray from the previous night. He'd never normally smoke first thing in the morning.

He inhaled a few lungfuls, then reached down the side of his bed for a bottle of Evian, which was empty. Scattered around the bed were some old photographs he'd been looking through the previous night. Stoned and with a bottle of red wine sloshing around his system, he'd indulged in self-pitying nostalgia.

Amongst them were pictures taken during his time in Ibiza, a series of girls, some of whom he could remember, some he couldn't. A few he had seen back in Britain, but it had never worked out. It was the Ibiza malaise: When people got back to the UK, suntans faded and with them the sparkling energy that, in the summer, made everything seem possible. The dour hue of responsibility, the deeply ingrained limitations of inherited belief systems, could be seen in complexions, attitude and even posture as the Ibizaphiles slipped back into the routine of UK life. The bright young big fish in the small Ibiza pond returned to their cities and villages, their offices and their factories.

Every month or two up and down the UK, intrepid promoters would hold Ibiza reunions where everyone could meet up and shine for a few hours more. Eventually though, it was only those going back the following year who would eagerly attend. For those that weren't, it was hard enough to accept the immediate future of pale skins, thick coats and traffic jams, without having their noses rubbed in it.

Connor knew he could never go back. But why? It was a question he had asked himself thousands of times. He had decided that to be happy he needed to be successful – and that was 'doing well' professionally and financially. In the last few months he had achieved it. With it though, came a whirlwind of backslapping, arse-whipping sales conferences and incentives. The advantage was that there was little time for reflection. This was just as well because Connor knew the truth: he was 'doing well' but he was not happy.

He reached down and picked up another batch of photos of a pretty, tanned girl. Mary.

She had been the closest thing to a soulmate he'd ever met. He'd been twenty-three at the time and only a couple of years out of university. He had yet to decide upon a career and the world was still his oyster. There was no hurry to do anything. Until this year, Connor had looked at all relationships as stepping stones. He was regularly shocked when a peer informed him that they were about to co-habit with their partner, or even worse, get married. Friends would speak of stability, starting a family and of being left on the shelf. Connor could only shake his head in disbelief and assume that they'd been reading too many of their partner's magazines.

Mary was pretty in a natural way, with long hair the colour of corn and the bluest eyes he had ever seen. She was normally reserved and fairly quiet, with an enigmatic charisma that attracted people. But she was also strong-willed, with a feisty side, and generally did not have to work too hard to command people's respect. Connor always felt it also had something to do with her magnificent posture, a straight proud back with her head always held high. Connor had considered her mature for her age (though on reflection it was perhaps that Connor was slightly immature for his), always having one eye on the future, whereas both of Connor's eyes had been fixed firmly on the present. It was mainly this attitude that caused him to be so dismissive when, on a weekend away together, Mary broached the subject of co-habiting. It seemed a natural progression to her but the idealistic Connor of then believed there to be big wide world waiting for him, full of opportunity and adventure. Mary was great but the timing wasn't.

After the rebuff Mary seemed to lose interest and things had gone quickly downhill. Not long after Connor went to work in Ibiza (something he had been considering even while seeing Mary) and although they kept in touch for a few months, Mary moved away, and that was that.

As the years passed, she often entered his thoughts. He now realized it wasn't so much that he hadn't been sure about her, more that he hadn't been certain about himself. He had felt as though he hadn't been a grown-up for more than five minutes and getting married or living with someone was most definitely something that grown-ups did. He'd wanted to have some fun, to enjoy life and, at that age, lovely though Mary was, he'd felt that the relationship path was not for him.

Although he never actually told her he loved her, he'd since accepted that he probably had. Experience had also made him realize how much his knee-jerk refusal to live together must have hurt her and it was this that in latter years made him feel sad, rather than the possibility he might have missed out on his own Big Adventure.

Connor dragged himself out of bed, showered himself into life and was just making some coffee when there was an impatient knock on the door. His heart leapt into his mouth. The Searles. Had they found out about the video? Worse, had they seen it? What conclusions might they have jumped to?

He cautiously looked out of the kitchen window, which overlooked the front door of his first floor flat. To his relief, double-parked directly outside was Luc's Mondeo. He had forgotten they were leaving for Ibiza that morning. He lumbered downstairs and let them in.

'Oh, we're going to Ibiza,' they sang in tormenting unison.

'Wankers.'

They bounded up the stairs, entered the living room and flopped into the armchairs, with Connor trudging behind them.

'So, are the two of you all packed and ready to go?' he said as cheerily as possible.

'Sure are,' replied Dex. 'Mind you, that miserable tosser keeps telling me how shit it'll be.'

'I just said that Ibiza isn't everybody's cup of tea.'

'But Luc, you've been back the last three summers.'

'Yeah, cos I've got a job to go to, I'm half-Spanish—'

'Yeah, the moaning half,' interrupted Dex. Bored with the baiting he turned to Connor. 'Heard anything from the Searles?'

'No, touch wood.' Connor reached for the coffee table. 'I must admit, I've been shitting myself the last few days but to be honest, if Gina was going to say anything she would've done it in a fit of anger after I'd left. If she sits down and thinks about it logically she's not going to want to let her brothers see what we were up to any more than I do.'

'Are you missing her?' asked Luc.

'A bit,' sighed Connor. 'I know you don't think much of her but her heart's in the right place.'

'Shame her brain's up her arse.'

'Easy,' said Dex.

'All I'm saying, Dex, is that, more than any of us, Connor's always gone on about meeting that special girl, and it ain't Gina. She's not bad-looking but she's not a patch on some of the other girls he's been out with. And he's not in love with her.'

'So, tell me, Luc, how do you know when you are in love with someone?' asked Connor.

'It's when you get butterflies in your stomach, a hollow feeling when they don't call—'

'That sounds more like indigestion to me. Anyway, this is the real world,' sighed Connor. 'Getting up and earning a living, paying bills, having arguments . . .'

'But you used to have the dream. Mate, you've lost your spark.'

'Leave the man alone.' Dex picked up Connor's weed. 'Don't mind if I nick a bit of this for the journey, do you?'

'Go ahead.'

'So, last time of asking . . .' said Dex.

'There's too many things I want to do here. Anyway, I've got this place to think of. I wouldn't have time to let it out and even if I did, it'd have to be for a minimum of six months and you're only going for three and a half.'

'If you really wanted to go, my sister would rent it. The place her and her boyfriend were buying has fallen through so she's back at Mum's,' said Dex.

'Yeah, well that's the point – I don't *really* want to go.' There was a moment of silence. 'Anyway, have you come round here to say goodbye, or to make me depressed?'

'Guess we'd better get going.' Dex stood up and gave Connor a hug. 'If you change your mind, you know where we'll be.'

'Jail or hospital?'

Luc shook Connor's hand. 'See you in October, Connor. Hope the Searles don't turn up.'

'That's what I love about you, Luc. You're such a happy bastard.'

'Only joking. Just make sure you don't get run over by a bus while we're away. The way you're going, I think old St Peter might be changing his opinion of you.'

'Ha fucking ha.'

'What's he mean by that?' asked Dex.

'I think he's trying to tell me I'm getting old and boring.'

'Tell me something I don't know.'

They walked towards the door. 'I'm not sure if I'm dreading or looking forward to this drive,' said Luc.

'Which way are you going?'

'Dover to Calais, through France, over the border at Perpignan, then down towards Barcelona. Stay in Lloret Thursday night – the season's already well under way there – then get the Friday night ferry from Barcelona to Ibiza.'

As they walked down the gloomy hallway, Dex tripped over the video recorder Connor had brought back from Gina's house.

'Shit – what was that?'

'The old video I lent Gina.'

'So it's spare then?'

'Yeah.'

'Any chance of letting us borrow it? I've got my portable TV in the car but the only video machine in our house belongs to the folks and I couldn't take that. Go on, buddy, I'll look after it.'

'Tell you what, give me ten minutes and I'll dismantle my fucking bed and you can stick that in the car too! OK, but don't break it.'

'Cheers, mate.' Dex picked the machine up, surprised at its weight. 'Jesus – they don't make them like this any more, do they?'

Luc drove the London to Dover leg. As soon as they turned on to the motorway at the Sun in Sands in Blackheath, Dex started skinning up.

'I hope you're not thinking of taking drugs across any of the borders,' said Luc when he noticed the spliff.

'Don't worry, Luc, this'll be all gone before we get to Dover.' Dex lit the spliff, took a long toke and passed it over. He picked up the video recorder, which he'd put on the floor in front of him, and reached over to place it on the back seat. 'I just hope that Connor hasn't left a porno in this. That'd be all we need at customs.'

chapter seven

'What the fuck do you mean, it's gone?' shrieked Rik Searle

'Just that. It ain't here,' replied Buster, looking in a pedal bin.

'Well, it's hardly going to be in there, is it? Check the rest of the flat. Maybe she's using the video with the telly in her bedroom. I'll give her a call.'

Buster walked out of the bedroom empty-handed just in time to witness his brother screaming into his phone.

'*What*? Fucking hell, Gina, when did he take it? Why did you leave it lying around? I don't care that it's his. It doesn't matter what the problem is, just give me Connor's address . . . *Gina*! Give me his fucking address!' Rik started writing on the back of a cigarette packet. 'Yeah, near Camberwell Green. I know it.' He pressed the button on his mobile to terminate the call then turned to Buster. 'The fucking video recorder belonged to Connor and he's taken it home. Here's the address. Go round there and get it from him.'

'What should I say?'

'I don't fucking know. Just take it. He won't argue.'

Connor had forgotten all about the Searles, being too wrapped up in his own thoughts, looking at his watch and wondering exactly where Dex and Luc were. Consequently, when he heard the knock at his front door, he was still trying to work out whether they would have caught the ferry yet, so opened it without even thinking who it might be. To his horror, the eighteen-stone frame of Buster Searle filled the doorway, eclipsing life in the road behind him.

'I want to talk to you about a video.'

Oh *shit*. The porno he'd made with Gina. Panic. It was too late for Connor to slam the door on the advancing Buster. 'You'd better come in,' he invited, as though he had a choice.

Connor stood back to let Buster walk up the stairs first, and contemplated running out of the door, jumping on a bus to Victoria, getting a train to Brighton then leaving all of his clothes in a pile on the beach along with a suicide note. Instead, he followed Buster and his size eleven muddy bootprints up the stairs.

'Right, where is it?' asked Buster briskly.

'Where's what?' replied Connor, as innocently as he could.

'The video.'

God, they knew. He couldn't believe she'd shown her brothers a copy of them having outrageous sex, but if Gina had shown it to them, why did they think he had it?

'Gina's still got it,' replied Connor, confused.

'No, she hasn't.'

'She has. I left it with her. She wouldn't give it to me.'

'That's not what she said. She said you took it with you the last time you left the flat.'

'She's lying.'

'Oi, watch who you're calling a liar. That's my fucking sister.'

'Sorry, no offence. Maybe she was a bit confused. We were both quite upset.'

'*You* might have been upset, but I if doubt if *she* was. She's had better.'

Connor was startled by this comment. Was it normal for Gina to show her brothers videos of her conquests? Did they sit round and watch them as a family, marking technique?

'Now, stop playing games,' continued Buster, 'and give me the video.'

'But what do you want the video for? When did you see it?'

'The last time was on Sunday.'

Bitch! She'd obviously shown it to them straight away. And by the sounds of it, they'd watched it more than once. But why had it taken them three days to pay him a visit? Connor decided to ask a direct question. 'How come you're so calm?'

'Because when we last saw it, we didn't quite realize its significance.'

Now Connor was mystified. 'What do you mean, *significance*? How fucking significant do you want it? What more could I do, for God's sake? I mean, *I* know that I didn't mean anything by it, but I didn't for one moment think *you'd* be this reasonable.'

Buster Searle looked at Connor as though he'd gone mad. 'What the fuck are you on about?'

'The video,' replied Connor. 'What are you on about?'

'The video.' They looked at each other for a few moments, then Buster continued. 'You lent Gina your old video machine, the one without a plug that was on the floor of her living room, and you took it back on Sunday.'

Connor's bottom jaw dropped. Inside his head, a choir started singing, 'Hallelujah!' They *hadn't* seen the video. He looked at Buster, almost wanting to kiss him. Then came an acidic feeling in the pit of his stomach as he realized how close he had come to disaster.

'Of course,' sighed Connor slowly, his face breaking into a relaxed smile.

'What did you think I meant?'

'Oh, nothing, nothing. Just got my wires crossed, that's all. Right, let's start again. What is it you want?'

'We left a . . . um . . . video, in the machine and we want it back.'

'Sure, no problem. I'll get it out for you.'

'*No*! No, we need the machine itself.'

'What do you need the machine for if you just want a tape out of it?' Buster looked instantly vacant and given that Connor was more than aware of the Searles' main source of income, it did not take him long to put two and two together. 'What have you put in that video, Buster?'

'It doesn't matter. Just give me the machine for a few hours and you can have it back.'

'Of course it matters. I've got a video with something illegal in it, sitting in my hallway, without – *oh shit!*' Connor clasped his hand to his mouth.

'What's up?'

'Oh fuck, the video recorder – I haven't got it.'

'Now don't start all that, if you—'

'I mean it. I've given it to Dex.'

'Right, well, let's go and get it.'

'We can't. Dex's gone to Ibiza with it.'

'He *what*!'

'They're already well on their way.'

Buster Searle started walking around the room in a blind panic. 'But he can't . . . I mean, what are we going to do . . . the Charlie . . .'

'So it *is* coke. I fucking knew it.'

Buster was flapping too much to think logically. 'We'd stashed a kilo in there. Rik's going to go mad.'

'More to the point, what about Dex and Luc? If they get caught with that they'll be in serious shit.'

'Yeah, and if they try to nick it, you'll *all* be in serious shit,' replied Buster, regaining some of his composure. 'Is there any way of getting in touch with them?'

Connor shook his head. 'They've taken their mobiles but said they wouldn't be switching them on because they'd have to pay for part of the call. They were going to buy Spanish SIM cards once they arrived in Ibiza.'

'Which way are they going? When will they get to Ibiza?'

'They're driving to Lloret, staying there for a night, then catching the Friday night ferry from Barcelona to Ibiza.'

Buster paced the room even more furiously, then picked up a glass and threw it against the wall. '*Fuck*! We already had most of that sold. Thirty fucking grand, *minimum*, that's worth. If those mates of yours nick it, I'll fucking kill 'em, and you as well.'

Connor began to lose his temper. 'Hang on a sec – what about my mates, eh? For all I know they could be in some French prison right now.'

'Yeah, well, if they are, I still want the money for our Charlie.'

'Are you serious?'

'Gear or the money – simple as that. If they get nicked then that's their lookout.'

'Are you totally fucking stupid? If I was—'

Before Connor could finish the sentence, Buster pinned him up against the wall. 'Who the fuck do you think you're talking to? I've a good mind to pull your head off.'

Although Buster was at least four stone heavier, Connor lost it. He summoned up all of his strength and pushed Buster away, sending him stumbling towards the settee, then dashed into the kitchen and picked up a large carving knife. He turned on the fast pursuing Buster, stopping him in his tracks.

'Go on. Get out of my flat.'

Buster glared at Connor. 'I hope you know what you're doing. Do you really want to be looking over your shoulder all the time?'

Logic was quickly replacing the flush of anger. 'I didn't ask for any trouble but what do you expect me to do?'

'I expect you to get our Charlie back.'

'How can I do that? I'd have to get to Barcelona on Friday, which I can't, because I've already been off work for nearly three days. Anyway, even if I did go, there's no way I'd carry a kilo of cocaine back through customs.'

Buster stared at him for a moment. 'Sit your arse down in the living room while I phone my brother.'

Connor dropped the knife and did as he was told. He could hear Buster's muffled voice, which rose in volume occasionally with 'Fuck off,' 'You're joking,' and 'Why me?' After a couple of minutes Buster returned.

'Fucking great,' he sighed. 'Rik reckons I've got to go with you.'

'What? Why?'

'Because we can't let you near that gear without one of us being there, in case you decide to take any out or put some bash in it. At least at the moment we're assuming your bum chums don't know about the cocaine, otherwise we'd just want the money and that'd be the end of it.'

'Can't you go on your own?'

'I don't know the score over there. You worked there.'

'I never worked in Barcelona – it was Ibiza.'

'It's still fucking Spain, innit? Anyway, it's up to you but I tell you this. If you don't come, not only will you personally be responsible for the money, but Rik says he'll give the Barcelona police a call and tip them off about your mates.'

'He wouldn't. What would be the point of that?'

'I don't give a toss. All I know is we won't be out of pocket and we won't be in trouble. It's your choice.'

'You wouldn't do that. If that's the case, why bother going out there at all? Why not just come after me for the money? You're bluffing.'

Buster wasn't listening, already making his way to the door. 'Give me a call when you book the flight.'

Once the door was closed, Connor sat on the floor with his head in his hands. There had to be a way to get the cocaine back and to keep his job (to say nothing of the Merc and the ten grand plus commission cheque).

He'd think of something . . .

Nothing. Not even on the loo (where he often had his best ideas). Another shower proved more functional then inspirational and on the drive to work barely a thought entered his head.

At his desk, he took a breath and picked up his phone. 'Can you give me a price for two flights to Barcelona please,' he whispered quietly, keeping one eye on Mr King's office.

There was no way of avoiding the trip. No matter how he viewed it, he simply had no choice.

Most of his afternoon in the office was spent ringing round travel agents then ringing Horne, Fleming and Mitchell, the large firm of accountants awarding him his big deal, to postpone the signing of the contract until the following week. For Mr King's benefit, he also tried to look as ill as possible, visiting the toilet frequently, and complaining that he wasn't yet over his stomach bug. Stuart King expected his staff to 'eat, sleep, and breathe the company'. Twelve-hour days were not uncommon and the walls of the office were plastered with motivational messages and target charts. Meetings were regular and high-energy, free trips and weekend breaks an elaborate cover for company bonding and brainwashing. King embraced and preached the Positive Solutions ethos with the fervour of a religious cult member. Positive Solutions was his life.

Connor was more than aware that his cavalier attitude annoyed him immensely as did the fact that Positive Solutions' MD had also studied English at the same university as Connor and seemed to like him. It made Mr King spout his 'it's what you've earned not what you've learned' and 'money is freedom' mantras to him all the more. Despite Connor's tenuous camaraderie with the MD, he was more than aware that were it not for his recent performance he would have long since been shown the door.

By 5.30 the flights were booked and everything seemed to be going well. All that was left was to tell Mr King he was still feeling ill and would be off work until Monday.

When the man's office was empty Connor went in.

'Have you got a minute, Mr King?'

His boss carried on writing for an eternal minute then looked up, raising his eyebrows to let Connor know he was permitted to speak.

'I'm really sorry, Mr King,' it stuck in Connor's throat to call someone he despised 'Mr', 'but I'm feeling terrible. I've tidied up most of the loose ends and I've re-scheduled tomorrow's appointment for Tuesday so I thought it would be best if I stayed off work until then so I can come back firing on all cylinders. If I'm up to it, I can even make some calls from home. It's probably best for everyone else in the office if I'm not here anyway, just in case it's catching.'

Mr King didn't say a word, but tapped out something on his desktop computer, then folded his hands, placed them on the desk and stared at Connor.

'Why are you flying to Barcelona on Saturday?'

For one of the few times in his life, Connor was dumbstruck. Mr King let the question hang in the air like the sword of Damocles, then stood up and continued.

'You see, Young, one of the unfortunate things about your absence from the office over the last couple of days is that you're a little behind on developments. As you are aware, I'm always trying to improve performance, trying to give my staff the benefit of my years in the business. You should also know that I trust no one. Now, if you'd been in for Monday's meeting, you would have heard about an exciting new device that's been installed. It enables me to help those who need it and chastise those who deserve it.'

Mr King leaned across the computer and pressed a key. Out of the two small speakers came Connor's voice, booking the flights to Barcelona.

'You see, we now have a call monitoring system.'

Connor slumped in his chair. 'Shit.'

'Shit indeed. I don't suppose you want to share with me why you plan to go to Barcelona and why you've been off ill when clearly there's nothing wrong with you that some basic psychiatric treatment wouldn't remedy?'

'It's hard to explain,' stammered Connor.

'If nothing else, I'm sure *that's* true, but try me anyway.'

'Well, I have been, um, ill, and, uh, you see, the er, Barcelona trip is, um, connected to that.'

'And what else is it connected to?'

Connor thanked his lucky stars that he hadn't made any other personal calls to do with the drugs. He had to come up with something big.

'It's a bit delicate,' he improvised. 'An old . . . an old girlfriend, yes, an old Spanish girlfriend, from my days in Ibiza, was over here for Christmas.'

'But you brought a different girl to the Christmas party – Gina, wasn't it?'

'Yes. That's why it's awkward, Mr King.' The lies were all falling into place. 'She came to see me on a trip to the UK over Christmas and one thing led to another, then she popped back over a couple of months ago and we, well, you know, and now . . . well, she's pregnant.'

'I see.'

'Obviously she can't tell her parents – good Catholic family and all that – and she didn't have the money for an abortion, which she's decided she wants, or anyone to stand by her, so I'm doing the decent thing.'

'You're getting married?

'God no . . . I mean, that's not on the cards right now. I'm paying for the abortion and taking her to the clinic just outside Barcelona. I didn't want anyone to know so I've had to come up with all this crap. I'm really sorry to deceive you, Mr King, but I promise you that I *have* been ill for the last few days.'

Mr King paced up and down the room some more then sat on the edge of the desk opposite Connor. He drummed his fingers on the table then stood up and walked back to his chair.

'Even if you are telling the truth – and it's just about far-fetched enough to be believable – it is yet another illustration of your attitude to life. You take no responsibility for anything. Life's a serious business and it's about time you treated it as such. Strictly speaking, I should sack you. At this very moment your future is in my hands.' He moved to his chair and looked at his hands as if to emphasize the point. 'Now then, what should I do? What would you do if you were sitting here?'

Connor wanted to make any number of facetious or derogatory comments. Instead he shrugged.

'Mmm.' Mr King rocked back in his chair. 'The silly thing is that on those rare occasions when you put your mind to it, you're actually a very good recruitment consultant. I think what we need to do is to break your spirit and mould you into a Positive Solutions man, a bit like they did to Richard Gere in *An Officer and a Gentleman*.'

'Was he the one who hung himself?'

But Mr King was in full flow. 'You can earn big bucks here, you know. Look at me – thirty-two, six hundred grand house, TVR with a Ferrari on order, in charge of all you lot. I left school without a single qualification – not like you with a degree. But as I always say, it's what you've earned not what you've learned that counts. It's not impossible, Young. It can be done and I'm going to help you. That's why I'm a good manager, you see. I know when to crack the whip and when to dangle the carrot, which is why I'm going to let you go to Barcelona . . .'

Connor was genuinely surprised and looked it.

' . . . But when you come back I want to see a different Connor Young. I want to see a company man, someone committed to this job, a man who's prepared to put his social life to one side. I want to see you getting involved with the best of us, not cynically raising your eyebrows in a corner. I want you to accept this as your world, to embrace it, to love it. That's what I expect of you, Connor, nothing less.'

Connor sat there, taking it in. 'OK.'

'Easy for you to say, but I'm going to make it easy to do. I've worked out that you should actually earn a little more than you were expecting from the permanent staff you're placing on this big deal – just under twelve thousand pounds. On top of that you'll have an income stream of just over a thousand a month for the next six months from the contract placements.' He paused to let the figures sink in. 'Money is freedom, Connor, money is freedom. Now then, while I'm happy to pay you on the contract staff I'm going to hold the permanent staff commission for six months, then if—'

'*What*? That's not fair.'

'Taking unauthorized time off work isn't fair. If in six months I see a change in your attitude and I'm convinced that you've got what it takes, then I'll release the money.'

'But you already know I've got what it takes. Look at the national target chart.'

'It's about more than just figures – it's about attitude, and yours isn't right. If you don't like it, then don't bother coming back on Monday. Personally, I'll be glad to see the back of you but nevertheless, I still think you'd be a bloody fool – jobs like this are hard to come by and this deal you've been working on is a biggie. The only other alternative is to show that Positive Solutions are top of your list of priorities by cancelling your trip to Barcelona.' Mr King stood up and walked to the door. 'Right, unless you've anything to add, I suggest you go home and chew things over. I'll either see you tomorrow or Monday.'

Connor left the office and five minutes later was driving home, deep in thought. Even if Buster Searle's threat to phone the Barcelona police had been a bluff – which he strongly suspected it was – there was no way he could allow his friends to risk getting the ferry to Ibiza with a kilo of cocaine on them.

Although there wouldn't be any more customs points to go through, Connor knew that police and sniffer dogs would often patrol the port at Ibiza, paying particular attention to cars with English plates and clubby looking occupants. No, he was going to have to go to Barcelona, then spend the next six months grovelling to a man he loathed.

Compromise, accept, capitulate, exist and die. Maybe not quite that bad, but that was how it felt.

chapter eight

Fighting, drugs and the recent operation on his rectum were Buster Searle's only topics of conversation. Connor had not been looking forward to the flight to Barcelona, but it was even worse than he'd imagined. Getting the time off work had been worse still. The only good part of flying to Barcelona with Buster was that familiarity had indeed bred contempt. Connor had previously been very wary of the younger Searle brother, but it was proving hard to be intimidated by somebody who was so stupid. He was like an overgrown child and providing one did not question his manhood, the most basic child psychology could be applied to manipulate him.

The only words of more than two syllables in Buster's vocabulary were those connected with things medical and anal. It had turned into something of an obsession and Buster spoke of the stitches still dangling from his anus with the same enthusiasm as a fisherman boasting of his biggest catch, or a football zealot discussing his team's best goal. It also became glaringly apparent that Rik called the shots. The journey would have been a good deal more unpleasant had the elder brother been his travelling companion.

After they'd landed and were in the terminal building of Barcelona airport, Connor's skin tingled when he saw the familiar airport signs, almost identical to those in Ibiza. The buzz of the airport, the casual way businessmen dressed, the Spanish voices over the Tannoy – he felt as though he had never been away.

As they approached the exit, the two customs officers eyed them suspiciously. Buster was blissfully unaware of their interest, whereas Connor was finding it hard not to look guilty, although as neither of them had any contraband, he had nothing to be guilty about.

'Excuse me, Señors . . .'

'Why are you visiting Barcelona?' asked one officer in a heavy accent.

'Holiday,' replied Connor.

'May I see your tickets?' Connor showed his ticket to the officer. 'It is a very short holiday, no? You return tomorrow.'

'Yeah, it's a . . . a shopping holiday.'

Buster was looking at them with utter contempt. 'What's the fucking problem?'

'Señor, we need to ask a few questions.'

'What sort of questions?' The officer said nothing and snatched Buster's passport away from him. When he looked at the skinny, spotty teenager in the passport photo, then back at the monster in front of him, his face almost broke into a smile.

'Señor Searle, the reason for your visit?'

'Do I need a reason?'

'You are here for only one day?'

'If I like it I might stay longer. Depends what the local women are like. You got any sisters?'

The officer turned to his colleague and said something in Spanish. He nodded then walked away.

'OK. I think we will ask you both some more questions separately.'

'Why are you hassling us? We're part of the European Community, aren't we?'

'Señor, if I were you—'

Buster was just warming up. 'We come over to your poxy country to spend good money and all you can do—'

'Buster—' Connor's interjection fell on deaf ears.

'Fuck 'em. We're British citizens. They can't do a fucking thing. Just because we stuff 'em at football.'

Within seconds, Buster was frog-marched to an interview room. The first customs officer invited Connor to accompany him to another.

'Sorry about him,' said Connor. 'He doesn't travel well.'

The officer wasn't listening and placed Connor's sports bag on the table.

'You come for a shopping trip, no?'

'Yeah, yeah. I love Spain. Used to work here.'

'In Barcelona?'

'No, Ibiza.'

The customs officer nodded slowly and continued rifling through Connor's bag. 'Which hotel are you staying at?'

'I'm . . . um . . . not sure. It's in the city centre.'

'So you like Ibiza? You go to clubs, take drugs?'

'Good God no,' said Connor hurriedly. 'I hate drugs. San Miguel man, me.'

The officer eyed Connor warily. Shit, thought Connor, I'm going to get a strip search.

It was then that the idea struck him. A plan so simple, so cruel, but so deserving that Connor was powerless to resist.

'Um, excuse me,' Connor coughed.

'*Sí*,' replied the officer without looking up.

'The other man in there, are you going to search him *thoroughly*?'

'Why you ask?'

'Oh, no reason.' Connor shuffled uncomfortably and tried to look suspicious. 'Do you, um, tend to look everywhere?'

'What do you mean?'

'Oh no, nothing . . . forget it.'

The officer stopped searching Connor's bag, lit a cigarette, and stared at him through the swirling smoke, which was drifting towards the nicotine-stained ceiling tiles. He pulled hard on the cigarette then rolled it between his bared teeth. Connor deliberately avoided eye contact. He knew there was a chance that at any moment the officer was going to don a pair of surgical gloves and ask him to drop his trousers, but if the plan worked, even that could be worth it.

Still in thought, the officer removed a few other garments from Connor's bag, then stubbed out the half-smoked cigarette and marched into the next room where Buster was being held. Connor let out a sigh of relief.

A few moments later there was a commotion from next door. Connor heard more footsteps running down the corridor and entering Buster's interview room. After the initial loud protestations from Buster asking why the officers were going through his bag, Buster's voice raised in volume and took on an increased urgency.

'What, what's up? What are you doing? Why are you taking my trousers off? No, stop it. No, you don't understand. I've just had an operation. An abscess. Abscess-o. Fuck off. I won't spread my legs. What are you looking for? Oh God, no. Please, not up there. No, leave that piece of cotton – it's not attached to anything. I swear it's not drugs. It's not what you think . . . fuck off . . . please . . . it's . . . stitches . . . *argh*!'

The scream was blood-curdling and the mental picture almost too unbearable to summon – although Connor enjoyed trying. He even felt his own butt-cheeks clench together in sympathy.

A couple of minutes later the officer returned. 'We made a mistake with your friend.'

'I heard,' replied Connor, trying to keep a straight face.

'It is unfortunate he tried to cause us problems. Now it is he who has

51

the problem. We have called for a *medico* to repair things, so you will have to wait here for a while, unless you wish to go alone?'

Connor very much wished to 'go alone', but he had estimated it was another five hours before Dex and Luc were likely to be at the ferry terminal and given what had just happened, he did not want to risk upsetting Buster further.

'I'll stay, if that's all right, thank you, Officer.'

The Spaniard nodded and poured two thick black coffees into small cups. He then reached into a drawer in his desk and pulled out a bottle of brandy, pouring a small amount into each cup. He handed one to Connor, his mouth twitching at the edges.

'*Salud*.'

'Cheers.'

chapter nine

From the small tapas bar near the Barcelona ferry terminal, Connor, Dex and Luc had a good view of the unattended Mondeo.

The smell of honeysuckle outside the bar was overpowered by the strong smell of diesel; the distant strains of flamenco drowned by the constant cacophony of juggernauts rumbling in and out of the docks.

Dex and Luc were still reeling from seeing Connor and Buster Searle waiting for them at the ferry terminal only twenty minutes earlier. At first, Dex was even convinced he was hallucinating, and that the weed he'd scored in Lloret was far stronger than he'd thought.

The three of them watched Buster hobble over to the car to retrieve his contraband from the video machine. Rather than go straight to it Buster had ordered some food and drinks, put three cushions on a plastic chair, and recounted his unfortunate experience with customs. As soon as he was out of earshot, the three of them collapsed in fits of giggles. The tension caused by realizing they'd driven through four border points with enough cocaine on them to make their planned stay overseas considerably longer, contributed to Dex and Luc's need to let off steam.

'So weren't you worried they'd strip search you too?' asked Dex finally, wiping tears away from his eyes.

'Yeah, but I figured it would be worth it. *You've* only had to listen to him going on about his arse for the last twenty minutes. I've had to suffer it for the whole fucking trip.'

'Serves him right,' said Luc, becoming more serious. 'That tosser could have got the pair of us nicked. What the fuck was he thinking of? And what's he going to do now – just walk through customs with it?'

'No. He's got one of his boys flying over in the morning to take it back.'

'He must be mad,' sighed Luc, shaking his head.

They all took a sip of their drinks and sat in silence for a few moments watching Buster rummage about in the car. Eventually he emerged and gave a thumbs up.

'Thank fuck for that,' sighed Dex. 'We owe you one for this, Connor.'

'You can be sure I won't forget.'

'So,' said Dex, changing the subject. 'Bet you wish you were staying now, don't you?' Connor said nothing. 'What happens when you get home?'

Connor poked his tapas around his plate. 'Back to work. Back to Gina, if she'll have me. I thought I'd give it one last shot.'

Luc and Dex shared a look.

At that moment Buster rejoined them. 'Looks like the queue for the Ibiza ferry is starting to move. Connor, I'm going to check us into that hotel over there and stash this. I suppose you'll want to kiss your buddies goodbye so I'll see you in the bar.'

Buster crossed the road. Connor watched him with contempt.

'Right then,' said Dex, 'we'd better go.'

They hugged each other. 'Don't let the bastards grind you down,' said Luc.

'I won't. Have a good season.'

'Check you when it's cold again,' laughed Dex.

They wandered towards the car. Connor sat back down and poured his beer into a glass. Luc turned and raised his hand. Within a minute, they'd reached the Mondeo and started the engine, then headed to the ferry.

Connor sat alone, sipping his beer, deep in thought, trying to push to the back of his mind the prospect of a night with Buster Searle and the journey back.

He loved the Spanish café culture. For him, the best parts of his time away had been spent sitting outside similar cafés in Ibiza Town, getting stoned and drinking *carajillos* without a care in the world. The beaches in Ibiza were gorgeous, the women incredible, and the clubs second to none, but on the whole it was just the relaxed, stress-free existence that he loved so much. And being away from it for so long, he'd forgotten just how much.

Perhaps that was what he needed. A little break, to recharge his batteries. A reminder that life wasn't always about canvass calls, sales targets, and other bullshit. He didn't have to be back until Monday after all, and it was Friday night.

He looked towards the ferry booking office then glanced at his watch.

Going back to Ibiza for a couple of days couldn't do any harm . . . could it?

The three friends leaned on the rail of the Barcelona–Ibiza ferry, gazed towards the approaching island and smiled at each other. The sun had risen just a few hours before. The sea breeze added a slight chill to the otherwise perfect May morning. As the island got closer, the small white dots amongst the thick green trees turned into buildings, clinging to the hillsides in isolated splendour. The Mediterranean lapped against the side of the ferry as it sliced its way through the calm waters to the port of Ibiza Town.

Connor's mobile rang and he ambled away to take the call.

'I tell you, Luc, I'm still getting over seeing him walk into the ferry bar,' said Dex.

'If I'd had the prospect of spending even another minute with Buster Searle I would have swum to Ibiza.' They both glanced over at Connor. 'What do you reckon, should we tell him?'

'I don't want to, but yeah, someone should. Especially now.'

'And I suppose that someone's me?'

Connor walked back smiling. 'Sorted. I've got a flight from Ibiza to Gatwick tomorrow night.' He sensed something was wrong. 'I thought you'd be pleased.'

'Yeah, we are,' said Luc uncomfortably. He looked to Dex.

'The thing is,' said Dex, 'there's something we've been meaning to tell you.'

'We've not been sure whether we should though.'

There was a pause.

'Come on then, out with it,' demanded Connor.

Dex took the reins. 'Well, you know you said you were going to try to smooth things over with Gina?' Connor nodded. 'I wouldn't bother.'

'Why not?'

Dex looked at Luc again, hesitating. 'She's sort of been shagging Rufus, that guy from the gym who works with her brothers.'

'What do you mean by "sort of shagging"?'

'Well, yeah, shagging,' said Dex, unable to think of a euphemism.

Connor appeared visibly shocked for a moment.

'How long's it been going on?'

'Apparently they've been on and off for years. I think she was trying to end it, but, well, you know what girls can be like. There's always someone they find it hard to get out of their system, especially if it's the bloke who popped her cherry.' The look Connor gave him suggested that this was perhaps too much information. 'I don't think she's been with him for a good few weeks though,' he added, by way of consolation.

'You could have told me.'

'We've been wanting to, Connor, but it might have worked itself out. We didn't want to get involved in a domestic,' said Dex, 'plus Rufus is about twice the size of the Searles and I know what your temper's like when you get angry. Anyway, I didn't think you were that serious on her.'

Connor leaned on the rail and let out a long sigh. 'I dunno. I suppose I always knew she wasn't really the Big Adventure. I also had this gut feeling that there was something . . . I guess I just kind of got used to her.'

'Are you going to call her?'

'I was going to try to sort things out, but now . . .' He shook his head. 'It was inevitable we'd split up one day. Maybe it's better something like this happened. Let's not forget she'd dumped me. Perhaps it's best left. I'd rather not have any more acrimony – especially given who her brothers are.'

They all looked towards the island again in silence for a few moments.

'Listen, mate,' said Luc, 'what you did for us, you know, coming over so we didn't risk getting nicked and all that . . . I just want to say again that we really appreciate it.'

Connor nodded, then turned through 360 degrees to take in his surroundings.

'There's something special about this place, isn't there? It's got a sense of destiny. I forgot what it was like.'

They listened to a Spanish announcement on the Tannoy.

'We'll be docking soon,' said Luc. They started walking along the deck and he put his arm round Connor's shoulder. 'Welcome home, Connor, even if it is only for a couple of days.'

The magnitude of what Connor had done really struck home as they disembarked. In their usual playful way, Luc and Dex had been telling him that he'd wasted his time and that if he hadn't said anything, they would have had a kilo of cocaine to play with.

Even Connor had been surprised at the number of police waiting at the port. The following week was when the clubbing season really got into full swing. With its English number plates, the Mondeo was one of the first cars pulled over. Luc's fluent Spanish only succeeded in making the policeman even more suspicious, to such a degree that he called over a colleague with a dog. They were kept there for nearly ten minutes before being allowed to proceed on their way. Connor didn't even need to say, 'I told you so'.

The first place they went to was Ibiza Town so that Luc could meet up with the bar-owner who was giving him a job. He had worked for him in a small San Antonio bar called Raffles ever since he first came to Ibiza, but this year the bar had expanded and he was to be manager.

Connor and Dex wandered around the old town for a few hours that afternoon. Most of the shops were closed for the *siesta*, although Connor was able to buy some toiletries, a T-shirt and a pair of canvas trousers to get him through his unplanned stay. Once they tired of window-shopping they headed for the hippified Placa del Parque to smoke a spliff and drink some coffee. Connor tried to talk to Dex about Victor James but Dex gave a dismissive wave of his hand, saying that he didn't even want to hear his name until September. Now he was in Ibiza he intended to enjoy himself.

In the early evening the three of them set off for San Antonio. For their first couple of nights, Dex and Luc had arranged to stay in a small apartment, and luckily, there was a settee in the living room for Connor.

Once they showered and got themselves organized, they made their way to the Sunset Strip, home of the legendary Café del Mar. It was an area that, in recent years, had become a meeting place for most of the workers, who were often the best way of discovering what jobs were on offer, and this was Dex's main priority.

Connor had no great desire to catch up with old friends who might still be in Ibiza. When working there himself, Connor had seen too many transient workers or returning holidaymakers greet a bar-owner they had not seen for a few weeks as though they had been flown in as the final *This is Your Life* guest. For the moment at least, this was Luc's domain and as they got closer, so more hugs seemed to be exchanged between Luc and various workers and locals.

Luc didn't bother introducing most of those he hugged and Connor correctly guessed that they were not close friends. The shared experience of working in Ibiza gave them a unique camaraderie, although they might have no more in common than with any other person one would pass in the street. This all changed towards the end of the season when everyone was potless and started scamming and stealing from each other – then the hug was as likely to turn into a headbutt.

Connor, Dex, and Luc stood in the road next to Mambo, soaking up the atmosphere and smoking a joint. As the smoke filled Connor's lungs, he started thinking about Positive Solutions for the first time since arriving in Ibiza.

He strolled away from the others and sat down on a small wall. He flicked the end of the spliff on to some rocks, rested his chin on his hands and looked wistfully out to sea.

'Ibiza,' he said, thinking aloud, 'what are you up to? Why have you brought me here?'

As Connor had just over a day in Ibiza, after their visit to the Sunset Strip he'd opted for an early night so he could spend the whole of Sunday in the sun, thinking it would be nice to go into work on Monday for his new beginning with a bit of a tan.

On Sunday evening they returned to Mambo. He'd always considered the place a great venue for people-watching. All around, excited, eager holidaymakers, laughing a little too loudly and showing a little too much white or sunburned flesh, mixed with recently arrived workers, displaying pieces of local jewellery and far too much attitude.

Connor realized little had changed in that respect. Even four years earlier it seemed that with some of the workers, the mere fact that they had not utilized the return flight ticket instantly elevated them to island expert and social magnet. They would adopt a wholly unfounded *savoir faire*, which if interrogated, would normally prove to be *savoir rien*.

Still, he couldn't help but feel a twinge of jealousy that they had the whole season in front of them, whereas his own immediate future . . . he looked at his watch.

'We're going to have to leave for the airport soon, Luc.'

'As long as you get there an hour before you'll be all right.'

Connor checked his watch again. There was still over half an hour to kill. He felt the need to be on his own.

'Listen, if it's all right with you guys I'm gonna pop for a drink in that little bar down by the port, where the San An ferries leave.'

'Yeah, I know it,' said Luc. 'Tiburon. We'll come with you if you want.'

'No, it's OK. I wouldn't mind having a bit of time to myself, you know, to sort my head out, prepare myself for Blighty.'

'Sure. What shall we say, about twenty minutes or so?'

Connor nodded. Luc and Dex watched him walk away.

'He doesn't seem himself, does he?' observed Luc.

'Do you think it's because of Gina?'

'I don't know. He's been really quiet. I'm not sure I've ever seen him like this.'

They turned their attention back to the people in the bar. From their terrace vantage point, Dex noticed a bald man in his early thirties, wearing fawn dungarees and no shirt, talking to three pretty girls. Everybody who walked past either shook his hand, or kissed him, depending on their gender.

'Who's that?' asked Dex.

'Kyle Goldwell,' replied Luc. 'He promotes a night over here and owns that new bar I was telling you about, Atlantis. Pretty sure he's heavily into knocking out Class A's too. Useful to know, but not the sort of bloke you want to get involved with. I met him a few times last year.'

'Do you reckon he might know of anyone who needs a DJ?'

'We can but ask.'

After several unsuccessful attempts, Luc eventually caught Kyle's eye and waved to him. Kyle made a point of continuing to talk to the girls before walking over with an arrogant swagger. Most new arrivals who intended spending the season on the island had the same three requirements: a means of income; free entry into clubs; and access to cheap drugs. As a drug-dealing promoter with his own bar, Kyle could satisfy all of these to those who found his favour. The added bonus of a fully loaded Range Rover and an established network of hangers-on meant that success with women and sycophancy from wannabe workers was something to which he had quickly grown accustomed. Kyle Goldwell was used to getting his own way.

'All right, Kyle,' said Luc, 'how's tricks?'

'Aye, no' bad.'

'I've only just arrived. Great to be back.'

Kyle nodded his head and scanned the beach, seemingly bored. Luc was embarrassed by this obvious lack of recognition and respect, but decided to be straightforward nonetheless.

'Kyle, I don't suppose you know of any DJ jobs going? My mate Dex here is red hot.'

Kyle stopped scanning the beach and held Dex's gaze for a moment. 'What sort of stuff do you play?'

'Mainly UK Garage, R 'n B,' replied Dex, 'But I play US Garage, anything with a bit of soul to it really.'

'So you don't play any of that banging trance stuff then?'

'Sorry, no.'

'Don't apologize. We get a lot of Londoners in my bar – could be just what I'm looking for. I've already got one DJ but I need two, and the second guy I had was shit, so I just sacked him. Have you got your records with you?'

'Yeah, back at my room.'

'OK. Go get them, then come to Atlantis in a couple of hours and we'll give you a try.'

'Great.' Dex tried to appear relatively indifferent although he wanted to yell with excitement.

'You jammy bastard,' exclaimed Luc, as Kyle walked away.

'See, told you it would be easy,' replied a grinning Dex.

'Do you know how lucky . . . what the chances . . . unbelievable! You can get me a drink for that.'

'Come on then. Let's catch up with Connor and get him to the airport, then we can pick up my records.'

Connor grabbed a quick beer and sat down outside the quiet and old-fashioned bar. Just over twenty-four hours in Ibiza and he felt as though he'd never been away. If only he had no commitments. If only he hadn't just turned thirty. If only he hadn't joined Positive Solutions.

He picked up a dated and dried-out English version of *Cosmopolitan* from a nearby table and started flicking through its pages. He'd always considered women's magazines to be a great source of information about how the opposite sex think. In between the plethora of fashion and perfume ads there were always a few interesting articles. However, the first headline that caught his eye was entitled, 'ENJOY WHAT YOU DO – AND KEEP ON DOING IT'.

He scanned it but at the end of the article was a bullet point that really struck a chord. It claimed that only 10 per cent of people live for more than three years after they retire. How shit is that? he thought. Most people spend all of their lives doing a job they don't really like, come home knackered, watch a bit of TV, get up the next morning, then do the whole thing all over again. They'll get a day or two free at weekends but even then, half of them spend it doing home improvements, and for what? Just so they've got a nest egg for when they retire and can at last do all the things they've always wanted. But when that day comes, apart from the fact that they either can't remember what it is they actually enjoy or are too old to do it, they fucking snuff it.

It was too depressing to contemplate further and Connor was depressed enough already. He threw the magazine back on the table then pushed himself back in his chair, determined to savour what would almost certainly be his last beer on Spanish soil for some considerable time.

The 1980s CD that had been playing in the restaurant moved to the next track. An old familiar chorus drifted over the speakers.

'Back to life . . .'

The tune carried on but that refrain spun around and around Connor's head, with his own bizarre video, flashing from Gina, to Mr King, to the Searles, all against a dismally grey London backdrop. This was Connor's life, Connor's reality, and even the imminent financial rewards from Positive Solutions felt more likely to imprison him still further, rather than give him the freedom Stuart King claimed it would.

He knocked back his beer and decided to sit on the harbour wall for a last few lungfuls of sea air.

Without thinking, as he stepped into the road, he turned his head to the right instead of the left. There was a loud blast of a hooter followed by a screech of brakes. Connor looked up to see a bus bearing down on him and just managed to leap out of its way.

He lay sprawled in the gutter and watched the bus pull up at a stop 50 metres down the road. Of all the things almost to send him prematurely to his Maker, it had to be a fucking bus. Luc wouldn't believe it.

He brushed himself down and sat on the kerb, gazing towards the sea and feeling the light sea breeze against his face. The wail of a police siren came from the harbour, but out of the inky blackness of the Med, another Siren was calling and had been for four years. Ibiza.

Connor stood up and slowly started walking. His pace quickened and gradually his face broke into a smile. With each step, he felt the burden of responsibility lift from his shoulders; the shackles of expectation break and fall, the safety net of routine disappear. Jogging now, grinning manically, then running, laughing out loud. The voice of reason screamed to be heard, a final desperate attempt to dampen the rebellion and to banish the usurping life force:

What about work? What about the big deal? What about the new Merc? What are you going to do about Gina? Her brothers? Your flat? How can you drop everything? You've no luggage? What are you going to do to survive? Where are you going to stay? What's round the corner?

For a moment, Connor reflected on what would have happened had the bus hit him. Would St Peter have still patted him on the back and told him he'd crammed a lot in? Or would going through life in a job he hated, perhaps even with a girl he didn't love, have caused St Peter to mutter, 'Chump'?

Connor had only one thing to say to the niggling, nagging voice. A word that had been his creed only four years before, and that he had all but forgotten. As he raced towards the sea, he yelled it at the top of his voice and leapt, screaming and grinning, fully clothed into the shallow water:

'*Mañana!*'

61

part two
if the bus doesn't get you . . .

chapter ten

Marina had not been looking forward to diving for the corpse.

Thankfully, the Guardia Civil had the task of retrieving the body. Marina was back-up, a safety diver in case anything went wrong.

She had never seen a dead person before. How would she react? Would she embarrass herself in front of her male, Spanish counterparts? Marina was fiercely proud and never expected any allowances to be made for her sex. She had stayed in Ibiza for the whole of the previous winter and for a couple of those months had even worked on a building site. With no make-up and her long straight blonde hair pulled back into a bun, she had still proved a major distraction for her Spanish colleagues. It didn't take long, however, for them to realize their advances were pointless, as were their attempts to embarrass or bait her. Ultimately, she won their respect, especially as she started to speak more and more Spanish, inflected with the local Ibicenco accent and dialectic idiosyncrasies, which only served to endear her to them all the more. Marina had made a number of good Spanish friends.

For the tenth time in as many minutes she glanced at her Suunto Spyder diving watch without actually registering the time. It was Monday morning, 9.37 a.m. and the tight knot in her stomach, caused by wondering what being on the sea-bed had done to a man's body, made her consider for a moment whether it had been wise to breakfast on slightly stale Frosties.

The weather merely added to the sense of foreboding. For over two weeks, Ibiza had enjoyed a glorious hot spell. Today, however, had started overcast, which elicited a kind of unnatural calm. The rockface of the nearby island of Conajera seemed more threatening and sinister than normal. The sea, which usually twinkled invitingly in the reflective rays of the sun, was now an ominous smooth grey swell, which lapped menacingly against the sides of the boat. The mix CDs that played throughout most of the dives for tourists were silent, neatly stacked in the wheelhouse where Pedro, the captain, chain-smoked and drummed his fingers on the radio receiver. Even the seagulls, which could always be found circling the boat on dives, were absent. Marina would have preferred to be elsewhere. Yet it was a challenge and she rarely backed down from one.

She sat on the starboard lip at the rear of the 12-metre diving boat and looked towards the Guardia Civil's Zodiac. The two police divers were already below surface.

A petite nineteen-year-old German girl emerged from the galley below deck with three cups of coffee. She gave one to Pedro as she passed him, then held out the other for Marina. It was glaringly apparent that she was a bundle of nerves. Nathalie had just qualified as a diving instructor. Marina took the coffee.

'Thanks, Nat. How are you feeling?'

'I wish I wasn't here. Why did Raoul have to get an ear infection?'

Marina shrugged. She would have preferred Raoul to be her diving buddy too, but Nathalie had the experience and, barring catastrophes, her role was fairly straightforward and well within her capabilities.

'We'd better go through our pre-dive checks,' said Marina.

They picked up their equipment from underneath the benches. Before putting on their wetsuits, they checked their regulators, breathing slower and more deliberately than usual. They had chosen full body wetsuits, to guard against the victim's remains, should they get that close.

After a couple of minutes, they put on their weight belts and adjusted them. They gazed over the water between them and the Guardia vessel, waiting for the buoy to pop to the surface indicating the body had been found.

'It'll be all right, Nat. We might not even see anything.'

Nathalie carried on staring at the sea. 'Do you know what happened to him?'

'It's all rather suspicious, something to do with drugs. His wife is at the harbour waiting to identify the body – it's her I feel sorry for.'

Just then, a gentle splash came from the sea a few metres away as the buoy popped out, then settled and bobbed on the surface. Pedro noticed it first.

'*Aquí,*' he yelled, pointing to the buoy.

The girls looked at each other, as he spoke to the Guardia on his radio. When he finished he relayed the information to them. 'They are at seventy-eight metres. The Guardia, they bring him up.'

'How far down will we have to go?' asked Marina.

'I don't know. You will meet them as they come up.'

Marina unfolded the steel steps at the rear of the boat and stepped on to the open platform with Nathalie, allowing Nathalie to lower herself into the water first.

Once in, she looked down into the bright blue depths below her, following the thin guideline attached to the buoy, not even wanting to contemplate what was at the other end.

It was not long before the silver bubbles from the Guardia divers were rising towards her. The leading bubble, larger than the rest, exploded like a subterranean firework, surrounding Marina with a frothy fizz. She was still acutely aware of all sounds and sensations. The bleep of diving computers grew louder from below. She checked her own and saw she was just above 25 metres.

Slowly, the two Guardia divers ascended. The first diver was holding something in his hand. As he drew closer, it became clear that it was the dead man's head. Before she had time to react, the second diver emerged with the rest of the body, one hand holding between the shoulder blades and the other his leg. The lower half of one arm was missing.

The body left an oily trail of white fatty tissue. As the second diver passed Marina, he made the 'OK' signal, which she returned. It was hard to tell, but he seemed fairly young. Marina wasn't as horrified as she imagined she would be by the sight of the body. It was so beyond her range of experience that looking through her facemask allowed a certain detachment, almost as though she were watching it on TV.

The same however, could not be said for Nathalie. Once the Guardia divers were above 20 metres, Marina looked round for her co-diver and noticed her drifting down. She quickly swam towards her. Nathalie's eyes looked vacant behind her mask about and the bubbles rising above her head indicated she was breathing very quickly and on the point of hyperventilating. Marina grabbed her arm and slowly pulled her towards the surface, carefully monitoring their ascent.

As they broke the surface, Nathalie wrenched off her diving mask, spat the regulator from her mouth and swam frantically to the diving boat. When Marina climbed up the steps a few moments later, Nathalie was sitting on the bench, sobbing. Marina put her arms around her and said nothing. She looked to the sea. There was an oily film on its surface producing a foul stench, so Marina replaced her just removed mask and regulator.

Once they had rolled the body on board, the Guardia started the Zodiac's engine and pulled up alongside. The second Guardia Civil diver smiled at Marina. He looked to be in his late twenties, with a kind, handsome face, made different from most of his countrymen by grey-blue eyes, which contrasted with his strong Latin features. He said nothing, but nodded towards Nathalie as a way of asking if she was OK. Marina smiled and nodded back. The diver pointed towards the harbour to indicate he would see her there. With that, the throttle of the Zodiac was opened as it executed a 180-degree turn, spraying a small plume as it sped away.

Back at the harbour, Marina found the Guardia Civil crew sitting in a small bar, drinking and eating tapas. The diver who had smiled at Marina was speaking to a uniformed policeman, his wetsuit rolled down to his waist. Marina avoided eye contact but noticed that his hairless torso boasted a finely chiselled swimmer's physique.

Marina took her time showering. By the time she had dressed, Pedro, Nathalie and the Guardia had gone. She got her things together and went to the bus stop, then changed her mind and decided to start walking back to her apartment. Although the sun was shining, there was a fresh breeze.

She had only been walking for a few minutes when a bright red Renault pulled up in front of her. Marina was used to both English and Spanish would-be Lotharios trying their luck, so she marched straight past with her head down, avoiding the Spanish-accented attempts to attract her attention.

After she walked past, the car overtook her and pulled up again. This time though, the driver stepped out. It was the Guardia Civil diver.

'Hi, I wanted to check you were OK,' he said.

'*Sí, bueno, pero hecha polbo y quiero mi casa,*' replied Marina.

The diver laughed at Marina's use of the Spanish equivalent of 'knackered'.

'*Ah, tu hablas español?*'

'*Sí.*'

'Good, but let us speak English – it is good for me. If you are tired as you say, then let me give you a lift.'

'No, really I—'

'I insist.' His voice had the authority that came with being a policeman, so Marina thanked him and got into the car.

'My name is Bartolo.'

'I'm Marina.'

They shared a smile.

'It was not a good experience for you today, correct?' asked Bartolo.

'Correct. I suppose you're used to it?'

'No, not really. I have seen dead bodies before but that is the most, how you say, *decomponersado?*'

'Decomposed. How was his wife?'

'That is the hardest part, always. My colleague, he dealt with her. By comparison, what I do is easy.' He smiled again and started the car.

'What happened to the dead man?'

'We are not sure. His arm was caught beneath a trunk. The trunk has much concrete in the bottom so it is probable that it was to be used for smuggling drugs. How his arm is underneath the trunk we do not know but he was not wearing tanks or a wetsuit, so is possible it was not an accident. There will be an investigation, I expect.'

'Oh dear.'

'Perhaps now is best we talk of something else, yes?'

Their conversation during the ten-minute journey moved naturally and easily from the morning's events to lighter topics, light enough for Bartolo to coax the occasional giggle from her. It was as if the bond caused by the morning's events had made her lower her guard. They pulled up outside Marina's apartment, then, as she said goodbye, she found herself holding Bartolo's gaze longer than she planned.

'Um, er, right,' she stammered, gathering herself. 'Thanks for the lift.'

She tried to open the door but couldn't find the handle, so Bartolo leaned across and opened it for her. She got out and reached back in the car for her bag.

'Would you like to go out, Marina – dinner tomorrow night perhaps? Some friends of mine run a fantastic restaurant near San José. It might help to talk things through.'

Marina hesitated a moment before replying. 'No, I don't think so. Everything's fine. I didn't have to touch the body or anything – you did that.'

'Yes, but I am a policeman. Anyway, even if we talk about other things . . . you perhaps?'

The twinkle in his eye made Marina blush slightly and look away.

'No, thanks all the same and cheers for the lift.'

Bartolo reached into his glove compartment for a pen and scribbled his number on an old receipt. 'If you change your mind, phone me.'

Marina thanked him and took the paper, watching him as he drove off. She had no intention of calling him, but put the piece of paper in her pocket anyway.

She climbed the steps to her apartment, opened the door and dumped her bag on the floor.

An attractive girl in an oversized Miss Moneypenny's T-shirt appeared in the hall, towelling her hair.

'Hi, Holly.'

'How was it?'

'Not good,' replied Marina. 'How was your day?'

'Depends how you look at it. Mr Wonderful has buggered off home.'

'Terry?'

'Yep. He decided that . . . hang on. Sorry, hon, we should be talking about you, not my sorry love life.'

'Don't be daft. To tell the truth, Holly, it might help to get my mind off things.'

'Are you sure? Do you want Holly to put the kettle on?'

Marina smiled and nodded. They walked through to the living room and sat down.

'So, how do you feel about him going?'

'I'm not bothered really,' sighed Holly.

'You weren't seeing him for all that long, were you?'

'Only a couple of months or so. I met him in Manchester. He wanted to come out here and I'd just finished doing my psychology MA, so I thought, why not? Coming to Ibiza wasn't a big deal, because I knew I could just fly back home or do my own thing, if we didn't work out. To be honest, I had a feeling he was a bit of a dickhead before we got here. A bloody good-looking dickhead though, it must be said.'

The two girls giggled.

'Anyway, the warning bells should have rung straight away. We got on too well when we met. He had loads of great one-liners but on reflection, I guess he must have spent most of his time practising them because he had bugger all else to say. I thought he had some depth but the only deep thing about him was the comas he'd go into on Sundays after a weekend out clubbing.'

'So what happened when you got to Ibiza?'

'When we got here it was obvious he was selling drugs. I had an idea he dabbled a bit back home, but he suddenly fancied himself as Tony Montana. Unfortunately, he was crap at it. Last week we were on our way to Las Salinas when he took a detour to a gorgeous villa in the Benimussa hills. I knew what he was up to. He even *told* me it belonged to some Spanish dealers he had to see.'

'Bastard!'

'Totally. I was furious at him for dragging me along. It's one thing knocking out a few pills to friends and that, but this was different and I didn't want to get involved. Anyway, I sat in the car while he went in and did whatever it was he was doing. Five minutes later, he walked out of the villa covered in blood.'

'Jesus. What happened?'

'The Spanish bastards cut the top of his ear off. He didn't say why but I'm ninety per cent sure he tried to rip them off and they sussed him out. Still, mutilating him like that . . .'

'Didn't you call the police?'

'I wanted to, but Terry wasn't interested. All he wanted to do was get off the island. I'd already decided he wasn't for me, so I guess that all things considered, I'm glad to see the back of him. I mean, obviously, I would have preferred it to be under different circumstances, but . . . '

'So what are you going to do now?'

'Well, I had an interview with your boss – Kyle Goldwell. He's another one who fancies himself.'

'You can say that again.'

'He was so cheesy. Even came out with the "I'm sure we've met before" line. Anyway, I'm doing some PR for that Smacker night he promotes. I'll need to find something else if I'm to stay though.'

'I'm sure a girl of your talents will have plenty of job offers.' Marina stood up. 'I'm going for another shower. I can't seem to get rid of the stench from earlier.'

'OK. There'll be a nice cuppa waiting when you come out. Are you sure you don't want to talk about it?'

'Not now. Maybe another time.'

Marina stepped into the shower and let the water run over her body. She recalled the sadness of the dead man's widow, waiting at the harbour for the inevitable news and the unenviable task of identifying her partner's body. At most, she could have only been a couple of years older than Marina, yet had three small children. Now, she also had a dead husband. It somehow brought home to Marina not only a sense of her own mortality, but also how quickly time seemed to be passing.

Marina knew that she had toughened up in recent years, if anything, playing up the hard-nosed, enigmatic, independent image that most took as the real her. Attacking life, travelling, broadening her experiences, she had discovered in New Zealand a taste for adrenalin and had literally thrown herself headfirst into any pursuit that gave her that rush, that buzz. The thrill it gave was greater than any she could remember in a relationship.

There seemed less chance of getting hurt too.

But was it the real her? Had she changed that much? Was it a defence mechanism or was that the person she had actually become? She knew that deep down, she didn't *really* want to be on her own. It just seemed easier, less painful. Was it now time to dip her toe into the relationship pool once again?

She stepped out of the shower and reached into her bag. She took a piece of paper and looked at if for a few moments.

'Sod it . . . why not?' She flipped open her mobile, and dialled a number. *'Hola*, Bartolo, it's Marina . . .'

chapter eleven

Dex groaned and scratched his hungover head. Shit, what *was* her name?

It had been a strange and very, very long Sunday night.

Dex and Luc arrived at Tiburon just in time to witness a madman jump into the harbour fully-clothed yelling, *'Mañana'* at the top of his voice. When a grinning Connor hauled himself from the sea, they thought he had cracked, and were certain he had when he told them he was staying in Ibiza for the summer.

They adjourned to another bar and spent a while discussing the whys and wherefores of Connor's seemingly impulsive and illogical decision. Although Dex and Luc couldn't think what was going through Connor's head they both later agreed that it seemed as though a weight had been lifted from his shoulders and for the first time in ages, he appeared to be genuinely happy and carefree.

Their collective mood improved still further when they all went to Atlantis where Dex ran through a set and was offered the DJ job on the spot. To celebrate, a bar crawl was suggested, but Connor declined; he wanted to ring Mr King first thing the next morning to resign and had things to think through before the dreaded conversation.

Dex and Luc subsequently went on a massive bender, which somehow resulted in the lumbering frame now sharing Dex's bed. He looked beyond her to his bedside clock. It was almost four in the afternoon. The previous night's proceedings slowly started coming back to him.

They had visited virtually every bar in the West End and in each one had been given several shots of differing liquors. They had ended up in an eighties revival club, where a girl almost twice Luc's size had swooped on him as if he were the last prawn vol-au-vent at a wedding buffet. Dex had ended up with her mate in a dark corner of the club, snogging, drinking, and trying not to throw up.

Dex remembered marvelling at the large girl's kissing technique – how Luc managed to resurface without suffering asphyxiation or some kind of serious injury was nothing short of miraculous. Luc had been unable to put his arm round her massive shoulders so ended up pinned against the wall with his limbs helplessly flailing. At one point, Dex was concerned that she was actually trying to eat Luc rather than kiss him. Luckily, when they got back to their apartment the plump friend discovered a Mars bar so Luc was probably therefore still alive or at worst, only half-eaten.

They had ended up in a Spanish bar until almost eight in the morning then taken a taxi home, coming in just as Connor was walking out to make the call to Mr King. Despite clearly having a lot on his mind, Connor had been unable to restrain his laughter at the state of his two friends and their new-found consorts.

Dex wondered how Connor had got on. Time to find out. He gave the girl a gentle prod, then shook her shoulders. She groaned into consciousness.

'Wakey-wakey. It's nearly four.'

She opened her eyes and tried to snuggle up to Dex.

'Sorry, but I'm going to have to kick you out, I've got to go to work,' he lied.

'Where's the bathroom?' the girl mumbled.

Dex pointed her in the right direction. She grabbed all of her things and trundled off. He heard voices from the living room so put on some boxer shorts and went to join them.

Luc was sitting there looking extremely sheepish. The girl he had brought home was on the settee, smoking a cigarette, eating a bowl of cornflakes and generally making Harry Enfield's Waynetta Slob character look like a refined debutante.

A couple of minutes later, Dex's own conquest emerged from the bathroom and despite freshly applied make-up, she was cast more from her friend's mould than anything a High Street shop would have classified as a 'standard' shape. Dex and Luc caught each other's eye and both pulled a face.

'Come on then, shall we piss off?' suggested Dex's ladyfriend.

Luc's conquest stubbed out her cigarette, took one last spoonful of cornflakes and hauled herself from the settee. Nothing much else was said. No suggestion of another meet, not even a 'see you around'. It was a familiar scenario for them all, that was clear.

As soon as they were out the door, Dex and Luc exploded into fits of laughter.

'Oh man,' said Dex, 'we must have been so wasted. That has got to be the nastiest girl I've ever slept with.'

74

'She was a beauty queen compared to mine.'

'What a bummer that Connor saw them – he's going to give us so much stick! Where is he now? Do you know how he got on with his call to Positive Solutions?'

'He just went back out about ten minutes ago. He rang them first thing this morning but that King bloke wasn't there. He spoke to the MD instead.'

'Isn't that the one Connor gets on with?'

Luc nodded. 'The MD told him to go away and dwell on it for a few hours and to call back at four. Said he was going to talk to Mr King about a new offer, or something like that.'

Dex looked pensive. 'So do you reckon he'll go back? And if he does, are we still going to take the apartment that Kyle offered the three of us last night?'

'I don't see why not. It's a bloody good price and we've each got our own room. If Connor leaves we should easily be able to get someone else in.'

'Assuming the apartment's OK, that is. He's not taking us up there until tomorrow.' Dex glanced at his watch. 'I think I might pack my stuff now – if we have another night like last night I'm not gonna fancy doing it in the morning.'

Dex walked back into his room. Magazines and clothes covered most of the floor so that only a small area of the grey-tiled floor could be seen. He started to tidy up and as he picked up a towel from beside the bed, was surprised to find a used condom underneath it. He smiled, pleased that even though he'd been wrecked, he'd remembered to use one.

The ants crawling around it seemed quite happy too.

Connor took a deep breath and picked up the phone. This time, he got straight through to Mr King.

'Ah, the elusive Connor Young. How's Ibiza?'

'OK.'

For once, Connor didn't have a smart reply.

'What happened to your Catholic girlfriend?'

'Oh . . . yeah, it all got sorted out.' So much had happened over the weekend that Connor had almost forgotten his original excuse. 'I was so close to Ibiza that I thought I might as well pop over for the weekend and, well . . . you know . . .'

'No, actually Young, I don't know. I understand you're planning on staying there. To do what, pray tell?'

'Um. I'm not sure.'

'Sorry? Am I missing something here? I assumed you'd met a famous female popstar, or won the Spanish lottery, or been offered a share in a bar, or at least,' Mr King could contain his irritation no longer, *'been offered a fucking job!'*

Connor contemplated simply putting the phone down; the call was proving even harder than he'd imagined.

'Just so I know I've got my facts right, allow me to summarize. You're turning your back on what could be a fantastic career, to say nothing of best part of twelve thousand pounds, a new Mercedes, a guaranteed bonus for the next six months . . . how much do barmen in Ibiza earn exactly?'

'Not very much.'

'Not very much,' repeated Mr King slowly. He let out a long sigh. 'Young, Young, Young. I doubt I'll ever understand you. What on earth is going through that head of yours? Some bohemian ideal? Thinking of reading classic literature, or writing poetry as the sun goes down, is that it?'

'I don't write poetry and—'

'How many times do I have to tell you, it's what you've earned, not what you've learned that counts.'

Connor had had enough. 'Actually Mr King, with all due respect, that's utter bollocks. There's far more to life than money.'

'As I keep saying, money is freedom, Young, money is freedom. Anyway, I'm not here to philosophize. You were fortunate that you spoke to the MD earlier rather than me, because I would have simply said good riddance. However, for reasons best known to himself the MD likes you and, based on your recent performance, he seems to think that losing you would be to Positive Solutions' detriment. So, between us, we have come up with a proposal.'

'Huh?' This was not at all what Connor was expecting.

'It's clear to the MD at least that you have certain unresolved issues. You must have because turning your back on the incentives that are on offer to you is plain bloody stupid. What the MD has decided is that you need time to sort through those issues. We are therefore going to keep your position open to you for two weeks.'

'Really?'

'Obviously it will be taken as unpaid leave, but otherwise, all of my previous conditions stand. You will be paid the twelve thousand pounds for the Horne, Fleming and Mitchell deal after six months – even though *I* am going to have to sign the contract with them tomorrow in your place – and you will still be paid on the contract business. Equally, *if* you come back, then I shall not be cutting you any slack at all until I am convinced your attitude has changed.'

Connor was speechless. Mr King continued.

'Yes, I thought that would get you thinking. I was, of course, totally opposed to the idea. But then, it's your dilemma, and it is going to be hanging over you for the next two weeks.' Mr King allowed himself a mirthless laugh. 'Enjoy yourself, Young – or rather, *try* to – it's only a decision that will affect the rest of your life. Don't forget. I'll be expecting a phone call from you on Monday, two weeks from today. If you decide to come back, we'll see you nice and early in the office on the Tuesday morning following that. Goodbye.'

Connor held the phone in his hands for a few seconds, dumbstruck.

For once Mr King was right. It was going to be constantly on his mind and meant, effectively, that his immediate future was still unresolved. Everything he did, all aspects of Ibiza, positive and negative, would now take on an added importance. They would not be enriching life experiences, but factors in a resurrected decision-making process.

The island that he had so long associated with a stress-free life, where he had had to make no greater decision than what bar to get pissed in or which beach to get brown on, had in some way been forever sullied. It had joined the real world. And in that moment Connor realized it was the real world he was trying to escape.

chapter twelve

'Hey Shuff, does this shirt look all right?'

A handsome 24-year-old, his head topped with spiky, white-blond hair, peered around the bathroom door.

'Grant, you look awesome.'

Grant smiled at the sarcasm and Shuff returned to his shaving. Grant inspected himself in the bedroom mirror a few more times and from different angles. He normally liked what he saw, but when he compared his features to the classic handsome symmetry of Shuff, no amount of squinting at mirrors could persuade him that any girl would prefer him to his best friend. He threw the luminous green shirt on to the bed next to the other half-dozen unsuitable garments.

'Those two chicks will let us stay with them for a few days, won't they?' There was no answer from the bathroom, so Grant continued. 'If this job tonight doesn't work out then we're going to have to think about going back to the States.'

'No way,' replied Shuff flatly. 'We're *not* bailing. Man, how many people back home have even *heard* of Ibiza, let alone come out here to work for a season, especially in San Antonio? This place is Brit Central and we've got novelty value, which is going to get us seriously laid.'

'I guess.'

'And you know how anti this whole trip our folks were. If you think I'm going to give them a call to bail us out . . .'

Shuff walked into the living room splashing on aftershave and wiping away a dollop of shaving foam that had dropped from his chin on to his deeply tanned and well-toned torso. Grant had just put on a well-worn dark-blue T-shirt with New Jersey Fire Department written on it.

'What about this one?'

'Yeah, might impress the chicks that you *used* to be a fireman. Still, it's not very Ibiza, is it?'

Grant took it off and replaced it with a tight-fitting red T-shirt.

'Yeah, dude, that looks better.'

Shuff rummaged through his wardrobe while Grant put on a pair of wire-rimmed glasses.

'The thing is, Grant, none of the clubs have even opened yet. We've been stuck in this goddam 18-30 hotel for two weeks – this isn't the only part of Ibiza we came for. You know how important it is to me that we see out the summer. Come on, buddy. Don't neg out on me now.'

Grant shrugged. 'OK. I guess we'd better make sure that this job tonight works out.'

They headed towards Atlantis, which was situated on a newly developed seafront promenade between the popular Café Mambo and another recently built development called Coastline. The rocky peninsula had remained a barren wasteland through years of tourism but now Atlantis had become the latest addition to the ever-growing Sunset Strip. Only two storeys high, its six luxury apartments above the bar were sold before a single breezeblock had been laid. During the day the small Atlantis diving school occupied the other unit at ground level and although it could be accessed from the bar during the day, glass doors partitioned it off during the evening.

As they walked down the slight incline towards the seafront bar Café Mambo, a lank-haired youth they had met a few nights before approached them.

'How's it going, lads?' he asked. It was clear he didn't remember their names.

'Not bad,' replied Shuff. He couldn't think what Lank-Hair was called either.

'Found any work yet?'

'Yeah,' said Grant, spitting his stale chewing gum on to the pavement. 'We went into Atlantis early last night asking for work and the manager told us to come down and try out as props – we're on our way there now.'

Lank-Hair started laughing.

'What's so funny?' questioned Shuff.

'Weren't you two with those cockney girls last night?'

'Katrina and Tasha,' nodded Shuff. 'Yeah. We had a few drinks with them.'

'Thought we were on for a jump,' smiled Grant, 'but they had to go somewhere. Probably catch up with them tonight.'

Lank-Hair shook his head. 'Well the best place to catch up with them is probably Atlantis.' Shuff and Grant looked puzzled. 'They started working there about an hour ago.'

'*What!*'

'But they can't . . .'

'We told them we were going to start working there . . .' Shuff's voice trailed off as he realized what had happened.

'Don't trust nobody out here,' said Lank-Hair. 'It's every man – or woman – for themselves.' He threw his cigarette on the floor and stamped on it. 'Got to go. Good luck.' He ambled down the road.

Grant turned to Shuff. 'Fucking bitches.'

'Let's go and see what's going on.'

As they approached the bar, they could hear the shrill voices of Katrina and Tasha long before they saw them.

'Come on, girls. Get yourselves into Atlantis. Two for the price of one. Hello handsome, loads of gorgeous girls in tonight . . .'

Both were wearing skimpy outfits. Katrina's huge freckly boobs were pushed together by a black low-cut T-shirt at least a size too small, tucked into tiny white lycra shorts. Tasha, who was less attractive, wore a short, see-through cheesecloth dress, transparent enough to show her small pert breasts and the tiniest of G-strings.

'Hi, guys,' said Katrina, sounding genuinely pleased to see them.

'What the fuck do you think you're playing at?' asked Shuff.

'I beg your pardon?'

'We told you last night that we were starting work here. Now you've taken our jobs.'

'It's not our fault,' said Tasha, sucking a chocolate-coloured drink through a straw.

'Oh, and how do you figure that?'

'After we left you last night we popped in here for a drink and the manager Paco asked us if we wanted to work here. He said he wanted a couple of girls propping so we didn't think it would affect your jobs.'

'So you're saying that all four of us are working here?' Shuff's tone softened.

'I guess so. Best you ask Paco.' The girls looked at each other uncomfortably.

The bar was quite busy, but it didn't take them long to find Paco, sitting at a table pouring tequila shots down the necks of two young girls, whose sunburnt faces showed them to be recent arrivals to the island.

'Paco, can we have a word?' asked Grant hesitantly.

Paco looked up. 'No. I'm busy.' He turned back to the girls. Shuff placed his hand on Paco's shoulder.

'We're meant to be working.'

Tutting and excusing himself to the girls, Paco stood up. He was of similar build to Grant, but a good four inches shorter than Shuff.

'You no work. I have two girls to do the job. Girls are better for business.'

'You told us we had the job yesterday.'

'And today I tell you there is no job.' He shrugged. Shuff grabbed his shirt. As he did so, he felt a sharp yank on his collar. He turned round and recognized Kyle Goldwell, the owner.

'What's your problem, blondie?'

In the two weeks he'd been on the island, Shuff had already heard lots of bad things about Kyle Goldwell. Though he could look after himself he was also streetwise enough to realize that a confrontation with Kyle would not be a good idea.

'We came to see him last night about working here as props. Now he's given the job to those two girls.'

'Aye, well, they're better looking.' He turned to Paco. 'Is that right, Paco, you offered these two Yanks a job?'

'*Sí*, but nothing is definite. The two girls say they work for less, so . . .'

Kyle nodded and Paco returned to his new arrivals. 'Looks like you've been outsmarted, lads.'

'It's not fair,' protested Grant. 'We've got no money, nowhere to live, we're thousands of miles from home, and now we've got no job.'

'Life's no' fair,' sighed Kyle. 'And where's home exactly?'

'Bloomfield, New Jersey.'

'Aye, that is a fair auld trek.' He paused for a moment. 'You've nowhere to live then?' He glanced towards Mac who was sitting in the shadows by the bar. Mac shrugged. Kyle smiled.

'I've a five-bedroom place just up by the Sa Serra apartments that I rent every year to people who work for me. Do you know where they are?' They shook their heads again. 'There's a wee slip road to the left of the roundabout just before the Port des Torrent road. Now if you want, you can stay there. There's a London lad DJing for me and two of his mates who'll probably be moving in. I'm taking them to have a look at it tomorrow. I'd only charge you two hundred and fifty euros a month each.'

'We appreciate the offer,' said Grant, 'but, as we said, we haven't got money or a job.'

'Maybes I can still help out. I've got a club night starting at Eden next week called Smacker. Heard of it?'

'Of course,' replied Shuff.

'Let me share something with you.' Kyle ran his hand over his bald head. 'One of the reasons I've done so well out here is that I'm a good judge of character and I trust my instincts. Now, I can tell that auld blondie here has got the gift of the gab. I can also tell from the way he just was with Paco that he doesn't take any shit – that can be a good quality out here. I can also tell that you,' he nodded towards Grant and lit a small cigar, 'are a stabilizing influence. Am I right?'

Flattered, Grant couldn't help but nod.

'Aye, I thought so.' He blew a plume of smoke into the air. 'Every year I have a small team that I let sell tickets for Smacker in advance. They've got to be trustworthy. As part of the deal I'd let you move into the apartment and pay me once you've the money. The only thing is I'd need one of you to give me a passport as security.'

'What sort of money are we talking?' asked Shuff.

'Depends how many people you get in. Being American could be a real advantage though. The way it works is I give the club tickets to you for thirty euros – the cost price. You sell them for thirty-five and we split the profit.'

'But we haven't got any money to buy them from you in the first place,' said Grant.

'That's no' the way it works. I give you say, fifty tickets. Once you've the tickets though, they're your responsibility – no sob stories about losing them or mates no' paying you. I've been ripped off like that before. But if you don't sell them, nae bother, just bring them back.' Shuff and Grant looked at each other. 'It's a bit quiet and you'll probably no' earn much money until July and August, but you'll still do OK even now. You'd probably only work a four-day week though, because people will only buy them in the days leading up to the night.'

'It's not bad,' said Grant, 'but it still doesn't sound like fortunes.'

'It is compared to what most make out here. Still,' Kyle lowered his voice, 'if you really want to make some folding during June, there is something else you can do.'

'And what's that?' asked Shuff.

'One of my boys over there needs a couple of people to knock out some bits and pieces. The pair of you look the part, right enough.'

Grant looked at Shuff then back at Kyle. 'What, you mean drugs?'

'Aye, just a few pills and a bit of Charlie.'

'We'd probably get caught.'

'If you're worried about the local police, then that's not necessarily a problem, if you ken what I mean.'

The boys didn't 'ken' what he meant. 'No, not for us,' said Shuff, knowing that Grant wasn't keen but, as always, being the voice of any mutual decision the pair made. 'Don't get me wrong, I'm more desperate to stay here than you could ever believe, but—'

'Oh well,' Kyle threw his small cigar on the floor crushed it underfoot, 'let me know if you change your minds.'

'We'll do the tickets though,' added Grant quickly.

'Nae bother but I'm telling you now, doing the other stuff is the only way you'll earn any real money here. Come on out the back. I'll sort you some tickets then we'll see if the London boys who you might be sharing with are here. The one who's a DJ is due on pretty soon.'

chapter thirteen

Connor got out of the Mondeo that had been following Kyle's Range Rover and looked at the two-storey building. It was nothing spectacular and he doubted it would have anything like the same home comforts he enjoyed in his Camberwell flat. Still, on the plus side, that meant no wrought-iron beds for girls to get their heads stuck in.

'Look guys – we've got our own orange tree,' observed Shuff as he stepped from Kyle's Range Rover.

And that was the other thing: Flatmates. When he originally contemplated staying in Ibiza he had accepted that he would probably share with Luc and Dex but not for one moment that he would have to share with strangers too.

The previous night in Atlantis, the Monday, Kyle had introduced the two Americans saying they were staying in the other two rooms of the apartment he was renting them. Until that point, Connor, Luc and Dex had assumed there were just three bedrooms – now they knew why it was so reasonably priced.

Once Dex finished his set they all agreed to go out in the West End to get to know each other, then, assuming they all got on, visit the apartment the next day and make a decision.

It was clear to Connor that Shuff was the more gregarious of the two, but he stopped short of being attention-seeking or annoying. He simply had a joy for life that was actually rather infectious and a considered enthusiasm that was neither bombastic nor all-embracing. Grant was a lot more laidback and was the perfect foil – it was clear why they were such good friends. Connor was fairly confident Shuff and Grant would be OK to live with but if that proved not to be the case then the worst that could happen would be one or other party having to find somewhere else to live. From Connor's point of view there was still the distinct possibility that in exactly two weeks he would be back at his desk at Positive Solutions.

'Rory here will show you round,' said Kyle, pointing to the swarthy twenty-something with a twenty-first-century mullet who got out of the passenger seat. 'I've got to make a call.'

A garage occupied the ground floor of the building, with a huge pair of light-blue corrugated doors providing the main access. The apartment itself was on the first floor, up a flight of terracotta-tiled steps.

'How long have you worked for Kyle, Rory?' asked Shuff in his usual breezy and uninhibited way.

'We go way back,' Rory replied, sifting through a bunch of keys.

'What do you do?'

The simple question seemed to throw the Scot. 'Oh a bit of this, bit of that.' He put a key in the lock and opened the door. 'Take as long as you want. I'll be downstairs with Kyle.'

They all walked down a long, dark corridor with oak-panelled doors on either side and a cheap, marble-tiled floor. The first of these doors on the left opened out to a huge living room. Most of one wall was covered with a blue and maroon rug, with a bemused looking stag staring out from the middle of it and what appeared to be mountains in the background. There were French doors opening to the balcony, which overlooked fields and orchards, dappled with young trees. There was another smaller balcony at the other end of the room, in front of which was a reproduction dining table with six chairs around it.

Opposite the living room were five doors, one to each of the bedrooms. There was a double bed, teak bedside cabinet and wardrobe in all of them, save one, in which there was a single bed. None of the wardrobes seemed particularly stable and most had Spanish or British graffiti scratched into them. There was a long balcony, which joined the five bedrooms and overlooked the small courtyard at the front of the building.

Next to the living room was a surprisingly large kitchen, with fitted units and a built-in oven and gas hob. The orange butane gas bottle underneath it was disconnected and empty. A fridge-freezer was tucked away in the corner, next to the sink. The kitchen felt very unused and unlived in, although stains on the wall and a punch hole in the door suggested that it had witnessed its fair share of excess during previous summers.

At the end of the corridor was a neat bathroom with an avocado suite. The light switch didn't work, so an old-fashioned table lamp had been placed in the corner, with an extension lead running to the hallway.

The two groups convened in the living room.

'What do you think?' asked Dex.

'It's better than I thought it would be,' replied Luc. 'If you saw some of the shitholes people stay in, this is like a palace.'

'We think it's great,' said Shuff.

They all looked at Connor.

'Yeah, it's fine by me.'

'So, are we all agreed?' asked Luc.

Everyone nodded.

'Cool,' said Shuff. 'I'll go down and let Kyle know. You guys choose which rooms you want then Grant and I will toss a coin to see who gets the single room.'

Connor was impressed and encouraged by this initial altruistic gesture, more so when Shuff returned and offered to make the ten-minute walk to the nearest shop to stock up on supplies.

Connor chose the room by the apartment's entrance, Dex the one next to him and Luc the bedroom at the other end, gleefully gloating that it was the closest to the bathroom and kitchen. Connor immediately discarded the rickety bed and put the mattress on the floor. There wasn't anything for him to unpack. He'd contemplated getting some of his things sent out by courier, but decided instead that his summer wardrobe needed updating and that a modest shopping spree in Ibiza Town should see him all right for the fortnight.

And there it was already. That *bastard* King. Something as simple as buying clothes was affected by the fact that he had yet to decide whether to stay in Ibiza or not.

Connor went into the kitchen to find Shuff and Grant having a light-hearted argument about who was going to have the room with the single bed (Grant), who was going to go back for the milk they'd forgotten to buy (Shuff, although Luc overrode the decision and went down in his car), then finally over who had first go on the hand-held computer game (neither, because the batteries had run out and Luc had already left).

Within half an hour, everyone was settled, so they got stuck into a traditional workers' feast of French bread, cheese, Spanish tomatoes, ham, cream crackers and strange crinkly crisps, followed by Danone yoghurt, washed down with a few bottles of San Miguel.

Their collective spirits were lifted still further when they discovered a swimming pool, which belonged to the adjacent Sa Serra apartments and looked as though it was rarely used.

Late in the afternoon, Connor felt restless and in a half-hearted attempt to convince himself that he intended to stay in Ibiza, decided to get himself a Spanish mobile. Dex and Luc needed one too, so went with him.

Shuff and Grant were left alone by the pool, delighted to have a job and to have met such compatible flatmates, but above all, just happy to be in Ibiza. Though neither admitted it, during the last few days, both had secretly felt that their Ibiza dream was coming to an end. Now though, soaking up the sun and tranquillity of their surroundings, they were at last able to visualize the season stretching out before them. Occasionally a dog would bark in the distance, prefacing a canine chorus as others answered, or a gust of wind would rustle the trees overhanging the pool. Other than that, they laid by the pool in almost total silence.

Their solitude was broken by the sound of a jet plane flying overhead. Both of them shielded their eyes from the sun, sat up on their sunbeds and looked skyward.

'Could be our plane,' said Grant wistfully. 'The first leg home.'

Shuff raised his Swatch. 'Probably is.'

They smiled.

'Well, that's that then,' said Grant. 'No money, no flight, rent owed, but the sun is shining and we've got a job.'

'Buddy, everything's gonna be just fine.'

chapter fourteen

'Come on Connor, drink up,' said Luc. 'The sun's down. Let's get to Atlantis and see Dex play his first set.'

They'd spent the afternoon buying their mobiles, then Dex, Shuff and Grant had gone to work for the evening, so Luc and Connor were looking forward to an evening of leisure and pleasure.

A few minutes later, the pair were walking along the seafront to the bar when they noticed a police car and several policemen surrounding two young men. Luc was the first to recognize them.

'Shit, it's Shuff and Grant.' Luc started running with Connor close behind. 'Leave this to me, Connor; at least I speak the lingo.'

One policeman had hold of Shuff, the other Grant, while a third sauntered over from the police car, casually smoking a cigarette. Shuff and Grant looked visibly relieved to see a friendly face, especially when Luc launched into perfect Spanish, which immediately seemed to defuse the situation.

After a brief conversation with the policemen, Luc turned to Shuff and Grant.

'They want you to turn out your pockets.'

Shuff and Grant did as they were asked. One of the policemen took a packet of condoms from Grant's hand, held them aloft to show his colleagues then said something in Spanish, which made them all laugh. But the laughing stopped when another policeman pulled out a bundle of Smacker tickets along with a wad of cash.

'What's going on?' mumbled Shuff.

The policemen checked the rest of their pockets, then simply walked off.

'What was all that about?' asked Grant.

'And where are they going with our money and goddam tickets?' demanded Shuff.

'You aren't allowed to sell them on the street – surely Kyle told you that?' said Luc.

'He just told us to sell them. He didn't say anything about—'

'Here he comes now,' interrupted Grant.

'What's the problem, boys?'

'The cops just took a load of tickets from us,' replied Grant.

'Fucking hell. What were you doing selling them out here in the open? Why wasn't one of you keeping watch?'

'You didn't tell us a goddam thing about selling tickets outside the bar being against the law,' exclaimed Shuff, his voice rising in anger. 'You just said get out there and sell them.'

'Aye, but when I said "get out there" I meant spread the word, get people into the bar where it's *legal* to sell them. If you're gonna do it this way then one of you should keep watch – everyone knows that. I thought you two were streetwise.'

'We are, but we're not fucking telepathic.'

'Och, you don't have to be telepathic, just have a bit of common sense. Think about it – who in their right mind is going to hand over cash for tickets on the street? You could be anybody. They could be forgeries.' Kyle shook his head in mock despair. 'How many did the bizzies take?'

'I'm not sure,' replied Shuff. 'At last count we'd managed to sell just over thirty.'

'You're obviously fucking good salesmen then. That would leave just under twenty, no?'

'Yeah, but they took the money as well,' added Grant.

'They what?'

'Everything – the money *and* the tickets.' Shuff had now become more forlorn than furious. 'Can't you do anything to get them back? Everyone says how well connected you are.'

'Away to fuck,' laughed Kyle. 'It's your problem – ken what I said? I gave you the best job I've got to offer, so don't blame me for no' doing your research.'

'But—'

'Remember?' Kyle cut Grant short. 'I said no sob stories. There's more tickets if you want them. Like I said, you're obviously good at selling them. I don't know how else you'll pay the money you owe me. I'm leaving soon so come in and see Rory if you want some more.'

'Now what are we going to do?' wailed Grant, as Kyle headed back to Atlantis.

'We've got no choice, have we?' replied an angry yet defeated Shuff.

Luc watched the two Americans trudge towards Atlantis, then turned to Connor.

'There was something not quite right about that little situation.'

'What do you mean?'

'I've never heard of anyone having their money confiscated – apart from dealers. Also, Kyle should have told them they couldn't sell tickets like that.'

'Maybe he just forgot, or didn't explain it properly.'

Luc shook his head. 'No way.'

'Why?'

'Because it's the *bar* that normally gets fined.'

'Shit!'

'I can't work it out, but something doesn't smell right . . .'

Connor didn't want to hang around Atlantis. There was something particularly unsavoury about Kyle – he hadn't taken to him when they first met, was wary of him when being shown the apartment and after what just happened with the police, wanted as little as possible to do with him. His sidekick – the smaller guy with the cravat – was even worse. It was as though he relished making people feel uncomfortable. Whatever it was that Connor was looking for from Ibiza, feeling uncomfortable was most certainly not it.

He borrowed Luc's car and drove into Ibiza Town. For most of Connor's second season in Ibiza he had worked in Say Chic, one of the small harbourfront bars. His main reason for driving to the more eclectic side of the island was to see Leo, an old customer, ex-pat and confirmed hedonist. Nobody was quite sure of his exact age – between forty and fifty-five – or even what he did for a living. It was rumoured that he was a doctor of philosophy, once worked for the secret service, had an IQ off the scale, and now made his money out of entering competitions and quizzes around the world.

His Swedish wife, Katya was an attractive woman in her early forties, who radiated a kind of sophisticated New Age warmth and positivity. There was still a freshness to their relationship that would not have looked out of place on a university campus; they were clearly very much in love and not afraid to show it. Connor could never imagine them arguing over trivia of everyday life. They just seemed so . . . happy.

Connor had formed a special bond with Leo. Many hours were spent just chewing the fat or putting the world to rights. When Connor returned to the UK they remained in touch by post, but during the last year they had not communicated. The truth was that Connor didn't like the person he had become back in London. Leo seemed to lead such a contented life that Connor did not want to be reminded how he had compromised his own.

Now though, there was the possibility of putting that life behind him. If there was one person who might be able to guide Connor towards making the right decision regarding his future, then that person was Leo, which was one of the reasons why he was so looking forward to seeing him.

Connor crossed the road to avoid the jostling, cosmopolitan hordes stopping at shops, stalls and bars. He passed the luxury cruisers moored by the ferry terminal. Some of the owners and their smug guests seemed to delight in having their haute cuisine served by waiters in crisp white uniforms just metres from the gawping 'have-nots'. For the most part, the diners would act as though they were blissfully unaware of the fact that they were on show. Some however, would perform like chimps at a tea party, guffawing loudly or gesticulating with exaggerated movements.

It all seemed a thousand miles away from the West End of San Antonio rather than just 17 kilometres.

Eventually, he reached the recessed promenade where Say Chic was situated. The bar had been extended and the layout changed. It was far busier than he remembered, too. The new owners had tried to attract a younger crowd and it had obviously worked. It should have made no difference in locating Leo though – he was as happy offering pearls of wisdom to the young as the old.

A waiter walked by and Connor was just about to stop him to ask if he had any idea where Leo could be found, when he heard a voice come from the corner by the door.

'Connor? It can't be – is that you?'

He turned round and sitting at a table with a book in his hand and a drink on the table was his Leo.

He barely recognized him. He was gaunt, emaciated, and clearly very ill.

Leo sighed at the shock on Connor's face. 'I know, I know – you don't have to say it.' His skeletal hand reached out and took Connor's. 'It's great to see you, Connor. It really is.'

Connor bent down and hugged the slender frame.

Leo smiled. 'Let me order us both a drink and I'll tell you about this great new diet I'm on.' To a passing waiter he said, 'Get me a beer with a large Hierbas chaser, and a JD and coke for this young man, assuming that's what he still drinks?' Connor nodded. 'Good.'

Connor took a resigned inventory of his friend. Typical Leo, breaking news in his own way.

'You can have alcohol on this diet then?'

'Essential.' Leo swigged back the last drop of the previous Hierbas still on the table.

Connor smiled. 'What other rules are there?'

'Eat what you want, when you want, and as much as you want. The real beauty of it, however, is that you don't actually feel like eating.'

There was a pause, as the waiter put the drinks on the table.

'On the slate, my good fellow. I plan to settle it at the end of summer, but don't hold your breath.'

The waiter – one of the co-owners – patted him on the shoulder. 'If you can settle it then, Leo, I'll happily wipe the slate for you.'

After he'd gone, Leo and Connor held each other's gaze for a few seconds, before Leo pursed his lips, sighed, and sat back in his chair.

'It's cancer, Connor – riddled with it. I found out at the end of last year.' Connor's eyes remained fixed on the table. He shook his head. Leo continued, 'Like I said, the good thing is I can eat, drink and do whatever I want without having to worry about the consequences.'

'Nothing new there then.'

Connor looked up, trying to imagine what his friend was going through, what he was really thinking behind the quips and the bravado. He couldn't. He didn't want to.

'Is it . . . you know . . . terminal?'

Leo nodded. 'About as terminal as it gets.'

'Jesus, Leo. I, I don't know what to say. How, how . . .' Connor couldn't get the words out.

'How long?' Leo sipped his drink. 'Well, put it this way, I wouldn't count on getting a Christmas card from me this year.'

Connor hung his head. 'Is there nothing that can be done?'

'Well, I could send you one now, I suppose, if it means that much to you.'

Connor managed a smile. 'Seriously, Leo, have you tried every avenue?'

'Every avenue, every alleyway, every ditch. I started off trying to will myself better, you know, the old Quantum Healing stuff we used to speak about.'

'What about chemo?'

'That came just after the Green Lip mussels from New Zealand and a few other weird and wonderful ideas. Chemo's the main reason I look like this. I always promised myself I'd never have it, all that poison in your body. The thing is, these complementary health remedies are all well and good in theory, but when it's your body that those bastard little cancer cells are spreading through, then who do you listen to – a Mystic Meg look-alike with a set of crystals, or a grey-haired professor with half-moon glasses telling you that chemo is your only chance?'

'I feel so guilty I haven't been in touch.'

'Ah, now that's the thing with death you see – guilt. The people left behind always feel guilty about something: Should they have spent more time together? Should they have gone to the hospital more, despite the person they love being so deep in a coma that they wouldn't know if it were Jesus Christ himself next to the bed? And if that loved one were conscious, the last thing they'd want is for you to go through the daily torture of seeing the life slowly drain from their wasting bodies. Or maybe it's something silly, like nicking a tenner from your dad's wallet when you were fourteen? That was the one that got me.'

Connor shook his head again. 'And I thought I had problems.'

'And what problems would they be?' asked Leo, sitting forward in his chair.

This was so typical. Leo always asked questions of others. It did, however, get them off the subject of Leo's illness and there was of course, the distinct possibility that Leo didn't want to talk about it.

Connor summarized the last four years and, more latterly, how he'd turned thirty, joined Positive Solutions and met Gina, but still didn't know where his life was going.

Leo loved a good story and his face came alive as Connor told him about the Searles and the cocaine in the video machine. He clapped as Connor described leaping into the harbour screaming, 'Mañana.'

'. . . but I really don't know what I'm doing here,' he finished.

Leo tutted. He rested his hand on Connor's forearm. 'Listen to me carefully, Connor, because what I'm about to say might sound obvious, but it's one of the most important things I'll ever share with you.' He gave a little cough to clear his throat, but it turned into a wheeze that rattled his whole body.

'Bloody hell, hurry up and tell me, Leo. You can't build things up like that then snuff it.' He handed him a serviette. 'Are you all right?'

Leo nodded, laughing and coughing into the tissue. Their relationship had resumed the dynamic of four years previously.

'There are a few really important lessons I've learned in my life,' said Leo eventually, 'and this is one of the most important. Now, as you know, I've mixed with people to whom one of those fancy yachts moored over there would be small change, and those who could probably carry their worldly goods in a little red handkerchief with white polka dots on the end of a bamboo cane. But they all want the same thing – happiness.'

Connor looked at Leo for a moment. 'And?'

'And what?'

'Leo, you've given me some pearls of wisdom during the conversations we've had in the past, but that's hardly one of them. I mean, it's so . . . so, well, yeah – *obvious*.'

Leo smiled. 'Exactly. Everyone *says* they want to be happy, but how many people actually think about it, I mean *really* think about it. You see, half the equation – maybe the hardest half – is discovering *what* makes you happy, the other half is working out how to get it. Ask most people what would make them happy and they'll say the obvious things like money, or health, or love. For some it might be power and popularity. Now they're all valid in their own way, but too general. It's *how* you earn your money, *what* you do with it, *who* you're in love with and *why*.'

Leo lit a cigarette, coughing instantly. Connor knew better than to chastise. He blew a plume of smoke in the air, coughed some more, then stubbed it out.

'So, when were you at your happiest, Connor?'

Connor thought for a moment.

'Lying on the settee with a porno on, waiting for the doorbell to ring and not knowing if it's a nubile wench turning up or a giant pizza and Tennessee Toffee Pie.'

'And the sad thing is you're probably not joking. Seriously though, when have you been at your happiest?

Connor sipped his drink and this time, gave it some proper thought. The freedom he felt after sitting his last ever exam? The hedonism of his first holiday with friends at seventeen? The pure excitement he felt at being seduced by his 25-year-old neighbour at the age of fifteen? The 'there-is-a-God' joy of his first threesome? The euphoria of scoring the winning try in a rugby cup final, just as he got booted in the groin and had to be carried off the field, clutching his prized assets to thunderous applause?

Actually, thinking about it, most of his *moments* of happiness involved him having his dick in his hand, in one way or another. Yet none of these were sustained *periods* of happiness, which he correctly guessed, was what Leo meant.

The answer when it came was obvious.

'When I worked here, in this bar. I wasn't earning fortunes, but I had enough to do what I wanted. I loved meeting people. I felt I was respected and liked.' He waited for Leo to make a quip, but he was nodding enthusiastically. 'I had great friends around me, I enjoyed what I did, I felt I was good at it, I didn't have a care in the world and . . . yeah, I was happy.'

'Good, that's work—'

'And the other time,' interrupted Connor, warming to the theme, 'was when I was with Mary. Do you remember? Yeah, on the whole, I was happy for most of the time we were together.'

'And that's companionship. It's simple. Most of our time is spent either at work or with a partner. The very least you owe yourself is to enjoy your work, and so you choose something that gives you a feeling of self-worth. You need to feel you are developing your potential to feel stimulated.'

'I'm not sure that working as a barman at this age would be a good idea.'

'Of course not, because you wouldn't be developing your potential.'

Connor reflected. 'So what's the answer? Sure, all that stuff would be great, but I also want to have nice things—'

'What you want,' interrupted Leo, 'is a nice *lifestyle*. There's nothing wrong with having nice things but I bet there are a percentage of the people who own those yachts who aren't happy. Possessions sometimes just fill a gap.'

'Mmm, makes sense, I guess, though I can't see where it's leading. And what about the companionship?'

'You need to ask yourself the same questions. You'll feel dissatisfied and ultimately miserable if you've aimed too low, but equally, if you are with someone who erodes your self-esteem, you'll feel insecure and unhappy.'

Connor followed the logic but he was unable to see how he could apply it to himself. Still, it had been an interesting conversation. He finished his drink. 'What do you want, same again?'

Leo sat up in his chair and glared at Connor, the fire, for a moment, back in his eyes.

'What do I want? It's not what I want, you buffoon. It's about what *you* want.'

'No, I meant what do you want to—'

'I *know* what you meant and yes, I'll have the same again.' With exaggerated exasperation, Leo tutted. 'For goodness' sake, man, think about this. You've come over to Ibiza on a whim and claim you don't know why. In the next breath you say that the happiest time of your life

95

was when you worked in this bar. For someone who used to be good with figures you're not doing very well at putting two and two together.'

'But I've already said, I want to be more than a barman.'

'This isn't about being a barman. What was it that made you happy working here?'

'I guess it was meeting people, having good conversations, just being in Ibiza . . .'

'Now we're getting somewhere. You need to work out *why* you were happy as a barman, then look at yourself and see how you've changed. Sure, for a lad in his early twenties, being a barman with no responsibilities is fine, but as you get older, responsibility can be a rewarding thing. Then look at *why* you were happy with Mary. Shagging round is all well and good, in a rite of passage kind of way, but I bet you'd be happier here if you could share it with a soulmate.'

As usual, Leo was one step ahead. Connor had been thinking along those lines since arriving on the island. Mary was history, of course, but certainly he wanted someone who made him feel like she did – the elusive Big Adventure.

'And,' continued Leo, 'I'll bet you'd not be chasing the fast car and the luxury flat if you were living here, would you?'

Connor remained deep in thought. Had he looked up, he would have noticed the faintest of smiles across Leo's lips. Suddenly, Connor sat bolt upright.

'That's it! I know what I should do.'

'And what's that?'

'Get my own bar!'

Leo nodded. 'Could be an option.'

'Only . . .'

'Only what?'

'Only,' reality check, 'I can't afford one.'

'Well, I'd love to help you, Connor, but unfortunately when I shuffle off this mortal coil I'll be doing so with insufficient funds to settle my bar bill, let alone buy the place.'

'Oh God, no!' said Connor, instantly aghast. 'Leo, I didn't mean . . . I don't want you to think that I was—'

Leo held his hand up. 'I know you didn't and I'll be more offended if you believe that I could think that of you than if you'd actually asked.'

Connor breathed a sigh of relief. 'Thank God. Well, I guess I'll have to start doing the Spanish lottery.'

'Maybe. Or perhaps you'll just have to look at things differently. You've pretty much said that you'd like to be with your Big Adventure, and that Ibiza is where you could perhaps settle. At least it's shown you that having the nicest car or biggest house isn't necessarily what will make you happy. That's a start. A lot of people don't even get that far.'

Connor picked at his beer mat. Leo downed his drink in one and with a grin on his face, called the waiter over.

'Same again . . .'

chapter fifteen

Despite so many things spinning round in his head, Connor fell asleep almost as soon as he got back from meeting Leo and didn't hear any of the others come in.

He got up before ten in the morning, feeling surprisingly fresh. The apartment was quiet apart from a girl coughing in Shuff's room. The TV was still on in the living room but there was a fuzzy screen with no picture, as though a video had been allowed to run out. Evidence of post-booze munchies littered the kitchen and all of the milk had gone.

Rather than walk down to the shop and back, Connor decided to make the thirty-minute journey by foot into San An and get something to eat there. The first half of the walk was down a dirt track with a few modest houses en route, mainly belonging to locals rather than tourists. In their front gardens there were either women hanging out washing, teenagers mending bikes, weathered men tending plants or inquisitive pre-school children peering out from the gates in wide-eyed innocence, trying to engage Connor in conversation.

Even if Connor's Spanish had been good enough to speak to a four-year-old (which it wasn't) he still wouldn't have said anything – he was replaying the conversations of the previous night. Poor Leo. Even though his old friend had insisted on discussing Connor's problems, they inevitably paled into insignificance compared to the cancer. Or perhaps, put them into perspective.

Connor soon found himself at the back of San Antonio heading for the apartment he'd shared with six other workers during his last year on the island. He figured that maybe a trip to the past might help to untangle the future.

As he weaved through the narrow, criss-crossing streets of San An, the memories came flooding back. He'd had close friends here and had always assumed that at least a handful would stand the test of time, yet he was still in touch with only one former flatmate and they had not seen each other for nearly a year. It was not even as though they were spread all over the UK – over half were within two hours of Central London.

He reached the apartment and stood there. It hadn't changed a bit. The washing line of the house next door even looked as though the same washing was drying on it – T-shirts with tour companies and club logos hung motionless on another hot, windless day.

As he reminisced, the door of the apartment opened and two guys in their late teens came out, calling back and asking if anybody wanted anything from the supermarket. He noticed how young they appeared. He watched and listened as they walked down the road, exchanging stories of sexual bravado from the previous night. Connor turned away in the opposite direction, not fully understanding why he felt a little sad and let down. Maybe he'd had his time. The Ibiza Connor knew now belonged to the likes of Shuff and Grant. Perhaps it was a mistake coming back.

Yet Ibiza was not populated entirely by those within the 18-30 bracket. There were many ex-pats, far older than Connor, happily settled, or who spent several months of the year enjoying the island. As Connor walked along the road, he began to realize the past was best left for visiting, not for refuge.

It was like treasuring the memory of an ex-lover, then trying to get back together after a few years as the same people with the same expectations. Cute little traits turned out to be annoying habits, the beauty spot an ugly mole, and the charming changes of mind the first stages of paranoid schizophrenia. Maybe Ibiza was as confused about its future as Connor was about his own. Seemingly torn between being a clubber's mecca, a yacht owners' playground, a spiritualist haven and a Balearic Blackpool, it was not sure which path to take. The status quo was not an option; something would have to give. In Connor's case, after the conversation with Leo, it felt increasingly as though this would be Positive Solutions.

Leo had shown him that Connor had been at his happiest in Ibiza. Connor now wondered if the island was the answer. Was this now about more than simply deciding whether to go back to Positive Solutions? Was it about not going back to the UK? Could Ibiza become his home? Leo had helped him identify what it was about being in Ibiza that made him so happy previously, but what about the older Connor?

He certainly would not be happy re-living the life he'd had, once more being the young guy he'd just seen leaving his old apartment bragging about sexual conquests. No, if Connor was going to renew his relationship with Ibiza, then he was going to have to find fresh things to keep it alive. A shared history was not enough.

Then of course, there were the practical aspects. Getting back to see family and friends wouldn't be a problem. But what of work? The season was so short and most businesses were tourist orientated. He had come to the conclusion that there were essentially three options.

The first was to find a way of making a living, twelve months of the year. It would need to be a business that did not rely on the tourist euro – virtually impossible unless he started planting almond trees – or alternatively, an enterprise in which location was unimportant, linked to the internet, perhaps. However, Connor had no skills in that area, despite working in IT recruitment, and moreover, being huddled over a computer all day hardly fitted in with the notion of meeting people.

The second idea would be to work in Ibiza during the summer and elsewhere in the winter. A lot of workers and business owners on the island did this, but Connor felt the transience of this lifestyle wasn't for him.

The third and best option was to find a business so lucrative that the earnings in summer would sustain him through the winter months.

Ah yes, the winter months. Could he endure a winter on his own?

With no money to buy a business, no idea of what business to buy in any case, and no Big Adventure on the horizon, the whole notion of coming to Ibiza for some kind of greater purpose seemed, frankly, ridiculous.

Maybe he needed another pep talk from Leo.

Or maybe he should just go home.

Thoughts of home reminded Connor that he had been yearning for an English breakfast. The world always seemed a better place after sausage, egg, bacon, beans, bubble, toast and a mug of tea, which he eventually found about ten minutes from his old apartment in a place called Fatso's. Suitably empowered after eating, Connor strode out and popped into a shop to buy a British paper, hoping its contents would remind him why he was considering abandoning its shores.

Certainly, one major advantage of living in Ibiza would be not having to constantly read about reality TV wannabes or former stars in decline. He scanned the papers on offer and picked one. Then the trace of a scent he recognized wafted by: Fendi perfume. It was what Mary used to wear. He would always remember it. He glanced up to see a girl with long, wavy black hair glide out of the door and wondered if she looked as good from the front as the back. Suddenly curious, he replaced the paper he was looking at, and followed her.

When she looked over her shoulder to cross the road, Connor's tongue almost hit the floor. Unquestionably Spanish, with large feline eyes and full lips, she exuded a classically sultry appeal; her pert backside wriggled in a turquoise sarong and her dark shoulders contrasted exquisitely with her lacy white halter-neck. A tour bus drove slowly in front of him, temporarily denying him his visual feast, and when it had passed, the girl was nowhere to be seen. It was as if she had disappeared into thin air.

He looked down a few of the side roads, then gave up and went into the small Hiper Centro supermarket to get some chocolate, bread and dandruff shampoo.

The supermarket was busy: locals buying fresh meat and fish; lads from the adjacent Club 18-30 hotel buying San Miguel and boxes of Sangria. Connor walked down the toiletries aisle and noticed a suntanned and perfectly shaped leg poking out of a turquoise sarong. It was the same girl talking on her mobile. Connor was too far away to hear what she was saying, but he was entranced by the way she twirled her long dark hair between her fingers.

He studied her features more closely. Connor liked confident, smart, strong women and there was something about her that suggested she had these qualities. Connor couldn't put his finger on what this was, but the sparkle in her lively green eyes gave her face an extra dimension. Perhaps it was simply that from underneath her fringe, Connor was sure she gave him a smile. He was no different to the majority of other men in that reciprocated interest immediately makes a woman ten times more attractive.

The girl finished the phone call and carried on shopping. Connor desperately wanted to strike up a conversation but he wasn't sure if their relative linguistic skills would enable them to communicate. He'd picked up some basic Spanish during his time in Ibiza but most of the locals spoke English and during the summer simply didn't have the time or patience to indulge someone struggling with the language.

Although the super-confident Connor in his daydream would have whisked her to the champagne fridge and had her sarong off before the cork hit the floor, the Connor standing in the supermarket just gawped. He glanced down to his shopping basket where a baguette, a big bar of Dairy Crunch chocolate and some dandruff shampoo were all incriminatingly displayed. When he was sure she wasn't watching, he put the baguette back and grabbed some fresh vegetables, swapped the Dairy Crunch for an apple, and replaced the shampoo with a moisturizer.

With a basket that now said 'Healthy Gourmet Socialite' rather than 'Lonely, Flaky Chocoholic', he proceeded to the checkout, where the girl was waiting to be served with one person behind her and one in front. Just as the Spanish man in front of her was paying, the girl groaned, slapped her head, and scurried back to the fridge. When she returned, she stood behind Connor instead of returning to her place in the queue. Connor actually thought he was about to blush.

As he approached the till, he had the idea that it might impress her if she thought he spoke Spanish – distancing himself from the beered-up Brits prowling the supermarket and making lewd comments.

But it had been so long since he'd tried and his knowledge was, at best, merely restaurant Spanish. On impulse he grabbed a copy of the local paper, *Diario de Ibiza*, which was on sale by the till – she would assume he could speak Spanish without him actually having to do so. Brilliant.

The shop assistant put his things into a plastic bag for him. When she picked up the *Diario de Ibiza* she said, '*Ah, tu hablas español – esta bien. Te gusta el* Diario?'

He thought he understood her but he didn't want to risk embarrassing himself by trying to reply He shrugged his shoulders and hoped he would get out before she spoke again. No such luck.

'*Yo prefiero* Ultima Hora. *Que piensas tu?*'

The girl and the shop assistant both stared at him, waiting for an answer.

Connor quickly gathered his things and mumbled, 'Um, *gracias*,' before fleeing the supermarket, only then realizing that he had bought none of the things he originally intended.

chapter sixteen

Marina had tried to open up to Bartolo – *really* tried.

Even with the unusual bonding that the day's events had given them, Marina had found it difficult to be anything more than charming and pleasant during their date. As soon as Bartolo became tactile, she felt herself tense up; as soon as he tried to talk about anything personal, she would seek refuge in the superficial.

The restaurant Bartolo had suggested, Casa Domingo, was beautiful. It was situated just past San José, about 10 kilometres before the airport, down a dusty track that meant no passing trade would have found it. The menu was amongst the best (and most expensive) the island had to offer and its reputation ensured that even early in the season and the evening, it was reasonably busy, despite its isolated location.

Marina had not been expecting anything so grand. Indeed, she had thrown on a simple, white dress, anticipating a visit to a tapas bar or just going for a drink. She was therefore slightly embarrassed when Bartolo led her in to the rather upmarket establishment. Sensing her discomfort, Bartolo had smiled, returned to his car, then changed from his neatly pressed trousers into an old pair of jeans from the boot.

Bartolo had been nothing short of charming during the meal, most of the time speaking English but allowing her to speak Spanish and gently correcting her where necessary, as she had asked him to do.

As Marina had walked home alone along the Sunset Strip – oblivious to the admiring glances – she wondered why she had not been able to kiss Bartolo on his doorstep, or accept his invitation for a nightcap. He was good-looking, easy-going, not pushy, interesting, and they had loads in common . . .

As always, there was something that stopped her. It was illogical and she was aware of it as a problem. Deep down, she probably even knew the cause of it.

Simply being aware of the reason however, did not mean that the remedy automatically followed.

And now she was back at work and trying to solve another problem. She banished thoughts of Bartolo and forced herself to concentrate.

'Mac, you haven't checked your air again,' she said. 'There's hardly any left in that tank. And I keep telling you that you shouldn't dive on your own. It's dangerous, especially as you haven't been diving that long.'

'Cavaliers are pioneers,' he replied, and slid into the water.

At least this was an improvement on the icy, hostile stare he normally gave her. Kyle and Mac had been accompanying her on the diving school trips for the last few days. It was clear that Mac had been shown how to dive by an incompetent friend, rather than taught properly. There was a lot of pretty basic stuff that he either ignored or didn't know. Protests to Kyle fell on deaf ears but each time she tried nevertheless.

'Kyle, he really doesn't know what he's doing,' she said now. 'He definitely shouldn't be diving on his own. He's only got enough air there for less than fifteen minutes.'

'Well, seeing as he's going to be less than fifteen minutes, he obviously knows what he's doing then, doesn't he?'

'But why does he keep coming out on dives with us, then going off on his own? We're always having to wait for him.'

Kyle scratched his head with a confused expression. 'Um, I'm getting muddled.'

'About what?'

'Well, it's just that I'd been labouring under the obvious misconception,' he dropped his hand from his head and leaned in, staring straight at her, 'that you were working for me and not the other *fucking way round*!'

Marina said nothing, although she was furious. She went below deck to help some of the students take off their equipment.

When she returned just over ten minutes later, Mac was back on board and they set off. Marina kept out of everyone's way, standing with Pedro, the captain, and practising her Spanish.

About halfway back, Mac joined three public school types he had been talking to on the outward journey. This was unusual for Mac as he usually sat on his own, making everybody else feel uncomfortable.

Marina had noticed that a posh accent was about the only thing that made an impression on Mac. He had joined the Hooray Henrys almost as soon as he heard their clipped vowels. Mac's voice and choice of vocabulary was bordering on the ridiculous, using long words in the wrong context with an accent that sounded as false as Dick Van Dyke's in *Mary Poppins*. At first, the three Hoorays were polite, perhaps seeing past the paunch and cravat to his potential for violence. Marina noticed the baffled looks they gave each other and the cravat did nothing to lesson their confusion as to whether or not they were part of an elaborate prank.

When the Hoorays realized that the way he spoke owed more to aspiration than education, they were clearly amused and started baiting him, to make even more mistakes. A couple of times they almost giggled. It became like a competition between the three of them to see who could be the least subtle in their teasing.

Marina had seen what was going on and now Mac was with them again, she felt decidedly uneasy. She sensed that Mac had cottoned on to their game.

From the wheelhouse, Marina saw the ringleader say something and the other two burst out laughing. Then, just for an instant, he diverted his eyes from Mac. That was all Mac needed. He pounced, exploding into a frenzy of violence. Marina had never witnessed anything like it before. Within seconds, he had launched a punishing hook into the ringleader's jaw, flooring him.

His friend tried to drag Mac off, but was rewarded with an elbow in his nose. As he crumpled to the ground, Mac heaved him overboard. Pedro almost brought the boat to a halt; Marina dived in the water to save her client. Just before she did, she saw, to her horror, that Mac was aiming a spear gun at the third member of the group.

It was fortunate that Kyle had been on board because as one of the other paying guests helped Marina haul the semi-conscious recipient of Mac's elbow back on to the boat, Kyle and Pedro had restrained Mac and were trying to calm him down. Marina was absolutely convinced that Mac would have fired the spear gun had it not been for their intervention.

Not much was said for the rest of the journey back to land. Marina had been considering going out with Bartolo again but now she just wanted to get home, sink into bed and put this horrid day behind her.

When they docked, a police car was waiting. The ringleader of the Hoorays spoke Spanish and, despite Kyle advising him against it, had called the police. Marina watched as he remonstrated with seemingly disinterested police.

Clearly disgusted with the lack of police action in response to their complaint, the three Hoorays turned their backs and began to walk away. Before they left, Marina noticed Kyle pull the ringleader to one side. By the look on Hooray Henry's face it was clear that Kyle had not invited him round for afternoon tea.

A few minutes later, when the group of Marina's diving clients had dispersed, the police sauntered into Atlantis bar with Kyle and Mac, laughing and joking.

If she had had any doubts about Kyle's influence before, she certainly hadn't now.

chapter seventeen

The opening of Space was always perceived as the 'official' start of the club season. Kyle Goldwell had very craftily tried to steal a little of their thunder, by having the opening night of Smacker in Eden on the Thursday night before Space's Sunday opening party.

The pre-party for the night was, naturally, in Atlantis. Dex took over from the chilled out sounds of the sunset resident DJ at just gone nine-thirty. He started his set with tunes from the vocal end of the UK Garage spectrum, and put the pitch control on a minus number for the first few records, which was unusual for him.

The pre-party in Atlantis was the first of the season and as such, the venue was rammed. Within half an hour, Dex had the crowd in the palm of his hand and by ten o'clock, the atmosphere was electric.

As Connor fought his way through the dancing bodies he spotted Luc in animated conversation with Carlos, the Spanish owner of the bar he was managing. Raffles was due to open the next night and Connor guessed that their lively discussion probably had something to do with why Luc's best friend was playing for a rival and why they were both staying in an apartment owned by that rival.

What *was* clear to Connor, however, was that Shuff and Grant were selling drugs. Connor watched, as Grant took money from a freckly-faced youth while Shuff placed their part of the transaction in the youth's hand. As soon as the deal was complete, Connor stealthily eased his way over and grabbed Grant's shoulder.

'*Policia*,' he yelled.

Grant jumped, then swung round petrified.

'Bastard! You scared the shit out of me, man.'

'How's it been going?'

'Real good.' Grant noticed the slight disapproval on Connor's face. 'We had no choice. We'd never have been able to pay him back and I'd given him my passport.'

'Oh, you mug. Not that old chestnut. Just be careful, eh?'

'We will.' Grant's face relaxed into a smile. 'Kyle's even been sending some of his regulars over. Maybe we've got him wrong, you know. We should make shitloads tonight.'

'What are the pills like?'

'I dunno. I've never taken a pill before.'

'What? You're selling ecstasy and you don't take it?'

'Yeah. Shuff doesn't either.'

'Really? Dex said he saw him necking a couple of pills together the other night.'

'Believe me, Shuff wouldn't do that.'

'Don't you take any drugs at all?'

'Yeah, I like a bit of Charlie and I've been smoking weed since I was fourteen.'

'So why not E's?'

'I've seen so many people who look complete jerks on it that I've never been bothered. Mind you, now I'm in Ibiza I'm gonna take my first one at the opening of Space on Sunday.'

Luc joined them, catching the tail-end of the conversation.

'If you're going to Space I wouldn't risk selling pills in there if I were you – the security's red-hot. I can't believe you pair of idiots have got involved in selling gear for Kyle.'

'If you think he's so bad, why have you moved into the apartment with us?'

'I love the smell of stale farts and smelly socks. Apart from that it's a good location and fucking cheap. Most other workers have to share a room, sometimes with more than one. You don't know how lucky you two are, your first season as well.'

'It's not luck then, is it? We've decided to do a bit of work with Kyle so he's done us a deal on the apartment, same as he has you cos Dex is working for him.'

'Yeah but Dex . . .' Luc decided not to pursue it. 'Let me just ask you one question: How much more money do you reckon you'll make tonight from selling gear rather than tickets?'

Grant thought for a moment. 'Dunno. Loads more.'

'Exactly. And all the time you don't get caught, all the time it seems like easy money, you're going to find it hard to give up, aren't you?'

'No way. All we're going to do is make enough to pay back Kyle, enough for a flight home just in case and a bit of spending money and that's it.'

'See what I mean?' said Luc holding up his hands. 'Before we left the apartment you said you were only going to do it until you could pay Kyle back.' He swigged back the rest of his beer. 'I'm going for a piss.'

Grant looked after him sheepishly.

'He's only worried about you,' said Connor.

'We know what we're doing.'

Connor nodded and moved away, not wanting to get involved. Then, as he scanned the room he did a double-take. It was the girl from the supermarket. His eyes followed her as she walked to the bar. She seemed to know quite a few people, even English workers. He gathered himself.

Connor had never been one for 'chatting up' women. Although he'd had more than the average number of partners, he had never been able to get his head around the conventional rituals. The interminably long walk across a bar, feeling everybody's eyes burning into you, the men willing you to be rejected, or even better, humiliated – it just wasn't dignified. The fact that by the end of some nights he could barely talk and would later invariably end up with kebab fat and chilli sauce down his shirt or round his mouth, did not to Connor, seem as undignified. Or rather, he'd prefer to be perceived as an undignified drunken slob than a socially inept saddo.

For fifteen minutes, Connor tried to position himself near her. He got reasonably close a couple of times, but felt himself tighten up and unable to think of anything to say. He put it down to the potential language barrier – how could he say something funny when his Spanish was pretty much limited to 'A beer, please', 'How much is that?' and 'Is there a supermarket near here?'

Eventually, she left her friends to go to the Ladies'. As casually as he could, Connor sauntered over to a pool table near the toilets. Nobody was waiting to get on, so Connor took some change from his pocket, crouched down, and put it in the slots. He didn't push them in to release the balls but crouched there, waiting for her to return from the toilets. Just as he was getting cramp, she emerged. He rattled the table, pretending that his money was not being accepted. He caught her eye. 'Por favor . . .'

She looked over.

'Por favor,' repeated Connor, 'money, no good, no es bueno. Table broken.'

She smiled slightly. Connor pushed the money in properly and the balls clunked out. He raised his eyebrows in mock surprise.

'A-ha. Now is good.' He looked at her a bit more closely, pretending to have just recognized her. 'I saw you in the supermarket yesterday, no? In *el supermercado*?'

She walked towards him, running her finger along the edge of the pool table. She stopped when they were face to face.

'That's right. I seem to remember you buying a Spanish newspaper though. I wonder why that was because you obviously don't speak Spanish – do you like the pictures?'

'You're English,' gasped Connor, stuck for anything else to say. 'But, I thought, I thought, you were . . .'

'Spanish?' Holly rested her right elbow on her other forearm and put her finger to her mouth. 'That wouldn't be why you bought the *Diario*, would it? Not trying to impress, were we?'

'What?' Connor tried to regain his composure. 'Of course not. Don't be silly. I bought it for the, for the, um, adverts. Yeah the adverts. Looking at villas, that kind of thing.'

Holly didn't need to say anything more for Connor to realize he'd been sussed. It was time to come clean.

'All right,' he laughed, holding up his hands. 'But you can't blame me. I just didn't want you thinking I was another typical beered-up Brit on his hols.'

'Oh, so it was me you were trying to impress and not the woman behind the till?' she teased.

'Yeah. It was close though.'

'Gee thanks. So then, are you?'

'Am I what? A millionaire? Funny? Good in bed?'

'On holiday?'

'No. You?'

'I work at Smacker; it's a night that the guy who owns this place runs. My name's Holly by the way – what's yours?'

'Connor.'

They shook hands and kissed each other on the cheek.

'Where do you work, Connor?'

'I don't.'

'So why are you in Ibiza?'

Connor started setting up the balls on the pool table. 'That's a question I've been asking myself since I got here.' Holly searched his face but Connor shook his head. 'Never mind. Fancy a game?'

Holly walked to the other side of the pool table and took a cue. 'So, are you?'

Connor got ready to break. 'Am I what?'

Holly twisted her hair round her finger. 'Good in bed.'

Connor took his shot and miscued, sending the white into one of the

110

middle pockets. Holly smiled and ambled round the table, chalking her cue.

'Well, you can't be any worse than you are at pool. Two shots to me, I believe . . .'

'What are the TV cameras doing here?' asked Connor as he managed to attract the barmaid's attention.

'MTV,' replied Holly. 'They're about to interview Kyle about the opening of Smacker. They've a couple of famous DJs in too.'

Connor paid for the drinks, ceremoniously waving a ten-euro note under Holly's nose.

'I hate losing, especially when there's money on it.' Holly playfully parried the note away. 'How on earth did you win? I only had the black to pot when you still had four balls on the table.'

'Oh, I've always been good at, um, coming from behind.' Connor gave the faintest of smiles and raised his glass. 'Cheers.'

Holly looked over at the Dex. 'Who's the DJ?'

'He's Dex,' interrupted Luc, 'and I'm his mate, Luc. Actually, I'm Connor's mate too, but I doubt if he'll introduce me, because I'm—'

'So you know the DJ, Connor?' asked Holly.

'Yeah. We all came over together. We live near each other back home. Good, isn't he?'

'He's great,' replied Holly. 'I've been dying to hear some decent music since I arrived in Ibiza. I'm sick to death of banging hard house. You'll have to introduce me.'

'Sure, come on over.'

Connor led her to the small DJ booth and climbed in next to Dex. As he bent down to help Holly up, a bright light shone on them.

'Dex,' shouted Luc, 'you're on MTV.'

Dex was in the middle of a mix so looked up and gave a shy smile and a little wave to the camera. The lights were only on for a few seconds. When he finished the mix, Connor introduced him to Holly.

Dex found it very difficult to be sociable when DJing. As such, he only exchanged a couple of sentences with Holly, who stood looking slightly awkward. Connor noticed this and was about to invite her to the bar for another drink when Rory came over.

'Holly. Get out of there and up to the VIP now. Kyle's about to be interviewed by MTV and he wants his girls to be round him to give a bit of glamour. C'mon, get your skates on.'

Mac was glad to get out of the bar.

111

Kyle had wanted him in the shot when he was being interviewed. Mac was more than aware of his own menacing demeanour and of the image Kyle liked to cultivate, which was the reason Kyle had asked him, three of the best looking PRs and two of the meanest looking doormen to be around him. As soon as the filming was finished, Mac strolled down to the dive boat, checking his watch. He hoped his contact would be on time – he hated people who were not punctual.

He stopped to roll a cigarette with one hand. Despite all of the other affectations he had adopted, rolling his own cigarettes was the one legacy of prison life he had not been able to shake off. Had he been convicted of all the crimes he'd committed he would have been even more adept at it. The attempted murder charge had been reduced to GBH, mainly, he felt, because he gave such a good account of himself in the witness box and the 'victim' was almost twice his size with his own violent past that included assault with a deadly weapon. He rubbed his neck through his cravat . . .

As he sauntered down the newly built jetty, where the diving school's boat was moored, he noticed that the lights in the wheelhouse were on. His contact had obviously arrived before him. When he got closer, however, he saw that Marina was on her hands and knees, scrubbing the deck.

Mac didn't like Marina; he particularly didn't like women who were popular with men, attractive, or flirtatious. Although Mac considered her to be none of these, he could see that Kyle was keen on her. In Mac's eyes, this gave Marina power, and he could not understand or tolerate powerful women.

He jumped on to the boat, his dusty shoes spoiling the just cleaned deck, which Marina was still scrubbing.

'Hey, what do you think . . . Oh, it's you.'

Mac stared at her, inviting her to be confrontational. After the events of the previous day Marina was now even more convinced that he would have no qualms about hitting her in the same way he would a man.

Slowly and deliberately, Mac dropped his dog end on the floor and stamped it out, knowing that Marina was scared of him. Where women were concerned, he liked nothing better.

Marina dropped the scrubbing brush into the bucket of soapy water and stood up, wiping her wet hands down the old T-shirt she was wearing.

'Don't let me stop you,' said Mac. 'I'm not taking her out for another five minutes.'

'That's all right, I'd nearly finished,' replied Marina, trying to appear unfazed. 'Pedro didn't tell me the boat was going out tonight.'

Mac simply held Marina's gaze, a slight smile on his face. Inwardly, Marina shuddered, but she walked towards the stern of the boat. A bulky South American looking man in his thirties was coming down the jetty.

'Can I help you?' Marina asked politely.

The man looked beyond her to Mac, who said nothing and nodded him on board. Exasperated, Marina let out a sigh and strode back towards Atlantis.

She fancied a drink, but knew that it was the pre-party for Smacker in the bar and was sure it would be far too busy. Sure enough, there was a crowd of people outside – TV cameras even. Before heading for home, she looked back towards the sea. The boat had started up and was slowly making its way out into the darkness.

Whatever Mac was up to she did not want anything to do with it.

chapter eighteen

Connor just *knew* she was going to say she fancied him.

It was the way she said, 'There's something I want to ask you.'

Also, it was her expression as she said it. Playful, coy, flirtatious, embarrassed . . . and bloody cute. Yet it wasn't just her appearance. It was more that he didn't have to 'dumb down' when talking to her. Witticisms, playing on words, topical humour, she effortlessly understood things that would have left Gina Searle scratching her head until she touched bone.

They had so much in common too, or at least, he felt that to be the case. She hadn't said in so many words that she wanted to live in Ibiza, or that she was looking for a soulmate, but he sensed it – in as much as he could sense anything with the extremely strong pill he'd scored from Grant doing its work. Luckily it hadn't really kicked in whilst talking to her in Atlantis, so he'd been able to maintain a detached laddishness rather than a fawning 'love-the-world' soul-baring.

He strolled alone along the harbourfront towards Eden, trailing behind Luc, fully expecting some metaphysical poet to hijack his thoughts at any moment. Encouragingly, this didn't happen, indicating that he wasn't quite as twatted as he perhaps felt, which also suggested that the signals he'd picked up from Holly were real and not obfuscated with an MDMA tint.

Destiny. He always had a gut feeling that whoever the Big Adventure turned out to be would be met through a chance encounter. Could it be Holly? OK, he'd only known her for a few hours. But every magazine article he'd ever read always said 'you'll know when it happens'. Was it happening now? Or was the hollow feeling in his stomach just nerves, or the preface to an ecstasy-induced projectile vomit?

More pressingly, what should he say when she asked him? In his head, he went through the likely scenario: He'd walk into Smacker at Eden and go straight to the VIP section, where he would see Holly sitting by the bar. She would be nervously sipping a drink through a straw, anxiously glancing towards the door, waiting for him to approach. He would take his time walking over, mainly because so many people would be stopping him to say hi (obviously, predominantly other beautiful women).

After she asked him whether he fancied her, he would tease her a bit. Then, he would become serious, look her in the eye, and tell her that he'd never felt this way about someone he'd only just met. She would smile and he'd lean forward and kiss her, heralding the start of what would possibly be the Big Adventure.

Of course, before this romantic idyll could be realized, they actually had to get into Eden first.

'Look,' said the picker for Eden, a suntanned skinhead with a big silver chain round his neck, 'everybody here says that they're friends of Kyle. If your name's not on the list . . .'

'Ah,' protested Luc, determined not to give in, 'so how come you let those three girls in just now – their names weren't down?'

'Because I know them and I don't know you,' he replied, the cadence in his voice suggesting that the dialogue had come to an end.

'But our mate Dex is DJing at Atlantis. He'll be here soon.'

'I don't know him and if his name isn't down, then he won't get in either.' He beckoned over a doorman and closed his clipboard. 'Now then, if you don't go and join the back of that extremely long queue then you won't get in at all.'

Luc held his gaze, cursing under his breath, before being jostled back a little as the next group of blaggers tried their luck. He was about to turn away when an ebullient Shuff whacked him on the shoulder.

'Luc, Connor . . . hi, guys. You just got here?'

Shuff was with Grant, Rory, and a small posse of about half a dozen male and female workers, all looking rather pleased with themselves for going straight to the front of the static queue.

'Luc's been trying to get us in but our name's not on his list, so . . .' Connor shrugged.

'No worries, I'll sort it,' replied Shuff confidently.

'And how are you going to do that?' asked a slightly incredulous Luc. 'I've worked here for three years and I can't persuade him. You're even bloody American. The guy on the door's obviously new.'

Shuff pushed his way to the front. 'Hey, pal, these are with me.'

The picker looked Shuff up and down. 'So? Who are you?'

Shuff turned and called Rory. As soon as the picker saw Rory, his attitude changed.

'This lot are fine,' said Rory to the picker, waving his hand towards

Shuff, Connor and the rest of his group, while having three other conversations with clubbers trying to curry favour.

Two of the doormen immediately created a corridor to allow the party with Rory to walk through unimpeded.

'Sorry about the misunderstanding,' said the picker to Luc and Connor as they walked passed. 'We get so many people trying it on that it's hard to know who's telling the truth.'

'No problem,' said Luc magnanimously.

'Here, put these on,' he said, giving them bright red wristbands, 'they'll get you into the VIP.'

As they walked along the short passageway between the entrance and the club, Connor turned to Luc.

'Thank God we got in when we did – I can feel myself coming up even more on that pill.'

The doors swung open and the blaring, offbeat bass thud of hard house hit them. Connor stood there with his mouth open. The club was nothing like he remembered it, thus eradicating the image he'd been playing of seeing Holly sitting at the VIP bar downstairs – the bar was no longer there. Luc led them through the crowd.

'Where are we going?' asked Connor.

'Upstairs to the VIP.'

Luc smiled and pointed to a balcony, a second level that had not even existed on Connor's last visit four years before.

They edged their way upstairs and through the crowd towards another room, with yet another doorman. Once inside, an older guy saw Rory and immediately scurried over to a group of clubbers sitting on sofas around a table and shooed them away, pointing at Rory as he did so. This seemed to negate any protests.

The table was quickly tidied and Rory sat down, inviting Shuff and Grant to join him, who in turn, invited Connor and Luc. Bottles of champagne arrived. Three girls from the group who came in with Rory were also at the table. Once everyone's glasses were charged, Rory raised his glass. 'Salud.'

Luc took a sip from his glass and leaned over to the beaming Shuff. 'How come you got in with this lot so quickly?'

Before he could answer, Rory tapped him on the shoulder. 'Shuff, come out the back a sec and bring Grant with you – we need to have a chat.'

Luc watched them walk away then shook his head and turned to Connor. 'I tell you what, mate, I don't think those two young men know what they're getting themselves involved in.'

'Oh, they'll be all right,' replied Connor, scanning the room for Holly. 'For their sakes, I hope so.'

Rory knocked on the office door. Mac opened it slightly. When he saw it was Rory, Shuff and Grant, he stepped back to let them in. Kyle was sitting behind a desk.

'Looks like a good night, Kyle,' said Rory.

'Aye, right enough.' Kyle reached into a drawer and pulled out a bag of cocaine and a ceramic tile. 'Any of you fancy a line?' Grant nodded. 'Go on then, set 'em up.'

As Grant put a small mound of cocaine on to the tile, Rory winked at Kyle.

'Auld Rory here was telling me you're thinking about moving up a league. Getting scales and all that – wise move, fellas.'

'Yeah,' said Shuff, grinning.

'Well, Rory was going to explain things to us a little more fully first,' added Grant, taking a credit card from his pocket to chop the cocaine.

'I can see you're the more cautious of the two,' smiled Kyle. 'Go on then, Rory, explain what's what.'

'Sure, but shall we let the boys have their line first?'

Grant had chopped out four lines and offered a rolled up note to Mac, who shook his head. Mac took cocaine, but didn't like to do it in front of subordinates. He felt it looked weak.

The rest of the group apart from Shuff all took a line, then sat down, Shuff and Grant on an uncomfortable two-seater settee.

'Right then, you might need this,' said Rory, throwing Shuff a calculator. He opened another drawer and placed a bag of cocaine and a leather pouch on the desk.

'One ounce of cocaine and one set of electronic scales. We sell the cocaine to you for fourteen hundred euros. There are twenty-eight grams in an ounce, so what does that make the cost price of a gram?'

'Fifty euros,' said Grant, before Shuff had a chance to use the calculator. He paused. 'I don't get it. You're selling it to us for fifty so how do we make a profit?'

Kyle tapped his nose. 'Bright lad – watch this . . .'

'So let's imagine, here I am, on holiday,' continued Rory, 'and I want a gram of Charlie from you two.'

He folded a piece of paper and put it on the scales, beckoning Shuff and Grant over to have a look.

'First, put the paper on the scales to keep the Charlie off them. Then we press the on/off button to re-calibrate the scales, setting them at zero with the piece of paper on.'

He showed them the digital read out of the scales, which read 0.0.

'Oh, I see,' said Grant, with Shuff looking over his shoulder, 'it doesn't weigh the paper, just the cocaine you put on it.'

'That's right. And now for the Charlie.' Rory dipped a card into the ounce bag and pulled it out with some cocaine on its corner. He tapped it on to the paper on the scales, added a bit then took some away, until the scales read 0.5.

'Now,' said Rory, 'we have half a gram of Charlie.'

'But you said you wanted a gram,' said Grant.

'And a gram ye shall have,' laughed Kyle, passing a tube of something to Rory.

'These are New Era homeopathic hay fever tablets,' said Rory, tipping five small tablets, about twice the size of Sweetex, into the palm of his hand. 'Five of these weigh about point three of a gram. We crush them up, add them to the Charlie, mix them together and,' he looked at the digital read out as he completed the short task, 'we've got point eight of a gram.'

He transferred the white powder into a plastic bag and held it between his forefinger and thumb.

'Hey presto, a gram of Charlie.'

'But it's not a full gram,' observed Shuff.

Rory gave it to him. 'So you can tell the difference, can you?'

'But what about those other things, the hay fever tablets?' asked Grant.

'Sprinkle the "gram" on the tile and tell me if you can see them.'

Shuff sprinkled it on the tile. 'Gotcha.'

'You don't have to use hay fever tablets,' said Rory, satisfied the point had been made. 'In fact, we've only just started using them ourselves. A lot of people use glucose. Anything'll do as long as it looks like Charlie and doesn't have any adverse effect or a strong taste or smell.'

'So what it means, lads,' added Kyle, 'is that the gram you're now selling for sixty or seventy euros, has actually cost you twenty-five.'

'Still think there's more money in pills?' asked Rory.

Shuff and Grant shared a look. Kyle noticed it, so pressed on, walking round the desk and putting his arm around Shuff's shoulder.

'I like you two boys – I knew soon as I saw you that you had what it takes. The girls like you and you can obviously look after yourselves. You've got the gift of the gab, the look. Plus you fit in. Didn't I say they'd fit in, Rory?'

'Straight away, Kyle, straight away.'

'Now, I don't do this for everybody, but give it a week or so and I'm prepared to let you have an ounce at a time on bail. I'll even give you a set of scales – you can pay for them after you've sold your first lot. Have I ever done that before for anyone, Rory?'

'Never, Kyle, never.'

'And you know what, lads? You're doing the clubbers a favour. Getting a gram of Charlie where point five of it is the real McCoy is fuckin' good going in a club over here. The Moroccans, the Senegalese and a lot of them scally fuckers serving up in clubs or down the Strip cut it far more than that, and God knows what they put in it. Am I right, Rory?'

'Right as ever, Kyle, right as ever.'

'So then, boys, are you gonna join us?' He nodded at Mac, who took a champagne bottle from the fridge. 'Are we gonna open this bottle of bubbly?'

He walked back round the desk, sat back in his chair and lit a small cigar. Shuff looked at Grant. For a few moments Grant just stared at the Charlie on the table. Slowly he turned towards Shuff, his mouth turning up at the ends to hint at a smile. Shuff knew Grant well enough to know what that meant.

Shuff reached on to the table and picked up the champagne.

'Would you like me to open it for you . . . boss?'

Connor was taking in the grandeur of the club – he could not believe how much it had changed. He was trying to remember what it looked like prior to the renovations, but they had been so extensive that in the end he simply had to give up.

The strength of the pill he had taken earlier did nothing to improve his concentration in this respect. Although the music was a little too hard for Connor's liking, it still compelled him to head for the dance floor on more than one occasion. This also allowed him to try to locate Holly.

He spotted Luc coming out of the Gents' loos.

'Great bogs for doing a line in,' said Luc wiping his nose. 'Is Dex here yet?'

'I haven't seen him.'

As they walked up the stairs, two Smacker promotions girls slapped a sticker on them with 'You've Been Smacked' written on it, then whipped them playfully across the buttocks with a riding crop. Both wore masks and catsuits, one red and one white. Contained within these catsuits were undoubtedly fit bodies. For a moment, Connor reflected that he could quite happily spend the rest of his life in Eden, being assaulted by Smacker promotion girls.

Once at the top of the stairs, Connor persuaded Luc to take the long way round to the VIP. Apart from enabling him to continue looking for Holly, the pill had made him feel really horny, so jostling through the crowd allowed him some surreptitious body contact.

Connor's whole body was starting to tingle. When he had first started clubbing and taking ecstasy, all he wanted to do was dance. A great tune, or catching the eye of other clubbers sharing the experience, would be enough to bring on a rush.

Now though, sex made him rush more than anything – having it, talking about it or, as now, just thinking about it.

The beginning of the current rush was being caused by the certain knowledge that some time in the near future, he would be watching Holly grind away on top of him, her thick hair tumbling over her face, biting her full, luscious lips in ecstasy each time he plunged into her and cupped her full, suntanned breasts, gently squeezing then pulling . . .

'Ouch!'

A Smacker promotions girl in a black catsuit had struck him with the riding crop much harder than any of her colleagues.

'You've Been Smacked,' she triumphantly declared, placing yet another sticker on his chest.

'Given half a chance,' said Connor, leaning into her ear with pill-induced bravado, 'I'll return the compliment and not only smack your bum, but pull your hair at the same time.'

The girl giggled, 'Ooh, promises, promises. Maybe later, Connor. Don't forget we've got to have our little chat first.'

'Huh?'

Holly lifted her mask. 'Remember, I wanted to ask you something?'

It took a moment for Connor to register.

'Holly? What are you doing here, wearing that, that—'

'Connor! Are you saying you didn't know it was me? I had you marked down as a fast worker, but I didn't think that you came out with lines like that to any old random bird,' she teased.

'I don't, I mean, well, you know . . . ' He tried to compose himself.

'I thought you knew I worked for Smacker.'

'Yeah, but I thought you worked in the office, or organized the flyers, or . . .'

'Sorry to disappoint you, but one of the things I do is dress up in this PVC catsuit and go round whacking blokes with a riding crop.' She struck a dominatrix pose and grinned, tapped the riding crop against her thigh. 'I quite like it really. Bit of a turn-on.' Connor gulped. 'I've got a break in half an hour or so. Shall we meet up in the VIP? I'll get us some champagne and we can have our little chat.'

'Yeah, sure.' Connor's mouth was so dry he barely croaked the words out.

'By the way,' she whispered before she left, 'how did you know I like having my bum smacked and my hair pulled?'

This was going to be one of the best nights of his life. London and Positive Solutions at the moment seemed as appealing as being on a plane to Australia with Buster Searle. He'd quickly thrown another pill down his neck – he was so turned on he was going to need all of the help he could get to stop himself from coming when they went home together. Holly was going to be a brilliant shag – he just knew it. Of course, he was more than just physically attracted to her, but for now, and after seeing her with that riding crop in that catsuit . . .

There were a number of reactions Connor was considering, when Holly told him how she felt. What he wanted to do was hold her hand, look deep into her eyes, and tell her that he'd never been so instantly fascinated by anyone before. How he'd felt an immediate bond with her, and how he had this strange feeling that there was a sense of destiny about his trip to Ibiza, and she was part of that.

On the other hand, he was buzzing and she probably wasn't. She might not be as loved up and find a speech like that all a bit slushy. Being prematurely full on was not something Connor could ever have been accused of before.

Therefore, maybe a cooler response would be better? A kind of, suck it and see. Yeah, suck it. Oh, yeah.

Connor's inner voice was racing away once more. Thoughts and ideas came quicker than his head could organize. Some in and out before they could be assimilated, others flying off at tangents, maybe a dozen or so steps away from their source in no time at all. Then trying to trace them back: Which subject had led to which, then completely forgetting the original idea, question or topic.

This time though, the inner voice kept coming back to Holly. Lovely Holly.

In love with Holly?
Great song playing.
Song lyrics make more sense when you're in love.
Lyrics are like poetry.

Never liked that metaphysical stuff.
John Donne. Wanker.
William Blake was cool.
Didn't mind Wordsworth.
English 'A' level.
Miss Cooke.
Great cleavage.
Slippery tit wank.
School discos.
Getting the skeleton key then shagging Bernadette from St Philly's on the headmaster's desk.
Shagging Holly.
Holly.
Oh yeah, school.
Shakespeare.
Age cannot wither her, nor custom stale . . .
Uh-oh. Here we go. Customs.
Buster Searle. Barcelona airport. Stitches up the bum.
Bum.
Holly's. Smacking it and pulling her hair. Tonight.
Night. Nightingale.
O Nightingale, thou surely art
A creature of a fiery heart . . .
Heart. Broken.
I was taught to feel, perhaps too much, The self-sufficing power of Solitude.
Not bloody Wordsworth again.
Sounds like Wandsworth.
Wandsworth.
Wandsworth prison.
Bars.
Chains.
Chain Holly to some bars.
Fuck her brains out . . .
OK, deep breath. In, out, in, out . . .
'Oi, hurry up, mate!'
Connor opened his eyes. Fuck.

There was another bang on the door. 'Come on mate, you've been in there ages. There's a big queue out here.'

He was sitting on the toilet.

Connor pulled up his trousers and tried to calm himself. He opened the door, avoiding eye contact with those in the queue, and bustled past into the sanctuary of darkness, where he headed straight for the bar to get some water.

Ten minutes later he was back in control, aided by a quick line of cocaine and popping out of the club for a breath of fresh air. He was getting himself another water when he felt a tap on his shoulder.

'Get me a JD and coke.'

Connor turned round. 'All right, Dex, when did you get here?'

'I've been here about an hour. I've seen Shuff and Grant. I got a pill from them. Have you had any?' Connor turned his head to the light so Dex could see his pupils. Dex laughed. 'They're pretty strong, aren't they?'

'I know. I was sat on the bog rushing my tits off for ages. It took me a few moments to realize where I was. I'm trying to straighten myself out because Holly wants a chat with me.'

'Yeah, the bird you introduced me to in Atlantis. She just came and said hello to me. She asked if I'd seen you. Boy, she looks all right in that PVC gear.'

'You've seen her! Where? Whereabouts was she?'

Dex chuckled. 'In the VIP.'

Connor took a swig of water and went to head off. Dex stepped in front of him.

'Whoa there. You're a bit keen, aren't you?'

'Wouldn't you be?'

'I'd shag her.'

'Shag her? You don't just shag girls like that. You walk off into the sunset with them, have babies, get joint bank accounts . . . '

'Is that the pills talking or have you been in the sun too long?' He tapped him on the head. 'Hello? Hello . . . is Connor still in there?'

'Fuck off.'

'Well, what do you expect? It's been a long time since I heard you speak like that. Holly's above average but I've had better.'

'And in what dream was that?'

'Anyway,' continued Dex, ignoring the comment and putting his arm round Connor's shoulder in a patronizing way, 'you don't get slushy with girls like her. You gotta seem like you ain't interested.'

Connor shrugged his arm off laughing. 'They'll be playing the "Birdie Song" in here before I need advice from you about women.' He finished his drink. 'Right, you mug, I'm off to meet my destiny.'

chapter nineteen

'Go on, have another drink,' urged Shuff, filling the champagne glass for the umpteenth time.

'Ooh no, I shouldn't,' hiccupped a tipsy Raquel. 'Oh, go on then. Just one more.'

Shuff winked at Raquel's daughter Patsie and filled the glass. He was sure Raquel was lying about being forty-two although, with Patsie being twenty-five, it was at least mathematically possible.

Raquel's deep tan accentuated the smoker's lines round her mouth. The frown lines on her forehead would have given Jeffrey Archer a run for his money. Shuff was sure she was pushing fifty, or had already pushed it. The best thing about her was that the large mammary gene had successfully transferred from mother to daughter and in Patsie's case, nature was holding out against nurture. Their size and apparent disregard for Isaac Newton's theories were responsible for countless debates over their authenticity that she never got to hear.

When Shuff had first spotted Patsie and made a move on her, Raquel had overcome her abject fear of house music and leapt to the dance floor like an over-protective lioness. To avoid being the centre of further derisory attention, Shuff quickly invited them both to the VIP bar in Eden. He was perceptive enough to pay the mother most attention while being secretly tactile and exchanging loaded glances with a more than receptive Patsie. It was obvious that Patsie had endured this type of situation with her mother on more than one occasion. She seemed grateful that Shuff knew how to play things.

'Come on then, Raquel,' said Shuff, putting his arm round her shoulder, 'Let's get you two home.'

He part carried, part guided Raquel to the nearby cab rank but the short walk in the fresh air had a mildly sobering effect on Raquel, which seemed to remind her that she had to protect Patsie's virtue.

'Yer a genhelman, but y'aint fu'in m'daughter, so piss off home,' slurred Raquel as she fell into the back of the cab.

'Which hotel you in?' whispered Shuff to Patsie.

'The Regale, round the bay.'

'Room?'

Patsie cast a furtive glance back to her mother, mumbling incoherently to herself on the back seat. Patsie gave Shuff a short, passionate kiss. Shuff felt himself start to grow hard instantly.

'Five two two.' She looked at her mother. 'She'll be dead to the world as soon as we get back.'

Less than fifteen minutes later, having borrowed Luc's car and managed to sneak by the hotel porter, Shuff was outside room 522 of the Regale, gently tapping on the door.

'Who's a clever boy then?' giggled Patsie, slowly opening it.

As he entered the room, a low rumbling noise came from behind him. A snoring Raquel was unconscious and half-undressed on the settee, surrounded by Pringles.

'Don't worry about her,' smiled Patsie, 'I doubt if she'll come to for a good few hours. Go and wait in there,' she instructed, pointing to one of the two doors that led off the compact lounge-diner. 'Put some music on but keep the volume down.'

Shuff looked at the long brown legs tapering out of the khaki green T-shirt, which rode higher at the front than the back as a result of her superb breasts demanding the majority of the material.

She gave a little giggle as she closed the bathroom door behind her.

It was obvious that they were not there to discuss the weather so Shuff took his clothes off and sat in the armchair, his considerable erection standing proud. A quickie was not even in Shuff's thoughts, but he was aware that he promised to return the car to Luc within a couple of hours, so didn't want to waste time with unnecessary small talk – he would rather have left there and then. Also, he got the impression that Patsie wanted to take control and he thought that sitting there with a hard-on might throw her. He was wrong.

The Patsie that edged round the door a few minutes later was a total transformation from the relatively quiet girl who had sat in the VIP at Eden.

The white G-string and top she was wearing were clearly not designed for the beach. She looked at Shuff's erection, licking her now glossy lips.

'I see you like my outfit then.' She edged towards him, her stilettos slowly clip-clopping on the tiled floor. She was fully made up with her hair down.

She turned round just out of arm's reach and bent over. Looking back at him, with the ends of her dirty blonde shoulder-length hair in her mouth, she ran her fingertips up the back of her thighs, then back down again, each time getting closer to the mound contained within her tiny white G-string.

Holding his gaze, she turned round and wiggling to the seductive music, squeezed together her magnificent breasts.

'I always keep these under wraps when I'm out with mum. She gets upset if she's not centre of attention. Do you like them?'

Shuff was drooling too much to speak, so could only nod. Patsie giggled and unhooked her top to release them, letting the sequinned and tasselled bra fall to the floor. Her breasts remained firm and motionless.

'They've gotta be . . .'

Patsie shook her head. 'No, honey, they're all mine.'

She ran her fingers down their curve, licking the tips of her fingers and gently circling her nipples, then passed them over Shuff's mouth, telling him not to touch. Shuff let his hot breath flow over, allowing his tongue the briefest and lightest of flicks. Patsie pulled back with a slight shudder.

She took the dark blue belt from a silk, Japanese kimono hung on the back of the door then walked behind Shuff, running her tongue along his neck to his ear, then whispered, 'Keep still.'

He thought she was going to tie him up, but instead she rested her breasts on his shoulders, held her arm out then lightly ran the silk belt up his thigh, then his chest. She let the belt dance around the tip of his bursting cock and walked round so that she was facing him.

She pulled the belt through her hand then deftly made a noose, which she slipped around Shuff's erection and tightened. Shuff let out a groan.

She put the other end in her mouth so both hands were free to expertly remove her G-string. Now naked and holding the other end of the silk belt tied round Shuff's rigid member, Patsie sat on the corner of the bed, less than a metre away. She spread her legs wide apart and started playing with herself. She tied two small knots in her end of the belt, causing Shuff's erection to be pulled slightly towards her each time. She started to put the knotted end of the silk sash inside herself.

'Come closer,' she whispered.

Whether the moan Patsie let out after a few minutes of self-gratification as she tugged the knotted belt hard from inside her, signified a real orgasm, Shuff couldn't tell and frankly, couldn't care less.

She lay back panting, then started running the other end of the belt over her trimmed mound. She sat up and slowly pulled the belt towards her, moving back on the bed as she did so. Eventually she pulled it hard

– Shuff needed no further encouraging – there was no doubt in his mind that this was going to be a memorable night.

A very, very memorable night.

Connor took a circuitous route round Eden to meet Holly. He was, in truth, a little nervous.

In the short time since Holly had said there was something she wanted to tell him, Connor had been through the conversation they were about to have hundreds of times. This made it difficult to behave naturally – as, of course, did the pills, cocaine and alcohol.

In the VIP, Holly waved and ushered away the person on the stool next to her by the bar.

She was no longer wearing the mask. Her black catsuit was unzipped slightly with her heavy breasts begging for the zip to be opened just that little bit further.

She leaned forward and patted the empty stool, causing the catsuit to strain even more. Connor eagerly, although now somewhat apprehensively, obeyed. She passed him a bottle of Heineken.

'Kyle wouldn't let me have any champagne unless I sat with him, so I got you this. I've been here ages, where did you get to?'

'Oh, er, just bumped into a few people.'

The coke and spliff he'd taken had put an edge on his buzz. It had made him self-conscious and over-analytical. He knew it would pass, but the temporary trough in his high could certainly have been better timed. Mirrors surrounded one of the columns opposite where he was sitting. He caught a glimpse of himself, and was not entirely happy with how he looked. What does she see in me?

Humility is only doubt,

And does the sun and—

'Like I said,' Holly began, 'there's something I want to ask you.'

Connor nervously swigged his beer.

She took a deep breath. 'God, this is harder than I thought.'

Connor felt a wave of excitement, snatching at his runaway pill-induced stream of consciousness, superseding the snippets of poetry popping into his head, replacing the rehearsed responses to the coming question. When she said she fancied him, Connor knew that acting cool was no longer an option.

He'd just grab her and give her a bloody good snog.

'OK,' said Holly, taking a gulp of her drink. 'It's like this. When I first came out here, I was seeing this bloke. I don't know why, but for some reason, he obviously thought I wasn't that smart. He was dealing gear and getting himself into all sorts of trouble. He just went home but I decided to stay. Apart from my flatmate I didn't really know anyone here, just some of his scally friends . . .'

I travelled among unknown men
In lands beyond the sea . . .

'. . . so, I'm kind of on my own . . .'

I wandered lonely as a cloud . . .

'. . . and to be honest, I'm not really one for going out loads. A lot of the time I'm happy just to stay in on the settee with a good book or watching videos . . .'

For oft, when on my couch I lie
In vacant or in pensive mood . . .

'But I'm still young, I'm in Ibiza and, well, you know . . .'

God, thought Connor. I wasn't imagining it at all. She is, she really is about to say she fancies me.

He moved to the edge of his barstool, ready to kiss her.

Licence my roving hands, and let them go
Before, behind, between, above, below . . .

'I wouldn't normally be this forward,' she continued, 'but I was wondering . . .'

She paused.

'Wondering what?' asked Connor, trying to control his enthusiasm.

'I was . . . Oh God! This is so difficult.'

'Just say it.' Connor smiled and took hold of her hands.

'OK, OK.' Holly squeezed his hands and swivelled round slightly so she was face on. 'What I want to ask you . . .'

'Yes?'

'. . . is . . .'

'Yes?'

She paused. 'Does Dex have a girlfriend and do you think he fancies me?'

'Huh?'

'He seems really nice. Please tell me he hasn't got a girlfriend.'

I was angry with my friend,
I told my wrath . . .

Connor sat there, numbly holding her hands while she searched his face for an answer. His stomach felt like it was going in so many different directions that Dyson could have patented it as a new spin dryer. He felt physically sick. What should he say?

The self-centred part of him wanted to say, Yes, he's got a girlfriend back home, he's fucking around over here, he's a really nice bloke but far too shallow for someone as smart as you. Plus he just wants to shag you, whereas for me, you're the first girl that's flicked my switch like this in nearly a decade and up until a few seconds ago, I thought you were my destiny.

On the other hand, Dex was one of his oldest friends. Yes, they'd grown apart, had different interests and views, but there was still that special bond between them that only growing up together brings.

To deny him the opportunity to be with someone as gorgeous as Holly by slagging him off would be the work of a vain, arrogant, egotistical, jealous, callous, selfish bastard.

It was a close thing.

Connor gathered himself as best he could.

'Holly, so far as I'm aware, I haven't seen Dex bump into things, so I can only assume that he has twenty-twenty vision and anyone who isn't blind has *got* to fancy you.'

Holly squeezed his hand and smiled.

'And so far as having a girlfriend is concerned . . .' This was the hard bit. 'No, he hasn't. The coast is clear.'

Holly let out a little squeal of delight and clapped her hands.

Connor felt drained. 'I need a line.'

Like an army defeated

The snow hath retreated.

'Can I ask you a really big favour, Connor?'

What now? he thought. Could she be about to offer a consolation prize; something to make him feel better? A quick shag perhaps, to be sure Dex will think she's up to scratch? Or maybe a request to pull out Dex's toenails one by one saying she loves me, she loves me not?

'Yeah, go on, what do you want me to do?'

'I'm too embarrassed to tell Dex myself. Would you mind telling him for me?'

Connor couldn't help letting out a long groan. He could already imagine Dex's smug face.

'Oh, go on, please,' implored Holly.

Connor sighed. 'All right.' Over her shoulder he noticed Dex coming into the VIP. 'Here he comes now.'

'Oh God,' yelped Holly, jumping off the stool. 'I've got to go. I'll die of embarrassment otherwise. See you in a bit.' She looked at Connor fondly. 'Thanks, Connor.' She kissed him lightly on the lips.

It wasn't the kind of kiss Connor had been bracing himself for all evening. It wasn't a kiss that said 'I fancy you'. It wasn't a kiss that heralded the start of the Big Adventure. It was just a kiss that one friend gives to another to say thank you.

And that was all Connor was – a friend.

Dex bounded up. 'I'm on a fucking wicked buzz.'

'Yeah? Well I think it's about to get better.'

'Why's that?'

Connor started the 'Birdie Song' dance.

'*Doodoo-doodoo-doodoo-doo, doodoo-doodoo-doodoo-doo . . .*'

The sex had been absolutely fantastic. Patsie had even unearthed some love balls; two small plastic balls with ying and yang symbols on them and joined with a piece of string. When these were still inside her, Shuff had shoved his cock in and gone hell for leather.

And that was where it had all gone horribly wrong.

Patsie tossed her hair back and glared at Shuff.

'What were you thinking of?'

Shuff shrugged. 'I figured you might like it.'

'Yeah? And I figure *you* might like coming to the medical centre to help me get these love balls out.'

'*What*? You must be joking.'

It was clear from the look on her face and the absence of one hand that she was not. He stood there bemused and in truth, slightly amused. He was confident that they would plop out – they would have to. There was no way he could handle the total embarrassment of having to take her to the Galeno medical centre in the heart of the West End of San Antonio.

'Yeaaghhh!' Patsie yelled.

'Got them?'

'No, I haven't bloody got them. They're stuck solid. You have a try.'

Shuff looked at her helplessly. 'Do you want to lie on the bed?'

'No, it's better if gravity lends a hand. I'll put one leg on a chair.'

Tentatively he started probing around. He remembered having early teen discussions about how gynaecologists did their job without constantly having an erection. Now he understood. There was nothing even remotely sexual about what he was doing. In fact, he found himself pulling the same kind of face he would if cleaning drains.

He could feel the balls, but the string between them had got knotted up, so couldn't be used to pull. Equally, it was impossible to get a grip on the balls themselves – particularly as they were covered in the lubricant Patsie had been using to assist their exit.

They stared at each other, Patsie hoping Shuff would come up with a solution, Shuff racking his brain for a way of getting out of taking her to the medical centre.

'They're stuck, aren't they?' Patsie confirmed what they both knew.

Shuff stood in silence for a moment. He wanted to leave her. He *really* wanted to leave her. But he couldn't. He only had a vague idea where the medical centre actually was. There was probably an emergency number somewhere for her rep, but how on earth would that conversation go?

'OK, OK. Get something on and I'll take you. I'll get the car – it's down the street.'

Patsie looked at him suspiciously. 'Don't you dare leave me.'

Five minutes later, as he waited in Luc's car, Shuff's foot was twitching over the accelerator pedal. Oh, how he wanted to put the car in gear and drive off. But he didn't.

Patsie came out of the hotel and carefully got in. Shuff was relieved to see that she had removed her make-up and put on a T-shirt, jogging bottoms and a pair of trainers.

'I half-expected you to be gone,' she mumbled, her voice bordering on sounding grateful.

'The thought never crossed my mind.'

The hotel drive, which led down to the main road, was about 50 metres long, and had several speed restrictors – not the traditional humps found in the UK that eighty per cent of drivers don't change speed for, but two savage metal mounds, made unmissable by the bright yellow bands painted across them.

As he drove over the first pair, he heard a clicking noise come from the engine.

'What was that?'

Patsie didn't reply. Clearly she was more concerned with what he had done to fuck her up, than what he had done to fuck up Luc's car.

He drove over the next set and the car made the same noise.

'There it is again,' said Shuff.

Over the next ones, the clicking noise seemed to be even louder. Shuff started to become perplexed as he considered the prospect of having to abandon the car, take Patsie to the medical centre in a cab, then make his way back to Eden and explain to Luc that he'd knackered his beloved Mondeo.

'I wonder if it's something to do with the suspension,' he said, more thinking aloud than anything else. 'It seems to be coming from the front wheel on your side.'

As they approached the final pair just before the main road, Shuff leaned towards Patsie's side of the car to listen more closely. Sure enough, he heard the same click. Immediately, he realized what it was.

Slowly, he sat back up and looked at Patsie, trying not to smile.

'Why didn't you tell me?' he asked.

Sulkily, she crossed her legs and put her hands on her lap, then turned to him.

'Because, Motor Mechanic of the year, I was embarrassed, all right? Now will you just take me to this bloody medical centre, or are you going to take *me* to a garage instead?'

Shuff couldn't look her in the face. 'Sorry, it just didn't sound like two plastic balls banging together . . .'

chapter twenty

Connor walked down the hill in the West End doing his best to avoid the PRs outside Mega Music trying to cajole him into taking tickets for the various club nights on offer. Head down, he strode past Simple and Play 2, avoiding eye contact with the props for the same reason.

He had not been on the island long enough for his face to be recognized by the PRs and props as a worker or as someone who was there for the summer, so he was fed the same lines and treated in the same way as every other holidaymaker. He knew that they were only doing their jobs but it still niggled him. The San An lifestyle suddenly seemed very shallow.

He remembered the first time he had turned into the neon bustle of the West End, the fizzing undertone of excitement and barely contained anticipation of sexual adventure. Now though, looking at the same bars, with the same type of people going through the same rituals, all he sensed was the dull and hackneyed aura of glossy repetition, a sow's ear made into a tacky silk purse so weighed down with the superficiality of attraction on the outside that it left little room for content within.

Connor had not been able to stay in Eden after telling Dex about Holly. Although he put on a brave face and tried to make light of the situation, the rejection made him feel ill. He drifted to the West End solely because the other option – returning to an empty house and waiting for a giggling Dex and Holly to come home together – was so unpalatable.

He needed company, more specifically, female company. The West End had, after all, been his successful stomping ground during his first summer on the island. One of the bars he had most success in had been Gorm's Garage, so he made that his first port of call.

Sure enough, there were plenty of girls in there, even though many of them suffered from the British Lycra malaise. When he had worked in San Antonio years before, Connor often wondered if there were certain parts of the UK where mirrors were unavailable. It was the only explanation he could think of as to why girls who were clearly several stone overweight insisted on squeezing themselves into Lycra dresses, skirts or tops that were far too small, resulting in pasty flesh squeezing out of their attire like dough through a baker's fingers. It wasn't that he was fattist – it simply puzzled him.

However, it wasn't only the more corpulent female customers that Connor had trouble approaching. Even girls whom he would have more than happily bedded during his previous Ibiza stints, for some reason no longer seemed quite so appealing. Sensing perhaps that it was just a change of immediate location that was required, Connor went into two other popular bars, Koppas and Capones. But in these too, he felt exactly the same. Lots of attractive, up-for-it girls, dancing round and giving plenty of eye contact, yet he had no urge to talk to them.

He therefore headed to a bar at the back of town, a venue that had changed its name so many times it was now known by everybody simply as 'the bar at the back of town'. It was popular with workers on a night off, had a relaxed atmosphere, good music, few tourists and, as Connor walked in and was pleased to note, a bloody fit barmaid.

Half an hour later, most of which had been spent chatting to Dianne (the fit barmaid) Connor was feeling a lot happier about things. However, there was something troubling him and he wasn't entirely sure what.

Watching Dianne wiggle up the bar a few minutes later, it finally hit him.

He didn't want to sleep with her.

Actually, that wasn't strictly true. He *did* want to sleep with her, just not necessarily straight away and it certainly wasn't his main priority.

The realization – and for Connor, it was momentous – was that he was now mainly interested in approaching girls he felt might be the Big Adventure. For most of his post-pubescent life the opposite had been true. Even girls that made it past the hurried 'see you around' or into his mobile's phone book, were girls he knew he was marking time with, who were fulfilling the role of 'girlfriend' in function only.

That was why the West End of San Antonio had suddenly felt so superficial – it was predominantly frequented by people on the hunt for casual and transient relationships and his agenda had now mutated into something entirely different.

It dawned on him that he had gradually become less forward and predatory towards women. It was as if he now wanted them to have qualities that matched his own (albeit just discovered), girls who were not interested in one-night stands, who looked deeper than a fashion-able haircut.

It was, in truth, part of Holly's appeal and the reason he was now so disappointed. Yes, she was gorgeous, but she'd seemed to have a depth of character, an intelligence, even soulmate potential. But it turned out she'd simply been after no-strings fun with a good-looking DJ. However, in a strange way Connor felt vindicated. He was going to carry on pursuing this alien path. He had to. If he was going to attract the kind of girl he wanted, then he couldn't waste any more months or years on pointless relationships like Gina Searle. She happened to come along at the right time. She was just the wrong girl. Now, if he'd met Mary a year ago rather than seven . . .

Still, that wasn't to say that he had to enter every relationship as though it was going to be his last, simply that the girl had to have certain qualities. Take Dianne the barmaid, for example.

She certainly seemed different to the average West End girl. Light make-up, a student of law, well spoken and a good conversationalist. Every time she wasn't serving, she would return to Connor to resume their lively chat. Even if it didn't go anywhere, it reassured him there were other women out there with a bit of depth who weren't about to sleep with every scally in Ibiza.

The bar started to get busier so Dianne was able to spend less time talking to him. An old Ibiza stalwart called Dutch Alex, who hired out boats for a living, walked in with a gorgeous girl on his arm. Connor hadn't seen Dutch Alex for over four years so was happy to join them for a drink. Speaking to Dutch Alex's girlfriend, further reassured him that there were plenty of women out there who could be the Big Adventure – he'd just not been looking properly.

'Seems nice enough,' said Connor to Dutch Alex, as she walked to the Ladies' to 'powder her nose'.

'Yeah, she's not bad,' he agreed, in near perfect English. 'What about you – any girl in your sights?'

'No one in particular at the moment but I'm sure there will be. That barmaid's fit.'

'Which one?'

'Her.' He nodded towards Dianne. ' She seems really sweet. I might ask her out, take her to dinner, something like that.'

Dutch Alex chuckled. 'I'd save your money. Just hang about in the bar at the end of the night.'

'What do you mean?'

' "San An Dianne" she's known as. Total slapper. I can name at least half a dozen blokes who have fucked her and we're not exactly that far into the season, are we?'

Connor groaned. 'You've got to be joking. Don't tell me that. Jeez, what's going on? There's got be a few nice girls left. At least you've found one.'

'What?' Dutch Alex threw his head back and laughed. 'If I didn't come out with at least two g's in my pocket she'd be with someone else.'

'Fuck off; you're winding me up. She seems lovely.'

'She is – she also loves cocaine and doesn't care who gives it to her. It's only the second time I've been out with her. Doubt I will again to be honest. She'll end up settling down with someone – just not me. I'd never be able to trust her.'

'Great! Just as I'm resolving to change my ways, you're starting to make me feel like *no* girl can be trusted.'

'Mmm. That'd be about right.'

'What?'

'Oh, come on, Connor. You've worked out here, you know what it's like – that's the problem. People like you and me, we're nearly always the "other man". We see girls do things that most other guys are clueless about. How can we trust them? We just have to accept things as they are. All that true love stuff – it's bullshit.'

'No, I'm not having that.' Connor shook his head. 'I'll never get that cynical.'

'That's because you already are, even if you don't see it.'

Connor downed his drink. 'Here,' he said, giving Alex twenty euros, 'do me a favour, mate, and sort out my bill with that – I need to get some fresh air.'

He walked into the warm night and round the outskirts of the West End towards the main promenade. Dutch Alex did have a point. The thought had often crossed Connor's mind that he had grown too cynical, or that his expectations for a future partner were too great. Yet at heart, despite his debauched and fairly depraved past, he was still a hopeless romantic. He still hoped for the thunderbolt, the chance encounter, but if Dutch Alex was to be believed, then Connor's own lightning rod had about as much conductivity as a rubber ball.

Feeling quite depressed, Connor sought solace in food, stopping at one of the restaurants along the front. As he sat and finished off his burger, there was a commotion at another table. A female diner was getting flustered because she didn't have any money. She was early twenties, quite attractive, but wasn't wearing any make-up and was dressed in a sweatshirt and jogging bottoms, so obviously hadn't been out in the West End – good start.

'Look, I'm sorry,' she protested, 'but I honestly forgot I didn't have any money. You wouldn't believe what a crap night I've had.'

'*José, Policia*,' instructed the waiter to his colleague.

'No, please. I swear I'll pay you tomorrow. Please don't call the police. All I want to do is go home . . .' She started sobbing.

Connor walked over. 'Are you all right?'

She looked up. She was actually even more attractive than he'd thought.

'I've just had something to eat and I haven't got any money. I genuinely forgot I'd left my purse at the hotel. Now they want to call the police.'

'It's OK, I'll sort it.' Connor took some money out of his pocket and paid the bill. 'Where are you staying?'

'Round the bay.'

'Come on. I live on the way. We'll get a taxi and when I get out I'll pay the driver to take you on if you want.'

'You don't have to . . .' She wiped her eyes. 'Thanks.'

In the taxi the conversation between them flowed easily, mainly about Ibiza rather than each other. They pulled up at his apartment and he asked the driver how much more it was to the girl's hotel, then paid him.

'Here,' said the girl, taking Connor's mobile from him, 'let me give you my name and number – shit, I don't even know your name.'

'Connor.'

'Thanks, Connor.' She punched hers in. 'Mine's on your phone. I tell you what. Rather than paying you back, maybe I could take you out for dinner? I promise I scrub up well.'

Connor smiled. 'I'd like that.'

She kissed him on the lips, which quickly and unexpectedly turned into something more passionate. The taxi driver tried to ignore them but after a minute or so, started tutting.

'Listen, Connor, I'd come in or invite you back to my hotel, but I'm here with my mum.'

'That's OK. It gives me something to look forward to.'

She gave him another quick kiss and he got out of the car. OK, she was prepared to sleep with him on the first night, but that didn't necessarily mean she couldn't be the Big Adventure. After all, they had met in rather strange circumstances.

Connor watched the taxi disappear over the brow of the hill then looked at the name on the phone.

In the cab Patsie smiled to herself. What a night! The sex with Shuff had been fantastic but she could have done without the love balls getting stuck. The consultation at the medical centre had been downright embarrassing, especially when that bastard disappeared. Then, to have ordered that meal and not have any money to pay for it – thank God for that guy.

He seemed really nice too. Connor. She would have definitely gone into his apartment had it not been for the fact that she was hurting so much from earlier. Hopefully, she could stall taking him to dinner for a couple of days to give it time to heal . . .

chapter twenty-one

'I'll chop out another line then, shall I?' suggested Buster Searle.

Rik Searle nodded, aiming the remote at Gina's TV.

'Not another bloody MTV in Ibiza programme,' moaned Blue. Brazen's main doorman had been invited to Gina's flat by the Searles for a post-club wind down and cocaine session along with two other bouncers. No one spoke. He felt edgy. 'Good gear, innit?'

He didn't get a reply. Cocaine paranoia had caused conversation to virtually cease apart from talking about the drug itself – its effect, origin and quality. Subsequently, the awkward silences became more notice-able. To alleviate this, more lines were chopped. Eventually, at least one member of the group was constantly hunched over a table with a credit card or razor blade.

'Looks like the Charlie's almost finished,' said Buster, hoovering up the largest line. He looked round at the disappointed faces. 'So it's just as well,' he reached under the settee, 'that we've got this.'

He pulled out the still sealed kilo bought from Mac. The three bouncers' faces lit up immediately.

'Fuck me,' they said in unison.

'Don't open it yet,' instructed Rik, reaching over the back of the chair for his jacket. He took a wrap from his pocket. 'Here, there's still a bit left in this. Do the honours.'

Buster started chopping again. Then the doorbell rang. Rik and Buster looked at each other and grinned.

'Better do another two,' suggested Rik, looking at his watch.

'Who for?' asked Blue.

'We've laid on a bit of a surprise. A special treat for the boys. Get the door, bruv.'

Buster left the room and returned moments later with two girls, dressed and made up entirely inappropriately for a Sunday morning.

'This is Lena,' announced Buster, introducing a girl with short brown hair, 'and this,' he said putting his arm round the other, a blonde, 'is Pippa.'

'All right, girls? Fancy a line?'

'Love one,' replied Lena as she took off her jacket before adding, 'can we sort out the money up front?'

'Fuck me, give us a chance,' protested Buster, 'you've only just got here.'

'Sorry, but you know the rules.'

Rik pulled out a wad of twenty-pound notes. 'There you go. I think you'll find there's enough there to give the boys a bit of a show first.'

Lena counted it and smiled. 'Right then – where's that line?'

Buster passed her a long silver tube. In a swift sweep she sniffed the cocaine then passed the tube to Pippa, who did exactly the same.

'I take it you two have done that before?' laughed Buster as he retrieved the tube.

'Where do you want us?' asked Pippa, brushing her nostril with her thumb.

'Over there'll be all right,' replied Rik, pointing towards a clear area in front of the stereo.

There was music on MTV so Rik turned the sound up. The girls were soon gyrating, lowering themselves down on their haunches, then lightly brushing their fingertips along their thighs as they wriggled back up – no mean feat given the four-inch stilettos they were both wearing. For the first few minutes they ran their hands over their own bodies, then seductively did it to each other. Their tongues entwined, an exaggerated caricature of a French kiss. Lena slipped the lacy bra-straps from Pippa's shoulders, her recently implanted 36DDs standing proud as the bra fell to the floor. Lena looked saucily at the boys and flicked Pippa's nipples with her tongue. She stopped for a moment.

'Got any more of that Charlie to spare, Buster? Promise it'll be worth it.'

Buster almost fell over the table to pass what was left.

'Here – and we've got loads more,' he said, pulling the kilo from underneath the coffee table. Rik frowned and kicked him. The two girls raised their eyebrows.

Lena took some cocaine from the wrap then, lifting Pippa's left breast, sprinkled it over her aureole and nipple. She licked all round the area and sniffed it, finally sucking the nipple to make sure none was left. Giggling, Pippa immediately returned the compliment.

The girls removed each other's clothes with practised seduction. Lena sprinkled more cocaine on to her finger and put it under Pippa's nose for her to sniff. Pippa snorted it, tossed her head back, then gently kissed Lena before lying on the floor. They were both totally naked, apart from their heels.

Lena took a small rock from the wrap then knelt between Pippa's open legs. She gently glided the cocaine around Pippa's clitoris, the moist warmth causing the white rock to quickly dissolve. Lena ran her fingertips over her gums, then reached into the wrap and put a line for herself on her own fingernail.

Pippa sat up, amused by her transfixed audience.

'So, have you given us all this money just to do a show?'

'Fuck no!' exclaimed Rik.

In a rather ungainly manner, the guys removed their clothes. They were so bulky that there wasn't enough room for them all to do so at the same time so inevitably, several items got knocked off the coffee table.

'Move over there, you clumsy fucks,' yelled Rik, pointing to a clear area by the door to the kitchen. Even though it was Rik who had knocked most of the things off the table the others didn't argue.

Once naked, the boys resumed their seats and the girls walked over. Lena opened a condom and put it in her mouth.

'What you using one of them for?' asked Buster, with a certain amount of indignation.

'Yoo-oh-I-owent-goo,' Lena took the condom out of her mouth so she could speak properly, 'you know I don't do oral unprotected.'

'Yes, you do! You sucked me off without a condom last time!'

'Yeah, but you gave me another fifty quid.' Buster shrugged his shoulders and reached for his trousers. The others followed suit. 'And,' continued Lena, 'the rest of you can put your money away, cos we'll only do oral sex without a condom for regulars.'

'Anyway,' interjected Pippa, as Lena took another fifty pounds from Rik and Buster, 'it would probably help if at least one of you had a hard-on first.'

'Tell you what,' said Lena, chopping out the last two lines from the wrap, 'give us a sec and we'll be over to see what we can do to help.'

As the girls snorted the lines, the lads surreptitiously stroked or tugged at their privates, carefully avoiding looking at each others'.

The girls walked into the middle of the circle.

'My, oh my,' teased Pippa. 'What's wrong, guys? Don't we turn you on enough?'

'Course you do,' replied Buster, 'but we've given you that other fifty – got to get our money's worth, in't we?'

Lena sidled up to Buster and knelt between his legs. Pippa moved

141

towards Rik, took hold of his manhood, then bent over and put him in her mouth. The other three had now abandoned discretion and were tugging furiously to get erections.

Five minutes later, the girls both stopped performing oral sex on the brothers and looked around the room. The other three had given up and were sitting with their arms crossed and a resigned look on their faces.

'Oh dear,' sighed Lena. 'Looks like it's catching.'

'*Fuck!*' yelled Rik, thumping the arm of the chair in a final vent of frustration. 'This never happens to me.'

'Nor me,' said Buster. The others mumbled the same and shook their heads. 'Must be the Charlie.'

'Well, if it is, then having a bit more isn't going to make any difference, is it?' said Lena. 'Why don't you crack open that big bag you've got under the table and we'll go into the kitchen, chop out a few lines and fix us all a drink? Then we'll see how you all feel when we come back.'

'I've got a better idea,' said Buster. '*You* go and sort the drinks out and I'll stick a small pile on this mirror tile for you to take while you're doing it – fucked if I'm letting you anywhere near this bag.'

Once the two girls were alone in the kitchen they burst into fits of laughter.

'Five men,' said Lena, 'and not a hard-on between them.'

'At least it was easy money compared to what we were expecting. And we got extra out of them . . . suckers. And,' continued Pippa, as she chopped out seven parallel lines, 'guess who the biggest two of these are for?' She smiled and handed the silver tube to Lena.

Lena bent over and took a huge snort. Immediately, she started coughing and tried to empty the contents of her nostril.

'What the fuck . . . ?'

'Oh God,' spluttered Lena. 'It's not cocaine.'

'What is it?' asked Pippa anxiously, grabbing Lena's shoulders. 'Those bastards haven't given us ketamine, have they?'

'No, no,' said Lena regaining her composure. 'I don't know what it is.' She rubbed some into her gums. 'Ugh! I think it's glucose.'

Rik heard the commotion and came into the kitchen. 'What's going on?'

'Are you on a wind-up?' asked Lena. 'What's with giving us glucose?'

'You *what*?'

'Go on – try it,' said Pippa.

Rik scooped some of the powder on to his finger and transferred it to his tongue. As soon as the taste was absorbed his face changed; first bewilderment, then rage.

'Aaaaaggghhhh!' Rik knocked the tile from Pippa's hand, sending it smashing to the floor. Still naked, the others came running from the living room. Buster got there first.

'What the fuck's up?'

Rik was unable to speak and barged past everyone making straight for the kilo bag. He plunged his hand deep into it.

'Rik, what on earth are you doing?' asked Buster running after him.

Rik's hand was covered in white powder. He took a long lick from his palm. 'It fucking is! It fucking is! Cunts!'

'It is what, bruv? What the fuck is going on?'

'Out! All of you . . . out, *now*!'

Everyone knew better than to ask questions. They quickly put their clothes back on and headed for the door.

Rik paced up and down the room cursing, while Buster stood there trying to make sense of it all.

'I – I don't get it,' said Buster, scratching his head. 'I mean, it was still sealed when I took it from the car in Barcelona. Vacuum packed.'

'They *must* have known,' insisted Rik.

'But how? Connor had no way of getting in touch with Dex or Luc. I could tell by the look on their faces that they were genuinely shocked to see us in Barcelona.'

'He could have found the gear in the video and changed it over before they left.'

'Yeah, he could,' agreed Buster, 'but why would he then put glucose in the video?'

'He must've known we'd be round to pick it up.'

'No, I don't think he did. When I went to Connor's that first time he looked like he didn't have a clue. He's got more sense than to stitch us up. Anyway, that still doesn't explain why he'd let his mates take a video recorder to Ibiza with a kilo of glucose in it – what's the point of that?'

'Fuck knows, but he's got to be involved somehow.' They looked at each other in silence. 'Fuck it,' said Rik, 'I'm going for a piss.'

He stormed out the room. Buster sat down on the settee and vacantly watched the TV. A music video came to an end and a bubbly female MTV VJ leapt on screen.

'Here I am for the start of another mega season in the dance capital of the world, the legendary white island, Ibiza. All through the summer, MTV are going to be out here bringing you the latest, greatest tunes, the best parties and

the top DJs. Tonight, I'm at Atlantis, a new bar, which is hosting the pre-party for Smacker, the first club night of the summer . . .'

The commentary continued over shots of the inside of the club. Amongst these was a quick shot of Dex Djing . . . and walking past him was Connor.

'Fuck me, talk of the devil,' yelled Buster. 'Rik, get in here. Connor and that Dex are . . . oh my God.'

Buster's bottom jaw dropped as the next image came on screen. It was of the small VIP area. On one of the tables sat a blonde girl, Kyle Goldwell, the presenter . . . and Mac.

'What's the matter?' came Rik's voice, along with the sound of a toilet flushing. He walked into the room still doing his trousers up.

'. . . but now I'm pleased to be sitting next to Atlantis owner and Smacker promoter, Kyle Goldwell . . .'

'Look, it's Jock!'

'What?'

'Look . . . look at the screen. Standing next to the promoter they're about to interview.'

At first, it was a close-up of Kyle. As the camera pulled away, Mac could be clearly seen next to him.

'Fuck me, it *is* him . . . the Jock!' exclaimed Rik. 'What the fuck's he doing in . . .'

Rik's voice trailed off as he realized the implications. For once, Buster was one step ahead.

'Ibiza, Jock, Connor, Dex . . . I mean, I'm not Hercule Poirot, but something doesn't smell right.'

'They've got to be in this together,' concluded Rik. 'Fuck knows how, but we've been tucked up.' His face fixed in a scowl. 'I think it's about time we took a holiday, don't you?'

part three

open season

chapter twenty-two

The Thursday night at Smacker had continued well into Friday. Nobody had slept much since then but despite this, everybody dragged themselves out of bed on the Sunday.

It was, after all, the opening of Space.

Although this in itself would normally have been enough to put a smile on Connor's face, there was another reason he surfaced with a spring in his step. Holly hadn't slept with Dex . . . yet.

After Smacker, Dex and Holly had stayed with everyone for a kind of after party in the adjoining Garden of Eden, then left together to spend a day on the beach. Dex had come home alone on Friday night, but teased Connor that he was going out for a meal with her the next night and was sure he was going to 'do the business'. It irked Connor that his friend was talking so casually about her. How could anyone look at Holly in that way?

On Saturday, not long after Dex had left to meet Holly for the meal, Connor went to bed, but found it impossible to sleep. Every time he heard a car pull up outside he'd stir, then listen to see who it was, fearing the worst.

At about four-thirty on Sunday morning his heart sank. Two car doors closing, a few seconds' silence, then the car driving away – a taxi. A girl giggling, then two sets of footsteps coming up the stairs. He asked himself why he'd chosen the room next to Dex? It would be too much for Connor to bear, hearing Holly moan in the throws of ecstasy and the mental image of a grinning Dex grinding away on top of her.

But the footsteps had carried on passed Dex's room and on to Shuff's. Good old, womanizing Shuff. Connor breathed a sigh of relief and chuckled to himself as he remembered Shuff's story about the girl with the love balls. Connor was sure Shuff had made up the bit about the speed bumps although he had definitely believed that Shuff ran out of the medical centre as soon as he had passed her on to the charge of the doctor.

And thankfully, Shuff had pulled again. Content it was not Dex and Holly, Connor had drifted into sleep.

A persistent knocking on the front door woke him. Initially he tried to ignore it, but his room was the closest to the apartment's entrance so, cursing, and with a sheet wrapped round him, he trundled down the passage to see who it was. His mood changed instantly when he saw Holly standing there – he'd fully expected to get up in the morning and be green with jealousy as she emerged from Dex's room.

'Morning,' she sang, as she breezed past.

'Good morning.' He looked at his watch. Eleven fifty-five. 'Well, *just* morning. How was your meal?'

'Fine. I told, sorry, *asked*, Dex if it would be all right to get changed round here for Space. I figured I'd get more bathroom time competing with five lads rather than another girl.'

So they hadn't spent the night together. Dex had obviously come in later and was asleep in his bedroom. Alone. Connor's heart lifted.

'I thought you said your flatmate wasn't into clubbing?'

Holly put her bag down and raised her eyebrows. 'Impressive.'

'What is?'

'The fact that you paid attention to what I was saying when we first spoke to each other. Not a lot of blokes do that.'

'Oh, sorry. Don't hold it against me – I *was* looking at your tits too, honest.'

Holly laughed. 'She isn't coming to Space – she's going somewhere else. Right then, won't be a sec.' She walked into Dex's room and Connor heard them chatting.

When she returned, Connor and Holly spent nearly half an hour of relaxed conversation, swapping anecdotes, teasing each other, and having a laugh. He couldn't help flirting with her but was careful not to overstep the mark. Like it or not, she was his mate's new girlfriend.

Luc was the next one to get up, so Holly headed for the bathroom before it was in demand. Forty-five minutes later, after she had been in and out of the living room five times to get opinions on which state of undress suited her best, she finally emerged in a little red PVC number to the applause of Connor, Luc, and the just-up Grant. The sight of her made Connor gulp. She was so damn sexy that it made it hard for him to put on a brave face.

As she paraded up and down the living room, Shuff used the distraction to try and sneak out of his room the 45-year-old Wigan barmaid he'd pulled the previous night outside The Ship in San An.

However, he wasn't quite sneaky enough. Howls of derision were aimed at him once she was out of earshot . . . well, probably out of earshot.

'You're all jealous!' he retorted.

'What, of her?' laughed Luc.

· 'OK, she wasn't the best looking I've ever had. You would have loved the girl on Thursday night though.'

'The one with the love balls?' asked Connor.

'Yeah. Man, it was fucking hilarious. She was absolute filth too. It was a bit of a mean thing to do, leaving her in the medical centre like that. I wouldn't have minded a second go at her either.'

'Have you got her number? I'll ring her,' said Luc, half joking.

'Yeah, there you go,' said Shuff playing along and throwing his phone to him. 'Her name's Patsie.'

Connor felt as though he'd been kicked in the stomach. His immediate reaction was to confirm if it was the same Patsie, the 'lovely girl' he'd given a lift to, who was meant to be taking him out to dinner the following evening. He'd gone on about it so much he knew he'd get slated so instead he got Luc to pass the phone over. Sure enough, when he compared them, the numbers were one and the same.

Maybe Dutch Alex had been right after all. Holly, Patsie, Dianne – maybe there was no Big Adventure. Maybe the only choice was to carry on à la Shuff or to accept a Gina Searle. With a week left to make one of the biggest decisions of his life, the scales suddenly tipped back towards Positive Solutions. Was he mad considering giving up twelve thousand pounds, a Merc and such a potentially lucrative job just to stay in Ibiza? Perhaps the island had called him in order to mock him, to remind him that he'd had his time. Maybe the reason was simply to confirm to him that his real destiny was to accept working somewhere like Positive Solutions, to purge him of any lurking idealistic notion of living somewhere else, doing something he enjoyed or even being with the Big Adventure.

Thankfully, with the opening of Space and hyped up friends around him, it was something he would not be able to dwell on for too long. If he had been unsure about getting completely twatted on pills before, then there was absolutely no doubt in his mind that he was going to now.

By three in the afternoon, Dex and Shuff were up and everybody was more or less ready. There was a mood of excitement and anticipation in the air.

'This is the day I've been looking forward to since I got here,' said Holly, checking her lipstick for the umpteenth time in the mirror.

'Us too,' said Shuff. 'We saw something about it on a documentary back in the US. It seems crazy having a full-on club during the day – especially when the weather's in the nineties.'

'That's what makes it so good,' said Holly, puckering her lips then putting a tissue between them. 'Trust me, you'll love it, and even more so when you've got one of these.'

She held up what looked like a credit card, but on closer inspection, was laminated with a recent portrait picture of herself.

'What's that?' asked Shuff.

'It's a Space pass – gets you in free.'

'How much is it otherwise?'

'Probably about forty or fifty euros.'

'Fuck that. I'll give Kyle a ring. He's given us a mobile.'

Connor and Luc shared a look, then glanced at Grant. He was happily ironing his shirt, oblivious to what was going on. Without conferring, Connor and Luc decided not to make an issue of it. They had spoken the night before and agreed they were not Shuff and Grant's keepers and that while they would obviously look out for them, it was best not to get involved.

Everybody was waiting for Dex, who could be heard singing along to the tape that was playing. Holly went in to his room to usher him along. Connor felt uncomfortable every time the singing stopped. That was another reason for returning to the UK – Dex and Holly being together could really fuck his head up.

Even if Dex stopped seeing Holly, then Connor knew he probably wouldn't ask her out, especially if it was her who ended it, or if Dex really liked her, or if they simply were together for more than a few weeks.

If the boot were on the other foot, Connor knew how he'd feel if one of his best mates started seeing a girl who had dumped him, or he'd really liked. It was an unwritten code. The only way it could be broached would be if one man's casual fling was the other's Big Adventure, but somehow, Connor couldn't see Holly ever being anybody's casual fling. No, like it or not, Holly was off the list.

Despite this, Connor couldn't help yelling out when Dex's singing stopped again.

'Oi, are you two lovebirds ready?'

'Nearly. Dex is just deciding what shirt to wear.'

In the main room, Grant had started to pace impatiently, taking off his glasses and cleaning them every few seconds.

'Are you all right, Grant?' asked Connor.

'Yeah. Come on. Let's just get there, eh?'

'All ready to go?' asked Holly, walking back into the living room.

Grant continued pacing. Connor and Shuff looked at each other.

'Grant – have you dropped a pill?'

'Yeah. I said I was going to do my first one today, didn't I?'

'It's not like drinking, you plonker,' said Connor. 'You don't have a few before you go out, you wait until you get to the club or just before.'

'I know all that. I just fancied getting one down my neck now. If I am gonna freak out I'd rather do it in front of you lot than in a club.'

Dex walked in, splashing on some aftershave. 'Oh well, what we waiting for then? Space, here we come.'

Holly was walking just ahead of the group, so Luc nudged Dex.

'Well,' he whispered, 'did you shag it?'

Connor winced at the reference. His mood improved instantly when Dex shook his head.

'Nah, man. She didn't want to come back here and said her flat looked like a bomb had gone off.'

'Shame,' said Luc and Connor almost simultaneously, although only one of them actually meant it.

'Definitely up for it though,' added Dex.

Luc hadn't realized that there would be six people in the car. Holly had a motor scooter with her but wasn't going to take it; the San An to Ibiza road was notoriously dangerous for two-wheel transport, even when their drivers were sober or drug free. Holly planned to be neither of these within a very short period of time.

Shuff and Grant had quite a lot of ecstasy and cocaine on them, so they all agreed that six in a car would be too risky, as there were nearly always police outside Space or on the main road. As it was gear from Kyle, Shuff rang Rory to ask for a lift, and was lucky enough to catch him as he was just about to leave. Rory told him he had room for one in his jeep, so they arranged a rendezvous at the petrol station just outside San An. The petrol station was only a five-minute drive through some back roads, so Luc was happy to let Shuff and Grant share the front seat for this part of the journey.

When they got to the petrol station, they only had to wait a few minutes more before Rory turned up driving a Renegade Jeep with three girl passengers. Shuff jumped into the jeep, telling Grant he'd see him there and would leave his name on the door.

Luc pulled out of the garage and on to the main San Antonio to Ibiza road. Dex passed one of his mix tapes to Grant to put on, then threw a

151

lazy arm round Holly. She leaned towards him and her thigh moved away from where it had been resting against Connor's. He felt a pang at being denied the body contact.

When they got over the brow of the hill at C'an Tomas, Luc put his foot down, filling the car with a refreshing breeze, while the occupants turned towards the windows to cool their glazed faces.

Unkempt orchards stippled with bare trees and irregularly shaped terracotta fields swept along either side of the road as it climbed towards San Rafael. Further back, nurtured in the hills, the *casas payesas* or old farmhouses turned luxury villas, glimmered in smug and self-contained solitude with their own generators, swimming pools and stony tracks, which kept away all but the owners of four-wheel drives. Coaches from the airport passed in the opposite direction, bringing their pasty and hopeful cargo into the former fishing port turned package holiday paradise, San An.

Every so often the Mondeo would overtake a moped, travelling at less than thirty miles per hour and whining like a bronchial mosquito as it struggled up the gradient. Invariably, a weathered local wearing an off-white or blue (possibly off-grey) shirt with obligatory sweat marks and Ducados cigarette dangling from his lips, would be happily meandering up the narrow hard shoulder, oblivious to both other traffic and the last thirty years of progress.

From San Rafael the road turned slightly to the right and started to descend. Just after they passed the San Rafael petrol station, they were greeted with the panorama of Ibiza Town. The cloudless sky seamlessly joined a thin blue strip of sea pointing towards Dalt Vila, the old town and its four square tower and city wall bulwarks, built to protect the island, centuries before, from pirate invasions.

To the left of the road they passed the massive club Privilege, then a few hundred metres further on the right, Amnesia, the club that in 1987 and 1988 hosted the eclectic sets of the likes of Alfredo, which had such an impact on the young Danny Ramplings, Nicky Holloways *et al* that they brought the idea back to the UK and kickstarted the ecstasy generation.

The newest recruit to this generation, Grant, had been very quiet for at least five minutes. Connor assumed it was just apprehension at the effect of his first ever pill. Some people would need to talk constantly and ask loads of questions, whereas others went into themselves for a while, trying to pick up on the slightest change in their physiological or psychological state.

'Are you all right, mate?'

'Yeah, man, I think so.'

'How do you feel?'

'A bit tingly . . .'

'Good.'

'And a bit sick.'

'Not so good. Anyone got a plastic bag?'

'I didn't say I was going to be sick. I just feel a bit queasy.'

'Grant, trust me. E's make some people projectile vomit and the last thing I want is for Luc to make you clean his windscreen before we go into Space.' He rummaged round the floor, found a plastic bag and passed it forward. 'There you go, mate – hold this.'

Grant took the bag. 'All right. But I don't see what all the fuss is about. I really don't think I'm gonna actually be – oh shit.'

With that he retched and catapulted the contents of his stomach into the bag. Everyone else in the car either laughed or screwed up their faces. He heaved again then slumped back in the seat panting.

'Oh fuck me – where did that come from?' He gulped some air into his lungs. 'Jesus, I've never known anything like that before.'

'You finished?' asked Dex, who was sitting directly behind him.

'Yeah, I think so.'

'Well, throw that bag out of the window – it stinks, man.'

'Dex, don't be so rude,' chastised Holly.

Grant flicked the bag out of the window, but his index finger got entangled in the handle. The oncoming wind forced the bag back against the car and most of its contents through the open back window and over Dex.

'Uh . . . uh . . . oh . . . yuk . . . watch it . . . fucking hell, Grant, you idiot!' yelled Dex.

Holly shrieked and moved away from him, almost landing on Connor's lap. Grant untangled the bag and it flew into the distance.

'You clumsy, dirty fucking bastard. Look, man – I'm covered in puke, you fool.'

'The proverbial ill wind,' Connor said.

Luc pulled over to the hard shoulder. He turned round, saw the state of Dex and was soon helpless with laughter, along with everyone else.

'What you all laughing at?' spat Dex indignantly. 'It ain't funny. If the man can't handle his drugs he shouldn't take them.'

'Oh, leave it out,' said Connor. 'It's just one of those things.'

'It's all right for you. You're not the one sitting here with his top ruined. Now what am I going to do?'

'I've got a T-shirt in the back,' said Luc.

'Open the boot so I can get it then, man.'

Dex got out and went round to the back of the Mondeo.

'Are you all right, Grant?' asked Luc as he pulled the boot release lever.

'Yeah, fine. I don't actually feel sick as such. It just seemed to come from nowhere.'

'So how do you feel now?'

'I've got a bit of a hollow feeling in my stomach and everything seems sharper, plus I've got a bit of a prickly feeling in my scalp. Other than that, pretty damn good.'

'What the fuck is this?' shouted Dex from the back of the car. He reappeared wearing a T-shirt with 'I Luv Ibiza' on it in sparkly letters. Holly put her hand to her mouth to contain her giggles, but Connor, Luc and Grant were less restrained. Dex was not amused. 'Are you trying to take the piss or what?'

'Course not,' lied Luc. 'I found it in the apartment. I was going to use it to clean the back window. It looks all right.'

'If you think I'm wearing this to the opening of Space—'

'I don't see you've got any choice. I'm not driving all the way back to the apartment, especially as Grant here's just taken his first pill.'

'Give me the keys when we get to Space and I'll drive back.'

'No way,' replied Luc, now on a wind-up. 'I might need the car and you know how untrustworthy you are. If it bothers you that much, just take your shirt off. You spend enough time in the gym.'

'You wanker.'

'Cheers. Right, shall we go?'

Dex soon calmed down, especially when, five minutes later, they turned off the main road towards Playa d'en Bossa, where a large sign on the main road pointed them towards Space. Passing the Bungee Rocket, they followed the road round the 90-degree turn and were on the home straight to the club. Small groups of clubbers were all heading in the same direction; walking, on bikes, or in cars.

The Space car park was full, although Kyle Goldwell's Range Rover had still managed to find a space right by the entrance. Luc was ready to find somewhere else to park when an old Citroën pulled out just in front of him, so he drove in to the gap before the scouting Vitara in front had even noticed it.

As they got out of the car a jet roared overhead, almost drowning the thumping music from the club's terrace. As was the custom, a loud cheer rang out.

Approaching Space, they all experienced the same tingle of anticipation, their steps quickening without them even realizing. The location of the club and its bizarre juxtaposition to a family resort, meant that bewildered couples towing even more bewildered offspring in the Sunday afternoon sunshine would stare at the colourful array of sunglass-clad clubbers as they preened themselves before being swallowed up by the mouth of the beast that was Space. Which group was more amused was open to debate.

There was a large queue outside. Holly caught the eye of the guy on the door and was ushered forward. They exchanged a few pleasantries, he looked down a list then nodded and waved them all forward. They were in.

Even without drugs, it was almost impossible not to experience a natural high on the atmosphere, with smiling faces, raised arms, beautiful people and upbeat music. Despite this, a chemical high was on all of their minds.

Shuff was standing near the bar with Kyle, Rory and a large group of people. As soon as he spotted them he ran over.

'This is fucking unbelievable. Come over to Kyle and the boys.'

'Maybe later,' said Luc. 'Stay here with us for a while.'

'Right then,' said Connor, a big grin on his face. 'We'd better sort out some pills.'

'Grant's got them,' replied Shuff.

'Fuck the pills, man,' moaned Dex, tugging at his shirt, 'I can't stay here wearing this thing.'

'You can't seriously want to go home.'

'Oh, don't go,' pleaded Holly. 'You'll be at least an hour and I've just taken a pill, look . . . ' With that she snatched a pill from her pocket and popped it in her mouth, grabbing the closest drink to her from the nearby table to wash it down. 'See. You can't leave me on my own. If it bothers you, Luc's right – just take your shirt off. There's plenty of other blokes who have.'

Dex tutted and took his T-shirt off. They all wolf-whistled. He turned to Grant.

'And you can shut up, you Yankee twat. If it wasn't for you puking over me I wouldn't be in this mess.' Dex half-smiled. 'Anyway, how you doing on that pill?'

'Yeah, I feel good. I don't think I've had one of those rush things yet though. Mind you, I only took half a Playboy and Connor was saying they're not all that strong. Maybe I should do the other half. What do you reckon?'

'Go for it,' said Holly grinning. 'Just make sure you're nowhere near me when you start coming up.'

Dex put a protective arm around her, and kissed her on the cheek.

Mac nudged Kyle Goldwell as he saw Dex kissing Holly.

'I know, I know. I've a pair of fuckin' eyes, but.'

'She looks nice in that red PVC, doesn't she, Kyle? Marvellous breasts.'

'Aye, I don't need you to tell me that . . . fuckin' wind-up merchant.'

'I thought you were going to ask her out? Wasn't that the only reason you gave her the job?'

'It wasn't part of the fucking contract, but there's no' much point in having her around otherwise, that's for sure. I swear I know her from somewhere though.'

'That's funny, because I thought I did too.'

Suddenly, Kyle clicked his fingers. 'Terry. That fucking idiot you did the Tarantino on. The one who turned up at the villa in Benimussa with the girl in the car.'

A look of recognition spread across Mac's face. 'Of course. She was the girlfriend. She didn't see us though, did she?'

'No. He reckons he told her we were Spanish.'

'So what are you going to do?'

'I was going to sack her anyway. Whore.'

Mac looked over towards Dex, Holly and the group around them. He never liked to get involved in Kyle's personal affairs. He preferred to keep their involvement strictly on a business level, sorting out bad debtors or scallies who were taking liberties paying their bills. The Balearic lifestyle was one to which Mac had quickly grown accustomed. Previously, the money had not been as good as they were used to making back in the UK, but Ibiza had captivated him in its own inexplicable way. He was a big fish in a small pond. His age, appearance, reputation, and contacts ensured that those that mattered quickly knew who he was. His relationship with Kyle was good too, although it was still nice to wind him up sometimes.

'She's obviously moved on to black guys,' he taunted. 'She was probably worried you wouldn't measure up, Kyle.'

'Aye, well if the wee bitch carries on like that, the only measuring that she'll be doing will be for her coffin – and one for that black bastard with her.'

'You can't sack him,' said Rory.

Kyle fixed Rory a steely gaze. '*Can't*? It's my bar. I'll do what I fuckin' like.'

'No, I mean, yes, I mean, I know you can,' stumbled Rory nervously. 'What I mean is, you've got that big garage night tomorrow. You've got his name on all of the flyers. It might fuck the night up, that's all I meant.'

Kyle grabbed Rory round the back of the head, pulling him forward, so they were nose to nose.

'That's what I like about you, Rory – always on the ball.' He kissed him roughly on the forehead and let him go. 'Right. We'll get tomorrow night out the way and kick him in to touch after that.' His face broke into an unpleasant smile. 'Still, you can tell that trollop in the red PVC she's no' got a job any more. I've got to sack *someone*.'

chapter twenty-three

In the UK Marina had only ever had two serious boyfriends. After splitting up with the last of these, she had travelled, following the well-trodden backpacking path, and spending two years in Queenstown, New Zealand, eighteen months diving in Egypt, and finally ending up in Ibiza, where she'd lived for almost a year. She had had a few short-term flings, but for the last few years, she had concentrated on her diving and had rejected all advances – of which there were plenty.

This had not been a problem; after a while, she didn't even miss sex. She thought she would yearn for the closeness and intimacy, but the memory of what it was like had become distant enough not to be a problem either.

Now though, something was stirring. In part, it was down to Bartolo's easy-going, pressure-free approach. Yet it was more likely the timing – the forgotten X factor that makes or breaks so many relationships – which was playing its part.

She had literally and metaphorically immersed herself in diving to the extent that it substituted other parts of her life that may have been missing. Now though, routine was taking over, and while she still loved diving, it was not so all-consuming.

This meant that she was beginning to examine those other parts of her life, realizing that the carefree existence she was leading would have to either come to an end, or develop into something more tangible. This kind of inward self-analysis was new to Marina and she wasn't sure what was causing it.

Maybe it was because she had spent so long away from home, or possibly being midway between the twenty-five and thirty milestones was having an effect. Perhaps it was the enduring memory of the fisherman's widow that had jarred her into thinking about her own mortality and life's direction.

While she was not broody, she also found herself considering motherhood. For Marina, there had always been a subconscious mental image of being part of a future happy family. Although this reassured her that her abstinence from men was only temporary, the Marina in her mental image was quite close in age to the Marina of now.

Learning to dive had been great, but in working for Kyle and Mac, the fun was fast disappearing.

Fun. That was what she needed.

And that was why, at the last minute, she had decided to accept Bartolo's invitation to the opening of Space.

'No, Dex, leave it!' yelled Holly.

She grabbed his arm, as Luc and Connor stepped in front of him. Clubbers in their close proximity backed away slightly, or decided to find a different part of Space to dance in.

'Who the fuck does he think he is?' Dex struggled to get free.

'He doesn't have to *think* he's anyone. He just *is*,' said Luc, holding him more firmly. 'What's the point in barging your way through all these people? He's right over the other side of the club – you can't even see him from here. It's not worth it.'

'But the man can't treat people like that.'

'Don't worry about it,' replied Holly calmly. 'I'm fine. It was a shitty job anyway.'

'Yeah, but this ain't just about the job. The man came on to you. Kyle's dissing me because he knows you're my woman.'

'Hold on,' said Holly, her tone changing, 'I'm *nobody's* woman.'

'You know what I mean,' snapped Dex. Holly raised her eyebrows. 'All right then – he knows that I'm *with* you. Is that better?'

'Much.'

'And it's because I'm *with* you that he's given you the sack.'

'It's got nothing to do with you. It's just that I'm seeing someone other than him. The fact it's you is probably irrelevant. It just means I'm not available any more.'

Shuff and Grant returned from the bar. 'What's up?' asked Shuff.

'That so-called friend of yours Kyle Goldwell has just sacked Holly because he fancies her,' replied Connor, 'and now Dex is trying to do his knight in shining armour bit.'

'What, he wants to have a go at Kyle?' Grant asked with an air of incredulity and the beginning of a laugh in his voice.

Dex noticed the inflection and turned his attention to Grant. 'What's that supposed to mean? Are you "one of his boys" then, eh? Do you wanna carry on his dirty work?' Dex pushed him. 'Come on then, tough man.'

Shuff stepped in front of Grant and shoved Dex. 'Hey, back off.'

Luc and Connor intervened.

'Leave it out, guys, for fuck's sake,' said Luc. 'We're supposed to be friends. This hasn't got anything to do with Shuff and Grant. They work for Kyle the same as Holly used to, and the same as you *do*, Dex.'

Dex realized his anger was misplaced. 'Sorry,' he mumbled to Grant.

'Don't worry about it,' replied Shuff, answering for his friend.

'I'm going for a walk,' said Holly. 'There's far too much testosterone in the air for my liking.'

After Holly left, Luc turned to Shuff and Grant.

'Listen guys, you're both grown men so can make your own decisions, but you're a long way from home and I'm telling you now, Kyle Goldwell is bad news.'

'We know he is if you get on the wrong side of him,' replied Shuff, 'but he's all right with us.'

'Now he is,' said Dex, 'but he was all right with Holly too until she started seeing me. You suit his purpose at the moment but don't expect any loyalty from him.'

'What else are we gonna do?' asked Shuff. 'I don't wanna go back across the Pond, that's for sure.'

'I could do with a couple of props at Raffles.'

'And how much are you going to pay us? Thirty, forty euros a night?'

Luc nodded, knowing what was coming next.

'I can earn that selling one gram. Why should I stand outside a bar all night, being told to fuck off by pissed punters?'

'Because at the end of the season you'll still be outside the bar and not in a hospital bed or a prison, like you will be if you carry on working for Kyle Goldwell.'

'Thanks all the same, Luc, but I'd rather take my chance with Kyle. If it starts to go sour I can always pack it in.'

'It'll be too late then,' added Dex.

'So what about you, Dex?' asked Grant, pushing his specs up the bridge of his nose. 'Now he's sacked Holly, are you gonna stop working for him too?' Dex's face remained set. 'No, I didn't think you would,' declared Grant, with an air of triumph. 'At the end of the day, we all need to work out here and when it comes to making a living, sometimes principles just take a back seat.'

'It's not about principles,' sighed Luc. 'It's about you two not being taken for a ride and ending up in the shit.'

'Look,' said Shuff, putting his arms round Luc and Dex. 'You're right – we *are* adults and big enough to make our own decisions. We've seen what Kyle can be like and I'm really sorry about Holly. But at the end of the day, I figure we know the score. So long as we keep selling gear for him, don't fleece him over, or tread on his toes in any other way, then we'll be fine. He's already told us our faces fit and if that changes . . . well, that's our problem.'

'Come on,' said Connor, 'let's talk about it another time. This is the opening of Space and I'm losing the buzz.'

'I couldn't agree more,' said Shuff, reaching into his pocket and pulling out some pills. He handed one to each of the group. 'Have these on me.'

Luc had a full beer, which they all used to wash back the pills. Not one of them even considered the irony of the fact that the pills had come from Kyle.

The queue for Space was massive.

Marina had never been before and was amazed at how busy it was. To the right were the paying customers or those with pre-paid tickets, snaking round the barriers five across for about 30 metres. Although excitable, they were positively sedate compared to the madness that was the guest list scrum.

At least a hundred people were all trying to attract the attention of the two guys on the door, who calmly listened to the genuine *invitados*, letting them through, or the blaggers, turning them away or re-directing them to the paying queue.

Marina looked at it aghast.

'Don't worry,' said Bartolo, sensing her concern, 'it is the opening and this is one of the busier times. We will have no problem getting in. The security man up there knows me.'

He looked towards a large Spanish guy with slicked back hair and a stern face, wearing a blue shirt. Handcuffs and a baton dangled from his belt.

It took less than a minute for Bartolo to catch his eye, and the stern face quickly broke into an eager-to-please grin, as he strode down the stairs to usher Bartolo and Marina through. The security guard towered over most of the jostling clubbers and his long arm and deep, authoritative voice ensured the guest list hopefuls soon parted. He shook hands with Bartolo, was introduced to Marina and made sure they were well into the club before he resumed his post.

They made their way through the crowd to the nearest bar. Bartolo got them both a drink then told her he had to quickly see a friend, promising to be back straight away. Marina felt uncomfortable as she scanned the alien environment. She was therefore pleased when a rather surprised looking Holly spotted her and came bounding over.

'You're the last person I expected to see here,' said Holly. 'What's brought this on?'

Marina paused, then smiled slightly. 'I came with Bartolo. That police diver I mentioned.'

'Go girl!'

'He's just had to go and see some friends. What about you? Did you come with that DJ?' Holly nodded. 'And . . . ?'

'Yeah, he's nice. Cute.'

Marina didn't think Holly sounded particularly enthusiastic.

'Just cute?'

Holly sighed. 'Oh, I don't know. When I first saw him and spoke to him, there were things about him I really liked. He's nice-looking, fit bod, a wicked DJ, self-assured – I probably filled in all the other things I hoped he'd be for myself. Y'know, like when you look at yourself in the mirror and aren't really happy with how you look so squint your eyes?'

'Did you come here with him?'

'Yeah. That's the other thing. I just got the sack so he's taking it on himself to—'

'You've been sacked! Why?'

'Because Kyle Goldwell's an arsehole. It's all right, I'm not that bothered. I'm not going to do a job I don't like, but . . . oh, it's this place. I'd just love to live here.'

Marina smiled. 'It happens to the best of us. I don't care what anyone says. I'm sure there are more beautiful places in the world, I'm sure there are easier places to live and I know there's loads to moan about, but it's just got something about it, hasn't it?'

Holly nodded. Marina turned the conversation back to Dex.

'What about this DJ's mate, the one you first met – I thought you said that you got on really well with him?'

'I did – too well. That was the problem. He just seemed to have all the right lines, it all came a bit too easily to him. In a way he reminded me of Terry. Actually, no, that's not fair. He's a lot smarter and more genuine than Terry, but . . . once bitten and all that. The more I speak to him though, the nicer he seems.'

'Sounds to me like you might have got off with the wrong friend,' observed Marina.

'No, I don't think so. I don't think he's the settling down type.'

Marina raised her eyebrows. 'That's the first time I've heard you say anything about settling down. What are their names? You've never said.'

'Haven't I? Well, that must prove a point. The DJ—'

Bartolo reappeared then, interrupting Holly. He turned to her. 'I am sorry, but do you mind if I have a word with Marina?'

Holly watched as Bartolo explained something to Marina. Whatever it was, it was serious enough for Marina to clasp her hand to her mouth. The conversation was brief, ending with Bartolo giving her a hug and kissing her on each cheek, before sprinting for the exit.

Marina returned shaking her head.

'What's up?' asked Holly.

'One of Bartolo's best friends – another policeman – he was off duty and has just had a really serious motorbike accident. Bartolo's dashed up to the hospital.'

'Oh God, no! Will he be OK?'

'Bartolo doesn't know. He didn't think it would be right for me to go with him, so I told him I'd be fine, seeing as you're here.' Marina took a deep breath and looked around her. 'Although to be honest, it's been so long since I've been anywhere like this, I'm not so sure.'

Holly put an arm round her. 'Don't worry, I'll help you rediscover those clubbing feet.'

'*If* you see me dance, I think it's more likely you'll be calling them *clubbed* feet.'

'Come on, let's get a drink down you and I'll take you over to meet the boys.'

Holly battled her way to the top bar on the Space terrace, towards the corner furthest away from the DJ stand. It was more or less where she had left Dex and the crew and even from the middle of the club, she could periodically see Shuff's distinctive white-blond hair in the crowd.

When they got there though, the only one with Shuff was Grant.

'Shuff, Grant, I want you to meet a very good friend of mine, my flatmate Marina.'

'Hi,' said Shuff.

'Where's the rest of them?' asked Holly, with a tone of concern. 'They're not causing trouble with Kyle, are they?'

'Of course not,' said Grant. 'Look, here they come now.'

Holly looked over Marina's shoulder to see Connor, Dex and Luc forcing their way through the packed crowd.

'I've been dying for you to meet them,' Holly said to Marina excitedly. They were almost directly behind Marina when she eventually turned round.

163

'Marina, this is—'

'*Connor.*'

It was the only word Marina could get out. Connor just looked shell-shocked.

'Fuck me,' said Luc, 'Mary – what are you doing here?'

'Will somebody tell me what on earth is going on?' Holly was confused.

Dex sidled up next to her. 'Connor and Mary used to go out with each other a long time ago. They split up just before he first came to Ibiza, what . . . six years ago?'

'Seven,' replied Connor and Marina simultaneously, still staring at each other in disbelief.

'Hang on, hang on. "Mary"?' Holly was still baffled.

'That's my real name. When I went to Egypt and worked at my first diving school, the guy who ran it thought it was funny – you know, *Stingray*, the old sixties puppet TV series like *Thunderbirds*? Mary sounding like Marina?' She was greeted with blank faces. 'No, I thought it was pretty stupid at the time too. Anyway, one of the girls who worked there got me the job at my first diving school in Ibiza so it's kind of stuck. Everyone calls me Marina so I guess you'd all better get used to it and join them.'

'When were you in Egypt?' asked Luc.

'Let me see, that must have been . . .'

Connor didn't really hear what she was saying. He just stared at her, utterly transfixed. She had been in his thoughts so often recently that it didn't feel as though it had been seven years since he'd last seen her. Physically, she had not changed that much. Yet there was something different about her. He could not put his finger on it, but whatever it was, it made her even more beautiful.

'. . . and that was that basically.' She turned to a mesmerized Connor. 'And what are you doing here? I thought the Ibiza chapter of your life was over?'

'I can't believe it's you,' was all he could say.

'Yes, it's definitely me.' She shuffled, slightly uncomfortable, as Connor continued to gawp.

'Sorry,' he said, coming to his senses, realizing what he was doing, 'I'm just stunned. You wouldn't believe it, because I've been thinking . . .' Connor checked himself – now was neither the time nor the place. He quickly moved to more neutral ground. 'So, when did you get here? Ibiza I mean, not Space.'

'Last August.'

'But that's mad because Luc was here last summer – this is his third season – how come he didn't bump into you?'

'I was working in a diving school in Santa Eularlia last August and September, then I actually stayed during the winter too. It was only a few months ago that I went to San Antonio for the first time.'

'But what about Ibiza Town, the clubs?'

'I've never really been into clubbing, have I? I spent most of my time last summer working or just hanging out near Santa Eularlia. I came into Ibiza Town occasionally, but not really to any of the trendy bars.'

'Right.' Once more Connor shook his head, still unable to believe his eyes. 'But of all places, why Ibiza?'

'Oh, it's a long story . . .'

Marina had not exactly been bursting with enthusiasm to go to Space. It was bad enough that Bartolo had to leave. Now though, to bump into the very reason she had gone travelling, the primary cause of her guarded attitude towards the opposite sex, the man who had effectively rejected her all of those years ago . . . it was too much to take in. Especially when her flatmate was going out with one of his best friends *and* – reading between the lines – had expressed a passing interest in the man in question.

She needed to get things into some kind of perspective and the terrace of Space was clearly not the place to do so.

'Do you fancy meeting up for a bite later?' asked Connor, as though reading her mind. 'You probably won't get much sense out of me here.'

'Um, I don't think I'll be able to tonight. A friend of mine has had an accident, so I've got to leave here too, I'm afraid.'

'Shit, I'm sorry to hear that. Give me your mobile and I'll call you to arrange something for later in the week.'

They swapped numbers, then Marina said her goodbyes and left, with Holly walking her to the door.

'Are you all right?' asked Holly once they were out of earshot. 'I thought you were going to stay. Bit of a shock, was it?'

'You could say that.'

'All roads lead to Ibiza, eh? Didn't you know Connor might be here?'

'No. When I was in New Zealand I heard that he was back in the UK permanently. That's why I kind of thought it a little ironic when the job came up in Ibiza. Of all the places in the bloody world . . .'

'That's right, I remember now – the guy you were seeing wanted to come to Ibiza and that was one of the reasons you split up. And that guy was Connor?' She shook her head. 'Amazing.'

'It wasn't just Ibiza, more that he didn't seem to want to settle down.'

'Funny how that was exactly my impression of him.' They squeezed their way out of the main throng of people. 'He does seem like a really nice guy though – maybe it was just the timing that was wrong,' suggested Holly once they were free of the masses near the exit.

Marina shrugged. 'Who knows?'

'Are you going to go out for dinner with him?'

Marina thought for a few moments. 'Yeah, I guess so. Maybe it's a ghost I need to lay to rest.'

'Maybe,' replied Holly, 'it's one you need to resurrect . . .'

Connor had not been able to enjoy Space after seeing Marina. He didn't take any more pills because he knew that his emotions were shot to bits as it was.

During the previous week he had become increasingly convinced that circumstances had bizarrely conspired to cause him to be in Barcelona, close enough to Ibiza to feel its magnetism once more and to pull him back. To almost be run over by a bus after talking about it with Luc and to have been poring over photographs of Marina *née* Mary only a few days earlier, *had* to be more than just a coincidence. Now, for her to actually be living on the island . . .

The more he thought about it the reason for returning to Ibiza was, to Connor at least, now perfectly clear. It wasn't to expunge all fanciful notions of a life abroad with the Big Adventure. Quite the opposite. It was as if fate was trying to tell him that this was a chance for a second bite of the cherry.

Marina *was* the Big Adventure after all.

Within a few hours the scales were tipping the other way, the Positive Solutions option moving quickly towards obsolescence. The mental picture of life in London was fading and draining of colour like Marty McFly's photo in *Back to the Future*, whilst Ibiza's was re-emerging in gloriously vibrant technicolour.

Connor desperately needed to talk to someone about the significance of the events of the last few days, of the last few hours even, and that someone had to be Leo. He had therefore left Space at just gone ten and jumped in a taxi to Ibiza Town and Say Chic.

Leo quickly dismissed Connor's polite attempt to talk about his illness, telling him they had no need for such social formalities – he wanted to know all the juicy gossip about meeting Marina/Mary again.

'. . . honestly, Leo, it's fucking destiny, I swear it is,' said Connor, on his second beer and warming to the topic. 'I knew there was a reason I came over to Ibiza. Don't get me wrong, all that stuff you said last week about finding something I'm happy doing and all that ... there's definitely some truth in it. But I just *knew* that there was more to it. I *knew* that it had something to do with finding the Big Adventure.'

'And that's what you think Mary – I mean Marina is, this mystical Big Adventure?'

'She has to be.' Connor ran his finger round the rim of his glass. 'It's funny though, because last week I met this other girl called Holly and I was half convinced it was her ... until she told me she fancied my mate Dex.'

'Ouch.'

'But that's the whole point, it obviously wasn't meant to be. It was Holly who just re-introduced me to Marina. That proves it was fate.'

'Or it proves that Connor Young has got to a point in his life where he's had enough of philandering and just wants to settle down, whether it's here, London or Timbuk-bloody-tu.'

'I don't know, Leo. Something's different though.'

Leo smiled. 'Dear boy, I think what's different is that although it may have taken you thirty years, you've just joined the world of grown-ups ...'

Dex checked his phone on the way to the car as he left Space and noticed three missed calls, all from the same number, a London number. Worried it might be family connected he moved away from the rest of the group and dialled.

'A-ha, Dex,' said a voice he didn't recognize.

'Who's that?'

'Victor James.'

'Oh ... shit.'

'Nice speaking to you too.'

'Sorry ... I mean ... how did you get my number?'

'It wasn't easy, believe me. Still, I've got you now though, haven't I?'

Dex was silent for a few moments. 'Look, Victor, about your car—'

'Ease and settle now. I thought you would have called me.'

'To be honest, I thought you'd want to kill me. In fact, I'm surprised you didn't get out the car and have a go when it happened.'

'I wasn't in the car. I'd left the keys at the studio cos I was staying around some absolute honey's place nearby. That little ragamuffin hothead who was DJing for me took it on himself to go get your aerial and "borrowed" my car to do it, with his doughnut sidekick. It's a shame you took it out on my car and not them. Still, at least I had the pleasure of doing that ...'

Dex gulped. 'Shit, I never realized. For what it's worth, as soon as I saw it was your car I yelled at my two mates to stop.'

'I'm sure it was too late by then.'

Dex paused. 'So Victor, don't mind me asking, but why have you rung me and how did you know where I was?'

'I'd heard a few rumours that you were in Ibiza. Then, by chance, I saw you on some MTV thing filmed there. Basically, I want to know if you'd be interested in playing for me because I still haven't found anyone that's right for the station. Plus, over the next couple of weeks I've got some pretty good gigs lined up and you'd be perfect for them. I've started up a DJ agency and you could be my lead man. What you saying?'

'Fuck.' This was the last thing Dex had been expecting. 'I dunno. I'm flattered. I'm glad you're not vexed about what happened too. That was one of the main reasons I came over here.'

'What?' Victor laughed. 'Man, I'm gonna have to do something about my rep. I've had a lot of bad press but I'm not as much of a roughneck as people think. I'm a respectable businessman and I'm ringing you with a respectable business proposition. How about it?'

Dex looked back towards Space. It wasn't his kind of music. In fact, there were very few places on the island playing his kind of music, so if he parted company with Kyle – which seemed pretty inevitable – where would he play? Then there was Holly. They got on well but hadn't really clicked and he felt it unlikely that things were going to progress past the kiss and cuddle stage.

'I tell you what, Victor. I've got a few things I need to sort out, people to talk to, that kinda t'ing. Let me give you a call in the morning.'

'OK, man, safe. Don't let me down though.'

Dex put the mobile in his pocket and smiled, having pretty much made up his mind already.

Which gave him one more night to try and crack Holly.

chapter twenty-four

Marina put away the students' tanks and equipment on auto-pilot. All day long, she kept asking herself whether agreeing to meet Connor for dinner that night was a good idea. Was Holly right about resurrecting things with him? Was Marina's own gut feeling, that Connor was still interested, correct?

Bartolo had asked her out too, to make up for leaving her in Space. She had told him she was busy working. She was such an unaccomplished liar that she knew he could tell and that he probably imagined it to be some kind of rebuke.

Marina's world felt as if it had turned upside down. Although she was aware that there had probably been a void in her life caused by having spent so long abstaining from men, she had hitherto been more than happy to ignore it. How bloody typical therefore, that having had no interest in potential suitors for so long, all of a sudden just like buses, two turned up at exactly the same time.

Bartolo (the first bus) had played things perfectly. He had not been pushy, yet was anything but a pushover. He was good-looking but not conceited, charming without being smarmy, intelligent without being patronizing. It might have gone further but for the arrival of the long gone and unexpected second bus.

What was she supposed to do? For ages after Connor had rejected her (because no matter how he'd tried to sugar-coat things, that's exactly how she'd interpreted it) she had been convinced that the love of her life, The One, her Big Adventure, had passed her by, had refused flatly to live with her then promptly disappeared to Ibiza.

Every morning that she woke up after Connor left, he would automatically enter her thoughts. Every morning, she got the same sick feeling in the pit of her stomach and more than anything else, wished that there was an 'off' button on the side of her head so she could stop thinking about him. But no matter where she went, something would remind her of their relationship and if Ibiza were ever mentioned, she'd feel an inexplicable stab of jealousy.

To keep her sanity, the only answer had been to get as far away as possible, which was why she had gone travelling. The irony was not lost on her when the opportunity later arose to work in Ibiza. With Connor completely out of her system by then, she decided working on the island would be the ultimate closure on their relationship, though she did discreetly make sure that he was back in the UK before she accepted the job.

At that stage she was happy with who she was and did not feel she needed a man. If she did, then it would be on her terms. Yet seeing Connor again, all of those old feelings (and insecurities) had effortlessly re-surfaced. It was the same emotional experience as turning up at a school reunion, a composed and confident adult, then being reduced to a quivering wreck simply by an old school nemesis yelling a long-forgotten nickname.

The only good thing about being so preoccupied was that it took her mind off Mac. Yet again she'd had to remind him to check his tanks and yet again he hadn't had enough air in them. Despite this being in Mac's interest, he still treated her with contempt. Irritatingly, he had also continued to come out on every dive, as had Kyle. Kyle had insisted that they go to the same site (something they had never previously done) and while Marina or Nathalie took the clients, Mac continued to dive on his own in the opposite direction, instructing Marina not to come anywhere near him. She had protested to Kyle, partly on the safety aspect of diving without a buddy and partly because Mac invariably kept everyone waiting. But Kyle had backed Mac.

She could tell that Mac took great pleasure in this confirmation of his superiority. Because of him, Marina no longer looked forward to going to work. Today was worse than ever – Mac had kept them waiting for over fifteen minutes. Some of the students were complaining because they had plans for after their lesson and needed to get back. Much longer and she would have to ring Connor to rearrange the meal. Marina moved to the stern to speak to Kyle.

'Kyle, some of the students are asking when we're returning to shore. What's Mac doing down there?'

'Go back to the bow and shut them up. We'll be leaving in a few minutes.'

No sooner had Marina skulked off than Mac broke the surface. He gave Kyle a thumbs up then removed his facemask. A grinning Kyle helped him on to the platform.

'Was it there?' Kyle asked.

'Yep. It's sitting between two rocks, weighed down with concrete. First small shipment delivered. All systems go.'

As Mac climbed back on to the deck and took off his tanks, he noticed Marina watching him. He fixed her with an aggressive stare. She looked away and busied herself with the students.

'I don't know why you employ her,' remarked Mac. 'She's trouble – I can sense it.'

'Och, away with you. She's harmless and a bonnie wee worker.'

'I take it that means you haven't cracked her yet?'

'I've no' tried. I've been too busy getting all of this little malarkey organized.'

'She hangs round with Holly. If you ask me you'll get about as far with Marina as you did with her.'

'Aye, well, I didn't ask you. And the reason she hangs round with Holly is because they fucking live together. Anyway, screw Holly, there are plenty more fish in the sea and nobody gets one over on me. I've sacked her and after tonight I'll be sacking Dex too.'

'While you're at it you should sack those other two daft fucks, Shuff and Grant. Why are you bothering with them? They're clueless. And they're fucking American.'

'I thought you liked them?'

'I don't like any of that little lot you've got staying at our apartment near Sa Serra.'

'But you know why we're letting them stay there as well as I do.'

'So why wait? Let's bring it forward. Now this first small drop's been successful it could provide just the diversion we need,' urged Mac.

'Mmm, you've got a point there, right enough.' Kyle ran his hand over his chin. 'Is Rory set?' Mac nodded. 'Fuck it. Let's do it then.'

'Good.' Mac allowed himself a small smile.

'Any particular preference for whose room we put it in?'

Mac shrugged his shoulders. 'I don't care. With any luck they'll all be there in the morning and they can all get done.'

Kyle helped Mac out of his diving suit. 'OK. Get Rory up to the apartment tonight. Shuff and Grant are out selling gear, Dex is DJing for me, the bald fella's managing that bar that's just opened so the only one who might turn up is Connor, and chances are he'll be down Atlantis watching Dex. The apartment should be all clear. Can I leave it with you?'

Mac looked over to Marina who was making a conscious effort to avoid eye contact.

'Consider it done.'

Even though Rory had sat outside the apartment for more than ten minutes and there was no sign of any activity, he knocked on the door just in case. When nobody answered, he put his key into the lock and slowly entered. Kyle was right – the apartment was empty.

Despite this, Rory tiptoed down the corridor and used a Mag-lite torch to find his way round, rather than switch on the lights. He could have easily negotiated the apartment blindfolded – unbeknown to its current occupants he was a frequent visitor. He went straight to the last bedroom along. He had a look round and saw a few photos of Luc.

'Your room it is,' smiled Rory.

He removed a bag of just under a thousand ecstasy pills from a small rucksack. They were all that remained of a batch from the previous summer that had proved particularly unpopular. He then took out a set of electronic scales that had actually just been bought to sell to Shuff and Grant. Finally, he added a small bag of cocaine to complete what would look like a dealer's arsenal, then put all of the drugs and scales into the bottom of Luc's wardrobe.

As he crossed the hallway into the kitchen he felt his mobile vibrate. It was Mac.

'Mac?'

'Have you done it yet?'

'I've planted the shit pills and the other stuff in one of their rooms. I'm just going to clear out all of the good gear. Where shall I take it?'

'The new villa that Kyle and I are renting. The one in Benimussa had nosey neighbours. There's a little outhouse – it'll be safe in there for a while. Give me a call when you leave and I'll arrange to meet you.'

'Cool. I'll see you later then.'

Rory went into the kitchen and knelt down next to one of the base units. He took a screw out of the false bottom then lifted it up. Packed underneath were several thousand ecstasy tablets along with a dozen or so separately bagged ounces of cocaine. He put them all in his rucksack then replaced the false bottom.

He looked round the rest of the apartment, finding Grant's room then Shuff's. He went through their drawers and in Shuff's found several hundred euros rolled up in a sock. Rory slipped the money into his pocket.

As he walked down the hallway to leave the apartment, a key turned in the front door. Scrambling back into the kitchen, he heard the voices of Holly and Dex.

'You knew nobody would be here, didn't you?' giggled Holly.

'Nah, honest,' replied Dex, switching on the hall light. 'I thought Shuff and Grant or Connor would be here.'

'Mmm.' Holly didn't seem convinced. 'I'm not going to change my mind you know. *Especially* now you're going back to London.'

'Oh well.' Dex laughed. 'You can't blame a man for trying. But would it have made any difference if I stayed?'

They stopped in the hallway. Holly turned to face him. 'You know I think you're really cute, but . . . well, we want different things.'

'Are you sure?'

'Well, I'm sure about what I want,' she laughed, 'and I've a pretty good idea what you want.'

Dex shrugged. 'Oh well.'

He went into his bedroom. He had barely unpacked so gathering his things together was a simple task.

'Anyway,' said Holly, following him into the room, 'this opportunity to DJ back in London sounds too good to miss. Plus it'll give you the chance to tell Kyle to poke his job.'

Rory strained to hear what was being said.

'Nah, fuck it, I can't be bothered with all that nastiness,' said Dex. 'I'd rather just leave Kyle in the shit. He's not worth the hassle.' Dex walked down the corridor. 'Do you fancy a quick cup of tea?'

When he heard this, Rory moved away from the fridge and stood behind the kitchen door.

'No thanks,' replied Holly, 'the cab's waiting outside. Come on, let's get back to Atlantis.'

'OK, let me just grab my weed.'

'What are your plans for later?'

'I'll pop into Atlantis to get my records then I'll get a cab, stop off here for my things then see if I can get a flight at the airport. There's one at about four in the morning and another at seven. I'd rather get the later one cos I don't want to get caught in the rush hour back in London.'

'Why don't we drop your stuff at the airport now? I've got a friend who's a rep there, so we should be able to leave it behind her desk. We can sort out your flight then go to Pacha – I think Sanchez is playing. I'll come back up to the airport and see you off after if you want.'

Dex thought about it for a moment then nodded. 'Yeah, sounds cool.'

'What about Connor and Luc – aren't you going to tell them you're leaving?'

'They'll only try to make me stay and to be honest, I could be easily persuaded. Anyway, Luc's working and Connor's going out for a meal with Marina.'

'Oh yeah, I forgot about that.' Holly kissed him on the cheek. 'Ah, I'll miss you.'

'I could always give you something to remember me by.'

'Stop it!' She playfully smacked him.

'I won't give up until I'm on the plane.'

'*That* I can believe. Come on, let's go.'

Rory breathed a huge sigh of relief as he heard them leave. He tiptoed over to Luc's bedroom, peeked out of the window and watched the taxi disappear down the dusty road. Once sure they were gone he took out his mobile.

'Mac, it's Rory again.'

'Job done?'

'Yeah. Bit of a close call though – that DJ came back.'

'I thought he was playing down at Atlantis.'

'That's why I'm ringing. I'm making my way down there right now but it might be a good idea to get a few of the boys to the bar . . . pronto . . .'

Connor poured the last of the champagne sangria into Marina's glass and smiled. All of the things she had wanted seven years ago he had more or less just offered her on a plate, along with a rather nice goat's cheese salad and rack of lamb.

He leaned across and kissed her. 'Just going to the little boys' room.'

After a couple of hours in his company, Marina had pretty much bought into Connor's belief that fate had conspired to give them another chance to be together. When they had first sat down at the popular Kasbah restaurant though, the conversation had been fairly stilted, both sizing each other up from the safety of the banal.

However, once they started talking about the past, Marina quickly opened up. She could tell that her simmering sense of hurt and frustration took Connor completely by surprise. It had clearly been suppressed and ready to explode as soon as a vent in her carefully constructed protective crust appeared. Just sitting alone with Connor was all she needed for seven years of anger, hurt and frustration to come hissing out. Conversations that she had gone through in her head hundreds of times, at last got an airing, and the only person more surprised at the strength of feeling than Connor, was Marina herself.

Cathartically cleansed, she then felt a little guilty. Connor looked genuinely shocked and upset by how he had apparently hurt her.

'I honestly didn't realize,' was all he could say.

But she had needed to get it off her chest. If they were going to build their relationship again – as Connor clearly wanted them to – then they had to be sure that there was nothing lurking in the foundations that would later undermine their progress and bring it all tumbling down. Encouragingly, she felt as though the feelings he'd had for her before had genuinely matured and taken shape. He was also prepared to go along with whatever she wanted in order to make sure that she didn't get hurt again. Most surprising of all though, he was ready to commit to her and even live together, the main thing she had wanted all of those years ago. It was all moving very quickly.

Connor had taken her initial outburst on the chin, including some of the things that she knew she'd only said to be spiteful. She could see that he had changed, or was certainly in the process of changing.

Most importantly though, Marina was happier with herself now. Even if Connor did prove to be bullshitting (which she doubted) then she would not be hurt in the way she had before. Having exorcised the previous pain, she was actually slightly puzzled as to how it had dominated her thoughts for so long; it had all been re-framed with a new perspective.

But how would it progress? For example, was she going to allow him to stay the night? This was hardly a conventional first date, after all. She pushed the remnants of her meal around her plate, still unsure what to do. The only thing she was sure about, was that first thing the next day, she was going to ring Bartolo and be totally honest about what had happened, then cool the relationship. But as for when she was going to sleep with Connor . . .

He came back to the table.

'Do you fancy some dessert?'

'Funnily enough, that's just what I was trying to decide . . .'

chapter twenty-five

Grant opened the door to the fridge and looked around the magnificent open plan ground floor, still finding it hard to take in the magnificence of the three-bedroom villa tucked away high in the hills overlooking the airport.

It was fairly small, but the modern geometric architecture and the minimalist glass and steel design set it apart from the more traditional villas that Shuff and Grant had hitherto seen, either firsthand or in magazines and photographs. Each bedroom had an en-suite that was double the size of Shuff and Grant's own rooms in the apartment they rented from Kyle.

The bedrooms took up the whole of the villa's first floor, but it was the downstairs living area that totally blew them away. It was huge, bright and open plan. At one end was a massive modern kitchen, and at the other, an indoor Jacuzzi next to a swimming pool that was half inside, then via an electronically controlled glass shutter, wound its way outside to a second section surrounded by wooden decking and Balinese furniture. The pool cascaded off the edge to infinity towards the sea and a view of Ibiza's sister island, Formantera.

As if that wasn't fantastic enough, the three girls who had invited them back after buying drugs from them the previous night, had immediately insisted on everyone skinny-dipping. Shuff and Grant could not believe their luck.

It had soon emerged that the reason they were staying in such opulence was that one of the girls, Sinead, had an Irish industrialist multi-million-aire father who paid for the holiday as one of her twenty-first birthday presents. Of the three, Sinead was the one that Shuff and Grant found least attractive, ironic given that she was the one who had been most instrumental in inviting them back in the first place. They sensed that she was used to getting her own way and that there was a high degree of tolerance and indulgence on the part of her two friends, Denise and Fiona.

Sinead had a full-on 'look-at-me' personality. If she were not centre of attention, she would either sulk or do something to re-focus the spotlight back on herself. As such, though the natural dynamic of the evening was drawing Shuff to Denise and Grant to Fiona, the two girls were reluctant to pursue things for fear of upsetting Sinead.

One aspect of Sinead's personality was an avarice for all things narcotic. She took more than everyone else and any lull in conversation had been filled with her demands for something else.

Shuff had had some GHB, which Sinead had never sampled before. Despite this, she had ignored Shuff's advice to wait a while after her first few sips, because she was adamant it wasn't affecting her. Just how far off the mark she was with this self-assessment became clear thirty minutes later when she had passed out in the Jacuzzi. This left the others free to pair off, though Shuff did the decent thing and pulled the plug of the Jacuzzi before they retired so she didn't drown.

Grant stepped now from the kitchen into the grounds. He hadn't really slept and had only just stopped buzzing, so was contemplating a quick swim to liven himself up. Shuff was already outside, energetically bouncing up and down on a small trampoline next to the pool.

'Thought I might find you on that,' said Grant.

'Saves me having to go to the trampolines round the bay,' replied Shuff. 'How did you get on with Fiona?'

'Yeah, great. She's really nice. What about you?'

'Denise? Filthy. Fucking great night. Is Sinead awake yet?'

'Don't think so.' He checked his watch. 'It's seven-thirty and she crashed out around three in the morning.'

'She should be coming round soon then.'

'I know. Fiona said she was going to check on her.'

'I can't believe what a spoilt brat Sinead is. I told her to take it easy.' Shuff stopped bouncing for a moment, coughing furiously then spitting thick phlegm on to the grass. 'It's a shame,' he continued, wiping some spittle from his lower lip, 'because I thought she wasn't bad at the start of the night, but she just got less and less attractive every time she opened her mouth.' He started bouncing again.

Denise emerged from the villa wearing a sarong. 'There you are,' she said rubbing her eyes as they became accustomed to the light. 'I was worried you might have gone home.'

'No way, babe.' Shuff did a somersault and Denise gazed at him admiringly. 'You haven't seen the state of the place we're living in. We're in no hurry to go back.'

'*You fucking bastards!*'

The three of them turned to see Sinead hobbling out of the villa with a worried looking Fiona walking next to her.

'What's up?' asked Denise.

'What's up? I'll show you what's up,' yelled Sinead, half screaming, half crying. 'Look . . .'

As she got closer, the others could see the source of her concern. On the top of her leg was a very nasty burn.

'How did that happen?' asked Grant.

'Which one of you took the plug out of the Jacuzzi?'

'I did,' volunteered Shuff, who had come to a standstill on the trampoline. 'You passed out on GHB. I told you not to take so much of it. I warned you that you'd be comatose for a few hours and that's exactly what happened. I let the water out of the Jacuzzi so you didn't drown.'

'You bloody idiot – why didn't you turn the Jacuzzi lights off?'

'What are you on about?'

Sinead let out a gasp of exasperation so Fiona took over.

'Um, when Sinead passed out, her leg was resting against one of the underwater lamps in the Jacuzzi. She must have been so far under on the GHB that she didn't feel anything. With the water drained out it's burned her leg . . . quite badly by the look of it.'

'I'm scarred for life,' wailed Sinead. 'I've got third-degree burns.'

'I've run her leg under cold water,' continued Fiona, 'but we really should take her to the hospital.'

'I'm going to get my things. You can take me down there right now,' ordered Sinead to nobody in particular as she turned on her heel and limped into the villa.

The others watched her disappear in silence. Shuff was the first to start giggling.

'Ssshh, stop it,' chided Denise, albeit only half-heartedly.

'Well, what do you expect?' protested Shuff. 'It was her fault for being such a goddam hog and taking so many drugs. I thought I was doing her a favour.'

'We'd better get our things together,' said Fiona. 'I'll drive her to the hospital.'

'We'll come with you if you want,' said Shuff.

'Ah, that's sweet of you,' said Denise. 'The forecast is that it's going to be a lovely day too. Are you sure you want to spend it stuck in a hospital?'

'Fuck that. She'll be in the hospital for ages. What I meant was we should drop her off, then go down to a beach near Figueretes – it isn't too far from the hospital.'

Denise and Fiona looked at each other for a few moments, then shrugged.

'We'll go and get our towels . . .'

Connor slid his arm from underneath the sleeping Marina, and crept out of her room to the kitchen. It was just gone seven-thirty in the morning. Tuesday. A week from now he could be just about to join the throng of London commuters, instead of looking towards the sea and another glorious day. At the moment it was no contest.

He was disappointed that he was still wearing boxer shorts. He was more frustrated, however, by the fact that Marina was wearing a T-shirt, bra, knickers (probably) and tracksuit bottoms, despite the stifling heat and lack of ventilation in her room.

If she had got into bed a few hours earlier just wearing a sexy thong, Connor would have taken her choice of nocturnal apparel as a green light; a thong with a T-shirt and no bra a probable amber; a thong with matching bra and a T-shirt an amber/red, but to go to bed wearing more clothes than she had been wearing all day . . . there was no doubting the colour of that light.

This hadn't stopped Connor from lying there in dry-mouthed anticipation, listening for any change in breathing, hoping for a positive response to his lightly wandering hands, praying for her to purr, cuddle up, and wrap an inviting leg around his. But no, they hadn't even kissed, at least not in the playground braggart sense of the word. And if his tender caress lingered too long or erred too close to any area that could be considered an erogenous zone, Marina shifted or even worse, moved his hand away.

Connor reconciled this in the knowledge that this was of course, a double-edged sword. Marina had never been a girl who easily surrendered her virtue. If she was not prepared to rush into resuming carnal relations with someone who had shown a willingness to live with her and with whom she had previously pushed sexual boundaries further than with any previous lover (or so she had told Connor and he had no reason to disbelieve her), then the chances were that she had not been particularly promiscuous in the intervening period since they had stopped seeing each other.

He took some water from the fridge. Looking back down the hallway he noticed that Holly's door was closed. He hadn't heard her come in. Did that mean she was back at the apartment with Dex?

He swigged the water and absent-mindedly looked at a picture, Blu-Tacked to the wall, of Holly and the other Smacker girls, taken on the opening night. How long ago that night seemed. Holly was a great girl but, clearly, not for him.

Marina, on the other hand, most definitely *was* the girl for him, even wearing half of her wardrobe in bed. He stepped back into the bedroom. How could he blame her for not sleeping with him after their first meal together in seven years? She obviously wanted to be sure of his motives this time round. He could wait. He'd waited for seven years. In fact, as far as searching for the Big Adventure was concerned, he'd waited all of his life.

A few more days would not be a problem.

Luc had only just about got to sleep when he was aware of a car pulling up outside the apartment, perhaps more than one. The digital display on his bedside clock told him it was 7.45 a.m. He had worked late because Raffles had not got off to the kind of start its Spanish owner Carlos expected and, as manager, the pressure was immediately put on Luc. He was even returning to the bar at midday to interview some new props.

If Shuff and Grant had come back to the apartment with a load of people, Luc resolved he was going to go ballistic. It was all well and good having a laugh, but now he was working so hard, there was going to have to be some give and take.

He strained to hear any signs of boisterousness but couldn't, so concluded that it was probably either Dex and Holly or Connor. He wondered how he'd got on with Marina? Content, Luc pulled the cover up to his chin and snuggled down for a nice few hours of much-needed sleep.

Crash!

The bedroom door flew open. Luc had barely opened his eyes when what seemed like a hundred policemen charged in screaming and shouting. The very real pain he felt as he was forcibly dragged from his bed shattered any doubts he had about it being a horrible dream. Before he had even properly woken up, two triumphant members of the Guardia Civil emerged from his wardrobe waving a rather large bag of pills, some white powder, and a set of scales.

Despite his protests, in both English and Spanish, Luc was bundled down the stairs and into a waiting police van.

Opposite, a surprised neighbour stopped hanging out her washing and lit a cigarette as she witnessed the several police vehicles speed down the road.

Sitting in his car nearby, Rory also lit up a cigarette, though the grin on his face was a fair indication that he was anything but surprised by the turn of events.

part four

*old faces and friends
in high places . . .*

chapter twenty-six

Dex rang the bell on the 171 bus, but didn't immediately get up from his seat. The Walworth Road traffic was moving at a glacial pace and the mid-morning shoppers were sitting in their usual glum silence. He cleared an arc in the window and looked out at the grey clouds sagging behind the Camberwell tower blocks. Skunk FM had just moved its studio into one of the blocks.

Rather than being depressed by the urban landscape, Dex felt a warm glow of familiarity. It was where he was brought up, where he belonged. People cared about him here, and he felt respected, popular and secure. He was home and being home made him happy.

What made him even happier was how Victor James was championing him, adopting him as his leading DJ, taking his advice on where to base the Skunk FM studio, promising him some prestigious gigs and introducing him to promoters and venue owners. Tonight he was playing a prestigious Friday night spot at a recently opened central London club.

However, Dex's upbeat mood was constantly punctuated by concern over what was happening to Luc back in Ibiza. Nobody had been back to the apartment on the Monday night prior to Luc's Tuesday morning arrest, which was pretty much when Dex was boarding a plane, happy to be going home but disappointed he never nailed Holly – how trivial that now seemed.

At first Dex assumed that the police had found Shuff and Grant's drugs stashed in the villa and that Luc was unlucky to be the only one there at the time. However, when he learned that 1,024 ecstasy tablets, 25 grams of cocaine and a set of electronic scales were actually discovered in Luc's room, the one thing he was certain of was that they didn't belong to his best friend.

Dex got off the bus, flung his sports bag over his shoulder and made his way to the gym, which he found to be therapeutic in releasing the anger he felt towards Shuff and Grant. It would have been bad enough for Luc to be carrying the can for their dealing, but storing drugs in a mate's room as Shuff and Grant had clearly done, was the lowest of the low as far as he was concerned. So much for American values. Dex had wanted to return to Ibiza to beat a confession out of Shuff and Grant, as they had, unsurprisingly, denied all knowledge of the drugs seized.

Connor had rung him on the Wednesday with the news of Luc's arrest, then later in the day with more details. During the second conversation, Holly's name briefly came up. Dex had given Connor so much stick following the opening night of Smacker when Holly said she fancied him (oh, how he'd enjoyed rubbing Connor's nose in it) that he knew Connor would repay the teasing tenfold if he found out Dex hadn't actually slept with her and that she had effectively dumped him. He was fairly sure that Holly wasn't the kind of girl to volunteer information about her private life, so he had simply told Connor that they were going to put things on hold but keep in touch, then maybe pick things up again at the end of the summer. Dex had also implied that one of the main reasons for their 'sabbatical' from each other was that he would be too busy with his DJing to give her the attention she would need, seeing as she didn't know too many people in London. That way, even if Holly told Connor that she had split up with Dex, Connor wouldn't know what had really happened. Anything to avoid Connor's piss-taking.

Dex took a baseball cap from his pocket and pulled it tightly over his head to offer some protection from the light drizzle. The rain started to get a little heavier, so he jogged the last 50 metres or so to the gym with his head down. He skipped into the gym's entrance, but bounced off someone standing in the doorway who was so big and solid they could have easily got a part-time job as a motorway crash barrier.

'Sorry, mate,' apologized a semi-winded Dex, 'Oh, it's you two.'

'We heard you were back,' snarled Rik Searle, as his brother Buster grabbed Dex's collar and escorted him towards a waiting car. 'Perfect timing too, seeing as we're booked on a flight to Ibiza tomorrow night. But, before we go,' he helped Buster bundle Dex into the car, 'we're going for a drive, during which you can tell us all about a certain Scotsman and a kilo of glucose . . .'

Connor watched the small pendulum on the cheap reproduction clock in Marina's flat swing back and forth. In the five days since Space, Connor's mind had swung from wanting to stay in Ibiza to going back to London almost as many times. Now the final weekend before having to make his decision was bearing down on him. He'd told Marina about

Positive Solutions' Monday ultimatum. In typical sensible Marina fashion, they'd agreed that things between them would still be workable if he returned to his job. With the money he would be earning he could pop back most weekends. The season ended in just over three months too, so it would fly by . . . wouldn't it?

Although there was still a residual gut feeling to stay in Ibiza, London *had* to be the right choice. Ibiza was not the responsibility free, hedonistic playground he'd remembered. When he'd walked near his old apartment the previous week he had worked out that to continue his relationship with Ibiza he needed to find fresh things to keep it alive. So far, all he'd found was a shallow lifestyle, a friend dying of cancer, a suspicious promoter, a girl he'd really liked getting off with one of his best friends and another friend in prison on drugs charges.

Yet on the other hand, there was Marina. The other part of the happiness equation that Leo had shared with him was being with the right person. Despite theoretically being able to have a relationship with Marina if he returned to London, he was not entirely convinced that it would progress in the same way as if he stayed on the island.

Especially as they had yet to consummate their reunion.

He had stayed at her apartment every night since the raid. Sex had taken on an added importance. He felt unable to make a true decision about his future until it happened, until that tension had been broken. It was there, ever present as a backdrop to everything they did, but Marina seemed reluctant to discuss it, perhaps because of their history.

'When it feels right, it will be right,' was her mantra.

Connor understood and didn't push things. But he knew he would be able to think clearer and get things in perspective once the deed was done.

Marina returned from the shop with Tanit, a puppy she was looking after for a friend. He tickled the yapping Tanit under the chin and picked her up. Marina gave the dog a kiss.

'So the puppy gets a kiss and I don't?'

Connor tried his own puppy dog expression, but Tanit's wet nose, floppy ears and inability to do anything on two legs other than beg, meant it wasn't exactly an even contest.

'I know what you're like this time of the day,' she said, taking the puppy and putting a small bowl of water on the floor. 'Before I know it you'll be trying to drag me into the bedroom.'

'You can't blame me. At the rate we're going, old Tanit here will be producing her own puppies before we . . . well, you know.' Connor could feel the wicket getting stickier with every word.

'Oh, so it *is* all about sex then?'

'Sorry. You know that's not true,' replied Connor, in a simper that would have given Tanit a run for her money.

Marina sighed. 'I know it isn't. I want to,' she held her hand up for fear that Connor might grow a tail and start wagging it, 'but it hasn't seemed right, what with everything going on, plus Holly's been in every night too . . .'

'It's OK.'

'So, you've put your stuff in Luc's boss's garage then?' Marina always had been good at changing the subject.

'Yeah, Carlos, the guy who owns Raffles. He's an absolute star. Luc rang him from the prison this morning. We're heading up there tomorrow.'

'You're not actually going in though, are you?'

'Don't be silly. I need to find out if I'm in the clear first. Even though the gear wasn't in my room, I *was* living in the apartment.'

'Why doesn't Luc just tell the police that Shuff and Grant did it? Or better still, why don't they admit the drugs were theirs? Have you spoken to them?'

Connor nodded. 'On the phone earlier. They're still denying all knowledge. Shuff even had the cheek to say we were out of order trying to blame them and that Luc should just admit it because they were in the shit with Kyle.'

'What did you say?'

'I can't remember exactly but it all got a bit heated and I ended up putting the phone down on him.'

'Oh dear.'

'They've been living on the campsite since the apartment got raided. It's more or less opposite the local police station, ironically enough. I reckon they'll probably piss off back to the States soon.'

'Good riddance.'

Tanit yapped for attention.

'She's a cute puppy,' said Connor. 'Who's the friend?'

'Um . . . the police diver I told you about, Bartolo.'

There was an uncomfortable silence. She had been honest with Connor and in a way, she supposed, this was a kind of test for him. If he repaid her honesty with suspicion, then it would not be a promising sign.

He appeared deep in thought. Suddenly, he jumped up from the table.

'That's it!' he exclaimed.

'What?' asked Marina, altogether unsure what he meant.

186

He walked over to her. 'Bartolo. He could find out whether or not the police want to question me, couldn't he?'

'I . . . I don't know, I mean . . .'

'And,' continued Connor, 'he might even be able to find out why the police raided the apartment in the first place.'

'It might have had something to do with you living with two drug dealers,' replied Marina sarcastically.

She fell silent for a few moments while Connor paced the room, his mind obviously racing. A few seconds earlier she was worried that Connor was going to have a jealous outburst at the mention of Bartolo's name. Now, he was virtually insisting that she meet him again. That was one thing about Connor; you could always count on the unexpected. It crossed her mind that if anything, a mild show of jealousy would actually have been quite welcome.

'What are you thinking?' she prompted.

Connor came to a standstill. 'Oh, it's just something Shuff said that keeps going round my head. He reckoned that Kyle Goldwell only ever laid on enough drugs for a night's dealing, certainly nothing like the amount of gear the police found.'

'Well, he would say that. He's not going to admit all those drugs were theirs, is he?'

'I know, except he told me that *before* the raid, several times in fact. He moaned that it meant more trips to Rory and therefore more chance of getting caught.'

'So?'

'So, just supposing Shuff and Grant are telling the truth? Like I said, I'm pretty certain the drugs didn't belong to Luc. Therefore, if they didn't belong to Shuff and Grant either, then it begs the question, who did they belong to? And, more importantly, how did they get there and why did the police choose to raid that night?'

'What, you mean someone put them there?' She was slowly catching on.

'It's the only other explanation, isn't it? And who does the apartment belong to? Kyle Goldwell. Who didn't like Dex because of him going out with Holly? Kyle Goldwell. Who probably doesn't like me because he's seen me hanging round with you? Kyle Goldwell. It's not exactly a case for Inspector bleeding Morse, is it?'

'But is that enough reason to plant drugs on someone? I know Kyle's unhinged, but from what I've seen he normally only does things that benefit him. I don't know a lot about drugs, but that kind of quantity would definitely set him back quite a bit, surely?'

'Hmm, the price Kyle would pay would probably be no more than,' Connor did some quick mental arithmetic, 'two or three grand.'

'That's still a lot of money. Why would he waste that on framing Luc?'

'I don't know. I'm probably way off the mark – the drugs more than likely *did* belong to Shuff and Grant. Still . . . '

He picked Luc's car keys off the worktop.

'Where are you going?'

'I'm just going to go and dig around a little. See if I can come up with anything.'

'Connor, be careful.'

'Aaah,' he kissed her on the lips, 'I could get used to you worrying about me.' As he was leaving he stopped at the front door. 'Don't forget to give Bartolo a call. He might even know whether or not the raid was the result of a tip-off.'

'Oh, Connor, I'm not sure. I'll probably have to meet up with him.'

'Fine. I'll see you later.'

Marina stood there.

Was just a teeny-weeny-incy-wincy bit of jealousy too much to ask for?

Shuff and Grant walked down the road to Atlantis in sullen and apprehensive mood. The early afternoon sun was already over 30 degrees and even close to the sea, there was hardly any breeze. A heatwave had been forecast and it looked like proving to be accurate. Not that the weather was at the forefront of their minds. Within the space of a few days their Ibiza dream had turned into a nightmare, though they had to concede that it was even worse for Luc.

They simply did not have a clue what was going on. All they knew was that the drugs found by the police were not theirs and that everyone, including Connor, had turned against them. It was, they agreed, understandable, as the fact that they were selling cocaine and ecstasy was hardly the island's best kept secret.

Luc had naturally denied having anything to do with the drugs, but they were surprised when Connor rang and told them that Luc had still maintained the drugs weren't his during the prison visit.

To make matters worse, Rory had advised them to keep out of Kyle's way. He was fuming that his apartment had been brought to the police's attention and also that as far as he was concerned, they had obviously been buying drugs from another supplier. However, they'd now been told he wanted to see them.

Fleeing Ibiza had been discussed as an option, especially now they had received the summons from Kyle. They had quickly tried to find out if there were any flights but it had proved a pointless exercise – they didn't even have enough money between them to catch the ferry to Denia, as their cash had been taken from the apartment. They were totally broke. Moreover, Kyle still had Grant's passport.

The door to Atlantis was ajar and they tentatively pushed it open. Inside, two jabbering Spanish cleaners busied themselves, mopping away the excesses of the previous night.

'Is it just me or is it cold in here?' asked Grant.

'Just think,' said Shuff, ignoring the question, 'less than a week ago we were walking round this very floor like kings of the castle.'

'Hmph,' grunted Grant. 'At the moment I feel like we've just come from the Tower and we're walking up the hangman's steps.'

They stopped outside the door to Kyle's office.

'Don't worry,' said Shuff. 'Once we explain everything Kyle will be all right.'

Shuff knocked on the door and heard Kyle yell, 'Come.' Gingerly, they walked in. Kyle was sitting behind his desk with a cigar in his hand. Mac stood behind him. Rory sat on a fake green Chesterfield near the door.

'Oh shit,' mumbled Grant, immediately sensing the hostile atmosphere.

Kyle nodded at them to sit on two chairs positioned in front of his desk. He took a long drag on his cigar, leaned back in his big leather chair and slowly exhaled. The smoke hung motionless in front of his face enveloping it like a shroud then drifting towards the ceiling. He said nothing, but fixed them with a stare that seemed to last as long as the ferry crossing to Barcelona.

'So,' he finally said in a calm and deliberate voice, 'I always knew you were smart. The problem is, sometimes smart people think they're smarter than they actually are. Getting drugs from another supplier, when I treat you like one of my own, how fucked is that? Lay gear on, give you somewhere to live for virtually fuck all – have I got "mug" tattooed across my forehead or what?'

'Kyle, I swear that gear wasn't ours,' said Shuff. 'It wasn't found in our room, was it? It was in Luc's. Luc must have started dealing. The bar he manages had just opened. Maybe he was after getting a little extra income.'

'The one thing you should have learned about me is that if you so much as fart on this island, I'll find out. From what I've heard you're no' too popular with Luc's mate . . . what's his name?' Kyle looked towards Rory.

'Connor,' replied Rory.

'Aye, Connor,' repeated Kyle. 'If Luc had been dealing, I'm sure Connor would have known about it.'

'He might not have, especially if Luc had only just started, which is quite possible given the amount of drugs that were found,' said Grant.

'Aye, the amount of drugs – that's the other thing. Where did you get the money to pay for 'em, eh?'

'But I just said, they weren't—'

'Don't take me for a fucking mug!' yelled Kyle, leaning forward and cutting Grant off mid-sentence. 'You're scum. Worse than scum, hiding drugs in a friend's room then letting him take the blame.'

'We *didn't*!' pleaded Grant.

'Then where's my fuckin' money then? Eh?'

'The police must have taken it with the drugs,' said Shuff.

'Oh, how fuckin' convenient.' Kyle laughed and looked round at his boys. 'What says you, eh, boys?' Mac stood impassive; Rory guffawed. 'Mac here knows the exact figure, but from what I remember there's a good few hundred euros owing. So where is it?'

'I swear,' said Grant, close to tears, 'it was hidden in a sock and after the raid it was gone. We've no money, not a cent. Do you think we'd still be here if we could afford to get off the island, or if we'd really tried to stitch you up? That's why *we* wanted to see *you*. We thought with your contacts you might know what's going on.'

Kyle sat back in his chair again. 'Oh, so the polis thought they'd have a wee poke around after the raid, go through you're undies and stuff, just to see if there was anything worth taking, is that it? Oh no, sonny Jim. Let me tell *youse* what's happened. You've used my money to buy drugs from another dealer and now those drugs are gone, you've nothing to sell so that's why you're skint.'

'That's not true!'

Kyle held his hand up. 'Stop greetin' like a bairn or I'll give you something to greet about. Now mebbes I'm going soft in my auld age, because God knows, a few years ago I wouldn't have been so lenient. The pair of you get your sorry butts off this island and never come back.' He reached into his drawer, pulled out Grant's passport and threw it across the desk at him. 'Here. If I see either of you again after *mañana* . . .' Kyle drew his finger across his throat. 'Go on, get to fuck.'

Rory got up and opened the door. Grant walked out, his eyes fixed firmly on the floor. Shuff left at a slower pace, holding Rory's gaze. Rory sneered, coughed up some phlegm and spat in Shuff's face. Then he looked at Kyle and smiled, so he didn't see it coming.

Thwack!

Shuff's forehead connected beautifully with Rory's nose, splattering it across his previously smirking face. Mac started towards Shuff, but Kyle held his hand up to stop him.

'Make sure that's the last thing you ever do in Ibiza, blondie.'

Shuff had been ready to sprint; instead he wiped the gob from his face and on to the simpering Rory's sleeve, then slowly and proudly he sauntered out of Kyle's office towards an astonished Grant.

As the door shut behind him, Kyle shook his head. 'Rory, Rory, Rory. How many times have I told you *never* to pick on someone your own size?'

'Why didn't you do something?' he wailed.

Kyle stood up and walked over to Rory, pulling his hand away from his bleeding and broken nose. 'Ooh, Rory son, that looks nasty. Tell you what. Give me that fuckin' money you took from silly bollocks' sock and I'll give some of it back so you can get yourself down the medical centre.'

'What money? I never . . .' Rory stopped as he saw Kyle pick up a heavy ashtray from his desk. 'I was going to give it to you. It just slipped my mind.'

'Aye, well, don't let anything slip your mind again. You've been fucking shite lately. That'll be coming out of your money, sunshine, make no mistake.' Kyle put down the ashtray and immediately changed his mood. 'I've got to say, boys, I almost convinced myself there that we didnae plant them drugs. RADA, that's where I shoulda studied, I'm telling you.' He clapped his hand together. 'So, it's all worked out nicely really. The nigger DJ's gone and those two daft wee American prats'll be right behind him. Luc or whatever his fucking name is, is banged up and Connor . . . well, who the fuck is he anyway? So, I guess now we can get down to more important things, eh, Mac?'

Mac nodded. 'The diving gear is all ready to go. The other gear should be there by now.'

'Excellent. See, boys, I told you it was going to be a great season . . .'

chapter twenty-seven

Marina jumped on to the diving boat to get her bag. Holly's eyes darted nervously between her and Atlantis.

'Hurry up. That's Kyle's car; he's obviously here.'

'He's probably in the bar. Anyway, I'm not doing anything wrong, just picking my bag up. I'm allowed to do that, for heaven's sake, aren't I?'

'Of course. I'd just rather not see him, that's all. Or Mac – he gives me the creeps.'

'The pair of them are definitely up to something. This is the third day running Kyle's called off the school and taken the boat out just with Mac. I wouldn't mind but it's almost sunset – we would have been back by now. Here it is.' She grabbed her bag and Holly helped her off the boat.

'So what was it you wanted to talk to me about?'

'I've got a meeting with Bartolo . . .'

Holly raised her eyebrows and smiled. 'Oh yeah?'

'No, no, nothing like that,' replied Marina, a little too hurriedly. 'I'm meeting him down at the little Spanish bar near the San An ferry terminal. I've asked him to find out whether or not Connor is in any trouble.'

'Why would Connor be in trouble?'

'He was living in the place that got raided, wasn't he? The police might think he's implicated.'

They carried on walking.

'So is that it? I get the impression you want to talk to me about something else.

Marina sighed. 'It looks as though Connor's going back to London on Monday. He keeps asking me if I've had enough of working for Kyle, how I'd feel about moving in together back in London, if I'll carry on having Sundays off in case he flies over every weekend . . . stuff like that.'

'It sounds to me like he's fairly committed – I thought you'd be pleased?'

'I am, I am. The thing is though it's almost like now that Connor has decided to settle down he's getting swept along with the whole notion of it. I feel as if I'm just slotting into his little masterplan. Him not wanting to move in together was the main reason I left him before, which is why I think he's so keen to suggest it now, to prove how much he's changed. It's rather sweet actually. It does feel right though, because we've got so much history together and it took me so long to get over him. You don't know how many hours, days, weeks, I dreamed of this very thing happening.'

'Yeah, but . . .' Holly hesitated.

Marina stopped walking. 'But what?'

'Well, maybe he does want all the things that you wanted then, but . . . do *you* still want those things now?'

'Of course.'

'Are you sure you haven't changed? You've travelled, done loads of different stuff. All I'm saying is to be certain you're doing it because you *want* to. You've got to look to the future, not live in the past.' They started walking again and Marina put her arm through Holly's. 'So, how come you're still in touch with this police diver? Does Connor know you're meeting him?'

'Yeah – it was Connor's bloody idea.'

'That's a bit cheeky, isn't it? One minute you're telling Bartolo you're back with your old boyfriend, the next you're using him to discover whether or not there's a warrant out for his love rival's arrest. If I was Bartolo I'd be tempted to slap the handcuffs on him myself.'

'Bartolo's not like that. I met him for lunch a couple of days ago just to put him straight. To be honest, he doesn't even seem like a policeman – not that I've much experience with them.'

'Even so . . .'

'Anyway, it's not as though anything's ever happened between us. Maybe I got it wrong and he just saw me as a friend.'

'Yeah, right,' laughed Holly. 'Have you looked in the mirror lately? You're an absolute babe – of course he fancies you. If I were into girls, *I'd* fancy you.'

'Oh shut up,' grinned Marina, embarrassed.

'He sounds too good to be true.'

'He is, he's lovely. Why don't you come and meet him properly? We're almost there now.'

'Yeah, all right . . . why not?'

They carried on down the hill past the Faro apartments towards the San Antonio Marina. Thirty metres up the road, Bartolo was sitting outside a plush bar and restaurant called Bel Sito, opposite the yacht club, Club Nautic. With his light-blue Ralph Lauren shirt, designer shades and immaculate jet-black hair, he looked more like a luxury yacht owner than a policeman. As soon as he saw Marina, he stood up and smiled, his perfect teeth seeming even whiter contrasted against his deeply tanned olive skin.

'I tell you what,' whispered Holly, 'if you're not interested, pass him my phone number.'

The two girls giggled.

Bartolo ordered a bottle of Marques de Carceres red wine and some water. They all chatted together for a few minutes until the waiter brought their drinks. Once the waiter left, Bartolo leaned forward in a conspiratorial manner, even though the closest other patron of the bar was some metres away.

'OK, I speak with some companions and they say that there is no problem for Connor or any other boys in the house. But your friend – Luc?' Marina nodded. 'He is in much trouble. The drugs they find are many. I hear they will make big example of him. Maybe five years . . .'

'Oh God!' exclaimed Marina.

'Sí. I know this is true because last year and the year before, in this month, the same thing happens to other English boys. They get found with many drugs too and this is the sentence. One, he is now in prison in Mallorca.'

Marina clasped her hand over her mouth.

'I am sorry,' continued Bartolo, refilling all of their glasses, 'but there is nothing I can do.'

'Thanks anyway,' said Marina, resting her hand on his, 'I really appreciate you doing what you have.'

Bartolo left his hand under Marina's and picked up his wine glass with the other, sipping it slowly.

'So tell me,' his expression became more serious, 'your friend Luc. I have the feeling that you think the drugs, they are not his.' Marina nodded. 'So, who do you think they are belonging to? Connor? Is that why you wanted me to see if he is in trouble?'

'God no!' exclaimed Marina. 'He just wants to know if they are intending to question the others in the house. I would never have asked you if Connor was involved.'

'Good,' replied Bartolo, visibly relaxing once more, 'I am pleased about this. So who do you think?'

Marina pulled her hand from his and picked at a beer mat. 'It's hard for me to say. You *are* a policeman, Bartolo.'

'Yes, but I am also your friend, besides,' he took an olive from the bowl on the table, 'I will not be a policeman next year. My friend, he offer me the chance to buy a diving school in Almeria on the mainland.'

'Bartolo, that's fantastic!' squealed Marina. 'You're so lucky.'

'Yes. I think this too, but I make mistake. I tell my friends at work. Now my *jefe*, he takes me away from diving. In a few weeks I have to patrol there.' He gestured towards the West End of San Antonio. 'My friends like to work this place. They like the English girls, they like their batons to use on the *borracho* English boys. But for me, this is no why I join.'

'Can't you do something else, do a different job, seeing as you're leaving the police anyway?' asked Holly.

Bartolo shook his head. 'I have to pay for many things and save. If I leave the police I also must pay for an *apartamento*. Is necessary for me to wait until the end of the *temporada*, the season.'

The table fell silent. Holly looked beyond Marina and saw two figures emerging from a bus.

'Is that Shuff and Grant?'

Marina swung round. 'Yeah.'

'These are the boys who were also in the house that have the drugs, yes?' asked Bartolo. Marina nodded. 'Is it they you think have the drugs?' Bartolo gathered his things before Marina could answer. 'It is not good for me to be seen with these boys. I will call you tomorrow. Maybe we can go to lunch again, or maybe dinner, *sí*?'

Marina nodded. Bartolo kissed her and Holly goodbye, then skipped across the road to his car, avoiding the need to pass Shuff and Grant. Marina felt Holly looking at her smiling.

'What? I'm only going for dinner with him.'

Holly held her hands up. 'I didn't say a word.'

The girls watched Shuff and Grant traipsing towards them. A very sullen and defeated looking Shuff nodded at the girls and went to carry on towards the ferry terminal but Grant stopped.

'Still talking to us?' asked Grant.

'Where are you two going?' Marina pointed at their backpacks and bags.

'We've had enough. We're outta here.'

'What, you're going back to the States?'

'Eventually. We're getting the ferry. Shuff's got some relations who are in France so we're gonna hitch up there then get some work to raise the fare home. Ibiza's beaten us but we don't want our folks to know that.'

'But the ferry doesn't leave for another three or four hours.'

'To be honest, we can't get off the island quick enough. We even had to sell some stuff to be able to afford a couple of ferry tickets.'

'And I can guess what stuff that was,' sneered Holly.

'It was clothes actually,' said Grant, 'and we just scraped enough together for our ferry fares. Like I said, we're going to have to hitch to France.'

'My heart bleeds for you. So, rats leaving a sinking ship, eh?'

Shuff, who had been on the periphery of the dialogue and unusually quiet, nodded towards the ferry terminal.

'Grant, I'm gonna make my way over there, I'll see you in a minute.'

'He doesn't seem himself,' observed Marina.

Grant turned to the girls, his normally placid and amicable features contorting to as close to a scowl as he could manage.

'You've no idea what going back means to him, do you?' he spat. 'This is the last thing he needed to happen.'

'Steady on,' said Holly. 'What's up? Is he wanted by police? Drugs again, I suppose.'

Grant shook his head. 'If you only knew what he's been through, what he goes through every day, then you'd . . . you'd . . . oh what's the fucking point! Our consciences are clear and that's all that matters.' Grant took a few deep breaths to calm himself. 'Marina, when you see Connor, tell him we said goodbye. We've been trying to ring him but his phone's off all the time.'

'He lost his mobile a few days ago,' said Marina. 'He's got a new one though. Do you want the number?'

'There's no point. I haven't got any credit left now anyway. Can you just say goodbye to him?' He gave her a piece of paper. 'If there's anything we can do, this is my email address.'

'The best thing you could do is admit the drugs were yours,' snapped Holly, not letting it go despite Grant's previous outburst. 'How can you let Luc rot in prison? Five years! That's what we've heard he's likely to get. Five bloody years. The pair of you—'

'Leave it, Holly,' interrupted Marina. She reached into her purse and pulled out a fifty-euro note and offered it to Grant. 'Here, take this. It won't get you to France but at least you'll be able to get something to eat on the way.'

Holly looked at her aghast but said nothing. Grant was equally surprised.

'I . . . I . . . don't know what to . . . why?'

'For my own peace of mind.'

Grant looked at her suspiciously. 'Is there something you're not telling us?'

'No.'

Marina shifted uncomfortably.

'You know something, don't you?' pressed Grant.

'No, of course not.'

'If those drugs weren't ours and you know who they belonged to . . . oh fuck me. How could I have fallen for it? It's so obvious . . .' Grant hit his forehead with the palm of his hand. 'Luc *was* dealing, wasn't he? They were his all along. You're just pulling together, closing ranks. What is it – all Brits together and fuck Uncle Sam?'

'That's not true and that's not what I said.'

'You might as well have. Fuck me. Have you any idea of the shit this has landed us in? Do you realize what Kyle could have done to us? And if I told you why Shuff mustn't go back . . . you fucking *bitches*!'

'It's not like that, you've got—'

'Here,' Grant threw the fifty-euro note back on to the table, 'keep your goddam money.' He turned on his heel and stormed away from them.

'What's going on?' asked Holly, once he was well out of earshot.

Marina sighed. 'I didn't want to say anything until I saw Connor, in case it all leads to nothing.' Marina went to pour some more wine but the bottle was empty. 'Connor's sure the pills and coke didn't belong to Luc. However, *before* the raid, Shuff was moaning that Kyle was only giving them small amounts at a time, certainly nowhere near the quantity the police found.'

'And?'

'Well, just that maybe, somebody else put them there.'

'*What*! Who?'

'I can't say. I mean, if I start spreading rumours and they all turn out to be wrong, then the shit hits the fan . . .'

'Who on earth would do . . . ?' Holly's bottom jaw dropped. '*No*! Kyle! Of course, that would make sense, he's—'

'Sssh! Nothing's definite. This isn't a game, Holly. You know as well as I do that Kyle's got eyes and ears everywhere. We might be way off the mark. Suppose those drugs did belong to Shuff and Grant after all?'

'Not by the way Grant behaved just then. And I've never seen Shuff look so down. I wonder why he can't go back to the States? God, I feel such a bitch now.' She grimaced.

'Look, I've got to meet Connor in Say Chic at midnight – he's been asking around all day. He's also catching up with Leo, the old boy who's got cancer.' Marina looked at her watch. 'That should just about give me time to get changed and grab something to eat. What are you doing?'

'I was going to pop down to Base Bar. I've got a short meeting with another promoter about doing some work.'

'If you can arrange to see him after midnight then we can go up there together. Connor said he'd probably be over the limit so I said I'd have a couple of drinks, then drive the car back. So long as you're not planning a late one, we can give you a lift back too.'

'Yeah, why not? I'm as intrigued by all this as you are. It's a shame we won't be able to get to the bottom of all this before Shuff and Grant leave the island.'

Marina looked wistfully towards the ferry port. 'I know . . .'

chapter twenty-eight

Connor sat outside Say Chic. The Ibiza Town promenade opposite the port was just getting busy. Clubbers and late night *bons viveurs* were taking over from *al fresco* diners, while the first procession of drum beaters, stilt-walkers and bizarrely made-up, semi-naked, over-enthusiastic PR boys and girls were doing all they could to attract attention to their night at El Divino, as they wove along the narrow streets and past the small bars and restaurants.

Connor had far too much on his mind to give them anything other than the most cursory of glances. First of all there was Leo, who was looking very ill. Despite this his mood was upbeat, and, as ever, he had got Connor thinking with his take on life, love and the universe. He'd just popped along the promenade for a pizza slice before returning to the bar for round two.

Then there was his hunch about the part Kyle Goldwell had played in Luc's arrest. Luc had hardly anything to do with Kyle, so the only explanation Connor could come up with was that the drugs may have been intended for Shuff and Grant. But he needed proof, which was why he'd made the decision to go and talk to the two Americans the next day.

The final thing on Connor's mind was Marina. She was so damn fanciable and her reluctance to get physical was frustrating him, though he understood her desire to take one step at a time. She was calling the shots and he realized it had to be that way because he was the one who had chosen to finish their relationship the first time round.

However, he was beginning to feel that because of their history and the way they got on so well, their relationship could drift towards the dreaded friendship zone. Would going back to the UK and returning as a weekend visitor help to avoid or to encourage that? There was tonight, tomorrow and Sunday night left before he had to make his decision. Surely something would happen between now and then? If not, Connor still felt that coming back as a weekend visitor might get their relationship back on to a more physical footing.

But to encourage that outcome before then, he needed to do something more direct to take their relationship to the next level, other than asking her outright or persisting with his hitherto thwarted nocturnal fumblings.

He looked at his new Nokia phone. Texting. There was something deliciously sexy about communicating via text. The slow build-up, the waiting, the occasional ambiguity of a reply. On a roll, the anticipation of opening a message was akin to the pre-pubescent excitement of opening a Christmas present.

First off, something straightforward to get things going. Using the predictive text option he keyed, *Hi Marina, how long til you arrive? X*

About a minute later his incoming message alert beeped.

Just bin dropd off. Wiv u soon xx

Now for something a bit more personal.

You look even sexier than you used to x

He could see Leo making his way back though the crowded street. The reply came back fairly quickly.

How do u no? U cant c me yet! x

Though Marina had just about got her head round using predictive text, she steadfastly preferred to use her own unique shorthand. Time to step it up a gear.

I love kissing you x

Nothing too dirty to start with. Marina put great store on kissing. Good tactics.

U2 x

Encouraging. Leo was almost back. They had been having a pretty heavy conversation and Leo was bound to want to carry on where they'd left off. One last text and he'd switch off his phone until Marina arrived. Fuck it. Why not? Something unambiguous and to the point.

I really want to lick your pussy x

There. Sent. Smiling to himself, he put the phone into his pocket and pressed the off button. It would be bad manners to carry on texting while talking to Leo. He knew though, that if his phone was on and he heard an incoming text, he wouldn't be able to stop himself from looking at it. Far better just to see Marina's face when she turned up. He could almost predict the cheeky 'you-naughty-boy' smile she would give him.

'Now then, where were we?' said Leo, sitting back down next to Connor and biting into his pizza slice.

'Near death experiences.'

'Ah yes.' Leo chewed a little more so he was able to talk without showering Connor in spinach and mushroom. 'I was saying that being confronted so directly with death makes one even more aware of life. Actually,' Leo swallowed the last piece, 'I was thinking that it should be made mandatory for everyone in their twenties to have the threat of death hanging over them.'

'Why's that?'

'Because if you actually knocked on death's door, tasted mortality, the world would suddenly seem a different place. You'd soon re-define your values and enjoy the moment. If you don't live in the past or the future but concentrate only on the present then it is far easier to be content and happy.'

'It's good in theory—'

'It's not just theory, my friend. It's what I'm doing now. And *you* were the one who used to say you could be run over by a bus tomorrow.'

'I know. But how many people actually *do* get run over by a bus?'

'I've always simply interpreted it as being true to yourself. Do what *you* want to do and what makes *you* happy. If you can temper that by treating those around you as you would like to be treated, then in my opinion that's not a bad way to live your life and it's pretty much how I've lived mine. I'm no angel – in fact I've been a right bastard at times – but if there is a God up there, then I reckon I've got an even chance of getting in to heaven. And if there isn't, then at least I've had an enjoyable life in the place I know exists and when my number's up, I'd like to think I've touched a few people's lives and won't be too badly thought of. Maybe sometimes, the odd person might even raise a glass to me.'

Connor put his arm round Leo's shoulder and kissed the top of his thinly covered pate. 'You can count on that.' Beyond Leo he could see Marina and Holly weaving their way through the crowd. 'Looks like you're about to meet the girls.'

But Marina wasn't smiling playfully as expected. If anything, she looked slightly annoyed. He made the introductions, after which Leo went to the loo and Holly went to the bar.

As soon as they were alone, Marina turned to Connor. 'What was that last text about?'

'Huh? I thought it was pretty self-explanatory.'

'It was meant for me then?'

'Of course it was.' Connor lowered his voice. 'I'm hardly about to send it to anyone else, am I?'

'Why did you send it?'

'Eh? For fun, I guess.'

'But what's funny about it?'

'Well ... um ... nothing – unless I wore a little red nose maybe.' Connor laughed, but Marina apparently didn't see the funny side of it. 'Bloody hell, Marina, lighten up.'

'So you did mean it literally? There isn't some kind of metaphor I'm missing, is there?'

'Of course not. What's the problem? Where's the harm?'

'Harm? Actually, I think it would be quite painful.'

This really threw him. Admittedly, he couldn't remember too much about their previous sex life together, other than it being good at the time and that Marina preferred a tender, gentle caress to swinging from the chandeliers and having her bum smacked. However, Connor had always thought that he'd got the oral sex part of things spot on with her. In fact, from what he could remember, short of changing his digits for feathers and tongue for a piece of satin, he couldn't have been more gentle. Shit. Did that mean she was faking it? Even worse, was he not as gentle or skilled as he thought? How many other girls had faked it?

Hang on though. Despite his experience, Connor's attitude to sex was quite unassuming, since he realized early on that what one girl loved, another might hate. He never went for the sex by numbers routine. He always let himself be guided, even verbally if the girl was as uninhibited as him. Marina (or Mary as he had then known her) had been no different. So did she think he was moving too fast?

'Maybe I'm rushing things,' he said, in a conciliatory manner. 'We'll let things take their course, and what will be will be.' He leaned into her ear and whispered. 'But I know you want me to really.'

Marina stepped back horrified. 'Connor, what has Ibiza done to you? God, I thought we were making progress but I'm beginning to wonder. You're actually quite sick.'

'What's sick about it? Everyone does it.'

'I don't know anyone who does. Perhaps it's different in Spain. After all, they kill bulls and push donkeys off high buildings.'

'What are you on about?'

Marina shook her head and held her hands up. 'Look, let's just drop it, OK? But if you ever try to do it, I swear—'

'Have you turned into a total prude? A lot of people would say it's just an expression of love.'

'Love? Good grief. How can hurting my little Tanit be an expression of love?'

'You've given your noony a name?' Connor started laughing. 'This is too much. You've named it after the *dog?*'

'What do you mean I've named it after the dog? We're talking about the dog, aren't we?'

Connor stopped laughing. 'Do what?'

'The text you sent me. You said you wanted to boot her, to boot Tanit. Look . . .'

She showed Connor the text he had sent.

I really want to kick your puppy x

'That's not what I sent!' Connor switched his phone on and went to the message composer. Using predictive text, he typed in, *I really want to lick your pussy.* In a few seconds he was laughing uproariously.

'What's so funny?'

Connor was laughing too much to answer. Holly and Leo arrived back at the table.

'What's got into him?' asked Holly.

'I wish I knew,' replied Marina.

'Sorry,' said Connor, catching his breath. 'I've just got to have a word with Marina on my own.' He put his arm round her shoulder and guided her a few metres away. He showed her the phone. 'When I sent the text I didn't check it. What I actually typed in was this,' he showed her the intended message, 'but lick came out as kick and pussy as puppy.'

Marina put her hand to her mouth and started giggling.

'So you don't want to kick Tanit then?'

Connor shook his head. 'Of course not.'

Both laughing now, they made their way back to the table.

'Come on then, what's so funny?' asked Holly. 'Share it.'

'I can't,' said Connor.

'Just a misunderstanding over a message,' added Marina.

Holly slapped her head. 'Shit, a message . . . I completely forgot. I spoke to Dex earlier.'

'How is the old scrote?' asked Connor.

'He's been trying to get in touch but said your mobile's permanently off.'

'It's not been off – I lost it the day after the raid. I've been meaning to ring him actually. Was he trying to get in touch about anything in particular?'

'It was a bit weird actually. He sounded as though he was whispering and in a hurry. He asked what was happening with Luc, then saying something about someone you knew coming over.'

'Who?'

'I can't remember. It sounded as though some friends came into the room because there was a bit of shouting then the phone went dead. He only mumbled it once. Whoever it was is on their way to Ibiza. I'm sure he said Earl.'

'Earl?' Connor shrugged his shoulders. 'I haven't got a friend called Earl.'

'Maybe it was Dex's friend, or just someone you know.'

Connor shook his head. 'Still means nothing.'

Holly tapped her forehead, trying to jar the memory loose.

'Oh . . . bloody hell . . . I'm sure it was Earl. Or maybe it was his brother? I'm sure he said something about a brother.'

'Earl's brother?' suggested Leo.

Connor froze. 'Earl's brother?' He screwed up his face as if preparing to take a spoonful of particularly unpleasant medicine. 'Are you sure it wasn't . . . the Searle brothers?'

'That's it! I'm sure that's what he said. The Searle brothers. The Searle brothers are coming over Saturday night, tomorrow . . .'

'It's gone twelve, so strictly speaking, tonight,' corrected Leo.

The colour drained from Connor's face. He had already told Leo and Marina the whole story of the Searles, but briefly went through it again for Holly's benefit. Why were they coming to Ibiza? It had to be something to do with him and, that being so, it was almost certainly going to spell trouble. He immediately rang Dex but the number was unavailable. Connor made a few more calls and eventually became involved in an animated conversation, which caused him to stand up and walk away from the bar. When he ended the call and returned, Marina noticed he looked even paler.

'What's up?'

Connor flopped on a stool and rested his head in his hands.

'This is not good. This is *so* not good.' He took a deep breath and sat upright. 'I just spoke to one of Dex's brother's friends. The word is that when Buster got the kilo of cocaine back to the UK from Barcelona it wasn't cocaine at all – it was glucose.'

'Oh God,' exclaimed Marina.

'But what's that got to do with you?' asked Leo.

'They obviously think we switched it. But I didn't even know it was in the video machine until Buster Searle turned up on my doorstep, by which time it was in Luc's car and on the way to Barcelona. Nobody touched it in my flat, so the only time anyone could have got to it was on the drive from London to . . .' Connor's voice trailed off as the implication grazed him. The thought was too unpalatable to do anything other than immediately dismiss. 'No, no way. Luc and Dex looked as surprised as me when we were at Barcelona and found out the gear was in the video. I know Luc better than anyone and like I've said before, getting involved in drugs just isn't him. And Dex . . .'

A flicker of concern momentarily registered on his face. Holly picked up on it.

'If Dex did change it over then I promise you he didn't say anything to me about it. In fact, he didn't even mention all this stuff with the Searles, or Barcelona, or the video . . .'

'Which in itself could be considered slightly strange,' suggested Marina.

'There's always the chance that if Dex did do something like that then perhaps that's exactly why he was trying to contact you,' offered Leo.

'No, he wouldn't be, he couldn't . . . he would have said something at the time. Dex can be self-centred but he'd never pull a stunt like that. *And*,' Connor slapped his head as another realization dawned on him, 'once they hear Luc's been banged up for dealing they'll put two and two together and get five.'

'Have you no other way of getting in touch with Dex?' asked Leo.

'The only number I've got for him is his mobile. His folks moved a few months ago and I haven't memorized their number.'

'He lives with his parents?' Holly sounded surprised.

'If it was that urgent, surely he'd call you,' said Leo

'Seeing as his phone's unavailable he might have lost it and all our numbers would have been in the phone's memory. I doubt if he's memorized any of them. And he wouldn't have my new mobile number anyway.'

'Are you absolutely one hundred per cent sure that Luc wasn't dealing and that there's no way it would have been him who changed the cocaine for glucose?' asked Holly.

'One hundred and ten per cent positive. I've not worked out the whys and wherefores, but I'm almost certain that those drugs the police found were something to do with Kyle Goldwell. And if Kyle can get the police to threaten to arrest people then he must have pretty good connections – maybe even good enough to give the police tip-offs about suitable places to raid.'

'What, surely you don't mean that it was Kyle who arranged for the police to raid the apartment?' asked Marina.

'Why not?'

'Wait, wait,' Holly raised her hand, 'who are you saying the drugs belonged to?'

'Kyle,' replied Connor.

Holly shook her head. 'So, Kyle somehow planted all of those drugs into your apartment, then called the police, who raided the apartment and confiscated the drugs . . . *his* drugs – why on earth would he do that?'

'I'm not sure, but the price he buys gear for means it wouldn't have made too much of a dent into his finances. And if he planted them, maybe they were meant for Dex. After all, he was well pissed off that you and Dex were together.' Holly looked horrified. 'Or maybe they were meant for me. He's not made any secret of the fact he's after Marina and he's seen us out together and knows about us. Or maybe Shuff and Grant did something to upset him. I really don't know, which is why,' he turned to Marina, 'I could do with meeting up with this police diver friend of yours.'

Now it was Marina's turn to look horrified.

'What Bartolo? I can't, he—'

Connor took her hand. 'Marina, honey, Luc's in prison and he shouldn't be there. I'm not going to ask Bartolo to do anything wrong, quite the opposite in fact. This whole situation doesn't smell right and I'll put money on that smell leading us straight to Kyle Goldwell. We need to find out just how far his influence goes. Most of all though, we've got to put our heads together and think of a way to get Luc out of nick. Kyle is the key.'

'Oh, Connor, I can't—'

'Please, babe. I wouldn't ask but we don't know enough people to do this without help.'

Marina sighed. 'OK. But let me meet him on my own first. It'll be better that way.'

'Before we go any further,' interrupted Holly, 'let me just be absolutely clear about one thing. Connor, are you saying without a shadow of a doubt, that those drugs didn't belong to Shuff and Grant?'

'Not without a shadow of a doubt, but if I were a betting man I'd put everything I own on it,' replied Connor firmly.

'Shit.' Holly sank her head in her hands, then looked at an equally concerned Marina.

'What's up?'

'Oh, Connor, we saw them earlier on. They were on their way to the ferry port. Holly had a real go at them too. I'm afraid they've left the island.'

'They've what?'

'They've gone back to the States. Well, actually they're going to France first. You can't blame them really, can you? We all thought the drugs were theirs so nobody's talking to them and like Marina said, I was an absolute bitch to Grant earlier. Apparently Kyle virtually threatened to kill them, they had no money—'

'When did they go?'

'They caught the Denia ferry from San An.'

'That leaves at about one in the morning, and it's quarter to now,' said Leo.

Connor punched their numbers into his mobile but both went to voicemail. 'There might just be time to stop them. Marina, where's the car?'

'Next to the croissant place. I'll come with you. What about you, Holly?'

'You go on. I've got to meet that promoter. I'll stay and get to know Leo here while I'm waiting.'

Connor and Marina set off through the busy streets and within a couple of minutes they were at Luc's car.

'Do you think we'll make it?' asked Marina.

'Maybe. The ferry often leaves a little late.' He looked at his watch and started the engine. 'I tell you what though – if we miss them I'll bloody well kick myself.'

Marina put on her seat belt. 'Don't you mean "lick" yourself?'

chapter twenty-nine

It was unbearably hot, even though it was not yet eleven in the morning. Eggs could easily have fried on the low concrete wall, the only place to sit near the small prison car park, so Connor, Shuff and Grant slowly paced around, reflecting on how, but for the grace of God, they could have been on other side of the mustard coloured walls in front of them.

'How long's Carlos been in there?' asked Grant.

'About half an hour,' replied Connor. 'Did you sleep much?'

'No. Getting up at eight o'clock to come here didn't help. It was well past three when we finished and there was so much going round my head after everything you told us, that it took me ages to crash out.'

'Plus Marina's floor isn't exactly the most comfortable thing I've ever slept on,' added Shuff.

'Still, it could be worse.' Grant smiled. 'We could be hitch-hiking from Denia at this very moment.'

'True enough. Good job the ferry runs as late as everything else on this island.' Shuff took a deep lungful of air. 'God, I'm glad we're still here.'

'Yeah, but for how long? We can't go to any bars or clubs, in case Kyle or his cronies see us. The money Connor's loaned us ain't gonna last that long either.'

'We'll be all right. The main thing is helping to get Luc out of there and somehow getting back at that bastard Kyle Goldwell.'

Grant nodded and they lapsed into a comfortable silence. The faint hum of traffic could be heard from the nearby Ibiza Town to San Jordi road, but other than that it was eerily quiet, apart from the occasional cricket chorus.

Family homes lined the roads leading up to the prison. A small white lookout tower and walls topped with barbed wire were the only indication of the building's purpose. Compared to the imposing, bleak, gothic façade of its London counterparts, it looked almost inviting.

When Carlos eventually emerged, they all but sprinted over to him.

'How's Luc?' they asked in unison.

'I hate that place,' replied Carlos. 'There is a glass panel with a small hole cut into the concrete at the bottom, so you have to stoop to talk through this.' He pulled a face to emphasize his disgust. 'Luc says it is actually not as bad as he thought it would be, but maybe I think he is putting on a brave face.'

'What did he say when you told him about Kyle Goldwell and that the drugs didn't belong to Shuff and Grant?' asked Connor.

'He was very pleased about Shuff and Grant as he said they are good people. He also said he had been thinking and had come to the same conclusion about Kyle Goldwell.'

Shuff and Grant were visibly relieved at this news.

'Luc also made a very good point. He said that the fingerprints of whoever planted the drugs should be all over the bags. If it came from Kyle there is a good chance his will be on them too. They did not fingerprint Luc and because he is saying he is innocent the solicitor thinks it could help when it goes to court.'

'Who got him his attorney?' asked Shuff.

'I did. Luc has worked for me since he first came to Ibiza. I know he is not drug dealer. I will do what I can to help. Now though,' he glanced at his watch, 'I must go. Connor, ring me later, yes?'

'Seems like a good guy to have on side,' commented Grant, as Carlos headed for his car.

'And then some,' added Connor. 'Ibiza's still pretty much run by a few families—'

'Like Mafia?' interrupted Shuff.

'No, not insofar as they go round shooting each other or anything like that. It's just that in Ibiza there are a few old family names: Ribas, Escandell, Planells, Tur, names like that. You'll see them cropping up in the papers or on the side of trucks and stuff all the time. Carlos belongs to one of those families. He'll almost certainly have contacts in government, police, virtually every profession you'd care to mention. Those families own hotels, land . . . If they need to get something sorted then you can be sure that they'll have a contact a phone call or two away.'

'Fingers crossed then,' said Shuff.

'In the meantime,' continued Connor, 'we've got to meet Leo in Talamanca in an hour and see the studio flat that belongs to a French friend of his.'

'Where's Talamanca?' asked Grant.

'You carry on past Pacha. It's a residential area, out of the way of all the clubs and bars, because obviously the last thing you need is for Kyle or any of his boys to see you. Only thing is, it's just the one room with three beds in it.'

'Beggars can't be choosers,' said Grant.

'I'm just glad to still be here. I'd sleep in a kennel,' added Shuff. 'Aren't you staying with Marina?'

'To be honest with you, I don't even know if I'm staying on the island. If I do though, the place in Talamanca is another option for me in case it all comes on top in San An.' Looking like he had the world on his shoulders, Connor trudged to the car. 'The only good thing is that Marina's meeting that policeman tonight. He reckons he's got some news for her.'

'That's great news . . .' Shuff noticed Connor didn't look too over-joyed. 'Isn't it?'

'Yeah, depending on what he says I suppose.'

The real reason Connor was not jumping up and down with enthusiasm was that Marina had suggested he stay with Shuff and Grant that night as she didn't know what time the meal would finish and also, due to the Searles' imminent arrival, it might be safer for him to be out of town.

'Have you had any luck getting in touch with Dex?' asked Grant, almost reading his mind.

'No. It's hard to believe that the Searles are going to be here tonight. As if I haven't got enough problems already.'

'Are they here because of the drugs or that video you made with their sister?'

'Neither, I hope. The only thing I *am* sure of is that they haven't come over here to get a tan . . .'

A couple of students from the diving school helped Marina take the last few tanks from the gently bobbing boat. She waved goodbye to them and approached Kyle and Mac; she had been conscious of them watching her. She dumped a bag at Kyle's feet.

'Right then, that's me done. Unless there's anything else you need me for, I'll see you Monday.'

'Aye, there might be actually. What are you doing later?'

'I'm meeting up with a friend.'

'Connor?'

'No.'

'You could do far better than him, hen.'

Marina was finding it increasingly difficult to hide her contempt for Kyle.

'Really? Who?'

'Like, if you wasn't seeing him I could whisk you up to Amalur for a slap up meal, take you to a wee bar I know in Ibiza Town, mebbes the VIP in El Divino after . . .'

'Thanks all the same, but like I said, I'm not seeing Connor anyway.'

'Don't tell me I've got another rival?' Marina said nothing. Kyle's expression went from smug to stung in an instant. 'I'm surprised Connor's still here. What's he doing for work?'

'He's on holiday.'

'Aye, I've heard that one before. He wants to be careful. One mate already banged up for drugs, his DJ mate sacked from my bar, and those American *dealers* he hung around with on the way back home as we speak.'

'He isn't selling drugs.'

Kyle laughed. 'Methinks the lady doth protest too much. I'm just saying it's a nasty business, that's all.'

Marina had to call on all of her reserves not to say, 'You should know.'

'Come on, Kyle,' said Mac, 'we've work to do.'

Kyle scanned Marina with contempt. 'With his pals gone I can't see anything *here* worth him staying for.'

Marina dearly wanted to tell Kyle to poke his job, but had promised Connor that she would stick it out. Working for Kyle might come in useful, and she was now the only one who did.

'I'm sure he has his reasons. Anyway, Dex wasn't sacked, he left.'

'If he hadn't left I was gonna sack the wee tosser.'

Marina simply raised her eyebrows. 'Must go.'

Kyle watched her walk away.

'I love a woman with a bit of spirit. I'll crack her, Mac, mark my words . . .'

The room was smaller than they expected; no more than fifteen by fifteen, with a tiny kitchen squeezed in at the end. The three rickety single beds fought for space, two parallel to each other and the third at a right angle along the top wall. There was one small window and a bare lightbulb in the middle of the room. It was dark and dank. Leo's friend Pascale had opened the window to get rid of the musty smell but it was a losing battle. He could see the boys were not impressed.

'It used to be a garage,' he offered by way of explanation in his soft French accent. 'Over here is a toilet and a shower.'

He opened a sliding concertina door to reveal a tiny windowless room. A few inches closer together and the toilet would actually have been *in* the shower. The overpowering smell of pine bleach indicated that Pascale had clearly gone to great lengths to clean it.

'Um, how much do you want for it?' asked Grant cautiously.

Pascale looked at him surprised. 'How much?' He turned to Leo and said something in French. They both smiled. 'I think you have misunderstood. I am doing this as a favour. I cannot charge you. It is free. Leo said you are good friends and that you needed somewhere for a few weeks. I am just sorry it is not better.'

Connor, Shuff and Grant perked up for the first time since entering the converted garage, the word 'free' immediately adding a star or two to the room.

'Here are the keys.' Pascale gave them to Connor. 'I have to go. If you need anything just knock.' He pointed to his house about 30 metres along a dusty drive.

'What a top guy,' said Shuff, as Pascale left. 'I can't believe you managed to arrange this so quickly for us, Leo.'

'Ah, no problem, boys. Now then, how are you two with a paint-brush?'

'Does Pascale want us to give this place a lick of paint for him?' asked Shuff.

'No, no. I've heard all about your little run in with our friend Mr Goldwell and that you can't work anywhere he might see you. You're obviously skint so I thought you could do with earning a little money. I've a small villa just a few kilometres from here and some of the rooms need painting. I'll give you a fair rate for doing it, if you're interested.'

'Of course we are! In fact,' Shuff scanned his new home unenthusiasti-cally, 'can we start tonight? We can't go to any bars or clubs because of Kyle, you see. Only if it suits you, that is . . .'

'Sure, why not? You can work until about three in the morning if you want. I'm going straight home from here so I can give you a lift too.'

'Brilliant. We'll get our bags from the car and we'll be ready.'

Leo watched them bound out the room.

'Seem like nice enough lads.' Connor said nothing and just looked at him with a big grin on his face. 'What? What's that stupid smile all about, Connor Young?'

'A few days ago you told me that you'd only just finished renovating your villa, so why does it need painting again?'

'I fancied a change of colour.'

'What colour is it now?'

'White.'

'And what colour are you getting them to paint it?'

'A very subtle off-white,' replied Leo with a glint in his eye. 'In fact you'll barely notice the difference.'

Connor patted Leo on the back. 'Thanks, Leo. You didn't have to. You don't even know them.'

'Like I said, they seem all right and besides, I'll be glad of the company. It's not going to cost me a fortune, I've already squared it with Katya and it'll keep their minds off all the nonsense they've been through in the last few days.'

'You're a star.'

'And, talking of having things on one's mind . . . any more developments with you and Marina? You looked very lovey-dovey last night. And what about the big decision – is London still in the lead?'

Connor sighed and scratched his head. 'When I'm alone with Marina she seems to go into herself a little, becomes withdrawn. It's doing my head in, Leo. I don't know if it's her, me, this place . . . it's not the same.'

'Of course it's not the same. Times change. Expectations change. There's nothing wrong with treasuring old experiences, but it's far more important to embrace future challenges, adventures and opportunities. If that doesn't seem possible, then perhaps it *is* time to move on to pastures new. And that's true whether we're talking about being in love with a woman or in love with a place.'

'Are you telling me I should forget Marina and leave Ibiza?'

'I'm not *telling* you anything. That's for you to decide. Just be aware that you can no more turn the clock back and for Marina to be the girl she was, than you can turn the clock back on Ibiza and for it to be how it was when you were here four years ago. It is for you to accept them as they are now and to then work out whether or not – with give *and* take – Marina and Ibiza are right for you.'

'I'm not sure either are at the moment.' Connor hesitated for a moment. 'She's meeting up with the diver tonight – the one she went out with for a meal just before she met me.'

'So? That was your idea, wasn't it?'

'Yeah, but . . . oh, I don't know. I've probably only got two nights left and I wanted to spend them both with her but she suggested that I stay with Shuff and Grant. She said that she didn't know what time she'd finish with Bartolo and that I'd be safer here because of the Searles arriving on the island.'

'Sounds logical. What's the problem? Surely you don't think something's going on with her and the diver.'

'No, of course not. Like I said, it's just that she's one of the biggest factors in deciding whether or not to stay.'

'In that case, perhaps you should be looking at other factors.'

Connor looked Leo squarely in the eye and started laughing. 'Leo, why is it that every time I talk to you, I feel as though you know something I don't, yet you never tell me what it is?'

'Because . . .' Leo put his arm round Connor's shoulder and started walking, 'life's lessons always sink in better when you work them out for yourself, rather than having a smart-arse like me explain them to you. Come on, let's go to mine and down a few beers while we watch Shuff and Grant do some painting . . .'

Marina wondered if Bartolo would notice that she had put fresh lipstick on as she sat back at the table.

'This is such a fantastic place, Bartolo. What's it called?'

'Pujol. Not so many tourists come here. Many Spanish.'

He poured her some wine and they clinked glasses.

'You really didn't have to go to all of this trouble.'

'As I said, I have to be careful. I did not want to go somewhere that people may see us together to tell you the things I know.'

'Yes,' agreed Marina, playfully slapping his hand, 'but this isn't exactly the most private place on the island.'

'I had to be sure we were not being followed.' The laughter lines around his eyes creased. He was teasing her. 'And this place is too expensive for policemen to come so we are safe. Do you want anything else to drink?'

'No, the wine is fine. I really do have to be getting back soon.'

'OK.' Bartolo paused then pulled his chair forward and leaned into Marina. 'Now, I tell you things I find out.' Marina leaned forward too. 'My *jefe*, my superior, is not a good man. He is called Oscar and I hear many things today about him. I must still ask more questions but my friend he tell me that Oscar is not happy because he knows already that I ask about him.'

'Oh, Bartolo, please don't get yourself into trouble. It isn't worth it. I wish I hadn't asked you.'

Bartolo held his hand up. 'Please. I not only do this for you now. I am supposed to do what is right. It is my job, my promise. Some of my *compañeros*, they forget this promise. Also, even before this Oscar makes for me *muchas problemas*.'

'Yes, but Luc is *my* friend.'

'This is true. But Luc is also friend of my uncle. Before I ask any questions for you I speak with my uncle and he says that Luc is good man, *muy simpático*. He tell me that he is certain Luc no is drug dealer. If this was not so, then no matter how much I like you, I would not help.'

'Who's your uncle?'

'Carlos, the owner of Raffles.'

'Luc's boss?' She laughed. 'Small world.'

'A small island. So now this is not just for you. This is for my profession, my job. Also, this is personal for me and my family because Carlos say the bar is suffering without Luc. But I think to get Luc from prison is not possible. However, if Oscar is doing what I think, then maybe is possible to stop him, I do not know.'

'So what's Oscar doing?'

'Every year he raids one or two apartments of English boys with many drugs. This makes him look very good and he gets promotion *muy rapido*. But people speak and they say that he is friends with this man Kyle Goldwell. Other police who no like Oscar, they tell me that it is Kyle who puts drugs in the house of English boys then tells Oscar.'

'That's exactly what Connor said!' exclaimed Marina a little too loudly. 'Sorry.' She lowered her voice. 'But why would Kyle use his own drugs. Surely he loses money?'

Bartolo shrugged his shoulders. '*Sí*, but is not much. Only a few thousand Euros. If he is selling drugs himself, then this is nothing to have a policeman who helps you. I hear also he gives work to the family of Oscar, to build bar, to do things like this.'

'But surely if Oscar knows Kyle's a major drug dealer he would do something about it? And suppose Kyle gets caught by somebody else? Wouldn't it look bad if Oscar was seen to be connected with him?'

'Of course. But Oscar is very careful. What I hear today is only rumours. Also, if he does help Kyle then he can warn him when there is a problem, so it is very difficult to catch Kyle, unless he is very stupid or careless and I think Kyle is not this.'

'Is there nothing we can do?'

'Only for the police to catch him with many drugs. Not just the amount they find in the apartment of your friend, but much, much more.'

'And do you think Kyle *is* dealing large amounts of drugs?'

Bartolo raised his eyebrows. 'I know this kind of man and if he is not bringing in many, many drugs, then I will – how do you say? – eat my hat. And have you ever seen the hats that we must wear in the Guardia. *Joder*. I would be sitting on the toilet for much time.'

They both laughed.

'Shall we get the bill?' asked Marina.

Bartolo looked round shiftily.

'I think if we run without paying this would be very funny, no?'

'You can't,' replied Marina, not for a moment believing him to be serious. 'You're a policeman.'

'They do not know me here. Come, it is something I have wanted to do for many years. We are on the terrace, the road is there, they are inside. It will be easy.'

'I can't . . .' Bartolo stood up. Marina realized he wasn't joking. 'Bartolo, *no*! We mustn't.'

'Come, if you don't, I go alone. *Rapido*.'

By now he was grinning broadly with his hand outstretched, urging her to join him. Marina looked towards the inside of the restaurant and there was no sign of any members of staff. She jumped from the seat, sending her chair flying backwards.

'Shit!'

Now she had no choice. Within seconds they were running along the road together hand in hand, giggling like schoolchildren. After about a minute they stopped. Marina was panting.

'I can't believe you did that! What was that you were saying earlier about taking an oath or making a promise or whatever it was?'

Marina shook her head and laughed in between catching her breath. Bartolo was laughing even more.

'Marina . . .'

'What?'

Still laughing Bartolo shook his head. 'I paid the bill when you were in the toilet and I tell them that we are going to run away. That is why they stayed inside. They are good friends of mine . . .'

Marina's shocked expression soon turned to one of mock anger.

'You sod! I might have known . . .'

She playfully attacked him, poking him in the ribs and trying to pinch him, causing him to yelp between giggles. He grabbed her arms to stop her. As she struggled, they came face to face. A moment passed between them and they kissed. Marina didn't resist, though when the kiss finished a few moments later she looked surprised at herself, which seemed to amuse Bartolo even more.

'What happened there?'

'Here, we call it a *beso* but I think you call it a kiss.'

'I know what it's called, but how, why, I mean . . .'

Bartolo went to kiss her again but she pulled away.

'No, Bartolo. I can't. You don't understand—'

'Sí, I do understand. I understand things that even you do not yet seem to. You are a very intelligent girl, Marina – this is one of the things I like about you – but there are some things you do not see. This is because the eye you see them with is not the eye you use today. It is the eye you have many years ago.'

A taxi approached and she quickly hailed it.

'You do not need a taxi, Marina. I can take you—'

'Sorry, Bartolo. I have to go.'

Before he could answer, she scrambled into the back of the cab. As it pulled away she rested her head against the seat and tried to compose herself.

She had made a point of keeping her feelings for Connor in check, to the extent that she was aware of being cold. But she had finally accepted that they had both changed and that just because he had hurt her before, it didn't mean that he would do so again. She had therefore made the decision the previous night to take things to the next level on what would probably be Connor's last night before going back to London.

Now it was clear to her that part of the reason for doing this was to prove to herself that her attraction to Bartolo was harmless. She'd enjoyed the attention of the handsome, thoughtful policeman suitor, but she hadn't led him on. She had been honest about Connor from the very start.

Connor was her Big Adventure. She'd dreamed of them being together for years and had pretty much accepted that denying her true feelings for him was simply a fear of getting hurt. They were destined to be together and that was all there was to it.

So why had she just enjoyed the kiss with Bartolo so much?

chapter thirty

'Aye, thanks. Mucho appreciated, amigo.'

Kyle put the phone down.

'Who was that?' asked Mac, picking a sandwich from the office desk and unwrapping the clingfilm.

'My very useful wee contact in the bizzies.'

'Trouble?'

'Mebbes. Apparently someone's been digging round asking questions.'

'Who?'

Kyle stroked his chin. 'That's the worrying thing. It was a Guardia diver.'

'A diver!' Mac stopped mid-bite into his sandwich. 'But how . . . I mean, we've been so careful . . . there's no way . . . is your contact sure?'

'It's probably nothing to get too excited about, just one bizzie trying to make a name for himself asking a few questions. Still, best we take no chances. Maybe we should do the big one at night. No probs with night dives, eh?'

'Of course not. But just how safe are we? Who exactly is your contact?'

'Sorry, Mac,' said Kyle tapping his nose, 'but there's some things I can't even tell you. Let's just say he's high-ranking enough and he's on our team. I mean, he doesn't know the full extent of what we're up to and it's no' like we're entirely above the law, but he gives me the nod on a few things. If I've a problem and let him know early enough he can normally help us out. He gets well looked after and of course, every year I make sure he gets a good raid or two under his belt to increase his promotion prospects.'

They both chuckled.

'It's a shame Rory didn't plant the drugs in Shuff and Grant's room,' said Mac. 'It would be them in prison now.'

'Och, it makes no difference. I know you were no' too keen on them but then again,' Kyle punched him playfully on the arm, 'you're no' too keen on anybody, are you? They've left the island and now that the other fella – Luc? I never could remember the cunt's name. Anyways, with him banged up it's one less of those London boys to worry about.'

'Yes, they've been a bit of a thorn in your romantic side, haven't they?' goaded Mac.

'You what?'

'First of all you had your sights set on Holly but Dex got her, and now you're after Marina and she's seeing Connor. It's probably no bad thing that Luc *is* in prison, otherwise he'd probably marry the next girl out here you fancy!'

'Away to—' Kyle noticed the faint smile on Mac's lips, which stopped him from rising to the bait. 'Ah, stop winding me up, you wee bastard. Anyway, I've been looking into that Connor laddie. He used to work out here a few years ago in Say Chic, that bar near Base in Ibiza Town and I've heard he still goes there quite a bit. In fact, I've heard her ladyship mention it too. There's some fella in there he's good friends with – even older than you by all accounts. Reckon I might make my presence felt. Might even go there tonight. Fancy it?'

'Why do you want to go there?'

'All part of my Marina Masterplan. Divide and conquer. Sow a few seeds of doubt and turn on the charm. In fact, I'll put a hundred Euros now on me getting her in the sack before August.'

'And I'll *give* you a hundred Euros if you stop trying. She's not worth it. She's trouble.'

Kyle picked up the other half of Mac's sandwich and bit into it.

'I enjoy a bit of trouble . . .'

It was Sunday night and in about twenty-four hours Connor would be getting on a flight back to the UK and the grindstone that was Positive Solutions. There didn't seem to be any other option.

The drinks he was currently downing at Say Chic with Leo, Shuff and Grant were as much in celebration as a sad farewell, however. Marina had called him after her meal with Bartolo the previous night and confirmed Connor's suspicions about Kyle Goldwell having planted the drugs. When she called, Connor was at Leo's and well over the limit but thankfully not drunk enough to plead with her to let him get a cab over and stay.

However, first thing that morning, Connor had turned up at her apartment unannounced. Marina was still in bed and Connor hated himself for even contemplating that the police diver might have been with her. Connor's 'I was in the area' excuse was accepted without question and they had spent most of the day together.

Marina seemed more tactile and, with a glint in her eye, asked him if he wanted to come back over later and spend his last night there. It was one of the easiest decisions he'd had to make in recent days.

Grant was as twitchy as an impala in a cage of lions, worrying that Kyle might turn up at any minute.

'Stop worrying, Grant,' instructed Shuff as he returned from the bar with another round, 'Kyle hardly ever comes to Ibiza Town and I'm sure he's never been into this bar, ain't that right, Leo?'

'Yes,' replied a well on the way Leo. 'I have yet to witness Kyle Goldwell darken Say Chic's door.'

'OK. But now we know for sure that it was him who stitched up Luc, then if he does come in I'll beat the crap out of the sonofabitch,' slurred Grant. This was so out of character that they all laughed. 'I fucking mean it. What a bastard! And you said it's not the first time he's planted drugs on someone?'

'Apparently he does it once or twice every year,' replied Connor. 'He's got a high-level contact in the police who he tips off. In return, he gets left alone.'

'Can't we tell the police what we think he's up to and get his villa searched?' asked a sober as ever Shuff.

'I doubt it. If he's that well connected they'll need more than just the accusations of a few Brits who have a friend in prison on suspicion of dealing. We somehow need to get them to catch him with a large quantity of gear.'

'But how will that help Luc?'

'Marina found out that a guy who got done a couple of years ago was also renting an apartment in Kyle's name. It's not much but for it to happen at least twice is a bit of a coincidence. It still probably isn't enough to get Luc off but if we had something firm, like Kyle's fingerprints on the drugs that were seized, then it would definitely help.'

'Haven't the police taken fingerprints anyway?' asked Leo.

'Not yet. I guess as far as they're concerned it's cut and dried. Besides, Kyle's not been in trouble over here and he's not a resident, so they don't have his prints on record. He needs to be arrested, preferably with shitloads of drugs.'

'But suppose Kyle's prints aren't on the drugs that Luc's accused of having?' Leo was paying attention to every word Connor said, even though he seemed almost as pissed as Grant. 'Is there any chance that Luc could still get out?'

'I honestly don't know.' Connor took a slug of beer. 'I can't exactly see Kyle owning up to it. If we do somehow prove that Kyle's a big-time dealer then I suppose it depends on the attitude the police take, whether they're happy to chuck a little fish back once they've landed a big one. Luc's boss Carlos carries quite a bit of weight so I'm sure he'd do everything he could to help. He comes from quite a powerful family – the police diver is his nephew as well.'

'Even so,' said Shuff, 'it doesn't look too damn good for Luc then, does it?'

'Are you even sure that Kyle's dealing large amounts of drugs?' asked Leo.

'Definitely,' said Grant, his voice louder and more belligerent that usual. 'When we were working for him I heard quite a lot of gossip and rumours – he's at it big-time.'

'Where do you think he gets the drugs from and how does he get them on the island?'

They all shrugged.

'Well, that's probably the first thing to find out,' suggested Leo.

They lapsed into silence.

'Here, look, the pool table's free.' Shuff dug Grant in the ribs with his elbow. 'Come on, let's have a game.'

Connor stole a glance at Leo. His complexion had taken on a sallow grey hue; the once handsome features of his lively face were now pinched and drawn. Worst of all, it was difficult to detect the old Leo sparkle in his sunken and hollow eyes, though it was undoubtedly still there. But there was clearly nothing wrong with his mind.

'Come on then, Connor Young, let's have it. What's up?'

'Nothing. Just wondering if I'm doing the right thing by going back to London. I know you think I should stay here.'

Leo shook his head and said sharply. '*I* said that people are happy when they've got a sense of worth, a sense of security, a sense of fulfilling potential. *Your* interpretation of that was living in Ibiza and being with Marina, not *mine*.'

'Oh.' Connor looked a little wounded; it was rare for Leo to admonish him in such a way.

'Connor, Connor, Connor . . .' Leo's tone softened. 'Dear boy, you do have a tendency to simplify and romanticize. Life's not a film, it isn't scripted. If you want to walk off into the sunset with someone it doesn't just happen – you have to work at it . . . bloody hard sometimes too. You have to make decisions, often difficult ones.'

Connor sat in silence for a few moments digesting Leo's comments, then took another swig of Heineken. 'She's a great girl. I don't want to lose her.'

'If you're talking about Marina,' boomed a voice from behind him, 'I reckon you already have.' Connor swung round. It was Kyle Goldwell with Mac and Rory. 'I reckon she wants me. Can't blame her really, looking at the competition.'

'What are you doing here?'

'Just passing by and thought I'd have a drink with my favourite worker. Where is she? I could've sworn she said she'd meet me here.'

'How did you know we'd be here?'

'I just said, didn't I? It's not you I've come to see. Sexy lassie, that Marina, very obliging. Spent a lot of time with her not wearing very much, if you know what I mean.'

'What the fuck are you on about?'

'I reckon your days are numbered, pal. Girls like Marina need more than the likes of you can offer. In fact, if you think about it, there's probably not much point in you staying in Ibiza. All your friends have gone – well, apart from one, and he'll be here for a good few years by all accounts. Ha, ha. You should be careful – something like that could happen to you. Aye, funny auld place Ibiza. Just when you think—'

Rory interrupted Kyle, pointing towards the pool table, where Shuff and Grant were inching towards the toilets.

A brief look of surprise flashed across Kyle's face when he saw them, quickly replaced by a snarl as he strode across the bar.

'Well, well, well. What the fuck are the pair of *you* still doing here? I thought you were long gone. That's one of the problems with you Americans – you don't listen. Didn't I warn you? Are you both fucking stupid or what?' He turned round to Mac and Rory. 'Boys . . .'

Rory and Mac started walking towards them, until Leo stuck his leg out, tripped Mac, then threw what was left of his pint of Guinness at him, glass and all.

'You'll do for me, you're the bloody smallest,' he slurred.

The glass missed Mac by a mile and its contents barely splashed over his shoe. Calmly, Mac took two paces, grabbed Leo's ankle and pulled him from his chair, an easy task as Leo now weighed so little. Very deliberately he pulled his foot back and with a sickening crack, kicked him in the jaw. In a flash, he had pulled a flick knife from his back pocket and was standing over Leo.

Connor ran at Mac and pushed him. As Mac fell towards the pool table, the knife slipped from his grasp and skidded across the floor to the other side of the bar.

Shuff swung the heavy end of the pool cue at Rory, hitting him full in the face. Claret splattered the green baize of the pool table and Rory staggered back, clutching his nose.

'Oh fuck, dot by dose again . . .'

The owner dashed outside to get the police. Kyle leaped towards Shuff and tried to headbutt him, but Shuff moved out of the way just in time and they fell to the floor, grappling and exchanging close-range punches.

Connor stared in disbelief at Leo, who could have just as easily been dead as unconscious. The red mist descended. He let out a scream, grabbed the nearby Heineken bottle from the table and, just as Mac was turning round, smashed him over the head with it. The bottle shattered and Mac stumbled. Connor slammed the sole of his foot against the back of Mac's leg, forcing him to the floor and aiming kicks to his body as he went down.

Kyle had managed to get the better of Shuff, pinning him to the floor with the help of Rory. Grant ran at Rory and shoved him off, then grabbed Kyle round the neck, sinking his teeth into his shoulder and drawing blood, causing Kyle to scream in pain and let go of Shuff.

As a dazed Mac tried to stand up, Connor started raining blows into his face. Suddenly, he felt arms grabbing him from behind. At first he struggled but once he saw the Guardia Civil pulling all the others apart and realized what was going on he calmed down, only trying to yank an arm free so he could point at the still motionless Leo and yell, 'Medico, medico, por favor!'

Kyle was altogether different. Still full of fight he struggled to break free.

'Don't you know who I am? Let me go, you bastards. You'll fucking regret this.'

It seemed that the more Kyle struggled, the more the Guardia enjoyed it, occasionally whacking him or digging him with a baton.

Once on the street, Kyle, Rory, Shuff and Grant all tried to kick out when they came within range, usually to be yanked away at the last minute by their restrainers. Mac, however, calmly walked to the van, letting the blood trickle down the side of his head and from his nose without attempting to wipe it away. As the police briefly let him go, he slowly removed his cravat and held it against his head to stem the flow of blood. The police gave a small gasp. As they moved away, Connor saw the huge scar across Mac's neck, which looked as though somebody had once tried to cut his throat from ear to ear. Mac's soulless eyes didn't even blink as they fixed on Connor. There was even the trace of a faint smile.

Kyle, blood on his shoulder, bruised and grazed about the face, was the antithesis of Mac. As he was bundled into the van, he screamed at Shuff, Grant and Connor, spittle flying from his bloodied mouth, the Schemie back in his voice.

'Ah'm gaunnae fuckin' kill ivray one ay yis ma'sen. Ah'll be waitin fir yis all when we get oot tae'moro and yeh'll no' huv thaim fuckin' bizzies tae protect yer, mark ma fuckin words, I swear tae God . . . yir all fuckin' *deid!*'

chapter thirty-one

Connor squinted as he stepped into the early morning sunlight. It was Monday. His last day on Ibiza. He had to call in to Positive Solutions today to let them know his decision to return.

Shuff and Grant were already waiting outside the Guardia Civil station. The policeman who had given Connor his things escorted him to the road, then walked over to a bright red Renault. To their surprise, he beckoned them over.

'Come. I will give you a lift into San Antonio.'

Connor, Shuff and Grant all looked at each other, baffled, but made their way over to the car as instructed. Connor sat in the front. The policeman turned towards him and offered his hand.

'I am Bartolo, the friend of Marina.'

'The diver?'

'*Sí.*'

All three relaxed immediately, then shook hands and introduced themselves.

'You are very lucky,' said Bartolo, turning left at a petrol station on to the main road to San Antonio. 'I come in to work this morning and I hear about the fight. If my *jefe*, my boss was here, then he would let out Kyle first. Then you have big trouble.'

'Where's your boss?' asked Connor.

'He is on very short holiday, back tonight. Fortunately, Kyle causes the guards much problems, so they make him and his friends stay a bit more.'

'So you heard what happened then?'

'Not everything.'

'How's Leo?' Connor looked extremely anxious.

'The old man? I speak to the *medico* one hour ago and his wife already collect him. The *medico* say that he was so drunk that he would probably be unconscious even if he no have fight.'

'But he was kicked in the jaw. It sounded terrible. Are you sure he's OK?'

'He probably has sore head but this is not through fighting. The only thing he break is his teeth.'

'You mean his dentures?' Connor gave a relieved laugh. 'Thank God for that.'

'So now, I take you to the apartment of Marina. Then you must decide quickly what you want to do and where you want to go. I think Kyle and his friends, they will be out soon. I speak with other police and they say that he no make any phone calls yet, so until he is released you should be safe. But there are other police there that know him and he will be out soon even if he no speak with my boss first.'

'Fuck, are you going to get in the shit for this?'

Bartolo shrugged his shoulders. 'Perhaps. But I leave this job soon. Also, my uncle is Carlos who owns Raffles and he wants for me to help your friend.'

'Small world.'

'Yes, Marina say this also.'

The rest of the short journey was subdued. Connor did occasionally feel as though Bartolo was looking at him rather than the road, but he was too busy replaying events of the previous night to pay it much attention.

When the barely awake Marina answered the door and saw the two men who had been in her thoughts for most of the weekend standing next to each other – one of them in uniform – with a bruised Shuff and Grant behind them, she wondered if she was still asleep.

'Sorry I didn't come over last night. There's been some trouble,' mumbled Connor. 'Can we come in?'

Once they sat round the small dining table it was Bartolo's face she searched for an explanation.

'I cannot stay long. I must return to work. I come in this morning and hear there was a fight and that we have some British boys and that one of them is Kyle. These three were in the cells too.'

'We were in Say Chic last night,' continued Connor, taking over, 'and Kyle turned up with his cronies.'

'Kyle? What was he doing there?'

'He said he'd come to meet you.'

'What?'

'He was trying to wind me up. Anyway, he saw Shuff and Grant and it all kicked off.'

Connor briefly explained the gist of the previous night's events.

'That Mac's an evil piece of work.' Marina shook her head. 'I keep telling Kyle not to let him come on the dives with us but for some reason he insists. All he ever does is go off diving on his own, in the opposite direction to everyone else. Just as well really.'

'He's probably doing it to annoy you,' said Shuff. 'I bet he only tags along when there's decent looking babes.'

'I'm sure he hates women. That's not to say he's gay. I think he just hates everyone. Anyway, he only ever bothers to come to one particular site. Maybe he's having a secret romance with a Grouper fish, they're just about ugly enough.'

'I think for all of you now San Antonio is a very dangerous place,' advised Bartolo.

Connor turned to Shuff and Grant. 'Listen, guys, if you two want to get off the island then I won't hold it against you. And if you're stuck for money . . .'

'No, we're fine for money, thanks to Leo,' replied Grant.

'Why don't we give it a few more weeks and see if there's anything we can do to help Luc?' said Shuff. 'If nothing gets sorted by then, well, maybe we'll just have to admit defeat and go back to dear old New Jersey a little earlier than planned.'

'What about you, Marina?' asked Bartolo. 'What will you do about Kyle?'

'I'm meant to be at work in an hour.' She lapsed into silence for a few moments. Everyone looked at her. 'I suppose the best thing is to carry on as normal. I'll make out I haven't seen any of you. I can handle Kyle . . . I think.'

'Bartolo,' Grant rested his arms on the table looking pensive, 'do you think that the diving school could be a front? Maybe it's got something to do with how he gets his drugs?'

'Of course.' Bartolo answered this as though Grant had asked him whether policemen have handcuffs. 'Many drugs come into Spain via boats. This is not so unusual. In fact, I would say that this is most likely. I have always believed this.' He turned to Marina. 'The man we bring up the day I met you. I look into his past and he has a record for small drug offences. I try to make more enquiries but my boss, he says this is not my job. It is possible that this is connected to Kyle.'

'Marina, didn't you just say that Mac only comes out to one particular site?' asked Connor. Marina nodded. 'So maybe, somehow, the drugs are being dropped there.'

'Assuming that the dive school is a front, of course.'

It may have been obvious to Bartolo but Marina had never even suspected that her job was merely a cover for a smuggling operation. She was momentarily speechless.

'It must be,' agreed Shuff, 'it makes total sense, doesn't it, Bartolo?'

'*Sí*. There is probably a trunk very similar to the one that trapped the arm of the dead man.'

'So why don't the cops just watch him and catch him at it,' asked Grant.

'As I say before, he has friends. They will warn him first.'

'What about if we find out more information? Surely that will help?'

'Of course. It is possible that *if* Kyle is caught then your friend *may* have a chance of getting out of prison, but nothing is definite. Maybe you should just wait until things follow their path. One day those that really control these things will have enough of Kyle and he will fall. And maybe your friend, if he says he is guilty to make things easy and my uncle Carlos speaks to the right people, perhaps he will only be in prison for two or three years.' The room fell into silence and Bartolo looked at his watch. 'I must go.'

Connor stood up, shook Bartolo's hand. 'Thanks for everything. If ever there's anything I can do for you . . .'

Bartolo smiled and looked faintly embarrassed.

'I'll see you to the door,' offered Marina.

'Don't worry. I'm off too,' said Connor. 'I'm going over to see how Leo is. Then I'm going to make The Call.' He started walking along the short balcony to the stairs with Bartolo. 'Shit, I forgot my phone.' He went back for it. 'Sorry about missing last night, Marina. I'll probably come back for a long weekend on Friday though. That's only five days away. Maybe, we can make up for last night.'

'Assuming you don't get arrested again,' she laughed playfully. 'I'll see you later. You'll still be here when I finish work, won't you?'

Connor nodded and made his way down stairs.

He'd just remembered another thing about her – she always made jokes when she felt awkward about something.

chapter thirty-two

Leo slowly hauled himself up in bed.

'I don't know what came over me,' he chuckled, shaking his head. 'Truth be told, I can't really remember very much about any of it, I was so bloody pissed.'

'Probably just as well. We all thought you were a goner.'

'I am.'

'You know what I mean.' Connor passed Leo the glass of water he was reaching for.

'I still find it hard to believe that this Guardia Civil chap – the police diver – pretty much accepts that the diving school is some kind of front for bringing in drugs yet can't do anything about it.'

'He isn't saying that the police are directly on the take or anything like that, just that Kyle's been very smart. As well as stitching people up like Luc, he tips the police off if there are any new kids on the block, any little firms that arrive thinking they can take things over. Then on top of that, he gives some of the police and their families legitimate work in his bar, for his club night or whatever. It's not that he's above the law as such, but there would have to be a pretty good reason for them to investigate him and even then, the chances are that someone would let him know he was about to be raided or put under surveillance.'

'Scandalous.' Leo sipped his water and gave Connor the glass to replace on the bedside table. 'Anyway, enough about Kyle – what about you? All set?'

Connor stood up and walked to the window. 'Yeah, pretty much. It's definitely the right thing to do. The Searles are here somewhere, Kyle's on the warpath, I've not exactly had the best time I've ever had in Ibiza. If I go to London I can still fly back most weekends, see how you are, do what I can to help Luc, let things develop with Marina, get my bonus. Yet . . .'

'Yet what?

'Yet the thought of going back to that job, leaving all of this . . .' He swept his hand across the panoramic view. 'But I've done the balance sheet thing. You know, where you write all the pros and cons of two options in different columns, like Napoleon did.'

'Yes, but he was a bloody frog and on the losing side. Actually, I think you'll find the balance sheet idea was Wellington's. Anyway, all that's irrelevant. You've got to do what feels right for you, Connor. I'll tell you one thing, though, Ibiza never ceases to amaze me. She really is like a woman. Once you believe you understand her, she'll come at you from leftfield with something that totally throws you. She's tempestuous, unpredictable, strong, moody . . . but very, very sexy. I suppose it all depends on one's taste in women.'

Connor stood silent for a moment, then clapped his hands together.

'Right then, I'd better get going.'

'You can phone from here if you want.'

'No, thanks all the same, Leo, but I need just a little more time on my own first.'

Leo rested his hand on his arm. 'Connor. You do know that you're a very special friend.'

'You are too.' He bent down and hugged his fragile mate.

'Everything will work out, Connor, you'll see. Just don't walk in front of any more buses.'

'I'll try not to. Call you later.'

Connor stepped into the scorching sun. In the thick dust on the rear window of the Mondeo, someone had written 'Clean Me'. It was impossible to keep a car clean for more than a day in Ibiza.

He called Marina to see if Kyle had gone on the day's dive with her but she was constantly engaged. Just as he came over the brow of the hill at C'an Tomas, a few kilometres out from San Antonio, he got through.

'At last, I was getting worried about you. Hang on a sec, I'll pull over.' He stopped in a lay-by opposite a boarded-up restaurant. 'Did Kyle and Mac show up?'

'No, thank God. Have you rung the office yet?'

'I'm driving into San An now. I'll have a coffee somewhere out of the way, organize my thoughts then make the call.'

'OK. I'll ring you a little later, my battery's almost flat.'

Connor turned the stereo up, closed his eyes and sat back in the seat, feeling the warm sun caress his face, pleasantly cooled by a gentle breeze through the car's open windows. The funky guitar riff of a seventies disco track he recognized but could not immediately name came on. He sat up to take a moment to look about and absorb the simple beauty of his surroundings. Before him, the small island of Conajera perched on the horizon. To his right, the undulating orchards of almond and olive trees stretching towards the hills of C'an Coix, behind which a few low clouds were slowly building.

Working at the car wash, yeah . . .

The tune swung into its catchy familiar chorus. Great song, funny-ish film. Fantastic style though, capturing the whole seventies disco scene perfectly. Used as a template for quite a few retro revival nights too.

He was about to start the car again and glanced over the road to the closed restaurant with the For Sale sign outside. In front was a massive driveway and a small shed on stilts. What on earth was that used for? He could imagine people sitting up there, waiting. But waiting for what?

It hit Connor like a thunderbolt.

A car wash. Not at the moment, obviously. But that hut. He imagined workers waiting there, ringing a bell and springing into action as soon as a car pulled up below. Maybe a DJ up there too, spinning tunes. Young, good-looking British workers in orange dungarees and roller skates. The Car Wash Café and Diner. Girls in orange bikini tops and shorts, washing cars and offering drivers snacks. American food. A bona fide restaurant in the evening, a car wash cum bar by day. Where else was there a large American bistro in Ibiza? And how many hand car washes were there? He could think of only one and he couldn't remember that ever being open. Labour would be cheap, with seasonal workers desperate for jobs, especially one where they could work different shifts, get fed and top up their tans. The location was perfect, highly visible on the main San Antonio to Ibiza road. Tourists and locals would love it. It could also operate during the winter with the restaurant bar part being open at weekends.

A DJ could play all the funky 1970s and 1980s classics. Special party nights, pre-parties for clubs. Or open at 6 a.m., a post-clubbing chill-out venue for those making their way back to San An from the clubs.

Spanish families with kids in the winter, more of a functional car wash during those quieter months.

Car valeting contracts from the hire car companies. Mailshot the corporate market. Discount vouchers in welcome packs given out to tourists through their reps. Backhanders for the reps if needs be. He was a good salesman, after all.

The ideas kept on coming thick and fast. It would be perfect, giving him the same kind of contact he had with people when he was a barman, but with the feeling of self-worth, of fulfilling his potential and all of the other pointers Leo had given him.

He could scrape together about twenty grand if he sold his flat. Not a fortune but a start. If the figures worked out, he could probably get a mortgage for the rest. Then there would be—

'Hang on, what on earth am I thinking of?' he mumbled to himself.

This was crazy. It was totally impractical. An impossibility. He'd made his mind up. Common sense quickly took hold. Still, it had to be worth making the call, even if only for future reference.

A male voice answered.

'*Sí.*'

'*Hola*. Do you speak English?'

'Yes.'

'Oh good. I'm ringing about the restaurant for sale. I wondered if you could give me some information.'

'It is you that wants to buy?'

'Yeah. Yes. Well, depending on the price.'

'OK. Inside there are seats for eighty-four people, plus a small garden at the back that could be used as a terrace. There is a hut on stilts outside, which is used for storing food, very traditional in the part of Spain that the present owners are making the food from. It has a new kitchen, fitted two years ago, which cost about sixty thousand euros and has hardly been used. It has all of the necessary licences. Inside it is clean but not very modern. It has air-conditioning. There is also a small two bedroom apartment underneath.'

'Sounds great. And how much is it?'

'Four hundred and eighty thousand euros, but we would need half of that in black money.'

'What do you mean?'

'Two hundred and forty thousand would have to be black, that is to say not declared.'

'Right, I see.' Connor was still confused by this but did not want to appear ignorant. The man seemed to pick up on this.

'We would need two hundred and forty thousand in cash. Then the bank would give you a percentage of the other money. Are you a resident?'

'Yes, well, I live here.'

'But do you have a *residencia*?'

'No.'

'Then the bank will probably only give you half of the two hundred and forty. So you would need about three hundred and sixty thousand euros to put down, plus about ten per cent of the white money for taxes and fees, say twenty thousand, then whatever money you decide to spend on renovations.'

A few moments of silence passed.

'Oh.' Connor could think of little else to say.

'To open the restaurant properly you would need maybe half a million euros in cash. It is possible that some banks might give you a little more but you would still need much. Is this the kind of money you have? Would you like to see the restaurant?'

'Um, no. I don't have quite that much. It sounds as though you've explained this before.'

'Yes, my friend. Several times and always to English. The price may come down a little but am I correct in saying that it would need to come down a lot before you could afford it?'

'Yeah, you could say that. I'll have to leave it for now, thanks all the same.'

It was a nice daydream, albeit short-lived.

Still, it showed him that there was potential on the island. All he needed was half a million euros or another idea that didn't involve quite as much money.

And he had neither.

Time to make that call . . .

Connor entered the dingy Colombian-run phone shop that advertised cheap international calls and sat down in one of the six small booths. The setting seemed wholly inadequate given the importance of what he was about to do. He picked up the receiver and dialled the number. Moments later he was through to Mr King.

'Ah, Connor Young. Had a good *holiday*?' He spat the last word with true venom.

'It's been eventful.'

'I'm sure it has. Well, you'll be pleased to know that I successfully signed up Horne, Fleming and Mitchell. Mr Horne sends his regards. The money is ready and waiting for you, assuming you come back and behave for six months of course. The Merc's here too.' He fell silent. 'Well?'

'Yes, thanks for that.'

'No, I meant, well, what have you decided?'

'Do you know what, Mr King? I'm actually going to be totally honest with you.'

'That will make a refreshing change.'

'When I came to Ibiza I'd made my mind up. That was it – I was leaving. Then, when you offered me these two weeks to reconsider, it obviously got me thinking.'

'I thought it might. It didn't ruin your time out there, I hope.'

Connor could hear the smugness in his voice.

'Actually, Mr King, there have been plenty of other things that have conspired to ruin my time out here; your attempt at sabotage comes quite a way down the list.'

'Connor! I'm hurt you could think such a thing.' Heavy on irony, light on sincerity. 'Anyway, you'll be glad to know that things have been going fantastically well here, as usual. We've even had a few days' sunshine, not that anyone in this office has really had a chance to see it, of course. In your absence, we're still running at almost one hundred and fifty per cent of target. Giles pulled in an even bigger deal than you so is back on top of the league. When – sorry – *if*, you come back, we've a big sales conference coming up in Weybridge, where I'll be launching a new incentive scheme. I'm calling it "Money is Freedom" and the top five salesmen get two weeks five-star treatment in Australia – that's connected to the "freedom" theme, seeing as the country was started by convicts. Clever, eh? And on the subject of incentives, I picked up my Ferrari yesterday and it's sitting in the car park as a reminder to you all as to what can be achieved, with determination.'

Hearing Mr King rant on about sales incentives, sales targets and being stuck in that dreary office, reminded Connor just how much he really hated the job, even though the financial rewards were clearly there. But if he got his head down at Positive Solutions he could earn enough for a bar in Ibiza, if not next year then maybe the one after. However, would his spirit be so badly broken that he'd even still *want* a bar, or consider ever returning to Ibiza? Would all future forays to warmer climes be as part of an air-conditioned ra-ra-ra whistlestop tour with hyped-up salesmen, their eager-to-please, avaricious spouses and the insufferable gloatings of Mr King?

'I probably could make a go of it,' said Connor, thinking aloud. 'Be the salesman you want me to be, earn loads of money . . .'

'But are you one hundred per cent committed? A hundred per cent is the *minimum* I require of you.'

Connor considered his response. The dynamic of his relationship with Mr King was going to have to change. He didn't want to just say the right thing or to keep paying lip service – he couldn't carry on working in that environment. Surely if he spoke to him as an adult, he'd be responded to in the same way, rather than the parent/child relationship they had previously seemed to fall into?

'Mr King, you often say that your door is always open, that you're a people person, that you like to think of your sales force as one big happy family. So, help me out here and try to get into my head for a moment. Let me tell you what's been going on in the last two weeks. Apart from meeting a girl who was, and probably is, the love of my life, one of my best friends has been framed and is in prison. I've also discovered that one of the wisest men I've ever known is dying of cancer. If I come back then—'

'And I suppose there's a Catholic girl you've got pregnant that you've got to take for an abortion, along with two French hens and a partridge in a pear tree.' Mr King tutted impatiently. 'I don't know where all this is leading, Young, but it's irrelevant. All I want to know—'

'Hang on, what do you mean, irrelevant? How can someone dying of cancer be irrelevant? For Christ's sake, here I am actually trying to open up to you for once, trying to give you an insight into what I'm thinking, into what I've been through, and you just throw it back in my face. I wanted us to get off on the right foot, for you to understand what—'

'Young. When I said I wanted one hundred per cent commitment I didn't expect any hesitation. Instead, you rambled on about the last two weeks – I'm not interested. I don't know what your angle is here, but I can tell you now that if it's some kind of plan to soften me up so that I give you the money from Horne, Fleming and Mitchell, then you can forget it. The choice is simple: You either get on that plane tonight and I see you bright and early in my office tomorrow morning, or you turn your back on more money than you'll ever have the opportunity of seeing again. Frankly, I don't care one way or the other. I've earned my money, I've got my freedom, I'm happy. It's up to you if you want the same. You can be like me. All you've got to do is get on that plane.'

Connor gazed out of the booth. On the wall were three clocks, showing the time in Colombia, Ibiza and London. Underneath the clocks, the shop owner had put a poster from each location. A rich rainforest in Colombia, a sunset in Ibiza and a double-decker bus on a rainy day going across Westminster Bridge in the rush hour.

'Come on, Young, I haven't got all day. I've an office to run.'

All that was missing was a poster of Mr King's self-righteous, pompous and rotund face.

'You know, it's funny. I really was trying to connect with you just now, but I'd have more chance of connecting with the seventy-year-old cleaner scuttling round this shop.'

'Let me tell you—'

'No,' Connor could feel the blood rushing to his head, 'shut up for once in your sorry life and let *me* tell *you*. You're not free, Mr King, and you sure as hell aren't happy. You're trapped in that office, surrounded

235

by things that make you feel successful. But look in the corner at that Ovation guitar, or on the walls at those pictures of you in a band years ago, Mr King . . . *Stu*. Tell me you wouldn't swap all you've got now just for that band to have got into the charts. And tell me that when you go to those lap dancing clubs and convince yourself that the girls really like you, that you wouldn't swap them fawning over you just to be able to go home to a girl who actually loved you for being you. Oh no, Stu, money isn't freedom, not in your case. In fact, it's quite the opposite.'

Connor could hear Stuart King blustering at the other end of the line and couldn't stop himself from laughing out loud. Stuart King snapped.

'Right, that's it, Young, I don't care what the MD says and I don't care what you want to do . . . *you're fired!*'

'Mr King,' said Connor, a grin creeping over his face, 'I was hoping you'd say that.'

Connor held the phone for a moment, listening to the silence, then replaced it gently in its cradle. All of that worrying, contemplating, cogitating and deliberating over what to do and the decision was made for him. And surprisingly, it felt like the right one.

Funny. Being the dumpee rather than the dumper worked with jobs as well as women . . .

chapter thirty-three

Marina avoided eye contact with Pedro. The captain must know she had been up to something, diving on her own for fifteen minutes when she continually admonished Mac for doing so. But Pedro rarely spoke to Kyle or Mac and was clearly none too keen on them. Marina had considered the opportunity too good to miss. And how right she'd been.

She had directed the boat to the dive site where Mac always went diving on his own. Thankfully, the students were all experienced divers so she had been able to leave them with Nathalie and explore the area where Mac always swam.

She was about to give up when she saw it – a large trunk hidden between two large rocks. Cautiously, checking that nobody was nearby, she opened it. Apart from concrete lining the bottom to stop it from moving, it was empty. There was no doubt in her mind however, that this was where Mac swam to and it was also pretty obvious what it was used for.

As soon as she got a chance she rang Connor, moving away from everybody to the bow. She couldn't wait to tell him her news but wanted to hear his news first.

'Hi, Connor. Did you ring Positive Solutions?'

'Yep.'

'And?'

'And it looks like you're stuck with me.'

'What happened?'

'I'll tell you later.'

'Fab! Well, it looks like it might be a night to celebrate then.'

'Yeah, reckon so.'

'You'll never guess what I – shit!'

Her battery had run out. Oh well. She'd have to tell him about finding the trunk face to face.

So, he was staying after all. It was now *her* decision time. After all the years of waiting, after all of the daydreams, the wish that Connor would

237

turn into the very man he now was, she should be doing cartwheels and buying bridal magazines.

Yet she wasn't and it was all because of Bartolo. When not in his company, logic would once more convince her that it was the situation, the way they met, the danger, the grass is greener element, the holiday romance factor . . . but the bottom line was that when she was with him, something happened. Something warm and indescribable that seemed to have its genesis in her very core. And it was a feeling she had hitherto never properly experienced. But logic was winning. That feeling could simply have been caused by starving herself of attention for so long. If being around Bartolo was the cause of her confusion then the answer was obvious: avoid him. Even so, she wasn't ready to sleep with Connor – not tonight at least. She needed just a little more time. She'd tried to appease the logical side of her character the previous night by inviting Connor over and resolving to do the deed. It was almost as though she needed to prove to herself that Connor was The One after the little kiss with Bartolo.

Anyway, it was Connor who was always going on about fate. So, maybe it was fate that he'd been arrested and therefore unable to spend the night with her, to allow her that little bit of extra time to be ready. Now she knew he was definitely staying she could adjust her mindset, remove the temptation of Bartolo. It would be easy . . . wouldn't it?

What wasn't going to be easy was dealing with Kyle and pretending she knew nothing of the previous night's events in Say Chic. As the boat drew closer to the shore she could see his Range Rover, which meant he had been released and was almost certainly at the bar waiting for her. She had rehearsed playing dumb for most of the afternoon, but she knew it could not prepare her for being confronted with the real life event, especially now she had also seen the trunk. She was actually quite scared.

As the boat pulled in she could already see Kyle striding towards the jetty. She busied herself tidying up; even if it didn't feel normal it felt comfortable.

Kyle marched on to the boat. 'Where is he?'

Marina acted surprised. 'Hello, Kyle. Didn't you fancy coming out today?'

Kyle repeated the question, slower and more deliberately with an air of restrained aggression. 'I said, where is he?'

'Who?'

'Who? Don't play the innocent. That fucking boyfriend of yours, that's who?'

'Boyfriend? Oh, you mean Connor.' Inside, Marina was shaking like a leaf but she forced a smile, a task made slightly easier when she noticed the swelling behind Kyle's sunglasses. 'I wondered what you meant the other day by "love rival". Connor's not my boyfriend. He was, but that was years ago.'

'Well, whatever the fuck he is, *where* is he?'

'I haven't got a clue. I don't think I've seen him for a day or two.' Marina was finding keeping up the pretence very hard so tried to change the subject. 'Kyle, is there any chance of sorting my wages out? I'm owed over two weeks' money and I could really do with it.'

Kyle looked at her for a few moments. 'Do you know when my birthday is?'

'I don't know, why should—'

'Well, I'll tell you when it *wasn't*, shall I? It wasn't fucking yesterday as in I wasn't fucking born then.'

'I don't follow—'

'You know, your no' a bad looking woman but you're nowhere near as smart or as special as you like to think you are. Now I haven't got time to piss about. Where is Connor?'

'Why are you being so nasty? I've told you I don't know where Connor is – what's the problem?'

'Get the fuck off my boat.'

'I beg your pardon?'

'Now!'

'Kyle . . . I don't understand.'

'No one takes me for a fucking fool, especially some wee radge of a bird. Now *fuck off*!'

Marina could see that Kyle's mood had changed so she quickly gathered her things and hauled them on to the jetty, avoiding eye contact despite the fact he stood watching over her.

'Where are you going with that diving gear?'

'It's mine.' Marina struggled to pull her equipment along the jetty, conscious of Kyle's gaze. Scared though she was, she was determined not to be totally intimidated by him. She stopped and looked him in the eye. 'I won't even bother asking for a week in lieu, so can you just sort me out the money I'm owed, please, because I haven't got a penny and I need to get a cab to take this lot back to my apartment?'

Kyle jumped off the boat and walked past as if she was no longer there.

'Kyle, I need that money.'

'*In lieu?*' he snapped turning on her. 'The only thing you're gonna get "in" is more shit if you're no' out of my sight in the next few seconds.'

'Fine. But I need money for a cab. How am I going to get home?'

'Fucked if I care, but when you do get there I can tell you one thing – Connor's definitely no' in your apartment.' His snarl turned into a gloating sneer. 'By the way, you probably won't be needing a key to open the door either.'

A smile spread across his face as Marina's expression registered what he meant.

'You bastard! If you've taken anything I'll—'

'Dinnae worry, hen. There's nothing worth taking. I'm surprised you live in such a shit-hole actually, I always thought you had more class.' He cast her one last withering look. 'But I guess I was wrong about that too . . .'

When Connor got to Marina's apartment, the door was open. It wasn't until he walked in and discovered the flat empty that he realized the door had been forced. He immediately tried to call her but her mobile was off. He rang Holly's but heard it, then saw it on the dining table. Bizarrely, the flat appeared to be untouched, with an expensive digital camera still on the table next to Holly's phone. Connor inspected the lock and was able to bend it back to virtually its original position, so it could close properly again.

The last thing he wanted was for anything to ruin tonight, especially after missing out following the fiasco of getting banged up. He couldn't wait. What was it she'd said? A night to celebrate? If that wasn't a green light, he didn't know what was.

Which was why ten minutes ago, he had taken his first ever Viagra.

He gave his dick a gentle squeeze through his shorts. There was definitely something going on, but it was as much a question of not knowing what to expect as anything else. The diamond-shaped pill had been in his possession for ages, waiting for a special occasion. There had been a recent article he had read in a Sunday supplement explaining that rather than going hard automatically, an erection would only occur if the normal stimuli were present.

With Marina yet to arrive, an absence of smut mags and a Millwall team unlikely to enter the Premiership, Connor felt that for the time being at least, his flaccidity was assured.

The reason for taking the Viagra was his concern that after not sleeping with her for seven years there was every chance that things would end prematurely. Connor simply wanted to be ready for action again far quicker than his usual recovery rate would allow. Not that she would appreciate coming back to find Connor sitting there with a raging boner. Some decorum had to be observed. Well, at least until they'd had their first shag.

He had not had sex for just over three weeks, since Gina Searle's wedged head set the chain of events in motion that led him to now be sitting in Marina's flat in Ibiza. Tonight he was going to re-join the ranks of the carnally active and though with Marina it was about far more than just sex, thinking about anything other than exchanging reservoirs of bodily fluid was proving extremely difficult.

Connor sat on the settee and the warm glow in his crotch soon turned into a hard-on that was almost painful. He pulled his shorts down and was sure that he had never seen his cock look so big. Chuffed, he stood on the settee so he could marvel at it in the mirror above the fireplace, changing position to admire it from different angles.

Luckily, he had the music on fairly quietly so heard the key when it turned in the lock. Marina was very early. Connor quickly slid back on to the settee, pulled his shorts up, placed a cushion over his engorged member and immersed himself in the very unsexy Spanish bike race showing on the small TV in the corner of the room, willing his erection to subside.

'You all right?'

It wasn't Marina but Holly, wearing just a tight red bikini top and a sarong. God, she looked gorgeous.

'Oh, er, yeah, fine. You?'

'Cool. Just been topping up the tan.' She threw her bag on to an armchair. 'Actually, things aren't cool. I've no job and I'm skint. The way things are looking I doubt if I'll be able to stay until the end of summer, let alone all winter as I wanted to.'

'Yeah?'

'I might have to start looking at flights back to the UK.'

'Yeah?'

Holly was surprised not to get more of a reaction. 'What's that you're watching?'

'Eh? Oh, um, just some cycling.'

'I didn't know you were such a fan.' He had barely looked at her since she came in. 'Shall I turn the sound up?'

'No, no, you're fine.'

Holly shrugged, baffled by his behaviour. Perhaps he was just nervous. Marina had earlier said that if Connor didn't return to the UK, she would appreciate it if they could have the place to themselves for a few hours.

'I know Marina's due back soon so I'll take a quick shower then make myself scarce.'

'OK.'

As she left the room Connor breathed a sigh of relief. Just looking at Holly still gave him a stirring at the best of times, so seeing her half-naked, glistening with suntan oil hadn't helped.

Just as he thought he was in the clear, she re-entered the room.

'I'll stick the kettle on. Could you do the honours once it's boiled?'

Connor waited until he heard the shower come on, then scurried over to the kitchen with the cushion in front of him, barely having to hold it. The more he tried not to think of Holly, Marina or anything else vaguely stimulating, the quicker such thoughts raced into his mind.

The old-fashioned kettle seemed to take for ever to boil. Connor made the tea and resumed his former position only just before Holly entered the room. This time she had just a towel wrapped round her. Dex must have been mad to leave her.

'Are you all right, Connor?'

'No, I mean yeah. Everything's cool.'

Holly sipped some of her tea then placed it on the coffee table. She'd never seen Connor like this before and it was a little unsettling.

'Right then, I'll get dressed and leave you to it.' As she stood up there was a knock on the door. 'Don't tell me Marina's forgotten her key again. It's all right, I'll let her in.'

Connor breathed an even bigger sigh of relief; he was in no state to answer the door without taking the cushion with him. But instead of Marina, he heard a male voice.

'I take it Connor's here, seeing as that's Luc's car outside.'

'Yes, but who—'

The Searles.

Before Holly could protest Connor heard their footsteps clumping down the short corridor. It was such a shock that he completely forgot about the effect of the Viagra and leaped from the settee.

'Well, well,' said Rik Searle, 'found you at last.'

There was silence in the room as the eyes of Holly, then Rik, then Buster, all slowly made their way down to Connor's crotch.

'Fuck me,' said Buster, 'I didn't think you'd be that pleased to see us . . .'

chapter thirty-four

'I ain't grabbing him,' protested Buster. 'He's got a boner.'

'So what?' said Rik.

'It's . . . I dunno . . . it's a bit gay. You do it.'

'For fuck's sake.' Rik pushed Connor back into the chair then turned to Holly. 'Looks like we interrupted something. Just about to give you one, was he? Lucky boy. Never mind. You can carry on later – assuming we don't chop his fucking balls off.'

'She's not my girlfriend. Leave her out of this.'

'Oh what, so you were knocking one out watching the TV, were you?' Buster swung round to see what was on. 'Cycling? I always knew you were a fucking weirdo.'

'There's no need for her to be here,' said Connor, ignoring Buster's comment.

'It's all right, Connor, I'll stay.' She glared defiantly at Rik.

Rik shook his head. 'You two have been watching too many fucking films. Sit your arse down there and shut up, Wonder Woman.'

Holly did as she was told.

'Why have you come here?' asked Connor, who could at last feel his erection softening.

'We saw your mate Dex on some MTV thing last week. He was standing next to a horrible little fucking Scotsman called Jock who ripped us off. You were there too. So, we figured that you had to be in cahoots and booked a flight over to pay you a visit. Then, the day before we're due to fly out, who comes walking into the gym bold as brass, but Dex.'

'He shit himself when he saw us,' gloated Buster. 'We bundled him into the car and trust me, there was no way he was going to tell us anything but the truth.'

'He kept on saying he didn't know anyone called Jock and that he didn't know anything about the stuff in the video being glucose,' continued Rik. 'He was close to getting a fucking good hiding. We took

243

him back to the flat and showed him the MTV thing. That's when we realized Jock and Mac were one and the same.'

'But I still don't see what I've got to do with it, especially if you think Dex was telling the truth. I can't stand Mac. We even had a massive fight last night and I ended up bottling him. We all got banged up.'

Rik and Buster looked surprised. 'Don't think you can wriggle out of this by trying to make out you're on our side,' said Rik.

'It's true, he did,' said Holly.

'I'm not trying to get on anyone's side, because I've no reason to. I don't know anything about the glucose—'

'Hang on,' said Buster jumping up. 'How did you know it was glucose then?'

Connor looked at him as though he'd just given the wrong answer to the hundred pound question on *Who Wants to be a Millionaire*?

'Because they've got this wonderful new invention called phones,' he replied sarcastically, remembering the contempt he felt for Buster when they flew over to Barcelona together. 'I heard that Dex had been trying to get in touch with me and that you were on your way over, so I made some calls. I couldn't get through to him so I spoke to one of his brother's mates.'

'How did Dex get in touch? We smashed his phone.'

'Don't you remember he was on the phone whispering to someone when we grabbed it,' said Rik.

'I don't know why you did that,' said Connor, 'we've nothing to hide. If you want to get back at Mac, we're on *your* side.'

'The reason we did it,' explained Rik, as though talking to a simpleton, 'is that with that amount of money involved we trust nobody.'

'Yeah, nobody,' repeated Buster.

Connor looked from one Searle to the other, thinking that if they weren't so big, they'd be almost comical.

'So you're saying that you, Dex and Mac all being on MTV together was a coincidence?' pondered Rik.

'Of course. It's not that unlikely. It's the start of the summer, everyone working here goes to the opening parties, Dex was DJing in Kyle Goldwell's bar and Mac works for Kyle. Dex had only been working there a few days. He had a massive fall-out with Kyle because Kyle sacked his girlfriend.' He nodded towards Holly. 'Her.'

'You didn't waste much time then, getting stuck into your mate's bird.'

'I'm nobody's "bird".'

'Oooooooh,' teased the Searles in unison.

244

'I hope you weren't fucking round behind our Gina's back,' added Buster.

Connor was tempted to tell them about Gina and Rufus but thought better of it. He glanced over to Holly who was blushing.

'So guys, we had nothing to do with the glucose. When I stopped seeing Gina she gave me back my video player, not knowing anything was stashed in it. I let Dex and Luc borrow it and they drove to Barcelona totally unaware as well. You saw how surprised and pissed off they were when we met them at Barcelona. And do you think for one moment I would have gone through all that if I'd known it was glucose? I even lost my job because of it.'

'Diddums,' said Buster.

'Hmm. All that pretty much ties in with what Dex said,' admitted Rik.

'Good, so you believe me then?'

'You might not have known about the video having anything in it, but you've still caused us loads of hassle.'

'How do you work that one out? You should be jumping up and down thanking us because if we hadn't come out to Ibiza then that little fucker would have ripped you off and got away with it.'

'We'd've found them somehow.'

This was as close to conceding the point as Rik would get.

'So now what?' asked Connor.

The brothers puffed their chests out simultaneously.

'We're going to do the cunts of course,' answered Rik for both of them, 'and get our money back then tax them for fucking us about.'

'Did Dex tell you anything about Luc getting banged up?'

'Yeah. A couple of scallies he lived with were dealing, weren't they?'

'No – we think Kyle set him up and that one of his lot planted the drugs.' Connor paused. 'So maybe we can help each other.'

'Listen,' said Rik, resting his massive forearms on his even more massive thighs. 'Just because we've decided you're telling the truth and not to do you, don't think we've suddenly become bosom buddies. Thankfully Gina's got herself a new boyfriend and thinks you're a prat, but we ain't about to invite you round for turkey and Christmas dinner. We're here to get our money back and that's it. Luc can rot for all we care.'

Connor had forgotten how much he disliked the two meatheads in front of him.

'So Dex didn't tell you anything about Kyle or Mac then?'

'We didn't ask him. When he was trying to persuade us that neither of you were involved he told us what car you were driving and the best place to find you and said you'd show us where to find the Jocks.'

Connor could just imagine Dex scurrying to get away as quickly as possible, doing his utmost not to get involved. He didn't blame him.

Buster clenched his fist. 'If it was left to me I'd just steam in to this Kyle's bar and beat the shit out of him.'

'I'm sure Rik agrees that wouldn't be a good idea,' said Connor as tactfully as possible. 'I mean, I know you're the main men back home,' this really stuck in Connor's craw, 'but things are different here. He's got a lot of influence as well as having quite a few people around him. I reckon you've got to be clever. Was it just the two of you who came over?' Rik nodded. 'See, if I were you, to be on the safe side I'd get a few more of your crew out. All I'm saying, guys, is don't underestimate him. You're off the manor.'

Rik and Buster looked at each other.

'Yeah, we were thinking that anyway.'

'And if I were you,' pressed Connor, 'I'd stay out the way so he doesn't see you. That way, you've got the advantage of surprise. There's a little island called Formantera – you can get a ferry from Ibiza Town. Spend a couple of days there to plan things. Give me your mobile number and I'll phone you with any info you need because even if you can't help Luc, I still want to see Kyle get his comeuppance.'

The Searles looked at each other. 'You two piss off on the balcony for a minute. Me and my brother need to have a little chat alone.'

'I'm really sorry you were here for that,' said Connor once outside.

'What, do you mean the Searles, or that?' She smiled slightly and nodded at his groin. 'To tell the truth, I'm not sure which was most scary.'

Connor laughed. 'You are one incredible woman. Does nothing faze you? You were so calm in there. Come here.' He put his arm round her and gave her a brotherly squeeze, but quickly let go as her breasts pressed against him and the Viagra started taking effect again.

'Why did you send them to Formantera?' she asked, thankfully turning Connor's thoughts to a less stimulating subject. 'I thought you would have rather seen the Searles and Kyle's lot beat seven shades of shit out of each other?'

'I would. But even though they're a big pair of lumps, Kyle can call on quite a few people. At least if they get more of their crew out then there's a good chance that the Searles *and* Kyle will get a kicking.'

'Right, you can come back in now,' yelled Rik. 'This is what we're gonna do.' He pointed at Connor. 'You're gonna come with us and show us where this bar is. If we can find somewhere we can't be seen I want to get a look at this Kyle geezer. Then, we'll follow you and you can show us where the ferry to this island leaves from.'

'But I can't, I'm meeting—'

'Don't give me no can't bollocks. You're lucky we're buying this story you and Dex have given us. We can easily change our minds.'

'Great,' said Connor. He traipsed behind the Searles as they turned to leave the flat, and turned to Holly on the way out. 'Tell Marina what's happened and that I might be a little late.'

The Searles dropped Connor off at the Mondeo, seemingly satisfied that Connor was telling the truth, happy to go to Formantera for a few days and content that Kyle and Mac had visible injuries from the previous night's fracas. Connor was pleased about all of this too, but he was decidedly unhappy about the conversation he'd just had with Marina.

In the Searles' hire car on the way to show them Atlantis's location, they had passed Marina trudging back to her apartment. Connor had tried to ring her again but her phone was still off. While Rik and Buster were sneaking around trying to catch a glimpse of Kyle and Mac and be as inconspicuous as two eighteen-stone lumps with sunburnt bald heads could be, Connor rang Holly's phone to speak to Marina. They exchanged brief details of their respective event-filled days, with Connor carefully omitting the part about taking a Viagra. When he mentioned the door being forced open, she told him it was Kyle. She also told him about getting sacked, but saved the good news, about discovering the trunk, until last. His joy at this turned to despair when he asked what she fancied doing to celebrate. Marina said that it would be better if he stayed at Pascale's garage in Talamanca, claiming that Holly was upset by the Searles and worried that Kyle or Mac might try and kick the door down again looking for him.

She also said that she couldn't do anything tonight because she was meeting Bartolo to see what the next move should be now she had discovered the trunk.

Connor knew that Holly wasn't upset enough to say something like that. If anything, she'd seemed less concerned by the Searles than he had. He was also pretty pissed off that Bartolo was the cause of not being able to see Marina, although the means justified the end because it was to help Luc.

It was clear she liked Bartolo and Bartolo was definitely keen on her. So why wasn't he more jealous? He wasn't exactly jumping up and down over their friendship, but the spin cycle stomach he'd experienced when

Holly said she fancied Dex was missing. Why was that? Was it because of their history? Was it because Dex was a friend?

At the moment it seemed as though there were plenty of questions but very few answers. How was he going to get Luc out of prison? How could he turn the Searles' animosity towards Kyle and Mac to his advantage? How could he stay out of Kyle and Mac's way? How long was he going to stay in Ibiza for? How long could he realistically remain on the island?

And, as he climbed into the car and felt a tingle in his crotch, how long was this poxy Viagra going to last?

'I'm sorry,' said Marina, 'it was all I could think of.'

Holly was not impressed.

'Whatever is happening between you and Connor is none of my business – and I'd like it to stay that way. That's *so* unfair using me as an excuse. Now he's going to think I'm a two-faced cow.'

'I'm *really* sorry,' she mumbled. 'Do you want me to call him back?'

Holly looked at the normally controlled face in front of her, ready to crumple, with a tear pushing over the brim of her eye.

'Leave it for now.'

The tear slowly ran down Marina's cheek, then the dam burst, and she was sobbing uncontrollably. Holly put an arm round her.

'Hey, come on. What's the matter?'

'Oh, Holly, I don't know what's going on.' She wiped her eyes and caught her breath between sobs. 'Yesterday I was so sure that I had this whole thing with Connor clear in my mind. I thought I was just scared: I didn't want to get hurt again.'

'That's understandable, but from what you've said and what I've seen, Connor's totally different to the man he was the first time round.'

'I know he is. That's why I decided to take the plunge last night – he's slept in the same bed as me since the raid, but we haven't . . . you know.'

'Poor sod.' She thought back to his erection. 'That explains a lot.'

'I've always known that he's The One,' continued Marina, missing the reference, 'but all of this stuff with Bartolo, it's confused me.'

'Even people who are happily married have admirers – there's nothing wrong with that.'

'Yes, but do married people go out for a meal with that admirer and kiss them?'

'Oops.'

'I feel so guilty. It was after that that I decided to go for it with Connor. We're meant to be together. I hardly know Bartolo. But he keeps coming

248

into my head and until he doesn't, I don't think I should sleep with Connor. '

'You shouldn't beat yourself up. It was only a kiss after all.'

'But I really enjoyed it!' she squealed, halfway between laughing and bursting into tears again. 'And if Connor wasn't on the scene, if this had happened last year, or even a few months ago . . . We've got so much in common what with the diving, he's not that big on clubbing, he loves travelling, his family even owns horses . . .'

'But just because you're thinking about him, it doesn't mean that you're going to do anything about it. It doesn't mean you shouldn't sleep with Connor. Maybe that's exactly what you need to do to get Bartolo out of your head.'

Marina stood up and looked at her tear-stained face in the small mirror by the breakfast bar. 'You're right. After all, I've kept that side of me shut off for so long and, now Connor's back, it's kind of opened again. Maybe I'm just vulnerable to a little attention and flattery. I hardly know Bartolo, do I? Whereas Connor . . .' She wiped her eyes, resolve returning to her face. 'No, Connor is definitely where my future lies.'

'Good. That's decided then.' Holly's tone was brisk. 'So I suppose you're going to ring Connor and get him to bring his things over?'

'No.' Marina hesitated, chewing her lip. 'It's probably best that he gets all of this stuff with the Searles sorted out first . . . don't you think?'

'What *I* think,' replied Holly, making her way to her room, 'is that at the moment, babe, you don't know your arse from your elbow . . .'

part five

as michael caine once said . . .

chapter thirty-five

Leo's stroke came out of the blue.

Thankfully it was a mild one, but it had still been necessary to keep him heavily sedated. Katya told Connor not to visit until Leo showed signs of improvement. It was hard to believe that the stroke happened only a few hours after Connor left him that afternoon on his way to make the call to Positive Solutions. It explained why he'd been unable to get through later that evening to tell Leo he was staying. Katya subsequently relayed the news, claiming it had helped perk him up.

In the three days since then Connor had moved into Pascale's garage with Shuff and Grant. He hired a Corsa and let it get back to Kyle that he had left the island, so, frustrating though it was, Marina's reluctance to let him near her apartment made sense. Bartolo had been useful too, agreeing to help where possible.

Connor had spent a lot of time with Marina during the days though, as they had been on a mission to follow Kyle or Mac, watching what they were up to and trying to gather as much information as possible. He had hired a motorbike for Shuff and Grant, so they too had been keeping tabs on the Scots' nefarious activities.

They had discovered the location of Kyle's villa, isolated deep in a forest a few kilometres from Santa Getrudes. More importantly, not far from the main building was a small *casita*, a single-storey outhouse. It witnessed considerable activity and Shuff and Grant managed to snatch a look inside when nobody was around. Electronic scales, plastic bags, and remnants of powder were scattered across the dining table. There was no doubt in their minds that the majority of Kyle's cocaine and ecstasy was stashed there before it was sold.

Bartolo was told of their find but his response was the same as it had been when told of the trunk – without catching Kyle in the act it proved nothing and was unlikely to prompt a raid or surveillance. He also advised against asking him to pass the information on to his superiors because in so doing, it would inevitably get back to Kyle and alert him to the fact that someone had taken it upon themselves to probe into his affairs.

Once again though, Bartolo's own contacts had proven useful. A friend had an unused apartment overlooking Atlantis and the diving school, in the Ali Bey block. However, during the previous three days, Atlantis had yielded nothing of interest.

Today was going to be different though. Connor had met up with the newly reinforced Searles. They were planning to reacquaint themselves with Mac and Kyle at around six in the evening, when Connor had assured them that the Scots would be there, even though the bar itself was closed to the public.

If everything went according to plan there was a chance of helping Luc too. Through watching Kyle over the last few days, they were now fairly certain that he would have handled the drugs planted in Luc's room at some point. If Kyle's fingerprints were on them, then the fact that the apartment Luc was staying in was in Kyle's name and that similar raids had occurred in previous years also at properties in Kyle's name, meant there could be a strong case against him. If Kyle was proven to be the big-time dealer that he undoubtedly was then with Bartolo's uncle Carlos testifying on Luc's behalf, there would be a reasonable chance of Luc being found innocent.

At six o'clock, Bartolo promised he was going to be on duty patrolling near to Atlantis, so that if the confrontation erupted in the way Connor expected, it would give him and other units the excuse to search Kyle's villa and outhouse.

It was just gone five as Connor approached the Ali Bey apartments. Had it not been for Leo being ill and the impending confrontation between the Searles and the Scots, Connor's thoughts would have been dominated by Marina. Despite the time spent together there had still been little progress.

As Connor pulled up outside Ali Bey he saw Holly hiding in the doorway. Ah yes, Holly. They were good mates now. At first he'd thought the chemistry was there with her but she simply wasn't partner material. She was at a different stage in her life, just after a good time. Even if Dex hadn't got to her first and Marina hadn't reappeared on the scene, there would have been no future for them, lovely though she was.

He pressed the remote to lock the car and walked towards the doorway. Holly gingerly poked her head out.

'Are you early or am I late?' he asked, taking the doorkey from his pocket.

'A bit of both, I think. I was getting worried hiding here in case anyone saw me.'

Connor opened the door and let Holly pass. 'I'll leave this bottom door open for the others – I'm not sure if the buzzer's working. Fourth floor.' He followed her up the stairs.

'How's Leo?'

'I'm not sure. Katya doesn't want me to see him because he's still heavily sedated. Apparently the stroke wasn't life-threatening but in his condition I'm sure it doesn't look good.'

'It had nothing to do with Mac kicking him, did it?'

'No. Katya asked the doctor exactly that and he said categorically that it wasn't connected. Leo seemed so full of beans when I left him, all things considered. I can't believe he had the stroke that same night.'

'He seems like a wiry old so-and-so. I'm sure he's got some fight in him yet.'

They got to the flat and entered. 'We've a perfect view of Atlantis from here,' he said, pointing towards a window.

Holly walked over to it. 'Are the Searles definitely coming?'

'Yep.'

'How many of them?'

'Six in all.'

'Will that be enough?'

'I would have thought so. Kyle's usually only got Mac and Rory with him in Atlantis this time of the evening.'

'Good. I'd love to be in that bar to see Kyle get what's coming to him, especially as I missed your little performance at Say Chic the other night.'

Connor watched Holly walk over to the settee. There was no getting away from the fact that she was absolutely stunning. Dex was a lucky man. It reminded him that he hadn't spoken to his friend for ages.

'Have you heard from Dex lately, Holly?'

'No, why should I?'

'I got the impression that you were going to catch up with him again at the end of summer.'

Good grief, thought Holly, don't men ever discuss relationships?

'I don't know why you thought that. I never made any such promise. When he went home, that was it really.'

It simply confirmed what Connor had suspected all along. Holly was after no-strings, no-commitment sex. Poor old Dex even thought they were simply having a sabbatical while she finished her season and he got his DJ career off the ground.

255

'So you won't be visiting London at the end of the summer then?'

'I doubt it. If I had my way I'd stay in Ibiza.'

'Me too. Mind you, I'm not sure I've got any choice. Fuck knows what I'm going to do when this is all over. Thankfully at the moment I haven't got time to worry about it.'

'Things are up in the air for me as well. I haven't even got a summer job let alone a winter one. Unless something drastic happens I reckon I'll be off very soon.'

'What, to the UK? I'm sure something will turn up.'

'Anyway, that's not the only reason.' She hesitated and picked at some loose thread on the settee. 'It's also because I've met someone.'

Connor felt a pang. He had assumed that she wasn't looking. 'Who?'

'No one you would have seen around.'

'But why are you leaving? Is he back in the UK?'

'No, no he lives out here. Or rather, he's out here at the moment.'

'So why are you going back?'

'He's seeing someone else.'

'Oh.' Connor walked over and sat next to her. 'And is he serious with this someone else?'

'I think so.'

'Bummer. When did you meet him?'

'A while ago actually.'

'Before you started seeing Dex?' There was a hint of surprise in Connor's voice.

She nodded.

Inside, he felt his stomach tighten still further. When he was convinced Holly was his destiny, not only had she fancied Dex but she was keen on yet another man. Thank God he hadn't got involved with her. His phone rang, saving them. It was a short call.

'That was Marina. Bartolo's just dropped her off and she's making her way up with Shuff and Grant.'

'Things are going well between you two then?'

'Yeah, great. We had a few hiccups but we've been getting on really well.'

He smiled and tapped the side of his nose. Having been so well and truly blown out by Holly the last thing he wanted her to think was that he was a complete failure with women. A little bravado to protect his pride wasn't the most heinous of vanities, after all.

There was a knock on the door.

'Door's open!' yelled Connor. An excited Shuff and Grant came bouncing into the room.

'All set?' Shuff rubbed his hands together. 'This is it then – payback time. I was just thinking, you have told the Searles that no matter what happens they mustn't mention that any of us are still in Ibiza, haven't you?'

'Of course – not that they'll be doing much talking with any luck.'

Marina was the last in. Her blonde hair was pulled back in a harsh ponytail. Connor felt something, but he wasn't sure what exactly. He went over and kissed her.

'Hi, gorgeous. Is Bartolo ready to go?'

She held up her mobile. 'Just press redial when we need him.'

'Excellent . . . now all we have to do is wait.'

An anxious Connor looked at his watch for the umpteenth time: 6:45 p.m.

'What the fuck is going on in there? I was expecting to see windows smashing, bodies flying out of doors . . . I've heard noisier libraries.'

'Maybe the Searles have tied them up, gagged them and are torturing them this very minute,' offered Shuff optimistically.

'Is it worth giving Bartolo a call?' suggested Grant.

'There's no point,' replied Marina. 'If they go in and nothing's happening, then all it does is put Kyle on his guard.'

'She's right,' agreed Connor. 'But there's definitely something . . .' Movement from outside Atlantis distracted him. 'What the . . . ?' He could not believe his eyes.

'What is it?' Shuff dashed to the window.

Kyle, Mac and Rory, along with the six-man Searle posse, were walking out of Atlantis all laughing and joking.

'Please tell me the Searles don't know we're up here,' said Grant, instinctively ducking back from the window.

'Of course not,' replied Connor. 'Look, they're getting into their cars. Where do you think they're going?'

'There's only one way to find out,' said Shuff. 'Come on, Grant. Let's jump on the bike and follow them.'

'They're probably heading for the villa,' said Connor. 'We'll drive up there. Make sure you give us a call because if they are there they'll hear our car as we pull up.' He looked to Holly. 'Are you coming?'

She shook her head. 'I've got things to sort out. I'll catch up with you later.'

As soon as they left, she punched a number into her phone.

'Hi, is that the Ibiza Travel Shop? I'm after a one way flight to Manchester . . .'

*

The Searles emerged from the *casita* smiling and shaking hands with Kyle and Mac, unaware that from the safety of the trees, four bewildered and horrified pairs of eyes were watching them.

The late sun cast long shadows across the clearing from the surrounding pine trees. On the warm bonnet of Kyle's Range Rover, two cats lazily purred, occasionally flicking their tails when a fly irritated them.

'So are you happy then, boys? No hard feelings, but?' The voice carried across the clearing.

'Nah, mate, more than happy.' Buster Searle was beaming from ear to ear.

'It's cost us a pretty penny, you know, but we worry more about our long-term relationship with customers than ripping people off – well, apart from those scum in Birmingham. Trust Mac to confuse the two packages and give you the glucose, eh? Especially with lumps like youse – Jeez, that's the last thing we need.'

'I must admit,' said Rik Searle, 'I was a bit surprised at old Jock – sorry, I mean Mac – trying to get one over on someone like us.'

'Like I said,' gushed Kyle, 'we were surprised when we didn't hear anything from those cunts in Birmingham. We were looking forward to telling them that we'd given them the glucose for trying to rip us off before. Thank God that young idiot who DJ'd for me told you where we were. Otherwise we'd've had a nasty surprise waiting for us when we came back down to London in October, eh?'

'Fucking right you would have,' said Buster, puffing his chest out.

'I suppose we should give Dex a little drink when we get back, for steering us towards you,' added Rik.

'Aye, well, don't get too carried away, eh?'

They all laughed.

'So these *two* kilos are one hundred per cent genuine?' asked Rik.

'You saw me test it,' piped up Rory, 'and besides, you know where our bar is, where we live – we're not going to be that daft, are we?'

'I don't know, you're daft enough to give us an extra kilo for nothing.' Rik Searle was only half joking.

'Hey, big man, in my books that's no' daft, that's fucking sensible, eh? This way we don't end up having an all-out war plus we keep you sweet for future biz.'

'And talking about future biz, when is that next shipment coming in?'

Kyle looked around as if to check that no one was listening. For once he was right to do so, although he would have been wiser still to have lowered his voice in the natural auditorium that the clearing created.

'Not sure exactly, but certainly within the next few days.'

'Fuck me, you've got a fair old bit stashed in there anyway, so you must be talking about a decent whack,' observed Buster.

'Aye, we are. Most of that stuff in there is sold anyway. It's no' where we normally keep it, obviously. This stuff'll be just as good as what you got there and like I say, even if you only want a little, it'll be the best price you've ever known.'

'Sounds good. What was the name of that hotel you recommended again?' asked Rik.

'Pike's.'

'Right. We'll book in there until this gear turns up. Then we'll have a look at it and let you know how much we want. That will also give us a chance to get one of our boys to come out and take this back for us.'

'Aye, wise move, fellas. It's nice dealing with pros. Rory, gimme that gear.' Rory passed the two kilos to Kyle. 'There you go, boys.' He placed it carefully into a holdall in the back of one of their hire cars. 'I'll give you a call as soon as I can confirm its arrival – probably be within the next two to three days, but might even be tomorrow, you never know. If you need anything at all between now and then, passes for clubs, a few lassies, whatever, just gimme a bell.'

They all shook hands. Kyle, Mac and Rory watched the Searles drive off.

'Why, Kyle?' asked Mac, shaking his head.

'Mac, I'd always put money on you in a scrap – you know that – and maybe they're no' the sharpest pencils in the case, but they are fucking big, nasty bastards. We always knew there might be a chance of them finding us, or sussing you on the day. That's why we've always had that Birmingham angle as an excuse.'

'But giving them an extra kilo?'

'Look, we chanced our arm and we got sussed. The MTV thing was just bad luck. That wee cunt Dex told them where we are and I wouldn't mind betting that now Connor's probably back in the UK he couldn't wait to tell them as well. It's just one of them things.'

'I know but two kilos!' repeated Mac.

'Chill out, Mac, for Chrissakes! They've paid us for one and the amount we're getting it for now means that what they've already paid pretty much covers two anyway. We're going to get more biz from them. We've kept the peace, we can stitch 'em up another time when we're back and if we are in London then maybe we can pay those bastards Dex and Connor a visit and thank 'em in person for telling the Searles where we were, eh? I'm sure after that bottle over your bonce you'd like to see

259

Connor again. Now, come on, let's leave Rory to tidy up here and we'll get back to the bar and make a few calls, OK?'

From the safety of the surrounding trees, Connor and Marina watched the Range Rover pull away – Shuff and Grant dashed off to the bike to follow the Searles.

'Great, did you hear that?' whispered Connor. 'Now I definitely can't go back to London.'

'I'm sure they'll have forgotten about it by then.'

'At least the Searles did as I asked so Kyle and Mac think I've left the island.'

Marina rolled over in the leaves on to her back and sighed.

'All of this is like being in a bloody film.'

Connor looked at her. Something that Leo had said in Say Chic on the night of the fight came back to him in a wave of realization.

Life's not a film, it isn't scripted.

That was it. It was the romantic idyll of his relationship with Marina that appealed to him: Boy meets girl, girl loves boy more, boy leaves on voyage of self-discovery, realizes mistake but loses touch with girl, a changed boy, he meets girl again after several years through chance encounter, resumes relationship, walks off into sunset to closing credits.

Except in this case the girl had changed too. And, although the boy was now ready for a relationship, there was no mistake the first time round. Back then, he simply hadn't loved her.

And he didn't love her now.

Yes, there had been that initial spark of attraction that he always felt vital to begin a relationship but it was a spark that never properly took hold, merely kindled brightly for a while. He'd experienced the stomach-knotting desire and the possessive yearning that he remembered with a rose-coloured tint as love, yet had they pursued it, would they honestly have still been together?

In the back of his mind he had always known that they actually had little in common – he even preferred brunettes to blondes and he knew she preferred the swarthy Mediterranean look to his Anglo-Celtic features. She was always outdoor and sporty whereas he was more into the club scene. Her family used to own horses; his used to bet on them.

Despite this she was undoubtedly attractive, smart, and with a host of other qualities he was now looking for in a woman. But he was not in love.

He was not in love.

And now he had to tell her.

'Marina. There's something really important I need to say.'

Marina felt her body tighten immediately. The last few days with Connor had been very difficult. Every moment, she sensed his need to become physical. On a few occasions she'd tried to let things develop, but had found it impossible to let go. No matter how she rationalized it, how much she convinced herself otherwise, she now knew the reason: Bartolo. Yet how could she tell Connor? His best friend in prison, all of this stuff now happening with the Searles and as if that wasn't enough, the Grim Reaper with Leo in his sights.

She had been waiting for Connor's 'big speech', his wanting to know why she'd been so cold, and she wasn't at all sure how she was going to react, or whether she would be able to tell the truth.

'Connor, maybe now isn't the best time.'

'It is – the perfect time.' He looked through the trees. Rory was back in the outhouse. 'Come on, let's walk to the car.'

Nothing was said until they were driving to San Antonio.

'Marina. You know I think the world of you, don't you?'

Marina nodded, worried as to what was coming next. Connor continued.

'You've no idea how many times I've thought about you since we split up. It took me ages to realize how much I must have hurt you when you wanted us to move in together. It was just that moving in together was something I hadn't even contemplated at the time – which was nothing to do with you, incidentally,' he added hastily. 'It was me. Living with someone was like getting married and getting married was something that grown-ups did and quite simply, I wasn't grown-up. But now . . .'

Oh God, thought Marina, he's going to ask me to *marry* him.

'Look, Connor, there's something—'

'Please,' he held his hand up, 'just let me finish what I was going to say. Now, I've changed . . . loads. Even in London I could feel it happening. Then, when I came out here, I was convinced that there was some kind of mystical reason for it, as if I was going to find my destiny.'

'Connor, I—'

'I've nothing to prove any more and if I'm going to be with someone, then she needs to be secure in herself with nothing to prove either.'

'That's good, but maybe I'm not that person. Maybe I still do have things to prove.'

Connor shook his head. 'I don't think so. But I also don't think – and I hope to God that I haven't got this wrong – you feel the same about me as you used to, do you?'

It took Marina a few moments to register that Connor wasn't in fact, on one knee, but was actually saying to her what she had wanted to say to him.

'If I've got this wrong, then I'm really, really sorry.'

'No,' Marina shook her head and looked almost guilty, 'you haven't got it wrong.'

Connor let out a sigh of relief. 'Thank God for that. I guess people move on and . . . have you shagged Bartolo?'

Oops. It just slipped out. It wasn't important to him and he probably wouldn't now even have minded if she had. However, prior to this realization, the question had been lurking beneath Connor's barely controlled façade for a while. He'd tried to bury the thought but it had been waiting, straining to burst out like Jordan in a trainer bra.

Marina looked at him, part confused, part shocked by the directness and incongruity of the comment, and part guilty that though nothing had happened physically, emotionally, at least, it had.

'No, I haven't.'

She searched Connor's face, which, with male pride intact, slowly broke into a smile.

'But you want to though, don't you? You like him as more than just a friend.'

Marina's features softened and she smiled too, then gently nodded.

'I think so.'

Connor indicated and pulled into a petrol station.

'He seems a really nice bloke.' He let out a long sigh. 'You know, strange though it may seem, I actually feel better knowing all of this. It's like a huge weight's been lifted off my shoulders.'

'Me too.' They sat in silence for a moment. 'So now what?'

'Now?' He switched the engine off. 'Now, I'm going to get some petrol then take you to see what I imagine will be a very happy young policeman . . .'

chapter thirty-six

Holly was packed and ready to go a good few hours before she needed to be. She'd said a quick goodbye to Marina who was dashing off to meet Bartolo.

'Connor will tell you all about it,' she'd said, before bounding down the stairs happier than Holly could ever remember seeing her.

When Connor turned up he suggested going for a farewell drink in San José, which was en route to the airport. It promised to be a busy day, because directly after dropping off Holly he was going for a meeting with Bartolo, Marina, Shuff and Grant to discuss the next move to help Luc, now they had discovered more about Kyle's activities.

As they shared a bottle of wine, Connor knew that he was going to be sad to see Holly go. It had come as a real shock that she was leaving so suddenly. True, he still fancied her like mad, but it said a lot about her personality that he was able to look beyond that and enjoy the relationship they now had.

He treated her to some tapas and told her about recent events with Marina. They'd allowed themselves a good couple of hours to enjoy each other's company for the last time.

After an hour Connor's mobile made them both jump as its shrill ring jolted them from their tranquil and relaxed afternoon in the sleepy village. Holly could tell instantly that it was not good news. The call ended. The colour had almost completely drained from Connor's face.

'What's wrong?'

'It's Leo,' replied Connor. He looked numb. 'He's just had another stroke . . . he's . . . he's dead.'

Half an hour later, with Holly waiting in the hospital corridor, a shaken Connor slowly walked out of one of the side rooms, his arm round a sobbing Katya. He whispered something to her, then kissed her gently on the forehead. Katya returned to the room and Connor came over to Holly.

'Ready to go? I'll take you to the airport.'

'Connor, don't be silly, I'll get a cab.'

'No, it's OK. Katya needs to sort out a few things here – forms and stuff. I said I'd take you to the airport then come back for her. I could do with getting out of here and having a friendly face to talk to, to be honest.'

Holly got the impression that Leo's death still hadn't really sunk in. They didn't say much until they were in the car. Holly drove.

'Apparently he had a thrombosis,' said Connor after a few minutes, staring blankly out of the window. 'A blood clot broke off and caused the first stroke. It was quite a small one but there was every chance that it would have had a long-term effect – well, as long-term as the lung cancer would have permitted. He was so weak that the second one finished him off . . .'

'Connor, I'm so sorry.'

'At least it means he didn't suffer the kind of end he would have had if the cancer had run its course, which is something, I suppose.'

Connor didn't speak for a while and turned away from Holly, watching the familiar landmarks pass by without any of them registering. She could tell by the slow, deep breaths he was taking that he was probably fighting back the tears. All she wanted to do was to stop the car, give him a big hug, then tell him what she'd wanted to for a long time.

That she was crazy about him.

She had been from the first time they met, though she'd tried to deny it to herself, scared that he was going to be another Terry, another smooth-talking wide-boy. But whereas Terry's lines were oily, well-practised and manipulative, Connor's were spontaneous, naturally witty and honest.

It hadn't taken her long to realize her attraction to Connor; it was why she never consummated her relationship with Dex. Well, that and the fact that Dex was more concerned with the contents of her G-string than her head.

Then, when Marina turned out to be the oft-talked of Mary, she could only stand back and watch their relationship develop, occasionally kicking herself for the missed opportunity, especially as Connor's hopes, dreams and attitudes seemed to increasingly mirror her own. Marina was a fantastic girl but it was clear to Holly at least, not right for Connor (nor he for her). Holly never once considered trying to influence either party or to sabotage their relationship though. She had been there for both of them and promised herself not to let her own growing feelings for

Connor influence any advice she gave, indeed she did her best to avoid giving advice at all.

When she'd found out earlier in the day that Connor and Marina were no longer an item, she had been sorely tempted to cancel her flight and stay. Though her heart told her this was the right thing to do, her head told her otherwise. There was too much going on. In all probability, Connor might have to leave Ibiza anyway if matters with Kyle were not resolved. Would things still be the same in the UK? More importantly though, he had literally only just split up with Marina; the last thing she needed was a rebound relationship. There were simply too many uncertainties. And with Leo's death clearly yet to affect him, it wouldn't be fair to suddenly blurt out all of her own pent-up emotions . . . he had enough on his plate already.

On the more practical side of things, if she decided to stay it would mean dipping still further into her savings. They had originally been put aside for a trip to Thailand at the end of summer with an old friend from university. The friend had rung the previous week to say that she was bringing the trip forward and going to Nepal, and asking if Holly wanted to come. It was only the next day – in the Ali Bey apartments watching Atlantis – when Connor had told her things with Marina were going so well, that Holly made the call ensuring a ticket to Nepal had her name on it.

Reflecting on that same conversation, she remembered Connor had even tapped the side of his nose, which she took to mean he was sleeping with Marina, but from what he'd said earlier, it never happened. What was all that about?

It was all too confusing, all too complicated. Trekking in Nepal seemed more appealing by the minute, sad though she would be to leave a man and an island she was fast falling in love with.

As they got to the San Jordi roundabout, a few minutes from the airport, they passed a huge billboard extolling the pleasures of Ibiza.

'He knew all along,' Connor mumbled. 'He just wanted me to work it out for myself.'

'What?'

'Leo knew the reason I ended up coming to Ibiza. I wouldn't mind betting the sly old so-and-so had me sussed from the first conversation we had when I came back.'

'What do you mean?'

'When I came over here on impulse, I got it into my head that some greater power was at work, as if there was a purpose to it all.' He sniffed then blew his nose. 'And I figured that this destiny was meeting the "Big

Adventure", the soulmate. Actually, when we first met, I thought it was you,' he paused for a moment and looked at Holly, but her eyes remained fixed on the road, 'then when I bumped into Marina again, well, it had to be her, didn't it? It was just too much of a coincidence.'

'I guess so.'

'But Leo . . . ha, ha. He knew that Marina wasn't the Big Adventure, that I'd just romanticised the whole thing. He knew that if there was a purpose to me coming to Ibiza then it was more about me discovering that my attitude to relationships had changed.'

'In what way?'

'It's hard to explain, but basically, I suppose I was always a bit like Shuff, not really looking for anything more than a laugh. Living each day as it comes and not really worrying about the future. Then I started seeing Gina Searle back home and I quite liked the *idea* of it, but even with her I knew deep down that things weren't going anywhere. I'd never really gone into any relationship expecting it to last more than a short while. But being somewhere like here, where every day's a Friday night, I knew I wanted more. I wanted someone special, I guess.'

'Doesn't everybody?'

'Do they? There's quite a lot of people who settle for someone who just seems compatible – I almost did it myself before I came here. Leo was even on the button with that one. He said that I was expecting a relationship to be like some great romance in a film.'

'There's nothing wrong with that, we all like a bit of romance. I guess the most important thing is being realistic about it.'

'Exactly – it's about give and take. And do you know what else he knew I'd work out? Leo knew I'd work out that *when* you meet someone is almost as important as *who* you meet.'

'Believe me, Connor, you're preaching to the converted on that one.'

'Exactly. If you'd met Dex under different circumstances, if he hadn't gone back to the UK, who knows where it might have led?'

Holly opened her mouth to say something but Connor carried on before she had a chance.

'And it wasn't just relationships Leo was right about. It was this place too: Ibiza. I was at my happiest here and he knew it, but that doesn't mean it's where I should be. Ultimately what's important is being happy in yourself and *then* you decide where you want to be happy and, if you're lucky, *who* to share that happiness with. At the end of the day, as Leo would have said, a problem is a problem if you're in London, Ibiza, or Timbuk-bloody-tu.' Connor sighed and shook his head. 'I wish, wish, *wish* that I'd got a chance to tell him, to let him know that I understood.'

266

'I'm sure he knew you'd get there in the end. You were special to him, even I could see that.'

Connor could feel the lump in his throat growing, and was relieved when his mobile rang. It was Shuff. They spoke for a few minutes. After the call he turned to Holly, who had just seen a parking space directly outside departures.

'Shuff and Grant are coming up to the airport on the bike. He was worried I might not be in a fit state to drive.'

'And are you?'

'Yeah, I'll be fine. They're halfway here so they said they'll come and say ta-ta.'

'That's nice of them.'

Holly parked the car.

'You go and get a trolley,' said Connor, taking the car keys from her, 'and I'll grab your luggage from the boot.'

He walked her to the departures gate, where there was quite a queue for her flight.

'I would stop,' said Connor, 'but I've got to get back for Katya.'

'I understand.' She stopped walking and turned to face him. 'Well, I guess this is it then.'

'I guess so.'

They stood there, one of them stuck for something to say, the other with too much.

'No eleventh-hour happy ending with this mystery guy then?'

Holly shook her head. 'I don't think so, no.'

'Still with his girlfriend?'

Holly took a deep breath. 'To be honest, I don't think she was the issue. Like you said before . . . timing.'

Connor nodded. There was a silence, which to Holly at least, seemed to go on for ever.

They stumbled towards each other and kissed awkwardly on each cheek.

'I hope you enjoy Nepal.'

'And I hope everything works out for you. I'm sure it will. Tell Luc and Katya I'll be thinking of them.'

'I will.' Another short silence. 'OK.' Another pair of awkward kisses. 'Have a safe flight.'

Connor walked away, thinking what a naff last thing to say to a girl he'd once believed to be his destiny. Leo was so right. Life wasn't like a film. If it were, then Holly would have fallen sobbing into his arms, hating herself for having slept with Dex, telling him that she wanted all of the things he did and finally proclaiming her undying love for him.

As he left the airport he turned and waved. It reminded him of a Clint Eastwood film where he walks away saying to himself, if she looks back, I've got her. Well, Clint old son, Connor thought, it just further goes to prove that real life isn't like that, because Holly's looking but I sure as hell haven't got her.

He walked out of the airport knowing that he was almost certainly never going to see her again. In the car, a trace of Holly's Fendi still lingered and it reminded him of when he'd first noticed her. He looked at his eyes in the rear-view mirror and started the car.

'If only . . .'

There were so many 'if onlys' but they all amounted to the same thing: Connor wasn't meant to be. That *was* the only certainty, so she hadn't even bothered exchanging email addresses. What was the point? Small consolation though it was, she had at least learned more about herself through the experience. Now she had to move on. There was every chance that she'd meet someone on her travels. Yet no one had made her feel like Connor before. He *was* her soulmate. Or was Leo right? Timing. Was it just that now she was ready to find one?

Shuff and Grant arrived just as Holly got to the front of the queue. Grant said his goodbyes then ran off to make some phone calls to the UK from a public phone using a cheap phone card, telling Shuff he'd see him outside in ten minutes.

Once she'd checked in, Shuff stood with her at the entrance to passport control.

'Don't go screwing any llamas, and if you do, make sure you film it.'

Holly laughed. 'Can I ask you something, Shuff?'

'Sure, what?'

'Well, it's not just to ask you something, it's also to apologize.'

'What for?'

'That day you were going to get the ferry to Denia – I was a real bitch to you.'

'Aw gee, don't worry. It was just a misunderstanding. All forgotten.'

'Thanks.' Holly stood where she was, so Shuff knew there was something else. 'At the time, Grant said something about you not being able to go back to the USA, about us not knowing what you go through every day. Tell me to mind my own business if you want, but I just wondered what he was on about? Now that I've got to know you better

I'd put money on you not being in trouble with the police – you're not, are you?'

Shuff smiled and shook his head. 'No, that's not it. And it wasn't so much that I *couldn't* go back, as didn't *want* to go back.'

'Hmm.' Holly frowned then her face broke into a playful smile. 'Oh, go on, Shuff, tell me. I'm not going to see any of them again. My lips will be sealed forever.'

'It's not something I normally—'

'I won't tell a soul.' Holly could tell he was wavering. 'If you tell me your secret, I'll tell you a huge one of mine, but you've got to swear you won't tell anyone either.'

Shuff slowly smiled. 'Is yours worth knowing though?'

'Oh yes.'

Shuff scratched his chin. 'And you won't tell anyone?'

'Nobody.'

He nodded towards the café. 'Come on then, let's grab a quick coffee. I never could resist hearing a secret . . .'

chapter thirty-seven

Nope, it definitely wasn't there.

Even when seeing Marina and Bartolo together – properly 'together' – the spin cycle stomach was still absent. If final proof were needed that he had never been in love with her, then that was it.

Connor was the last into the room. The meeting was being held out of the way in the Talamanca garage-cum-apartment. Bartolo was attending in full uniform, as he had to go straight to work, which was a little disconcerting for the others. Connor was slightly taken aback by how warmly Bartolo greeted him, which he put down partly to Leo's death and partly to the fact that he was so happy to be with Marina.

Bartolo didn't underestimate Connor's role in that. Even though Connor and Marina were not together, Bartolo was aware of how he could have still made the situation difficult rather than actually encouraging it. Marina had told Connor of the genuine respect Bartolo had for him and Connor got the distinct impression that if Bartolo wasn't totally committed to helping before, then he was now.

The meeting had been progressing for about forty minutes and Connor felt it was getting off-track, with different people having their own conversations at the same time.

'Listen, guys, why don't we just summarize where we are?' Connor looked at an exercise book he had been making notes in all evening. 'We're pretty certain that Kyle is getting drugs dropped in the trunk that Marina found at the dive site. We also know that some drugs are kept in the outhouse by his villa, although we heard him tell the Searles that's not where he normally keeps them.'

'Yeah, but he might have just said that because he was worried the Searles would come and try to do the place over,' suggested Shuff.

'Possible,' agreed Connor, 'but at the moment at least, we've just got to assume that there are sufficient drugs in there to warrant him being arrested, if we can somehow find a way of getting the police to go there. We heard Buster say there was quite a bit stashed there now.' The room mumbled its agreement. 'We also know for sure that Kyle handled the two kilos that were put into the boot of the Searles' hire car and I wouldn't mind betting they haven't touched it themselves since.'

'True, but we can't exactly go and ask them if we can have it, can we?' stated Shuff.

'Can't we buy it off them?' suggested Marina hopefully.

'If we had fifty or sixty grand, then yes,' replied Connor. 'I mean, it would probably actually be worth that to get Luc out, but we just can't lay our hands on that kind of money in time.'

'Oh.'

'We also know that at some point soon Kyle's got a shipment coming in,' continued Connor, 'because that's why the Searles are staying. If we knew when then perhaps—'

'Oh God, I've just remembered something really important,' interrupted Marina, flapping her hands up and down as though the winning answer to a game show question were on the tip of her tongue. 'I was speaking to Nathalie from the dive school earlier. She told me that Kyle was hassling her to work on Sunday – we *never* work on Sundays. He even offered her *double* money. I didn't think, or make the connection, what with Leo and all that.'

The four guys looked at each other.

'That's got to be it then,' said Shuff. 'That must be when the gear's coming – in less than two days.'

'But Bartolo's already said that even if we know when the drop is, he probably won't be able to organize a raid or anything,' said Connor, looking at Bartolo.

Bartolo nodded. 'This is correct. We need to somehow attract attention to Kyle when he has drugs on him.'

'What about if we rammed the car after he's picked the drugs up?' suggested Grant.

A few eyebrows were raised and positive gestures made.

'That would certainly attract attention,' agreed Bartolo.

'But how can we be sure we get the right car?' Connor looked round for answers. 'It's unlikely that Kyle would move it himself and if he isn't caught with it then we're not going to be able to get his fingerprints, so it won't help Luc.'

'And if we did ram his car and he saw it was us,' pointed out Shuff, 'the police would have to get there pretty darn quick – otherwise he'd fucking kill us!'

There was another short silence, broken by Connor snapping his fingers.

'I tell you what though. The good thing about knowing when he's doing the pick-up is it means we know when he *won't* be at the villa. We also know from watching him those few days that if Kyle and Mac aren't there, none of the others will be either.'

'So?' Shuff wasn't keeping up.

'So,' explained Connor, 'all we need to do is find a way of attracting attention to the villa to get the police to search it, am I right, Bartolo?'

'*Sí*. I can be in a car very close to the villa. There is a bar nearby that my *compañero* and I can sit in and have a coffee, so if we get a call we can be there in minutes. Marina knows how to ring to the police, she can tell you.'

'I reckon it would be useful if we could watch them at Atlantis too,' suggested Shuff, 'maybe even take some pictures or something, if we can use that apartment again.'

'Yes. If you want to use it then I can speak to my friend. I am sure this will not be a problem.'

'But we still need to find a way of attracting attention to Kyle's villa though,' noted Connor. 'From what you're saying we can't just break in then call the police and say, "Hello, Mr Policeman, we've just broken into this nice man's villa and found loads of drugs", can we?'

'We could always blow it up,' said Grant.

There were a few dismissive laughs.

Shuff added, 'Um . . . I think you'll find he's serious.'

'Don't be silly.' Connor turned to Grant. 'How on earth are you going to blow up a villa?'

'Well, it could be done in several different ways actually. First . . .'

Bartolo stood up and interrupted him. 'Listen, my friends, I think this is a good time for me to leave. It is probably best I do not hear the next bit. If you arrange something then let me know and I will be near the villa – I promise. I will do everything I can to help you but it would be better if I do not break the law myself, yes?'

They all said goodbye to him and Marina saw him to the door.

'Go on then, Grant,' said Connor. 'I've got to hear this.'

'Well, there's no need to use Semtex or anything like that. We could put petrol in a lightbulb, but then someone could get injured.'

'Your point being?' said Connor sarcastically.

Marina walked back in. 'Have I missed anything?'

'No,' Connor nodded towards Grant. 'Only old Guy Fawkes here giving us a rundown on blowing up villas.'

'Ah, but that's the point, we don't actually want to totally blow up the whole villa, do we? Just a big enough explosion to make the police come along so they've got an excuse to search the outhouse. And we obviously don't want to blow up the outhouse, because that would destroy all of the drugs.'

'OK, OK,' said Connor. 'Carry on.'

Grant continued. 'The best idea would simply be to get some of those big orange Butane gas bottles.'

'How do you know all of this?' asked Marina.

'I used to be a fireman. Not for long, but long enough to know how to start one.'

'How would we blow them up without us killing ourselves?' asked Connor.

'I reckon the best way would be to go into that kitchen to the right of the villa. It looks like it was built as an extension and we should be able to kick the door in easy enough. First of all we'd quickly mask all the windows to make it as airtight as possible. Then we'd put the bottles in and open up the valves on them. Then the clever bit.' Grant sat forward on his chair. 'What we need is some kind of fuse. Something that would give us a minute or two before the thing goes off. Basically, we'd get a cigarette, then about two-thirds of the way down, poke a little hole in it. Into that hole we'd put the fuse of a firework. As the cigarette burns down, it would set light to the fuse, the fuse would set off the firework and . . . *bang*! Job done.'

The others all looked at him in open-mouthed amazement as he sat back in the chair with a little smile and sipped his Heineken.

Connor jotted down some notes. Shuff patted Grant on the back. Marina shook her head.

'So how about this for a plan?' said Connor as he stopped writing. 'Grant and I will get the Butane and take it up to the woods overlooking Kyle's villa. They're heavy fuckers but if we can get the car right up that little dirt track then we won't be seen and we won't have too far to carry the bloody things. I'll have to swap that hire car for a small van.' He wrote himself a little reminder.

'Wouldn't it be easier with three of us?' asked Shuff.

'Probably, but I think you were right about keeping watch on Atlantis and it's best if Marina's not on her own just in case.'

'OK.'

'Once Kyle's left, we'll give it a little while then start putting the gas bottles into the villa and getting that all prep'd up. How many do you think we'll need, Grant?'

Grant shrugged his shoulders. 'I've never blown anything up before. Half a dozen?'

'What about nine or ten, just to be sure,' suggested Connor.

'That would definitely do it.'

Connor made more notes and turned to Marina. 'Once Kyle and the dive school have set to sea, call us. Old Butane Bob here will set off the explosion and then we'll call the police. Hopefully, once they find the gear in the outhouse, Bartolo can inform the powers-that-be about the drugs pick-up and then they'll have to listen to him, so if all goes according to plan they'll be waiting as the boat comes back and they'll get caught red-handed at that too.' Connor shut the exercise book with a self-satisfied grin. 'Brilliant.'

'It sounds brilliant, but actually doing it . . .' Marina sighed.

'Fuck it,' said Shuff, 'I'm game.'

Connor looked at Grant, who nodded. Marina had no choice really but to give her seal of approval too.

'You're all mad.'

'So is that a yes, Marina?' asked Shuff, grinning from ear to ear.

She raised her bottle. The other three did the same and they clinked them together.

'*Ba-boom!*'

chapter thirty-eight

'Oh God,' mumbled Connor, sitting with nine highly explosive bottles of butane gas, a firework and a perspiring ex-fireman, 'what the fuck am I doing here?'

Sunday. Kyle and Mac had just left the villa in two separate cars. Grant scurried down the shallow bank from the safety of the trees and cautiously edged along the walls of the villa, poking his head round every corner to check that there was nobody either in the buildings or the grounds. When he had completed the circuit, he signalled for Connor to come down.

As predicted, the door that led from the kitchen to the outside simply needed a good kick to open it. Once in the villa, Connor couldn't help having a look into the living room.

'Fuck me – have you seen this place? The bastard's even got a plasma screen.'

'Come on, Connor. We haven't got time. Start dragging the gas bottles down and I'll tape up the windows.'

Connor was both surprised and pleased by the sudden change in Grant. The easy-going sidekick had transformed into a focused and authoritative decision-maker.

Although they had managed to park fairly close to the villa it was still quite a way to carry the bottles. By the time he had hauled the second one down, he was sweating more than Grant . . . just.

'Do you reckon we'll need all of them?' he asked, rather hoping to get out of carrying any more.

'It's all right, I've finished here – I'll give you a hand. Let's put them all in . . . better safe than sorry, eh?'

'Safe,' muttered Connor, trudging behind, 'is hardly the first fucking word that springs to mind . . .'

Back at the Ali Bey apartments, Shuff kept his binoculars firmly focused on Atlantis and the surrounding area. The dive boat was as ever the only one moored at the small jetty. Unlike the nearby Coastline and Kanya bars, Atlantis wasn't open during the day and as it was recently built in the middle of long-established wasteland, it had a deserted and solitary feel to it, with a dust track leading to the nearby tarmac road that pointed towards the West End.

From the information Nathalie had given them, the dive school was due to leave at any minute. Unaware she was being watched or what was being planned, Nathalie had turned up about fifteen minutes earlier and was sitting outside the bar on her scooter, talking into her mobile.

While he looked through the binoculars, Marina was explaining how she'd found the trunk.

'. . . and it's between these two really distinctive rocks, one quite jagged, about two metres high and the other more like a boulder, about half as high. There's some plants growing out too so it's quite hard to see unless you're looking for it. The bottom looks as though it's been lined with concrete.'

'I'm surprised you found it.'

'It wasn't that difficult actually. I knew it had to be in the opposite direction to where I took the students because that's where Mac always used to go. I figured it also had to be near a noticeable feature so that whoever's doing the drop could easily spot it.'

'It's a shame all this shit happened; I would have loved to come out diving with you.'

'Have you got your PADI?'

Shuff nodded. 'How're things with Bartolo by the way?'

Just the mention of his name still brought a warm glow to her spirit and a smile to her face.

'Fantastic. As soon as the summer's finished he's leaving the police. He's asked me to help him set up the dive school in Almeria, on the mainland.'

'Really? I bet you're excited.'

'I can't wait. Carlos has given me a job in Raffles for the summer, so if Luc gets out I might be working with him . . .'

'Shit.' Shuff moved closer to the window and focused the binoculars. 'I wouldn't count on that just yet.'

'Why not? What's up?'

'I've just seen Nathalie jump on her bike and take off.'

'What?'

Marina ran to the window and sure enough, Nathalie's scooter was throwing up a plume of dust as she headed for the main road.

'Quick,' urged Shuff, 'give her a call and find out what's happening.'

Marina dialled the number whilst Shuff followed her progress.

'She's not answering.'

'She probably can't hear you. Wait a sec. She's coming to a junction. There's a truck coming. Hopefully she'll stop and hear the . . .'

'Nathalie, it's Marina. I thought you'd be on the boat by now?'

'So did I, but I got a call from my friends who were meant to be coming on the dive. They had just got back from clubbing and did not want to come. I just rang Kyle—'

'What did he say?'

'He went crazy, as if it was my fault.'

'Do you know if he's still taking the boat out?'

'I don't think so. He said they were already in San Antonio and he would have to drive all the way back to his villa. Listen, Marina. I am on my bike so I must go. Give me a call later, *ja*?'

Marina looked at Shuff in a panic. 'Shit. They're on their way back to the villa; the boat trip's off. I'd better warn Connor and Grant.' She dialled quickly. 'Come on, Connor, pick up the . . . oh shit.'

'Now what?'

'It's gone to voicemail.'

'Try Grant's.' Shuff walked to the door.

'Where are you going?'

'If Kyle and Mac are going back to the villa, then that means they won't be on the boat. I'm going to have a rummage round.'

'But we don't know for sure that they've gone back to the villa. Suppose Nathalie's got it wrong? They might change their mind.'

'Don't worry. If Kyle and Mac were on the outskirts of San Antonio, then by the time I get downstairs they'll already be here. In which case, we just go ahead as we were planning to. But if they are on their way back to the villa, then there might be some useful stuff on that boat. If today is gonna fuck up then any other information or evidence might come in handy for next time.'

'Next time?' squealed Marina, as she punched in Grant's number. 'I don't think I could go through this again.'

As he came into San Antonio, Mac kept glancing at his rear-view mirror, not to check that Kyle was still following, but because he couldn't believe his appearance. He cursed himself for being so weak, but he was not as lucky with women as he liked and this one had been an absolute darling. Unfortunately she was a darling who adored cocaine, so Mac had been up virtually all night with her on a massive sex and cocaine binge. It reminded him of the other reason he rarely took it – once he started, he couldn't stop.

He knew that being in that kind of state was not the wisest thing to do before diving, but he had dived after cocaine sessions once or twice before, although admittedly, never after taking quite so much or on so little sleep. It wouldn't be a problem though. Mac considered himself a good diver, a natural. When more experienced divers told him he had a cavalier attitude he took it as a compliment. Even so, he was glad that Kyle had agreed to come down with him, despite Kyle's own inexperience.

He once more looked at his red-rimmed hollow eyes in the rear-view mirror and noticed the lights of Kyle's Range Rover flashing him. He pulled over and got out.

'What's up?'

'What's up?' snarled Kyle, as he stepped from his car clutching a bottle of Evian as if it were a cosh. 'I'll tell you what's fucking up. Here we are about to pick up the largest amount of drugs either of us has ever seen when I get a call from Miss Hi-de-fucking-Hi—'

'Who?'

'The fucking Kraut bint at the diving school! Those div-arsed friends of hers have gone out last night and necked too many fucking pills and don't want to come on the dive! No wonder the cunts lost the fucking war.' Kyle angrily threw the Evian at the wall. 'Vy are you shouting at me, Kyle, ven I voz trying to do you a favour,' he mimicked. 'The fucking wee slut. That's her out of a job too. Now what are we going to do? I don't want to risk leaving all that gear there for another day.' He paused. 'Is there any chance of you going out on your own? I need to get back to the villa and make some calls.'

There was no way Mac would allow the weakness of a cocaine binge stop him from doing something so important, but he would have preferred not to go alone.

'Don't you think it might look a bit suss?' he offered half-heartedly.

'Of course it won't. You've been out enough times, no one will bat an eyelid. Why don't you pop into the supermarket on your way and get a few beers, try and straighten yourself out a bit. Maybe get a couple of Sunday papers and make it look like a nice Sunday trip.'

Mac nodded his agreement. 'What time will you meet me?'

'Let's see, forty-five minutes for you to get to the dive site, fifteen for the dive, forty-five back ... why don't I get Rory to meet you in two hours at Atlantis? He can take the gear up to the place by Cala Salada. Did he move the rest of the gear from the outhouse to there?'

'Yeah, yesterday I think.'

'Good.' He noticed Mac still looking slightly anxious. 'Chill out, Mac . . . what can possibly go wrong?'

Grant felt the phone vibrate in his pocket.

'Grant, it's Marina.'

'Hi, Marina. What's up?'

Connor had just brought the final gas bottle into the room. As soon as he heard Grant say Marina's name he knew something was wrong and felt a hollow feeling in his stomach as the adrenalin emptied it of blood and sent it surging to his already aching muscles.

'The dive's been called off.'

'What?'

'We saw Nathalie leaving. I'll explain later. If Kyle and Mac were still going out on the boat they would have been here by now so that means they're coming back to the villa. You've got to call it off.'

'But we can't! All the bottles . . .' Connor was frantically gesturing to him to find out what was going on. 'I'll call you back.'

'What . . . what?' Connor looked more likely to explode than the gas bottles.

'Kyle and Mac are on their way back – the dive's off.'

'Aaagh!' It was a half-scream, half-yelp. 'When did they leave?'

'Atlantis to here can't be more than twenty minutes . . . half an hour tops. We've got to get out of here . . . come on.'

Grant weaved between the Butane gas bottles that filled the kitchen, heading for the door.

'Wait!' yelled Connor. 'What about all of this? We can't leave it here.'

'We haven't got time to take it with us. It's taken us over quarter of an hour to get this all set up and that was flat out, downhill and feeling fresh. It'll take us twice us long to take them back and get everything looking normal.'

'But if we leave this here Kyle will know we're on to him. Plus it's got all our prints everywhere.'

'So? Neither of our prints are on record and Kyle doesn't know we're on the island. He's got to have other enemies. He might even think the Searles did it.' They both stood motionless in the kitchen for a moment. 'Fuck this,' said Grant, decisively. 'I'm out of here.'

'No, wait!' Connor stood in front of him. 'Let's do it anyway.'

'What? Are you mad?'

'Think about it. If we blow it up just before they come back, then what's the first thing they're going to do? They'll move all of the drugs from the outhouse. If Bartolo turns up according to plan then he might even catch them in the act. Perfect.' Despite his enthusiasm, his expression betrayed the fact that he wasn't convinced of his own plan.

Neither was Grant. 'I don't know.'

'It could work, couldn't it?'

'Perhaps.'

They faced each other, both urging the other to make the decision. Grant looked at his watch.

'We're running out of time.'

'Come on, Grant, yes or no?'

'It's your call.'

'But you're the expert.'

'Luc's your friend.'

'Fuck.' Connor frantically drummed his hands on the side of his legs, trying to make a decision.

'Connor, we've got to get out of here.' Sweat was pouring down Grant's face.

There was another moment's hesitation, then Connor leaped forward and turned on a gas bottle. Grant stopped him from opening any more.

'No wait! Let's set the fuse first or you'll kill us both. Here, light this cigarette.'

'But I don't smoke.'

'Neither do I. You smoke spliffs though, don't you?'

'Yeah, but that's different.'

'*Well, fucking sorry,*' yelled Grant in an uncharacteristic display of temper, 'but I don't think we've time to roll a fat one, unless you were thinking of maybe waiting until Kyle gets here . . . you know, pass it to him for a toke before you blow his *fucking kitchen to smithereens*!'

'No, I just—'

'So, if you wouldn't mind . . .'

Connor lit the cigarette and passed it back to Grant, who aggressively poked a hole into the side of it about two-thirds of the way down.

'Anyway, a spliff would be no good because it would go out, whereas cigarettes are designed to continue burning.' He inserted the firework fuse into the hole and placed it on the worktop. 'Now, I suggest we get the fuck out of here!'

They opened a couple more valves for good measure, wedged the door shut behind them and sprinted for the trees . . .

Kyle was not a happy man, although as he threw the car round the twisting dirt track that led to his villa, he had begun to calm down somewhat.

Fucking women. They were useless. All he'd asked the silly cow to do was get some friends to come out on a dive. What made matters worse was that he'd given them a great deal and was going to pay her double her normal rate, plus a commission. Taking them diving was actually going to cost him money! Well, apart from the several hundred grand he'd make from selling the cocaine that was at this very moment sitting in a trunk on the seabed.

Ah yes, it was the thought of that, which put a smile on his face. His first foray into the big league. The Schemie from Coatbridge made good. Not that he'd done bad up until now. But it had all been leading up to this, the Big One. And it wasn't going to be the last. He'd already been over to Marbella the previous winter and a little trip to Morocco was planned to see if it was worth getting involved in the other stuff. Maybe just a little investment. Let some daft Cockney or Geordie actually bring the stinking cargo back. But fuck the hash, it was the good auld Colombian Marching Powder that always rocked his boat. There was something glamorous about it. The crackheads – they were another story altogether. He knew some eventually found its way to them but he had a convenient blind spot where they were concerned. As for the Ibiza party scene though, he was the man. Untouchable. The King.

As the King made the last turn to his castle it was the flash that he saw first. The huge noise and the rubble that rained down upon his Range Rover came moments later, seemingly in slow motion, he would later recall. He slammed on the brakes and ducked behind the steering wheel. When he was sure that it was all over, he gingerly raised his head above the glass-strewn dashboard.

'Fuck!' He fell out of the car, fumbling for his mobile. 'Mac? Mac, it's me. Oh Jesus. You're no' gonna believe what's just happened.'

Shuff had waited almost ten minutes before tentatively boarding Kyle's dive boat, sufficient time for them to have arrived if they were coming. Satisfied that Kyle and Mac were both on their way to their villa, he went downstairs to the small cabin and started rummaging.

After five fruitless minutes he was about to go upstairs on to the deck when he almost jumped out of his skin. A mobile rang, so close it had to mean somebody else was on the boat. When it was followed by the unmistakable voice of Mac, Shuff understood for the first time in his life the expression 'frozen with fear'.

It was clear that Mac was on his own and talking to Kyle. From the

281

one-sided conversation, all he could make out was that the villa had been blown up. In truth, he was more interested in finding a place to hide than listening to the phone call. In the corner was a dank and smelly tarpaulin and he quickly scurried under it. As Mac was on his own, he prayed his visit would be short. It also suddenly occurred to him to switch off his own mobile, just in case someone tried to call while Mac was in earshot.

'Shit!' he hissed, under his breath. He'd left it in the apartment.

From beneath the tarpaulin, he was unable to hear Mac's conversation, or pretty much anything else for that matter. He was just about to poke his head out to see if the coast was clear when, horror of horrors, the boat's engine fired up and within a few minutes it was obvious that they had put to sea.

So far as he knew, nobody other than Mac was on board.

But that was more than enough.

'You fucking knob!' hissed Connor.

'Don't blame me,' retorted a defiant Grant. 'At least the place went up, didn't it?'

Connor had to agree with him on that one. Virtually the whole of one side of the villa had been razed to the ground. The other half wasn't exactly about to appear in *Home and Garden* either, with flames licking what was left of the roof.

'You were only meant to . . .' Connor stopped mid-sentence and started laughing. He changed his voice to a poor impression of Michael Caine. 'You were only meant to blow the bloody kitchen up.'

The nervous energy caused them both to collapse in giggles – until Connor saw the Range Rover.

'Kyle's here.'

They moved deeper into the forest.

'Shall I call the cops?' asked Grant.

'I don't think you'll need to. Bartolo's only down the road. He could have been in fucking Mallorca and still heard that.'

Sure enough, within a few minutes, a Guardia Civil car turned up and Bartolo stepped out with another policeman.

They couldn't really hear what was being said; miraculously the house burglar alarm was wailing. There was also quite a loud crackle as the fire quickly spread from the roof to the trees on the opposite side of the forest to where they were located.

'Mac's not with him,' observed Grant. 'Where do you think he is?'

'Fuck knows. Anyway, it's that bald fucker there I want to see get done.

Mac would be a welcome bonus. Come on, Bartolo,' he urged from the safety of the trees, 'search the outhouse.'

As Bartolo and the other policeman questioned Kyle, several more Guardia cars turned up along with some from the local police. It wasn't long before Bartolo and his colleagues escorted Kyle into the outhouse.

'Yes!' mouthed Connor, punching the air.

Their optimism turned to impatience, their impatience to curiosity, their curiosity to concern and finally their concern to disbelief as the policemen eventually filed out with a relaxed Kyle talking to them.

'What the fuck's going on?' hissed Connor.

A couple of fire engines turned up. From the other side of the villa, a hundred metres or so from their hideout, thick smoke was rising from the forest.

'That fire's looking pretty serious,' said an increasingly anxious Grant.

Sure enough, over the next few minutes, the priority seemed to move from Kyle and what had happened to his villa, to the safety of all of those in the vicinity. Police cars started speeding away and in the distance they could hear the sound of more fire engines arriving.

'We'd better get away from here, buddy,' suggested Grant. 'The fire's going in the other direction but I can tell you now, it's turning into a biggie. If the wind changes we could be well and truly fucked.'

'I don't believe this,' said Connor, as they scrambled up the bank.

Once in the car, they took the handbrake off to let it roll down the hill so as not to be heard (though the fire was raging so fiercely that it was unlikely it would have been anyway) then started the engine and within minutes were on the main road. Connor immediately rang Shuff. Marina answered.

'Connor. What on earth happened? I've just had Bartolo on the phone. He told me that there's hardly anything left of the villa and that there's a major forest fire. They've just called up one of those planes that dumps water.'

'Shit. I didn't realize it was that bad. We overdid it. Did Bartolo say anything about Kyle?'

'There weren't any drugs in the outhouse.'

'What? But there must have been. Oh no!' he wailed. 'What, none at all?'

'Nothing. Not a trace.'

'What an absolute disaster. Could things have gone any worse?'

'Um, actually yes . . . much worse.'

'What do you mean?'

'When Shuff heard that the dive was off he waited to check that Kyle and Mac weren't coming then decided to have a look around the boat. I was watching from the apartment and Mac turned up.'

'Oh, fucking hell!'

'I tried ringing him but he'd left his phone here.'

'Yeah, I figured that one out, seeing as we're speaking on it. So what's happening?'

'They've put to sea.'

'Jesus! Was there a fight or anything?'

'It didn't look like it.'

'So is Shuff still on the boat?'

'He must be.'

Connor quickly gathered his thoughts. 'Listen. Pop down to where all the boats and yachts are moored and see if there's a little speedboat we can hire. We'll meet you outside Club Nautic in about fifteen minutes.'

'I'll do my best. What are you planning?'

'Planning? I'm making this up as I go . . .'

chapter thirty-nine

After five minutes of tucking himself as far under the tarpaulin as possible, screwing his eyes up and barely daring to breathe, Shuff relaxed enough to peek out from his hiding place. He heard the hiss of a can of beer opening and as he cautiously looked up the stairs he could see Mac's outstretched legs, obviously relaxing next to the wheel. He heard the distinctive sound of a credit card chopping on a hard surface, then two long and loud sniffs. Until then, he never even knew that Mac took cocaine.

Most of the diving equipment was with Shuff downstairs. He did however, remember seeing a couple of tanks, a wetsuit and flippers on deck, so he hoped that maybe Mac would have no need to enter below.

One thought that crossed Shuff's mind was to run upstairs and steam into Mac. He was reasonably confident that on a one to one, he would come out on top. But he had seen Mac's type before and unless he either knocked him out or killed him, he knew Mac would just keep on coming. It was all well and good in James Bond when a half-hearted karate chop to the back of the neck sent a villain tumbling to the floor, or a heavy object over the head conveniently made him instantly keel over without a mark. In real life though, Shuff could visualize the latter course of action leading to an even angrier demented lunatic attacking him, albeit with a bloodied, fractured skull. There was a spear gun on the floor, but when it came to the crunch, would he honestly pull the trigger? Though he was fairly sure the answer would be yes, why risk it?

Eventually, he decided to sit tight, but he did pick up the spear gun just in case. He listened carefully for any movement but only heard the chop-chop-chop of the credit card every few minutes.

After what seemed like an eternity, the engines on the boat came to a stop. Shuff's whole body tightened. This was it. If Mac were going to come down below, it would be now. Though it was dark down there and Shuff was reasonably well covered, it was a fairly small room so there was every chance he would be found.

He waited; all senses ultra sharp, listening for footsteps down the stairs with his finger on the trigger of the spear gun. He could hear Mac clumping round on deck. When he heard the rattle of air tanks and the short bursts of air as Mac pressed the purge button, he started to feel optimistic for the first time. Then, the clumsy steps of someone wearing flippers, followed by a gentle splash as Mac entered the water.

Quicker than he should have, Shuff edged up the stairs. It wasn't until he was about to poke his head out that he realized he didn't have the spear gun. Nevertheless, the silence encouraged him to press on. Sure enough, nobody else was on the boat. He took a 360-degree inventory of his surroundings, recognizing the white buoy gently bobbing nearby to be the marker for the dive site that Marina had described. On the horizon was their original departure point, to his left, the island of Conajera. Further out to sea were a couple of pleasure craft, sailing away from the coast. Even though he was a reasonable swimmer there was no way he'd make it to shore.

He scanned the boat to see if there was a better hiding place, but the tarpaulin still seemed favourite. He contemplated just pulling off, but that would be tantamount to murder and besides, Mac would inevitably hear the engine start and the anchor coming up, before he had a chance to get away. No, sitting tight was the only option.

He waited, and waited, and waited. A couple of times he thought he saw bubbles and dashed to the safety of the tarpaulin, but both were false alarms. When he came up from below deck the second time there was an almighty roar that literally made him duck. It was a plane sweeping low overhead that skimmed the top of the sea scooping up gallons of water then sharply rising and banking back towards Ibiza.

Half an hour passed, then an hour. Shuff once more contemplated sailing off, but looking at the controls, realized he didn't have a clue how to operate the boat anyway. During the hour, a couple of other yachts pulled up and dropped anchor for a short while, but they were a good distance away. Shuff was torn between trying to attract their attention or staying out of sight – he chose the latter.

After an hour and fifteen minutes though, Shuff knew that Mac's air would be long gone. Where was he? The plane had scooped up water but far, far away from the dive site, so appealing as the idea of Mac being dumped on a forest fire somewhere was, that scenario was highly unlikely. Perhaps he'd picked up the contraband and boarded one of those other yachts, double-crossing Kyle? Yet the yachts had been a considerable distance away and as Kyle's number two, surely he'd be in for a good cut anyway. Or maybe, he hadn't checked his tanks and had run out of air and panicked.

Shuff went below deck and grabbed a wetsuit, tanks and the spear gun.

There was only one way to find out . . .

It took Shuff a few moments to recognize the figures on the speedboat waving at him. His sense of relief at seeing his friends was enormous.

They pulled up alongside, Connor brandishing a spanner and Grant something that resembled a small baseball bat.

'Where is he? Are you all right?' asked Connor.

Shuff stepped on to the six-seater speedboat Marina had managed to hire, hauling a bag on with him.

'What's in there?' asked Marina.

Shuff opened it slightly to reveal a wetsuit. The spear gun was resting across the top.

'Just a few bits an pieces I nicked from the boat that I thought might come in useful. Anyway, never mind that. What happened? Has Kyle been arrested?'

'Not exactly,' sighed Grant. 'I used too many gas bottles – either that or Spanish construction work is as crap as everyone says.'

'But what's that got to do with the outhouse? Surely you didn't blow up that as well? All you were doing was attracting attention to the place.'

'He did that all right,' said Connor. 'He blew up half the sodding villa, but the outhouse was fine. The police searched it and found nothing.'

Shuff put his head in his hands. 'So Kyle's still free.'

'As a bird.'

The sound of a mobile phone ringing came from the bag.

'That's Mac's,' said Shuff. 'It's been ringing pretty much since he went in the water. I had a look on the display and it's Kyle. He must be trying to let him know what's going on.'

'So where is he?' asked Connor.

'I don't know. I was below deck, hiding under some tarpaulin when he put to sea. One thing I can tell you though is I heard him taking shitloads of Charlie, and I mean shitloads. Anyway, the engines stopped, I heard Mac put his diving gear on and go in. After a bit, I came up on deck to see what was going on, ready to hide again when he resurfaced.'

'How long ago was that?'

Shuff looked at his watch. 'Not far short of two hours.'

'His air would have run out after about half an hour or so on a dive like that,' said Marina. 'He should have come back up ages ago.'

'There were a couple of boats that moored for a while, quite a way away though. I wondered if maybe he'd double-crossed Kyle and got on one of those with the gear. The only other thing,' continued Shuff, 'was a fire plane picked up some water. I just wondered if maybe . . . you know . . .'

'What, you think the fire plane scooped him up?' asked an incredulous Marina.

'Now that would be the ultimate irony,' laughed Grant. 'We blow his villa up – well, Kyle's villa, strictly speaking – the forest catches fire, a fire plane gets called and scoops Mac up, then uses him to help put out the fire by dumping him on it.'

'But that can't be right,' said Marina, not joining in the laughter. 'Planes wouldn't scoop up from anywhere near a boat. Anyway, I've heard something like that before. I'm sure it's just one of those urban myths.'

'The double-cross theory is believable though,' noted Grant.

'So have you been down to see if you could find him?' asked Marina.

'Are you joking? Man, I wouldn't fancy facing Mac underwater any more than I would on land. Anyway, I can't dive.'

'But you told me you had your PADI.'

'No, I didn't.'

'Yes, you did. When we were in the apartment earlier you said you wished you'd come diving with me.'

'Oh yeah.' Shuff paused. 'But I didn't say that I could dive though.'

'I asked you if you had a PADI and you said yes.'

'I must have misheard you. I thought you asked me if I *wanted* to get a PADI.'

Grant and Shuff shared a look, but nothing was said.

'Yeah, well, whatever,' said Connor. 'The thing is, what do we do now?'

'Well, I'd better go down in case he is still there,' said Marina.

'You can't go on your own.' Connor stopped untying the rope that was connecting them to Kyle's boat. 'I'll come with you. I haven't passed any tests but I've been diving a few times. Were there any spare tanks?'

'I think so,' replied Shuff.

Connor and Marina climbed across to Kyle's boat.

'Two of these tanks are almost totally empty and the others are all very low indeed,' noted Marina. 'When Nathalie knew her friends weren't diving today she must have decided not to bother filling them. We won't be able to stay down for more than five minutes, but we might as

288

well have a look anyway. Visibility's good so we don't have to go down too far.'

As soon as Marina and Connor were in the water, Grant turned to Shuff.

'What was all that about? Why did you lie about not having a PADI – you've done plenty of dives? What really happened?'

Shuff ran his fingers through his hair then sat on the side of the speedboat.

'Pretty much everything I said was true. Marina's right as well, there's no way that plane would have scooped him up. And I honestly can't see him double-crossing Kyle. Those other yachts were a fair way from here. If he was meeting someone then there was no reason for them not to get closer. I was just thinking of options. Man, I reckon he's just fucked up. Marina told me he always went diving alone and you should never do that. She said he was reckless, always forgetting to check his air. He was totally wired too, so . . .'

'OK, OK. Let's just suppose that Mac's had an accident. I still don't get why you lied about having a PADI.'

Shuff fidgeted nervously. 'Look, I'm about to tell you something that could really land me – possibly us – in the shit, big style. It's something I did on the spur of the moment. But now I've had another idea, which might get Luc out of trouble and put Kyle where he belongs . . .'

Slowly, Shuff opened the bag and moved the dive suit to one side.

When Grant looked inside, his mouth fell open.

'Jesus H. Christ . . .'

Kyle was going crazy.

He'd arranged to meet Rory at their safe house near Cala Salada, rented after the apartment near Sa Serra had been raided.

'I've been trying to ring the wee psycho since the bizzies left me alone. Not a fuckin' thing. It keeps ringing but there's no answer.'

'Do you think he might have been arrested?' asked Rory.

'I don't see why, but even so, I spoke to my man in the Guardia. Fuckin' mistake that was. He's gone garrity at me, wants to know what the fuck I'm playing at, getting half his men over to my exploding villa plus half the island's fucking fire brigade. I lost it with him a bit, I says it's hardly my fuckin' fault that my fuckin' villa blows up, is it? He seems to think it wasn't an accident and I've got to say, I tend to agree with the cunt. Anyways, he goes that it's no' the kind of attention I should be bringing on ma'sen, so he's no' gonna be able to help me in the same way for a while, till things blow over at least. The only good thing that came out of the conversation was that he's no' seen or heard anything of Mac. Mind you, maybe that's *no*' such a good thing.'

'Why?'

'I would of thought that's fuckin' obvious! Mebbes the temptation of all that gear was simply too much for him.'

'What, you mean the bastard's fucked off with all the drugs?'

'In one, Einstein. Why else would he no' be answering his phone? There's no sign of the boat either. I've just been trying to borrow or hire one, but everywhere's closed and it's almost dark so it looks like I'll have to wait until tomorrow. This is doing my fuckin' nut in. I hope to God there's another explanation and he turns up. I swear, I'd be so relieved to see him walk through that door right now that I'd kiss the wee fucker. Otherwise, I swear, head case or no', I'll have the bastard topped.' He called Mac's number for the umpteenth time. 'C'mon, Mac, answer the cunting phone . . .'

'You're mad,' said Grant, once more peering into the bag, ignoring the ringing of Mac's mobile. 'You've done some crazy things and had some crazy ideas in the past, but this . . . it's a different league.'

'Why?'

Grant shook his head in disbelief. 'Have you any idea what that's worth? Have you any idea what kind of trouble we could be getting ourselves into? Not just with Kyle, or the Searles, or maybe even the people that dropped it off, whoever they might be. But what about the police?'

'Of course I know how much trouble I could be getting into and of course I know how much it's worth!' said Shuff, raising his voice. 'That's why I said we could be landing ourselves in the shit with this before I told you.'

'What about Mac? What about if he is still down there? What about if he somehow swims to shore?'

Shuff shook his head. 'No way. You heard Marina – his tanks would have run out after half an hour. And she's right, all of the tanks were practically empty. I had to go down twice. That's why those two she picked up *were* empty. I nearly bought it on the second one. Scary shit, dude.'

'So as far as you're concerned, that's the end of Mac?'

'Gotta be. Think about it. The gear was still in the trunk. OK, it's just possible that he might have taken some out, but if he did, then he obviously got in trouble with it. I couldn't find any buoyancy aids or jackets on the boat and like I said, it took me two goes to get this little lot.'

Grant squeezed the bridge of his nose, trying to take it all in.

'But suppose he was wearing a buoyancy jacket? He could still be floating around somewhere.'

'If you wear a BCD then you normally throw it in the water, then jump in and put it on there. I would have heard two splashes instead of one. It is possible but I'd put money on him not having one.'

'OK. Let's assume Mac hasn't somehow made it to shore. Let's also assume that he hasn't double-crossed Kyle or been scooped up by a plane. What about if Connor and Marina find his body? Then what?'

'They won't! He would have drifted miles away by now. If he wasn't wearing a BCD then the tanks or maybe even the weights would have pulled him down. Even if they hadn't then he would have probably drowned. I'm telling you, man, in a few days he'll be fish food.'

'OK.' Grant finally accepted his friend's explanation. 'What do you want to do?'

At that moment, Connor and Marina broke the surface.

'Listen,' Shuff spoke quickly and quietly. 'When I tell them what I'm planning, just go along with it for now.'

An exasperated Grant nodded.

Connor took the regulator from his mouth and yelled, 'No sign of Mac.' He took a few strokes towards the speedboat. 'And there was nothing in the trunk either.'

'Well, there's a fucking surprise,' whispered Grant into Shuff's ear, with more than a hint of sarcasm.

chapter forty

Connor had no idea how exactly Shuff and Grant had managed to get the two kilos of cocaine from the Searles, but there they were. Sitting in front of him, hopefully bearing Kyle's fingerprints.

It was Tuesday evening, two days since they had left Kyle's boat anchored at the dive site and had all made a pact to say they had been nowhere near it. They did not foresee this causing a problem. The owner of the boat they hired had no idea where they were going and no other boats were in the area when they picked up Shuff and looked for Mac. If Mac had disappeared, then given the nature of his activities, it was unlikely that Kyle or anybody else would report him missing.

They had returned to Ali Bey the following day to see if there were any developments. Later that afternoon, Kyle went out on another boat and returned with his own one. There was still no sign of Mac.

Just after that, Shuff had gathered everyone together and explained that he had a plan to get the two kilos of cocaine bearing Kyle's fingerprints from the Searles. Connor wanted to know the details but all Shuff would say was that he needed to borrow some money to hire a decent car.

Now they were all sitting in Marina's apartment (having decided that with Mac out of the picture and Kyle most definitely preoccupied, it would once more be a fairly safe place to meet), staring incredulously at the two kilos of cocaine.

'So, come on then,' asked Connor yet again, still baffled by how Shuff and Grant had managed to pull it off, 'how did you do it?'

'You promised you wouldn't ask,' replied Shuff. 'That was the condition, remember?'

'But there's stuff we need to know, like do we have to stay out of the Searles's way? Did you steal it from them? You've got to tell us something.'

'No, we didn't steal it and no, you don't have to stay out of the Searles's way. In fact,' he allowed himself a self-indulgent smile and glanced across to Grant, 'I'd say that the Searles are extremely pleased with the way things have turned out.'

'And this is *definitely* the same two kilos that Kyle gave to the Searles.'

'Definitely.'

Connor shook his head. 'This is confusing the hell out of me. Still,' he looked at the cocaine, 'having that is the most important thing. Now all we've got to do is find a way of planting it on Kyle and getting him caught with it.'

'And how are we going to do that?' asked Marina.

'I reckon the idea Grant had before of ramming his car would actually work. Mac isn't going to be around, so we should be all right.'

'And then what?'

'Kyle's bound to get out of the car once it's been smashed into, especially when he sees it's me. While we're arguing or whatever, Shuff or Grant can chuck the Charlie on to his back seat. Then all we need is for Bartolo to be nearby again with a colleague or two. He is still going to help, isn't he, Marina?'

'He said he would, although he did say that next time it would be nice if you didn't do something that meant involving half the island's fire brigade.'

'I'll try. Would you be able to wait near the Curry House and let me know when you see his car?'

Marina nodded.

'Don't forget,' said Shuff, 'that there's no villa for him to live in any more, so he might come in a different way.'

'Good point. In that case, you and Grant had better wait at the other end of the road, near Tomas's Bar. I'll be in the road opposite the wasteland that leads down to Atlantis, engine running, ready to ram the bastard.'

Grant shook his head. 'Wait, wait, wait. This idea sucks, man.'

'It was your bloody idea in the first place,' exclaimed Connor.

'I know, so if I say it's shit, then it must be shit. Suppose the doors are locked, or he doesn't get out of his car, or someone sees us do it?'

'I'll admit it's not the slickest idea,' admitted Connor, 'but from where I'm sitting it's the best we've got and we really don't have the luxury of time to plan anything more foolproof. Anyway, you know what Kyle's like, of course he'll get out of the car. There'll be loads of confusion and everyone loves watching two drivers having a go at each other, you'll be able to do it easily.'

'Oh, *I'm* doing it, am I?'

'Well, you can drive the van and have a ruck with Kyle if you prefer.'

As Connor suspected, this idea held even less appeal to Grant. 'And in the unlikely event that someone does see you do it, don't forget we've got Bartolo on our side. He'll be there straight after the accident. Just make sure you wear gloves.'

'When are we going to do it?' asked Shuff

'I guess there's no time like the present,' said Connor looking at his watch, 'and I'd rather have that stuff about us for as little time as possible. It's seven-thirty now, Kyle should be coming down in an hour or so. I suppose the green light is all down to whether or not Bartolo can be in the area.'

There was a moment's hesitation, as the gap between talk and action closed before them. They all looked at Marina, who realized the next move was hers.

'I'll call him now,' she said.

It wasn't like Kyle to dip into his supplies that often, but this was an exception – not that there were all that many supplies left.

He had barely slept for two days. His eyelids were red and puffy, his nose raw and constantly running. He looked a mess. He was a mess.

Despite phoning virtually every mutual contact he and Mac shared, Mac had seemingly vanished. When Kyle had sailed out to the dive boat on the Monday morning it was just anchored there, like the *Marie Celeste*. On the seabed the trunk was empty although the suppliers confirmed they had made the drop. Kyle immediately regretted asking the question because the suppliers became instantly suspicious and had warned him in no uncertain terms, of the consequences should he not come up with the balance of the money owed.

He was in deep, deep shit and at the moment, all roads led to Mac.

What tipped the balance in Kyle's paranoid state was a phone call he'd received a few hours earlier from Rik Searle. He had been in touch to say that they were no longer interested in buying more cocaine. Yet there was no way they could have known what had happened and Kyle felt sure he detected something in the tone of Rik Searle's voice. Kyle had got it into his cocaine-fuelled mind that Mac had gone behind his back and done a deal with them. The Searles were leaving the next day so Kyle had called together as many boys as he could to meet him down Atlantis to drive up to Pike's and confront the Searles.

It had taken some pulling together, which was why he was running late for the meeting at Atlantis.

'What's the time, Rory?'

'Just gone nine. Are you sure this is a good idea, Kyle? Suppose it's just a coincidence that the Searles rang? Suppose something happened to Mac and he hasn't had you over?'

'Are *you* in on it too!' yelled Kyle, slamming his foot on the brakes and turning on Rory as they came to the Curry Club junction.

'No, of course not. Take it easy, amigo.' Rory was pressed as close to the passenger door as he could, knowing that Kyle could explode at any moment. 'I was just saying—'

'Aye, well, don't "just say". In fact, don't do anything other than shut your fuckin' hole.' Kyle took another line, oblivious to the traffic building up behind him. Eventually, he turned right on to the main road. 'I'm telling you. Somebody has met Mac by the dive site and brought him back in. He's taken my Charlie and . . . what the—?'

A small white van screeched out from a side turning and rammed into the front passenger side of Kyle's Range Rover. It swung the car, causing the seatbeltless Rory's face to knock against the just replaced windscreen, not too hard but hard enough for his still tender nose to make contact.

'Ow!'

The van looked as though it had come off worse though; there was steam coming out of the crumpled bonnets of both cars.

'Never mind your nose, you fuckin' bairn, let's teach this fuckin' idiot a lesson.'

When Kyle saw who the driver of the van was he looked gobsmacked.

'You! What are you still . . . have you got anything to do with . . . this time I'm gonna fuckin' kill you!'

He ran at Connor, screaming. Connor met Kyle straight on and with his slightly larger build, grabbed him round the neck and swung him to the floor, immediately getting the better of him.

'Rory,' yelled Kyle, 'get this cunt off me.'

Rory took his hand from his nose and stepped towards the grappling pair. He wasn't expecting the driver of the approaching motorbike to stick his fist out and connect with it squarely once more.

'*Yeeaargh*!' The pain was excruciating and Rory fell to the floor clutching his battered beak with tears streaming down his face.

Grant jumped off the back of the bike while Shuff rubbed his fist.

'Ouch,' he said, 'that hurt my hand.'

Looking round, and wearing gloves, Grant opened the back door and threw the two kilos of cocaine into the Range Rover. He did it only just in the nick of time as a local police car turned into the road. A few moments later, approaching from the other direction, was Bartolo's Guardia Civil car.

Shuff looked over to Connor, who was by now sitting astride the semi-conscious Kyle, punching him and banging his head against the pavement.

' . . . and he could be in prison for years. *Whack*! And do you know where I'll be Friday? *Crunch*! Burying my fucking friend, the one Mac laid into.'

Kyle's face was a bloodied mess. Shuff grabbed Connor's arms.

'Leave it. Come on. It's all over.'

Bartolo and another Guardia policeman helped pull him off, but Connor broke free and landed one last satisfying kick in Kyle's ribcage, before being restrained once more. A groaning Kyle rolled over, blood dripping on to the pavement and unsuccessfully tried to haul himself up.

The two local police shone their torches into the two cars. Within seconds one yelled out.

'*Mira!*'

All of the police gathered round. One of the police went to pick up the bag of cocaine but Bartolo had the foresight to yell at him not to touch it because of fingerprints.

'Who does this car belong to?' asked the bearded local policeman.

A panting Connor pointed at Kyle, who was still struggling to get up. The two local police strode over and handcuffed Kyle, then, after a word from Shuff, Rory as well. Several more police cars and a police van had quickly arrived on scene.

Bartolo went over to the other group of police who had congregated around the Range Rover. A few of them moved away to disperse the growing crowd of onlookers. After a minute or so Bartolo came back over, winking at Marina who had joined the mêlée.

'OK. It is good because the Policia Locale were the first to find the cocaine. He also had another bag of a few grams, a rolled up note and a CD cover with cocaine on it in the car. I think for Kyle now it no looks good. I also think, thanks to Connor, *he* no look good either.' Bartolo chuckled. 'Now I must leave. I will call my uncle Carlos and he will start to see if we can help Luc. I think if Kyle's fingerprints are on this bag, then this will help very much. Also, maybe the other boy will tell us more.'

'What, you mean Rory?'

'*Sí*. He is not very strong. I think maybe, with a little pressure, he will tell us much.' He turned and whispered something in Marina's ear, who smiled. When he was sure no other police were looking he gave her a quick kiss. 'Don't worry, my friends. We have him now. This time there will be no people in high places to help Kyle. They will turn their backs on him – he is going to prison. We will also now make it difficult for any of those who work for him. Very soon they will all be gone. Trust me.'

'And Luc?' asked Connor.

'I make no promises but I think he will be OK . . .'

Half an hour later, Connor, Marina, Shuff and Grant were sat at a table just down the road from the crash, outside David's pizza restaurant.

'What do you reckon will happen?' asked Shuff.

'I don't know,' said Connor. 'It sounds promising though. I doubt if Luc will get out overnight, but fingers crossed, we'll get there in the end.'

'And what about you?' asked Grant.

'To tell the truth, I haven't even thought about it, what with all of this and Leo's funeral coming up on Friday. I reckon I'll just spend a bit of time soaking up the island, catching up with old friends, then deciding what to do with the rest of my life. Nothing important really.' He laughed. 'Maybe see if I can persuade a beautiful lottery winner who loves ironing to part with a few hundred grand to start up that Car Wash Café and Diner. Who knows what's round the corner, but that's half the fun, isn't it? And you? What are you two going to do?'

'I figure we'll hang out here a bit longer,' answered Shuff. 'We'll pay our respects to Leo on Friday, that's for sure. Then we'll probably take off and check out a bit more of Europe and aim to be back in dear old Bloomfield, New Jersey by October time.'

'I thought you were skint?'

'We were, but the folks wired me some money over, so we're cool now.'

'Why didn't you get them to wire some over when you were going to get the ferry home?' asked Marina.

'I didn't want to ask them then. But I finally swallowed my pride. Needs must and all that.' The waiter brought over a bottle of wine. He changed the subject. 'And I hear you're going to be opening a dive school in Almeria. Sounds wicked.'

'Yeah. I'm looking forward to it.'

The waiter filled their glasses.

'Right then,' said Connor. 'Time for a toast. How about to the future, as uncertain as it might be?'

Connor and Marina raised their glasses, but Shuff stopped them.

'Actually, let's do it to something else. How about to friendship, freedom and following dreams?'

'Sounds like a lot of fucking f's to me,' smiled Connor, 'but why not?'

Once they'd all taken a drink, Connor leaned forward.

'I know I said I wouldn't ask, but come on, guys, how did you get that gear off the Searles?'

Shuff and Grant looked at each other.

Shuff spoke. 'Sorry buddy, but like I said, it has to remain hush-hush. I'm not saying you'll never know, but now's not the time. Maybe Grant here will tell you one day in the future.'

Shuff and Grant shared a smile.

'Another toast I think,' said Grant. 'To secrets . . .'

part six
secrets

chapter forty-one

Originally it was going to be a simple service for family and friends. However, they had underestimated his popularity. The small chapel had twice as many people in as it could comfortably cope with.

As the organist played the final cadence and the vicar slowly climbed the pulpit, the room fell into a hushed and respectful silence. Most focused on the teak coloured coffin, swamped in flowers and eulogies, finding it hard to believe that a man who had in his own way given so much, who had possessed such an incredible life force, could be contained within. It would have come as less as a surprise to the mourners if he'd suddenly leaped from the coffin with a huge smile on his face than if the cremation had actually gone ahead.

Luc sat next to Connor a few rows from the front. His clothes hung off him, but at least they were his own. It had taken a little longer to be released than he'd hoped for but looking at the coffin a few metres in front of him, his experience took on a different perspective. It was just a shame he hadn't got to know him better. Still, he was there and he was sure his attendance would have been appreciated.

After all, New Jersey wasn't exactly round the bloody corner.

A late mourner crept into the chapel and the East Coast November winter whistled through the door until she closed it behind her. It was a sharp contrast to the mild and temperate winter Connor had flown in from two days earlier. After a few words of introduction, the vicar concluded, 'Shuff's best friend Grant would like to say a few words about the dearly departed.'

He stepped to one side and Grant tapped the small microphone. He acknowledged the looks of support from various people around the room, giving Connor and Luc a small smile.

'As many of you will know, this time last year, Shuff and I were talking about going to Europe. In particular, we'd heard about a special, magical island in the Mediterranean called Ibiza.

'I guess it was an appropriate place to go. Legend has it that Hannibal, a leader of men, a conqueror, was born there. In his own way, Shuff was a conqueror too. He never let his illness defeat him. He conquered expectations about how he should live his life. He conquered pre-conceptions about the quality of life he should lead. He embraced every day and lived it to the full and it was something that inspired me and made me proud to be his friend.

'Legend also has it that Ibiza is a place where all elephants went to die. So many things happened to us in the summer just gone, that the elephants probably had the right idea – over there, you can almost cram a lifetime into just a few months.'

He gave a small cough to clear his throat.

'Shuff knew that with Cystic Fibrosis he had less time on this earth than most. That was probably why he attacked each day as his last. That was also probably why he wanted to try so many different things. Yet he never wanted to make an issue of it and for the most part, never told anybody. If he went trampolining he'd be doing somersaults and saying it was a way of meeting girls, rather than loosening the phlegm in his lungs.' There were a few laughs. 'Actually, looking round today, I'm glad to see a lot of his old girlfriends here.'

Connor glanced round the chapel. Almost half the mourners were young attractive girls, some smiling and some burying their faces in handkerchiefs.

'I suppose the fact that you are here means that those of you he may have been less than chivalrous towards have forgiven him, or at least understood him. Shuff simply didn't want to get too close to anybody because he didn't want them to suffer the pain of loss when he'd gone. Being a bit abrupt, or sometimes downright rude, was just his way of making that easier to achieve. Well, that and the fact that I think he sometimes enjoyed being abrupt and rude. His illness also meant that he wanted to sample as many things as he could. He looked at the world as a sweet shop and he just wanted to try as many sweets as possible, if you know what I mean.'

There were a few laughs and one or two claps.

'But underneath it all was a man with a big heart, who cared about his friends. And it's a privilege that he regarded me as one of his best and that during last summer, we became closer than ever.'

Grant glanced down at a scrap of paper he had jotted some notes on. He fought back the tears and took a deep breath, biting his lip as he felt the warmth grow behind his eyes. He straightened his tie.

'It's an indication of the impact Shuff had on people's lives that two friends we made in Ibiza have flown over to pay their respects. Another friend, Leo, who sadly passed away during the summer after suffering with cancer, said that Shuff was the most inspirational man he'd ever met. To this day I am sure that meeting Shuff made Leo's own passage easier to bear.

'Leo and his friends used to say a bus could run you over. In other words, we should try and do all of the things we want because we might not be around tomorrow. Shuff was lucky. He knew that his bus was never that far away, so he lived life to the full. But we've all got our own bus out there, revving its engine, ready and waiting, yet most of us choose to ignore it, or pretend it's not there, although in truth it could come and run any one of us over at any time. And if it does, how many of us could honestly say we'd tried all of the things we'd wanted to, had a go at all of those dreams that somehow get lost in the day to day business of just existing? If Shuff were sitting here, he'd be one of the few people putting his hand in the air to that question.

'So as sad a day as this is, maybe we can all learn from the short but inspirational life of my best friend. One day, we're all going to be the star attraction at an event like this, we've all got our own bus ready to run us over.

'I guess the only difference is, Shuff had a rough idea when his bus was coming.'

Most of the mourners had filed back into their cars to go to the wake at Shuff's parents' home. Luc was outside, having a rare cigarette and enjoying the crisp air and snow after the few months in prison. He'd told Connor he was going to get into one of the cars in the cortège with Shuff's extremely attractive 22-year-old sister.

Connor was in the room adjoining the chapel, where all of the tributes to Shuff had been laid out. It was an amazing sight. He spotted one from Bartolo and Marina, who had just gone on holiday to the Great Barrier Reef before coming back to set up their Almeria based diving school.

Tucked away near the top, he was surprised to see a wreath from Holly and a card:

Shuff,
Thanks for sharing your secret with me. Wherever I am in the world,
I think about what you had to go through every day and it makes
any problem I have seem unimportant.
  Holly x
  PS I never did tell anyone your secret; I bet you told Grant mine.

Connor picked the card from the wreath.

'I thought you might see that.'

It was Grant.

Connor hugged him. 'That was some speech. Shuff would have been really proud. He would have loved seeing all those babes crying over him too.' They both smiled. 'Do you know what this is about?' Connor nodded at the card from Holly.

'Shall we go for a little walk outside?' suggested Grant. 'It's stopped snowing.'

They turned away from where the last remaining mourners were gathered and walked out to the grounds, which other than a few cleared zig-zagging paths, were covered with several inches of snow.

'Yes, I do know what the card means,' said Grant finally. 'Shuff told me towards the end.' They took a few more paces. 'Remember the day Leo died, when you took Holly to the airport, when Shuff and I went to say goodbye to her, just before she left.'

'Of course.'

'After I said goodbye to Holly I went to make some calls so Shuff walked through to passport control with her. On the way, she asked him why he was so desperate not to go back to the USA, what the big deal was. Shuff never liked to tell anyone about the Cystic Fibrosis so said it was a secret. Well, you know what Holly's like. She kept on at him to tell her, saying it didn't matter because they probably wouldn't be seeing each other again – she didn't quite know how true that was at the time. Basically, Holly said she also had a big secret and suggested they swap. Shuff thought, what the hell, so they went for a quick coffee and he ended up telling her all about the Cystic Fibrosis, how the sell-by date on his life expectancy was pretty close and how that affected his attitude to everything. To tell the truth, I think it did him good occasionally to get it off his chest.'

'That's understandable. And what was Holly's big secret?'

'From what I can gather she felt a bit stupid after that, because obviously, her secret was never going to compare. Still, Shuff got it out of her in the end.'

'So what was it?'

'There's some other shit I need to tell you first. Let's get in the car.' Grant let the engine run for a few minutes. Connor felt this action had as much to do with creating tension as warming the car. 'We'll take the scenic route,' said Grant, pulling away and negotiating the slippery crematorium lane. He pulled out a spliff and lit it. 'Shuff would find us remembering him like this far better than eating sandwiches. He passed it to Connor then pulled onto the main road. 'Contrary to what Shuff told Marina, he had his PADI and was a pretty good diver. So, he *did* go down to see if Mac was there, or rather, to check he wasn't. Naturally, he decided to have a swim round to find the trunk . . .'

'Marina having given him a fairly good description of its location.'

'Exactly. He looked inside . . .'

Grant paused, his mouth twitching at the edges. Connor suddenly realized what Grant was getting at.

'No! The drugs were still in it? Fucking hell! How much?'

Grant slowly turned round to Connor with a barely contained smile.

'More than twenty-five kilos.'

'Twenty-five fucking kilos! Jesus,' whistled Connor. 'That must be worth, what . . . half a million quid.'

'Pretty much, yeah.'

Connor was still trying to take it in. 'Twenty-five kilos.' They carried on driving whilst Connor digested the huge amount and its implications. 'So what did you do with it?'

'I'll tell you in a minute. I thought you might be interested in how we got the two kilos with Kyle's fingerprints from the Searles – it's kinda connected.' Connor swivelled round in his seat with the excited look of a child about to be read a bedtime story. 'They truly were a pair of muscle-bound dolts.'

'Yeah,' said Connor, 'but I'm more interested in you telling me stuff I *don't* already know.'

Grant chuckled. 'OK. Now, what you've got to remember is that the Searles had never met Shuff or I. We rang them on the Monday – the day after Shuff took the twenty-five kilos – saying we'd heard some bad things about Kyle's firm and we were keen to get their business. Obviously, they were highly suspicious to start with but I guess the American accents helped. Basically, we offered them three kilos for the two they had in the boot. The more stupid of the two brothers was going crazy with excitement after they tested it. He was saying something about starting with a kilo of glucose and ending up with three of the finest kilos of cocaine he'd ever seen.'

'But weren't you scared they'd just take it off you?' asked Dex.

'Shit yeah! But we had to take the risk, plus Shuff played the part of a big-time dealer brilliantly. Then, we sold them a couple more kilos – real cheap too, I've since discovered. Then, just before we left Ibiza and toured round Europe they came over with some other guys and bought most of the rest. We did a few other bits here and there. Looking back on it, we must have been fucking crazy, man, but, that's basically it.'

305

'So how much did you get?'

There was a long pause. 'Not far off the figure you said.'

'Half a million quid! Over three-quarters of a million euros. Shit! What did you do with all that money?'

'Well, we had a ball round Europe. Shuff must have kinda sensed there wasn't long left. We lived the life, that's for sure. Then we brought some back, but as you can see, his family are fairly wealthy anyway. My folks are the opposite end of the scale, so I sorted out a car for them and paid off a few bills – told them we'd won a bit gambling in Monte Carlo. They loved the story I made up almost as much as the money. Much more though and it woulda been kinda hard explaining where it came from, plus they say money makes money, so I'm taking a longer term view on it.'

'So where's the rest of it?'

'That's one of the things we need to talk about. Shuff insisted that if we hadn't spent it before his time came, that I should have it. We buried it in Ibiza.'

'You've done what?'

'We couldn't take all of it round Europe with us. We couldn't put too much of it in a bank. It seemed the only sensible thing to do. If Shuff had lived, then we were gonna check out the island again next summer. You weren't the only one smitten with Ibiza.'

'Well, I hope it's well hidden and you remember where you've put it.'

'No worries there, amigo. But listen, let's talk about all this tomorrow. I guess you also wanna know about Holly.'

Connor nodded.

'If you don't mind me saying, Connor, you behaved like a real dumb-ass.'

'What?'

'You assumed that Holly had slept with Dex, so you figured her just to be a good time girl, correct?'

'Not exactly but I could tell she wasn't interested in serious relationships. Plus it's not my style to stir a mate's porridge.'

'Excuse me?'

'You know, sleep with a girl after a friend has. Actually, no, that's not strictly true. But certainly I wouldn't go out with a girl if a mate had been having a relationship with her.'

'And that's what you think Dex and Holly had, a relationship?'

'Of course.'

'Wrong, you moron. Jesus, don't you British guys ever talk about that stuff? At least in the States we're a little more in touch with our feelings.

I mean, fuck, if what I've heard is right, on the day she was leaving she even told you that her and Dex weren't going anywhere as a couple, correct?'

Connor was getting confused. 'Yeah, I think so, but . . . oh, I don't know. I can't remember. I was sure they'd slept together. Anyway, she also said something about a mystery guy that she fancied, who was seeing someone else so it was irrelevant anyway.'

'Ooh, and who do you think that might have been?' asked Grant sarcastically.

The penny slowly dropped. 'No, not . . . ?'

'Remind me never to put you down for phone-a-friend, asshole! Yes . . . *you*! And why do you think Holly never slept with Dex?' This time Grant didn't wait for Connor to catch up. '*You again*! Holly wasn't interested in sleeping around. She wanted a soulmate and she wanted to stay in Ibiza.'

'But that's exactly what I . . .' Connor sank his head in his hands and groaned. 'Oh, fuck.'

'To make things worse, you even told her that things with Marina were going great – that was the final nail in the coffin. What was she supposed to do? That's why she left.'

'But why didn't she say something?'

'She tried but it was too late. She said what Leo told you was right – it's all about timing. You were her Big Adventure, buddy, but you blew it.'

'How do you know all of this?'

'Shuff told me – it was her secret. She was mad about you. ' Grant had a twinkle in his eye. 'And I've exchanged a few emails with her.'

'You're still in touch?'

'I thought that might interest you.'

'Where is she?'

'At the moment I think she's in New Zealand, which, from your point of view, is both good and bad.'

'Why?'

'It's good because they've plenty of Internet Cafés but it's bad because a decent looking woman over there is so damn rare that if they see one walking down the street they'd probably stop her and have her stuffed. On the other hand, the guys are athletic, good-looking . . .'

'OK, OK. I get the picture. Seriously though, do you think I should contact her?'

'From where I'm standing, you both want exactly the same things and from the way you seemed when you first met her . . . Leo was right – the only thing wrong was timing.' Grant looked at his watch to emphasize the point. 'And the longer you leave it . . .'

Connor thought for a few moments. 'I don't suppose it would be good form to be late for Shuff's wake, would it?'

'It's exactly what he'd expect, if you ask me.'

'What do you say we go back to the house, demolish the sandwiches, tell a few stories about him, maybe even shed a few tears, then after everyone's gone, me, you and Luc find a bar with internet access where I can send an email explaining what a prat I've been, then we can sink a few sherbets in his memory?'

'Sounds cool to me.'

'Good. Right then – let's get back to the wake and see if we can fuck up Luc's chances with Shuff's sister . . .'

epilogue

the following may . . .

Ain't nobody gonna tell you what to do, Gonna be your judge and jury too . . .

The classic Chic song brought a big cheer. A few champagne corks popped and the engine of Leo's old TR6 roared into life.

The hundred or so guests sang and clapped. Connor walked over to the car wash entrance, where a yellow ribbon was ceremoniously tied. He held aloft a pair of scissors like an Olympic torchbearer, theatrically cut the ribbon, then waved the driver of the TR6 towards him.

Katya smiled, put the car into gear and edged it forward.

Connor stepped out. Scuttling behind him, still trying to do up the buttons at the front of her bright orange overalls with 'Car Wash American Café and Diner' emblazoned across the back, came Holly.

'Leave them undone, you spoilsport,' yelled Dex. Leanne, his latest girlfriend of three months' standing, gave him a playful slap.

Connor and Holly set about the car with soapy sponges.

'Oi, Dex, get over here,' called Luc from the DJ box set up in the hut on stilts. Dex climbed up and the friends put their arms round each other's shoulders. Luc nudged Dex and nodded towards Holly.

'She could have been yours, mate,' he teased.

'Nah man,' said Dex shaking his head. 'The girl's cool an' t'ing, but she wasn't my type really.'

Luc raised his eyebrows. 'No?'

'OK, maybe I wasn't her type either.' Dex smiled and ran his fingers through his hair, his dreads now grown back to their former glory. 'I knew Connor fancied her from the start. Why do you think I went after her?' They both giggled. 'I didn't realize he was that serious on her though. I thought he just fancied her in the same way I did.'

'What, as in just wanting to bone her?'

There was a short pause then they both laughed, because that was exactly what Dex meant.

'So, it looks like our man's found his Big Adventure at last. Thank God for emails, eh?'

'Oh, I'm sure he would have found some other way of getting in touch with her after Shuff's funeral. It's a shame you couldn't come, Dex. Grant gave a great speech and Shuff's family are really nice . . . his sister is badly fit.'

'You didn't . . .'

Luc gave a wry smile. 'She said she might come over here for the summer. Carlos has bought the bar next door to Raffles and knocked it through, so I might need more staff . . .'

'Go on the Luc!' laughed Dex. 'I tell you though, I felt bad about not paying my respects, but November's one of the busiest times of year for DJing and Victor was really pushing me.'

'I'm sure Shuff would have understood.'

'Yeah, man, the brother was safe.'

They stood and reflected on their departed friend for a few moments, interrupted by Luc receiving a hearty slap on the back.

'Hola, amigos. So what do you think of our humble establishment?'

It was an extremely excited Grant, also wearing bright orange dungarees.

'Wicked,' replied Dex. 'I just wish I had rich parents like yours who'd buy me a restaurant in Ibiza. Connor must be over the moon too.'

'Yeah, well my parents put most of the money down and we borrowed a bit from the bank. It was his idea though so hopefully it'll be a good partnership. Anyway, I don't think it's just this place that's making him happy . . .'

Connor and Holly were splashing each other with soapsuds as the TR6 slowly drove through the rinsing jets.

'Yeah man, they look well into each other. Sweet.' Dex pointed to a Spanish man standing behind them. 'Isn't that your boss Carlos, Luc, the one who really helped you out?'

'Yeah, he was a star. Shit,' Luc slapped his head, 'I meant to tell you. He just said that apparently Kyle was transferred to a prison on the mainland last week. He'll probably get deported as well when he does eventually get out.'

'Excellent news.' Grant took a drink then started laughing. 'But even more important, how's Rory's nose? Me and Shuff always used to have a scream about that. The poor bastard got it in the hooter every time.'

'I don't know about his nose but there was certainly nothing wrong with his mouth, was there?' said Luc. 'Once the police put the pressure on he couldn't talk fast enough. Carlos said I would have probably got out anyway, but him owning up to planting the drugs on Kyle's instructions, then telling them about more gear in the safe house near Cala Salada, well, it didn't exactly do Kyle any favours or me any harm. Still, two months in that place was more than enough for me, so I doubt if Kyle's exactly having a picnic.'

'Even so, I reckon he got off lightly compared to a UK sentence,' observed Dex, 'I mean, take the Searles, fuck knows what they're looking at . . .'

'What about the Searles?' Grant's smile immediately froze.

'Didn't Connor tell you?'

'Tell me what?'

'I let him know as soon as I got here this morning. They got nicked last week. I could see it coming – everybody could. It was obvious they were up to no good. They were driving round in fuck-off cars, had designer clothes, larging it with wads of cash. It turns out they'd gone up a few divisions and got caught bang to rights with loads of fucking nosebag. I heard it was ten kilos or something like that. Enough for them to be locked up for a long time, anyway. Good fucking riddance.'

Grant smiled in relief and climbed down the steps to join Connor.

'So,' asked Connor, 'have they bought the line about your folks fronting the money for this place?'

'Hook, line and sinker.'

'What are you smiling at?'

'Dex also just told me about the Searles.'

'Bastard! *I* wanted to tell you. I was going to save it until after this. Good, eh?'

'I suppose so. After all, they didn't know who Shuff and I really were even if they did start talking . . . and there's no evidence.'

'Exactly. And now there's absolutely no danger of them coming out here for a good few years – enough time for us to make a fortune from this place and retire, with any luck.'

'I'll drink to that.'

'So will I. Which reminds me . . . I'd better go and do the toast.'

Leo's TR6 was looking the cleanest it had been for a long time. Connor walked over and stood next to it then Luc threw the microphone over to him. He picked up a glass of champagne.

'OK, folks, if I could have your attention please.' Gradually everyone stopped talking. 'First of all, thanks for coming to the Car Wash American Café and Diner.' There were a few cheers and whistles. 'Thank you, thank you. But before I officially open it I think a few words are in order. I could go on for ages – though I promise I won't – because there are so many things I could say, mainly about the people who have helped to give us the opportunity to realize this dream,' he looked at Katya, 'or to even know what that dream was in the first place. I think Grant and I owe all of this to a couple of very special people and most of us know who they are. So, rather than ramble on, I think we can sum it up in two words.' Connor raised his glass. 'Absent friends.'

The toast was repeated back, there was a big cheer and the music started. Holly kissed Connor and went to mingle. Connor took Katya's hand and walked into the empty café with her.

The diner part of the café and the kitchens were not quite finished. Connor passed through to the just completed bar and poured them both a drink. In pride of place on a small shelf were three framed photos, one of Leo, one of Shuff and one of the group, all together, from the previous summer.

Katya's eyes rested on the picture of her deceased husband for a few moments.

'He was an incredible man, Katya,' said Connor, handing her a drink, 'but I guess you already know that. I promised him I'd raise a glass to him sometimes. Shall we?'

They toasted Leo.

'He would have loved all of this, Connor. He would have been so proud of you.'

Connor felt his eyes tingle. 'Thanks.'

Katya reached into a shoulder bag she'd brought in from the car. 'He told me to give you this, but only if and when I was sure you were going to stay in Ibiza. That's why I didn't give it to you at his funeral, seeing as it was only a few days after Kyle was arrested and what with everything still being so up in the air.'

'Yeah, mainly Kyle's villa,' joked Connor.

'When you told me about this place,' continued Katya, 'I thought I'd wait until the opening.'

She pulled out a large toy model of a London double-decker bus. On the front was an engraved plaque. Connor read the words and smiled. He hugged Katya, providing him with an excuse to wipe the tear that had crept over the bottom of his eye.

'Thanks, Katya. Shuff would have really appreciated these words too.'

'I think Shuff was partly the inspiration behind choosing them, to be honest.'

'Leo always did have a knack of being able to sum things up.'

Katya smiled. 'I asked him if he wanted the words put on his tombstone. He said,' Katya mimicked Leo's voice, ' "Pah woman, nobody will read it there. Connor will find somewhere for them to be read by the masses." '

'Well, I can't guarantee masses exactly, but fingers crossed, we'll have a few people walk through those doors.'

He took the bus and placed it next to the photo of Leo. He read the engraving once more:

> To my dear friend Connor
>
> Happy the Man, and happy he alone
> He who can call today his own:
> He who, secure within, can say,
> Tomorrow do thy worst, for I have liv'd today.
>
> John Dryden 1631-1700

acknowledgements

Craig Beck is an Ibiza legend and long time island face who holds a number of dubious records, the kind of records that make some people turn their noses up in disgust and others green with envy.

If ever the Cystic Fibrosis Association need an advert for how important a positive mental attitude can be for challenging this terrible illness, it is Craig. Despite seeing his sister die from it in her teens, he copes with his own CF in a matter of fact way, taking it in his stride and in all the time I've known him I have never heard him whinge about it. Personally, being someone who thinks every headache is a brain tumour and every bout of indigestion the beginning of a heart attack, I find that pretty humbling.

Craig has a go at everything, from songwriting, to learning instruments, to taking up golf and playing off a 12 handicap within two and a half months, to DJing and landing a spot at God's Kitchen, to being a male stripper (is there anyone in Ibiza who hasn't seen the bastard's dick!) . . . the list is endless. He's in the gym every day and has the kind of physique that could easily see him star as Tarzan, if another re-make were made (although I can't imagine that many would understand him yelling to Jane, '. . . get tha'sen over here lass, we'll have a reet good neet.' Mind you, Christopher Lambert got away with his accent, so who knows?).

Anyway, all of that aside, I not only want to thank Craig for being the inspiration behind a few anecdotes that found their way into the story, but also to thank him for just being an inspiration . . . period.

Other thanks for anecdotes and inspiration go out to his old partner in crime, Andy Matthews, to Eelco Muntinga, Greg Graham (RIP), Paul Louden, Gary Ivison (glad you found your Big Adventure), Jason Lorimer, Mark Sharrock, John Salthouse (I won't be giving Daniel Day-Lewis any worries but watch out Vinnie Jones), Richard Furber, Rachel Ives, (or your friend who made that great texting observation), Danny

Whittle (if ever Pacha blows up, I'll know who did it), Shivs (mainly for diving info) & Paretta.

To Rachel Leyshon for fairly painless pruning and some great ideas.

To my two oldest friends Steve Lawrence and Dave Thomas, as well as Mick Crowley for our own life, love and the universe discussions.

To Dave Wilson and Steve Mosquito for those days in the mid-90s when we had nothing better to do than sit around taking the piss out of each other and anyone unfortunate enough to come within range.

To Fitzroy Lawrence and Kenny Hawkes for the glorious days of Girls FM and all of our 'reciprocal' arrangements.

And finally, to various girls from my chequered past. Even if I've inadvertently missed out on my own Big Adventure somewhere along the line, please rest assured that none of you was the inspiration for Gina Searle.